Also by I. Allan Sealy

The

Brainfever
an illusion **Bird**

I. Allan Sealy is the award-winning author of three novels,
The Trotter-nama, for which he received a Commonwealth Writers
Prize, *Hero* and *The Everest Hotel*, as well as a travel book, *From
Yukon to Yucatan*. He lives in the foothills of the Himalayas.

The
Brainfever
an illusion
Bird

I. ALLAN SEALY

PICADOR

First published 2003 by Picador

This edition published 2004 by Picador
an imprint of Pan Macmillan Ltd
Pan Macmillan, 20 New Wharf Road, London N1 9RR
Basingstoke and Oxford
Associated companies throughout the world
www.panmacmillan.com

ISBN 0 330 41143 8

A CIP catalogue record for this book is available from
the British Library.

Typeset by Intype London Ltd
Printed and bound in Great Britain by
Mackays of Chatham plc, Chatham, Kent

All Pan Macmillan titles are available from www.panmacmillan.com
or from Bookpost by telephoning 01624 677237

To my father
Irwin Sealy
exemplar

Contents

Prologue

Youth is a country. I used to live there. The inhabitants are determined to emigrate, exiles long to return. But the borders are sealed, as if plague had broken out there and the United Nations had sent highly paid soldiers to patrol the passes.

The year my voice broke I began to dream of the capital. I first used a razor on the slow train south from our dusty town. Ticketless milkmen hooked their cans to the window-bars and sat on the roof under the sky that a high jet carefully cut in two. I looked out of the windows and urged the countryside back, but only the nearer trees obeyed. The ones at the horizon dogged the train, and somewhere in the middle was a tree that stood still.

The train arrived at night when the city lights were blazing. Only the porters were old. There were jugglers in the street at midnight; waiters brought iced coffee and dateless newspapers. I learnt to talk and smoke and look at a man from a great height. I became a singer in a restaurant. Every night I sang the same sad song. Those who listened shed tears, but none of us understood the song. I was paid in gold and had no use for it. There was dancing in the Cellar and at dinner they served fine long-grain rice from the valley of my childhood. Zinnias grew out of letter boxes, the wastepaper baskets were full of IOUs. So beautiful the girls of youth! I thought to look for a pattern, but every one was different.

One morning I saw from my window that the clock tower was not where it should be. It was much further away. I was living in a colony when I should have been in the centre where all radial roads converge. No taxi would take me to the heart; the buses all ran the other way. At lunch the rice was coarse and I had to fetch it myself. The next day there were mountains where the city had been. I found myself in a convoy of refugees making for the border. You can keep your film, my neighbour said, but they confiscate your camera. The UN was at the wrong pass and we simply strolled through the gates.

Why do I pretend the lost capital is not Delhi? It is. The best things in my life happened there. Of all loves city love comes slowest. Compare country love: quick, hot, easy. Or the sudden deep love of a woman.

Across the border things move faster. Paper currency carries you to the flashy port. You sail west and the dhow runs aground at the Monkey Pillars. After that there are any number of airports. All they ask is to see your onward ticket and evidence of funds. You may not return. Rumours of a second chance are loose talk; the price of going back is high. You become a toy of fate, you become a puppet. Refusing puppetude, I preferred to stay away. Accustomed to the stage I became a puppet master instead, master of puppetry, things puppetish, kathputli.

But some do go back. Here is the story of one who did and paid the price. Listen.

Imagine, then, an aeroplane trailing two white clouds cut

out of styrofoam. (A plane is also a puppet held up by strings.)
Imagine a backdrop of sky with cities down below, two cities.
At first, of course, there's no stage, no sky, nothing. Out of
nothing, on that firm black foundation, we raise a kathputli
theatre. Here, in this dusty narrow cul-de-sac that two muni-
cipal sweepers have swept because a police chief is involved,
a stage begins to exist. Piles, joists, boards, come together
and a durree spread over the whole. The street will do for
seating, durrees spread there too. The night sky is a black
marquee, sequinned with dusty city stars. There's a row of
palmyra pots on the ground along the front. Then a single
step up, one step from nothing. I climb it, move to the centre
and turn to face you. There are no footlights, just a row of
bulbs overhead with brushed aluminium shades strung along
a bamboo pole. As the lights come up I draw from them
shape and substance, and also comfort. Believe me, I was
once a singer. Hear me.

I sing two cities, red and white. Behind me is a backdrop
of both, not especially convincing. It is done on the flat, with
walls and towers and windows that obey medieval laws of
gravity and extension, and sidelong roofs that keep out a
strictly horizontal rain. The master puppeteers of the north
stipulate that the two sides of a stage shall not be of the same
colour. By antique tradition if one side is black, the other is
white, if one is blue the other is yellow. Formerly this was
managed by the colour of the curtains, which even when
parted showed on either side. In the present story the colours
are red and white.

The city to the right is oriental. It was built in the seven-
teenth century by the Mughal emperor Shah Jahan. The
principal buildings, fort, mosque and palace, and the city gates

are faced with red sandstone. To this day it is known as the Red City, although you can also see domes and dovecotes – and flocks of circling pigeons – in black and white. Delhi is its proper name, Old Delhi, formerly Shahjahanabad. Below it flows the River Jamuna, a shrunken much-molested stream. In summer the river boils and you may cook on the city's red stone.

On this side is the White City. It was called Sankt Peterburkh, after its founder the Tsar Peter the Great, more properly after his patron saint. Founded in 1703, hardly fifty years after Shahjahanabad, it was deliberately occidental, Asiatic Russia's window on Europe. Its spires and golden angels look west, its weathercocks have no other point. The many branching canals of the backdrop are actually arms of the River Neva as it flows out into the Baltic Sea. St Petersburg sits on a delta, and in winter the canals are covered in ice. Then the White City glitters like a stranded iceberg in the moonlight.

A horned moon hangs over the city on the left; a many-tusked sun over the right. Look! They are shared: the pale moon washes the nearer walls of the Red City with its soda-water light, and the whole eastern face of the Finland Station is bathed in dawn red. In between the sky is an indeterminate colour, and truly the cities mingle in the twilight. Look at where a red sandstone bridge ends in iron lace on the far side of the confluent river. See how the baroque mouldings of that white rampart peter out in blowzy arabesques where the Red Fort begins.

In the very centre, you will see a young woman with her arms raised up and her head thrown back, looking up at the sky where an aeroplane is painted. Her mouth strains open, her throat is stretched and vulnerable. She could be rummaging in the clouds for something or simply doing her yoga. She wears mostly yellow.

The colours of the old puppets, the master puppeteers say, were much the same, except for the tunic or the sari. Long flowing skirts covered the legs of king and commoner, man puppet and woman puppet. (You never saw their feet, and often there were no legs.) His crown of gold stuff would have distinguished the king; if he met another king in battle the other crown was shaped differently. The battle of kings was the climax of the show. All puppets fought, a child in the audience learnt: that was their nature. They danced and they crowed and they fought. On horseback or off, they fenced cordially for a moment; then, abandoning dignity, they hurled themselves at each other. Their bodies met with a thud you could hear at the back of the theatre, over the sighing of the crowd and over the tiny piping reeds in the mouths of the straining puppeteers. The reed was two slivers of bamboo with a rubber membrane stretched between them, like a tiny harmonica held between the teeth. It was a demonic sound, sharp as pain, vicious as a razor. More than the astonishing movements of their arms, more even than their birdlike cries, so at odds with their humanity, it was the thudding of bodies that you carried home and meditated on in the dark as you lay waiting for sleep.

How the kings fought when all their men lay dead! Here was their essence, in this eternal turning and hurling of oneself at the other, so that every terrible thump turned to flesh and bone the cottony wadding you knew was inside, turned also the birdlike cries into a voice which could easily be yours, thinned and twisted in pain. Till you saw that the strings by

5

which they swung, far from being proof of their unreality, as your older cousin whispered, were the very stuff of their suffering. The pain was in the strings.

But what if (and this thought pricked you hard so you woke up and lay there staring with your hands clapped on your ears) what if some of the *people* in the audience who had sat watching with you, who brushed your arm or leaned against you, were also puppets – had *cloth* in them? What if – impossible! – someone in your family . . . ? And then your eyes went quite round with terror as the possibility sank in.

What if you yourself were a puppet?

Lev is the name of the white puppet in this story. He is not a king but an ordinary man from that country which deified the ordinary man. A scientist with special knowledge, he has come down in the world, in that new Russia where physicists wash windows and engineers drive trams. (In the old Russia they could too.) Dropped from research and unhappy with chauffeuring, he decides to take his knowledge abroad. Many of his colleagues have gone West. Lev decides to go the other way. Because in his childhood there was a painted box with a picture of the Taj Mahal. By such slender threads hangs our fate!

In India he meets a red puppet who is not a queen but an ordinary woman in that country which has never deified the ordinary woman. Maya is herself a puppeteer. She has a roomful of puppets she has made herself of bits and pieces. She has rough hands and dreams of telling the irreducible puppet story. How they clash, these two, when all the world is asleep! How they hurl themselves against each other under the painted sky!

With cloth puppets the heart is of lead. A centre-weight

is vital to manipulation so the strings remain apart and the sweeping and swooping actions are clean and swift. Heavy work for the puppet master, who must hold the cradle out and away from his chest, beyond the backcloth. He is holding up a lump of lead padded with lint and wound about with bandages, a mummy stuffed with rags. Red gabardine about the heart, yellow calico where the liver might be, grey string balled in the head.

Imagine for a moment that the person sitting beside you is built differently. Look at him – go on – out of the corner of your eye. What if behind the eyes that return your furtive glance there lurks a ball of grey twine? Suppose you pinned him down and unbuttoned his shirt and clawed and punched and scraped. What might you find? The puppet-maker must be a brave man or woman to keep those unfinished figures in his house. Imagine the twitchings in the workroom when the door is shut on them. Or at night, when they lie there half formed, the first stirring of dreams in those bandaged heads.

Suppose one night one of them, nearer completion than the rest, with the beginnings of eyebrows and a hint of fingers under the fabric, were to sit up in the dark. Turn its head this way and that, straining to hear with the rudiments of an ear. Rise up, unsteadily. Its hand grips the door as it finds its balance, finds itself grown in that dreaming interval to human dimensions. Drawn by instinct, which is no more than a kind of gravity, it detects the warmth of your sleeping body in the next room. Imagine it creeping silently up the hallway to your door. Resting there as it absorbs the rhythm of your breathing. Then coming up sudden as a dream to your bedside and waiting in cottony silence, waiting for your recognition. And when your breath, that priceless exotic gift with its strange accompanying rise and fall of the chest, does not return its homage with an answering modulation, the mannequin bends over you as you sleep, its blind eyes searching the double dark. The ear cocked as it waits for the birth of sound beating in your chest. Imagine the temptation it resists to pluck at the harp of your body with its bandaged hand!

And what if the faith that carried it there should suddenly fail it, so it fell across you, all wadding and bandages and leaden weight crashing into your dreams?

You cry out and sit up with a start. Heart pounding, you sit there as your eyes adjust to the dark, making out the familiar shapes of cupboard and window. And your feet carry you to the bathroom where you stare at the puppet in the mirror till the eyes in your head have retreated to the remotest slimes of evolution. The harder you stare the more trumped up you seem. Can this red-eyed figment hope to love, to pray? Or is there simply stuffing in there, a dunnage of lint and brown paper with two glass lights that have learnt the trick of seeing?

And when you have drunk your draught of cooling water and returned to bed there is no sleeping. You lie there listening to all the unconvincing sounds of life sifting through your body, whose impress the mute sheets take. Until the first tentative birdcalls mark the dawn and a pale remorseless light fills the window. Life begins again to slip like proof, like the finest chiffon sari drawn through the gold ring of your given self, and at last you sleep.

Nightly the figure, visible only in the dark with your eyes shut, haunts you with its longings, nightly you haunt the mirror with your doubts, till you are no longer sure which of you is real, the yearning puppet or the doomed dreamer.

Come. The lights have gone down. The cities on the screen come up, white and red. Delhi I sing, St Petersburg I scat. Here is a spoon, here is a custard apple; spit the seeds where you like.

White City

As the needle slips in Lev feels the sting of spirits like a finer pain threaded inside the jab. He looks away out of old habit, the boy inside the man, till the scientist forces himself to look directly at the spot.

Meschersky. God! First the pricked finger, then the face, then the whole disintegrating man. Tracking so quickly he has to blink away the vision. Think of the nurse, he tells himself, concentrate on her.

He's brought his own needle in: he refused the one she started to unwrap, ready to stand his ground if she threw policy at him and went for the doctor. But she simply put the clinic needle back, broken seal and all, and there was nothing in the shutting of the drawer to suggest pique. His hackles, as usual so painstakingly raised in advance, stood uselessly on end for a moment before lying back down.

At the pharmacy too he'd gone prepared for battle and met with indifference. He had asked for two boxes and checked the seal, then in a charade of changing his mind returned the more shop-soiled of the two. As a sop he panto-mimed remembering the malaria pills already on his list.

After the pharmacy he'd sat in a bus shelter opposite the

Vitebsky station and smoked one and a half cigarettes, then carefully put out the second, tucked the stub back into the packet and taken the needles home. This morning he boiled one in an enamel saucepan for twenty minutes, entranced by the tinny underwater rattle.

The needle trembles in him and he looks up at the nurse. He is joined to this big woman for that small eternity. She is pushing something into him and he must trust her. So much fear invested in that moment from childhood on! And with good reason. The nurse is a chalk-white woman with dyed black hair that shows purple lights where it catches the table lamp's fluorescent glow. The tip of her index finger wears a grubby dressing of surgical tape. Flesh droops like smooth pastry over the point of her elbow; the nearer ear lobe is a downy meadow. Her immense grey eyes wear dark rings; nothing would surprise her.

'Hepatitis coming this way, is it?' she murmurs as the serum empties into Lev's arm. 'Or are you going that way?'

'That way,' Lev answers and checks his instinct to elaborate.

She allows her eyes to bulge at the implications of *that way* and Lev observes the strength of tribal solidarity. She still sees pestilence as belonging outside. In the old days his journey to it would have been a mission of mercy, state mercy; today it's foolishness. When there are troubles enough at home. If you want to escape you go the other way, West.

An image of skyscrapers flits through Lev's mind; he lets it die. At once a shadowy album invades that space, images that have hovered there like reflections on dark water since he first had this idea of going to India. Reflections, he realizes, without an original. When he lifts his eyes from the water, there's nothing up above.

Over the months the images have coalesced into a single iconic dome, with a ragged palm tree in silhouette. One or two concrete images he'll carry there: the dancer from the June recital at the Nehru Cultural Centre with black-rimmed eyes and fingers that mimicked a butterfly – for that matter the figure of Nehru himself from boyhood news photos, grainy and indistinct. (He snorts. A dead prime minister and a classical dancer will be a lot of help.) But it comes down to the japanned box his grandfather painted with the Taj Mahal and palm trees. Straining, he dredges up a blue jackal in a childhood storybook: he can still see the overturned pot of washerman's blue. But not the washerman, or maybe just the turban.

The nurse presses a cotton swab soaked in blue meths to his arm and removes the needle. Lev's eyes follow the needle on its journey to the bin by the drawers. Who disposes of the contents at the end of the day and where and how? Is there a bright-eyed collector who carries the syringes to his factory for repacking? A New Russian.

And what a joke if the clinic's needles are new and his are not! He stands up from the frayed stool while the nurse rummages in the top drawer among the rubber stamps. The flesh on her ring finger bulges around the ring, almost hiding it. Big soft women tantalize a man married to a sylph.

'Will you be needing the meningitis?'

'No.' He takes a seat in the waiting room. He'll go some-where else for the meningitis. A poster on the opposite wall lists the benefits of giving up smoking. Within a minute your blood-tar levels are halved; in two minutes your oxygen intake has doubled; in an hour you're breathing more deeply; in twenty-four hours scars on your lung tissue have begun to mend; in a week, in a month, a year . . . His eyes glaze over. In a year you're lifting derailed trams back onto their tracks. He looks out at the late afternoon light, the sky a yellow-ish formaldehyde colour, the brownstone buildings stiff and unyielding.

Always at this hour it's impossible to believe in the change. The big change or the little one which it brought and turned his life upside down. In the evening, in this pickling light, life goes on as before, for the city, for the country, for him. The street hangs suspended in a glass jar like the specimen jars at the medical faculty across the river. Two years he spent there, preparing to enter medicine. Until they found him.

Sometimes he returns in his mind to those jars of soused organs, diseased tissue on display: the riddled liver of a serf who wrestled for Tsar Nicholas; a Decembrist brain withered in dementia to a coral; a pair of eyes that saw defeat at Mukden reddened to maraschino cherries. A lung in cross-section with asbestos deposits rich as marrowfat peas. And often he returns to the moment of his claiming, so that over time the two have begun to overlap. As if it was there, by the jars, that they took him up, into militant biology.

'Your card.'

The nurse has returned. Her big body and deliberate walk spread a kind of calm.

'If it's cost you're thinking about, with the other shots, I sometimes work from home.' Her voice is lowered as Lev pays.

Lev opens to the page and checks the entry for hepatitis, rubber-stamped and signed.

'The stamp is no problem.' She lowers her voice further. She fishes one out of a pocket and wags it. 'Take my number anyway.' Outside, she watches Lev light a cigarette. 'My brother can give you a special rate on those.'

'I'm trying to stop, actually.'

In the old days he would have added 'Comrade Nurse' to fix her, but then in the old days she wouldn't have dared. Strangely, the comradeship is more real now. He feels a dangerous solidarity: she's not of his class, but he has slipped somehow into hers. Only for now, he feels sure.

He steps into the street, his synthetic sole scuffing on unchanged stone. In the old days it was Italian leather for him, the party shop for Alla. He notices with a slight lift of eyebrow that his trousers are beginning to keep the bulge at the knee.

'Mr Repin.'

It's the nurse again, beckoning him back. His instinct is to walk on but she turned away so confidently he's drawn back in. He blinks in the dark vestibule. She's not there. Not in the waiting room either. He tries the reception room, her domain, where a brackish light filters through the street-facing window, darkening the furniture.

He starts violently. She's in there, hanging from the ceiling, in the centre of the room. But no, she's pushing, not hanging, her arms lifted straight up in the air as if she were changing a light bulb.

'Aaaa-*ahh*!' she sighs, over the voluptuous cracking of bones, and turns to him. 'Every hour one should stretch the whole body.' She dips into a large carton on the floor and scoops up a black rabbit. 'Do you have room for him?'

Lev stares. First at the rabbit, then, lifting his eyes, at her. She meets his gaze.

'Isn't he sweet?'

Lev shapes his eyebrows into question marks, in italics. Here? In a *clinic*!

But she nuzzles the black fur and won't be deflected. 'Did you ever see the like? Soft as soft. Here.' She holds the creature out with a magician's authority.

The rabbit stops its nibbling and withdraws into itself, its whiskers stilled. Lev strokes its back once, with the knuckle of his middle finger, his other hand up against the rabbit's flank, to mark a limit.

'He's yours, if you like.' The nurse takes the smallest step towards him and immediately Lev's hands are buried in fur. They stand there a moment joined together by the warm creature. A little while ago it was a needle, Lev can't help thinking. The rabbit's whiskers stir in a random-seeming way and one whole side of it shudders so he's uncomfortably aware of hot pulpy life beyond the ribs. What have these soft bones to do with him? He pushes its blood heat away from him and encounters under that fine long-staple hair the shock of skin, hers.

'Isn't he a proper little gentleman?'

The rabbit expels a stream of dark pellets that fall to the floor around her white shoes. The seconds pass. Lev is standing up against a woman he expected never to see again. They are looking at the rabbit and the rabbit absorbs the energy of their concentration like a black hole.

'What's your future? Eh?' The nurse's mouth has softened as she brushes her lips against one long satiny ear. She could be a fortune-teller. The rabbit's ear leaps up at the sound then slopes back down mildly, trustingly.

Of course he must refuse. Alla would have a fit. Her allergies, for a start, and him flying on Friday.

'My future?' The nurse answers in a droll puppeteer's voice. 'Rabbit pie!'

Lev knocks lightly on the rabbit's forehead between the two bulges that he remembers in monkeys too. 'It would be nice, but I think no.'

She makes a disappointed rabbit face, two incisors biting into the lower lip, and returns the creature to his cardboard box. The box the office computer came in, lined, Lev sees, with grass and wilted lettuce leaves. 'My daughter brought him home, but my husband won't have him.'

Back in the street, Lev turns to wave. 'Sorry!'

Her hand flutters, the ring finger wagging. He watches the white nape of her neck disappear.

Again he's reminded of the gap between them. The job at the Indian Consulate is an aberration, a necessary one; it's never touched him. Research scientist Repin. It's why he's never envied Viktor the consul's Mercedes and is happier driving the runabout Volvo. The Volvo keeps him provisional; the Mercedes would mean he's a lifer. Embassy driver Repin – it's a uniform, not a skin. That's why the nurse is dangerous: she is her uniform. Her touch contaminates, makes him common. Lev Repin, who had access to a car then and has one now; black then, red now. They bought the Mitsubishi Galant before the axe fell. Now it stands in the yard waiting for a buyer, cat prints across the roof. But it's still his. He walks for the exercise, he tells his friends.

Yesterday, unable to sleep, he went downstairs at four in

the morning. In the chill white light the car stood there, its red skin mantled in dew, its wheels sullen and still. The skin glowed where he stroked the dew from it; he could almost imagine it shivering in the cold. The terrible endurance of things: such stubborn lonely persistence! It could wait for ever, for the key, the crowbar.

Sell it, he was thinking when a noise in the raspberry canes startled him. A fretful snuffling broke from the undergrowth and didn't stop till it had reached his feet. There the hedgehog sensed danger and went still. You poor sod. Don't you know you're in the open? What are quills good against? Dogs? Owls? The hedgehog didn't stir. Lev stared at the uselessness of its defences and felt the mood spread. To be going all that way on a single lead!

Now, with the vaccine pulsing in his arm, he realizes he should have driven. The truth is, driving is now tainted for him. Too many hours in the Volvo parked outside the market waiting while the vice consul's wife picks over foreign cheeses. Now there's irony: nowadays it's Alla who buys from the old women on the street; the stalls inside are an extravagance.

Deflected by a red light he lets his feet lead him up Shcherbakov Lane. Already a couple of Georgians are setting up a steel corral at the corner for the season's first watermelons. Empty, the cage looks big enough to hold a bear. A gypsy woman carrying a child on her hip watches the invasion of her territory but spares a glance for him as he goes by. Picky, he sniffs, annoyed even as he's relieved at being passed up. The mother sits leaned up against the wall with her legs straight out and a velvety purple skirt bunched up around them. Wearing a sweater in this weather. The alcove behind her stinks of urine. Mother and daughter have the same reddish-brown skin and reddish-black hair. He steps around the woman, staring at her black tight-cuffed pyjamas. Will Indians look like this?

A breeze stirs and the air seethes with birch seeds. The lane has brought him out on the Fontanka where there's a bench under a tree. He sits down, leans back and yawns. At once he hunches forward blinking, a birch seed in his eye. It's egregious, house-sized. First he can do no more than press, but then he tugs at his eyelashes, draws the upper lid down over the lower and works the eye sideways till it's out. He sits there wet-eyed, staring at the blur of paving stones between his feet. They are outlined in gold seed. Dunes of seed have formed around the iron paws of the bench, gold framing dull metal.

As he stares last night's dream returns to him. He's holding a gnawed-at piece of watermelon rind that's rotting in the heat. *Where do I throw this?* he asks a woman in a sari, and she points outside the door. In the twilight he sees a ruin spread out below the house where he's lodging. As he makes his way down to the site he sees it come alive with rows of lights like a runway. The grid is to orient him, he knows as he approaches. He has only to dig and it will yield gold beyond his wildest dreams. Strange!

On the air comes a deep bass thumping from across the canal. That will be the concert in Dvortsovaya Square. Alexei and his friends will be hanging out there already before the show begins. Lev is tempted to go and check on the boy. But Alex would think he was being spied on. Would waste a cigarette. Would be embarrassed too by his father's jacket, not black, or the wrong black, or his haircut. He gets up, dabbing at his eye and walks the other way, falling into step with the Fontanka, rubbing shoulders with the old dank winy air of it.

He draws a deep breath. Back in Petersburg! It was the one consolation when he lost the job. Losing Moscow, coming back home. Back to Peter. The streets, the sea, the empty skyline of his boyhood city. This canal especially, its moods changing with the sky, with the seasons, with the hour of the day. He leans his dull body, this silent brooding thing, against the parapet and peers at the water. Today the surface is restless, riffled by the same warm southerly whose gusts shake down the birches. Every few minutes a whole dark raft of mirrored windows silvers over, and then another and another as far as the Lomonosov Bridge while the gulls ride the unsteady air just above. In Moscow Lev used to think that what he missed most was the mewing of seagulls and the reek of bladderwrack, but now he realizes it was this canal. He knows every block of honey-coloured coping stone. As a boy he'd come here after school and walk along the top for a dare. He's seen Alex do the same.

He's shot up suddenly, Alex. Taller and more distant. The boy who could come up to you after a haircut and say: 'What's different about my hair?' So you couldn't help but say: 'It's longer. You've had it curled. It's not combed. It needs washing.' As he danced around you in mounting agony.

Doom, doom, the concert bass dents the languid air.

He steps across a trench dug to take a sewer. Sections of black pipe lie distributed along the cut; where the trench ends the remainder have been stacked in a pyramid. A spider has built a web across the mouth of the topmost pipe and caught a confetti of winged birch seeds, every seed die cut in gold. Plague cells shivering.

He crosses at the Lomonosov Bridge and waits for the lights even though there are no cars coming. Has he become a chauffeur, then? The thought sends him out into the street straight away so that a car that came up while he waited must brake sharply to let him by. The driver gives him a sour look and Lev responds with a finger. The man brakes hard to show he could get out and settle things and Lev sees the whole plan coming loose. The plane ticket in his pocket, snug with the passport he paid good money for, the whole brave scheme he's pondered and sweated over and pinned his hopes on. He lifts both hands in mock surrender and goes on his way.

At the Admiratelsky corner he looks significantly in the window of the Indian Tandoor where the waiters are busy with nothing. He looks significantly at the menu posted on the plate glass but it has no message for him. He's never cared for Indian food, for any food other than the food he grew up with.

The music hits him as he turns the corner. In the square the concert crowd is a horde of black ants with fair heads; the only colours are on strolling tourists. Where the stage is, under the column, the crowd is a phalanx and the music a fist in the chest.

Sod off, sod off, sodoffsodoffsodoff!

He scans the early birds up front. A solitary headbanger there, a big man, and right beside him, miracle of chance, is Alex. A full head taller than the rest at sixteen. Lev steps back instinctively, pushed also by the music. He'll go now. The boy is all right. He hasn't been trampled, he's not drunk.

But what's he up to now? A group of girls has come up,

friends. Alex and his mates greet them one by one with a ritual embrace. A loose clasping of arms about the other's neck, like Laplanders embracing. Alex performs his part with great formality, a long slow embrace with his hands folded behind the girl's neck, hardly touching her except where his wrists rest on her shoulders. It's a minimal encounter, mirrored by the girl and gravely performed, but the very solemnity of it in a pair so young is vaguely sinister, more than a groping hug and kiss might be.

Lev turns away unwilling to witness any more. This is the boy who just the other day asked with his eyes shining: *Shall we try the striped toothpaste?* He's crossing the great square when he hears footsteps catching up. The boy has come up behind, his face oddly hidden. His fingers are curled into two tunnels that he holds up against his eyes and he's staring at Lev without uttering a word. Binoculars, like.

'I wasn't spying on you, you idiot. I came to check out the concert. Who's playing?'

But Alex simply stands there with the glasses trained on his father.

'All right, I did see you. I just didn't think you wanted to be disturbed, with your friends and all.'

Alex comes up close without dropping his hands. The stare is unnerving. Trained in silence, the hooded eyes offer unbearable insolence. A wave of anger sweeps over Lev. He's tempted to shove the boy aside. But he masters the impulse and pats him on the cheek.

'Right. I'm off.'

And he turns away. But Alex doubles around and keeps up the stare, like a persistent cameraman. Lev surprises himself by breaking into a run. He's laughing, but he can't touch the boy.

Alex chases him for a bit, then falls back and returns to his friends, who are looking on. Lev turns, still grinning an unnaturally wide grin, and waves. His son hesitates, then flashes one hand from the waist. Lev ducks through the Morskaya Tunnel and slows down on the other side. Little Alex!

The music pursues him through the tunnel:

Fall down, fall down, falldownfalldownfalldown!

He takes the tram down Nevsky, avoiding the conductor like any twelve-year-old and getting off one stop before the Fontanka when he sees the man coming. He walks along the right bank of the canal this time, noticing how the water looks green from this side against the buildings that face the setting sun.

At the Rossi corner two young girls are feeding a mouldy loaf to the gulls. What mould? he wonders casually. The girls shriek louder as he approaches, their audience. They're too young for the concert, whose sounds must tantalize them here. The pretty one, poised on a boundary, looks up as he draws level, an open face accustomed already to tribute. Her plain companion's small cross face is tightly shut. He withholds the required look; Alex's embrace is still on his mind.

He carries her face with him as he turns the corner. But the turning shakes loose in him another face, Meschersky's. Superimposed on that healthy young face, Meschersky's ravaged mask, a network of burst capillaries risen to its surface. Or the face sunk to that subsurface, on its way down to a depth that life cannot endure. The odd thing is that the look on these superimposed faces is identical: it's a look of entreaty, a brave look. The girl's is brave and questing,

Meschersky's was brave and doomed. That was the hardest part to take, the recognition in those bloodshot eyes that he was past the point of return.

Nobody at work could concentrate that week. Not on work; they concentrated beautifully on Meschersky. Specifically, obsessively, on the pricked finger. They went about their jobs like automatons, could think of nothing but the accident.

'Morning.' Grigoriev looked away as he spoke.

Lev watched his colleague's arm slip cautiously into his lab coat as if a scorpion lurked there.

'How is he?' They'd stopped using his name.

'Same. Still waiting.'

All week they waited with him. Not one of them who didn't find himself staring into space as he ran thumb over fingertip, over and over. Tension so rich it communicated itself to the animals in their cages. A monkey that would ordinarily stop in its tracks as you went by and stare drop-jawed at you now hunched glumly grinding its teeth, eyes glazed with the ceiling's white light. Its neighbour sat and frigged itself listlessly.

On the fifth day Meschersky developed a temperature and they knew.

If there'd been a guillotine as Lev had once proposed, Meschersky would have sacrificed the finger instantly. Or would he have? Instead he took the prescribed route: red button, telephone, airlock 5, elevator to the decontamination chamber at Circle 4. Going up the levels someone had named from Dante when the building was new.

And all the while the virus coursing through his veins.

Kurile-D, the living face of death. Another face in the gallery Lev carries with him from his vanished career. Faces he watched over till they were as familiar as Alla's, more familiar than Alexei's – which after all kept changing. Sifting faces was what he did in those years after the induction when, led past immunology, he found himself seconded into research he could not speak of to anybody, not even his wife. Years when, still a young man but already slightly hunched from sitting over a microscope, he had watched his qualities vanish one by one till he seemed to himself invisible. Fading was what you were doing, since what you were doing had no official existence. You did as you were told, responsible for your programme, not for yourself. What self? You had leached out of yourself.

Every time he put his eye to the microscope Lev felt himself falling. The fall was fantasy, something at last he could control. A free fall into inner space, down an infinitely graded scale from larger to smaller, a fall checked at the day's micro-setting. He fell into the circle of light at the bottom, walked on that bright water, pure surface stretched above bottomless depth. He fell in silence, into silence. Put to mutate a cell he widened the game. The cell's horizon saw the threat, the agitated tumescence in its wall a plasmic response. You were firing blind, through slits in the wall, aiming for the nucleus, aiming to change its disposition. You singled out a gladiator in the arena and deployed him to infiltrate the ranks, to change the face of his kind. Here Lev would lift his eye from the microscope and look around sheepishly. It was a sort of video game he shared with nobody.

The game made the fear manageable. Because to watch Kurile-D multiply was a terrifying spectacle. It all but sprang out of the dish, its hordes pouring in every direction from a black hole that welled up continuously out of nowhere.

Medicine would cap that well; at Biosecuritat his job was to harness its power.

Porridge, they called it. You never lost respect for it. The nickname was the respect, a scientist's totemism. It placated the dark god. It kept the fear, as much as the virus, from breaking out. Just be careful. It came down to that. And luck. Meschersky's ran out.

They isolated him at once. On Circle 6 where the nurses wore spacesuits and even Circle 5 staff were forbidden entry without permits.

'He's my neighbour,' Lev said the first day.

'No visitors.'

'I work here.'

'And what do I do?'

Next morning he went to the director. 'His wife wants to see him.'

'Impossible.'

'Not even in a spacesuit?'

'Would he want to see her in one?'

Lev agreed. Why would she put one on anyway? The point was to be with him, not around him, he thought as he took his off in the decontamination room. In the isolation chamber Meschersky had taken him for one of the doctors. Better to talk to him through the fish tank glass; at least you were both recognizable.

Meschersky was sitting very still in an upright chair as if concentrating on the questions of an unseen interrogator. He must have caught a glimpse of movement beyond the glass because he turned his head with a studied calm. Lev was thrown; he'd expected to find him in bed. What to say? How are you feeling? Are they looking after you? Is there any pain? He discarded each in turn as he moved towards the glass.

'Meschersky! Hi.'

Meschersky gave his eyebrows a quick hoist. The hoist said: *Repin. Yes. Here I am.*

'How do you feel?'

The man shrugged. 'Nothing. How is Elena?'

'She wanted to come right away.'

Meschersky sipped water from a paper cup. 'They won't let her, I've asked. Tell her it's routine, not to worry.' He drained the cup and looked vaguely for a bin, like a man in a foreign room. There wasn't one so he held on to the empty cup with a puzzled look.

'Can you sleep?'

'They give me something. I'm OK, so far. No pain.'

No pain, just the waiting. Five days, sometimes six, from what was known of the disease. Meschersky kept a diary, wrote letters. By the seventh day there was only pain.

The next time Meschersky was in bed, the bed pushed up against the glass. His eyes were red, hundreds of capillaries bursting in there, but focused. As the red mesh spread over the whites, a gummy fluid collected in the lining and oozed from the corners. Every ten minutes a nurse in a spacesuit padded into the room and swabbed the wings of his nose. Meschersky's head was propped up to prevent him choking on his catarrh. He looked at Lev and began to weep. Lev was shown out. He did not return.

The known symptoms began to appear. Blood leaked from Meschersky's nose and ears. Blinding headaches flooded his brain and pushed on downwards to rack the spine; he was put on morphine. He ran a high fever that came down in the afternoon and then climbed higher before falling in his daily sweats. His sheets wanted changing with every shift, dumped wet in the incinerator at Circle 7. By the ninth day the duty nurse found the skin to blotch when he was lifted. Blood and tissue had begun to run together. Presently his blue-white redhead's skin with its high pink tones turned grey, then it turned black. It began to give in places, so he looked like the victim of a stabbing, not the jab of a needle. Towards the end the abdominal organs began to come away from their moorings. When he turned over they tended to remain where they were, like parcels in a sack. Gravity was tearing him apart, from the inside.

Germ warfare is the opposite of firebombing. It works from the inside out, in silence. It takes its time.

Back on Circle 5 they were firing blind. Looking for Kurile-E, or F or G. Something the enemy couldn't fight. The load delivered, Lev could sit biting his nails (a delicate gnawing with the hand turned away, an almost balletic gesture) till the cell showed acceptance or rejection of the foreign body. And there was still the climb back up, ducking the debris of dead cells, fighting assorted gravities. Organelles plucking at his sleeve as he went. Up higher, fungi stroked his midriff, parasites nibbled at his fingertips like goldfish. The shock of deliverance as he lifted his eye from the eyepiece was sometimes greater than when he stepped out of the last airlock into the outside world. As if he had taken up dual citizenship.

Sometimes he saw a tremor pass over the face of the deep. Matter, or simply optics? He imagined an eye opening in the void and staring gravely back at him. He looked away, checking on the world up above, his lips moving gently, enumerating: bench, cuff, test tube, napkin. These eccentricities did not go unnoticed by those who watched the watchers. In time their cumulative weight would count against him. Security risk Repin, unsteady puppet.

Towards the end the frisking as he left the campus was especially thorough. There were whole worlds an unhinged mannequin might be tempted to purloin.

Lev's head turns slowly as an astronaut's. Dark suns, winged seed, cool jelly, stardust.

He feels the proud flesh at the hepatitis shot buzz; the whole muscle is stiff where the serum went in. He's leaning on the parapet staring into the green water of the past. Eased out after twenty years for reasons of state security. But all those worlds came out with him after all. What frisking could hope to keep back the chain of sequences he carries in his head? Like a soldier back from a frontier war he hoards dark images. He moves among civilians who have no inkling of how the war is prosecuted, who don't see the wounded. For a moment he feels the veteran's baffled rage.

'Repin!'

It was bound to happen. There's no mistaking the blunt cranial mass and shambling round-shouldered walk of Isaak Tikhonov. Lev hasn't seen him since they were students together. Even at twenty Tikhonov was neckless. They called him St Isaak after the domed cathedral across the river.

'Tikhonov, my God!' Lev uses his proper name because St Isaak is with a woman.

'My wife, Katia,' Tikhonov introduces her. 'Katia, Lev Repin, who disappeared to Moscow and left us disconsolate in the bad old days.'

'These are good days?'

'You wait and see. You still live opposite the bandstand?'

'No, but we're not far away. You still on Rubinshtenya?'

'Of course. Come on home with us.' Tikhonov collects a hard look from his wife. 'Or maybe we'll go to the beer garden here.'

'OK, but I can't stay long. Alla will be waiting, my wife.'

'Go get her!'

'She'll have just got home from work.'

'Even better.'

'You haven't changed.'

'I was just thinking the same.'

'I'll let you boys catch up,' Katia announces at the corner under the yellow neon outline of a cocktail glass.

'Oh, come on,' Tikhonov urges half-heartedly.

'And dinner will cook itself?' She pats the back of his plump hand, not convinced by the disappointed droop he's given it. 'See he doesn't misbehave,' she says to Lev and shoos them both down the short flight of steps.

'Nice?' Tikhonov says, turning to Lev when she's gone.

'You always got the pick, St Isaak.'

'Hey, you did all right as I recall. But you should have seen her twenty years ago.'

'Maybe I did.'

'Bastard! She's smart too, you can't imagine.' When Isaak shakes his disbelieving head the shoulders and the whole torso are involved.

They find a corner in the railed-off patio under a grotesquely pollarded cherry tree. Isaak shoves the table black and forth on the grey paving stones till it's steady before sitting heavily down. Then he gets back up and shambles off to the bar. He's wearing expensive shoes but even in brogues he'd look prosperous. There are squashed cherry stains under-foot and a litter of sticky stones. He comes back with a pitcher.

'Vodka later.' His voice sounds fat and rich; he makes his jowly unshaven cheeks look fashionable.

Now you *do* walk for the exercise, Lev finds himself thinking. 'Practising?' he asks.

Isaak spreads his podgy hands. But the gold glints off his small oval spectacles belie the helpless stance. His skin is scrubbed and scented and the scent cuts cleanly through the beery fug. For the first time Lev is conscious of his old frames.

'You had the ground floor, right?'

'The upstairs folk moved out. That was what, 94?, when they were selling titles. We bought up front and back. Katia knows the market, don't ask me how. So, what, you up here for a breather?'

'You could say.'

'Still in Moscow, though?'

'The institute is not quite in the city, you know.' It's got to come out, Lev thinks, just like I had to run into him, or someone. He's surprised it took so long. 'You report to Moscow, but the labs are—' He fans a hand out so any one of the fingers could point into the heart of Russia.

Isaak looks that way as if he expected to see something. 'All hush-hush, eh?'

They're briefly uncomfortable, not at the danger but at the fact that *hush-hush* can now be said out loud. Strangely, now that the old danger is past, the obliquest reference to secrecy is a kind of embarrassing admission.

All week long Lev has felt a shifting in him, as of long-settled layers preparing to buckle. This sundown hour, coming at the end of a day of upheavals, represents a kind of summation, as if the cracks in his life have suddenly converged. In a way he finds his career to be simply a figure of a greater fall, his country's, which was after all the collapse of secrecy. He studies his old friend and is suddenly swamped by a craving to confide. Isaak reads the look on Lev's face and puts out a feeler.

'We figured you'd gone into defence. And when you didn't write we knew.'

'I'm not there any more.'

'How do you mean?'

'I quit.' He can't bring himself to pronounce *redundant*.

Isaak's jowls lengthen in astonishment, but he waits. When Lev appears to lapse into moody silence he pushes out: 'Just like that?' Lev says nothing again so he softens it with: 'When was this?'

'A couple of years back.'

'You set up on your own?'

'Sort of.' Lev is drawing an endless spiral on the tabletop. 'A couple of us thought we'd set up a lab. Pathology, testing, that sort of thing. Everyone was setting up at that time. You remember Vozhakov? There were three of us. He was in it. We had it all worked out. I would do the testing, Vozhakov would sell us, and this guy whose idea it was, he would steer.'

'And capital?'

'We put up a third each, I thought. The funny thing is it could have worked. It would have been paid back by now: there are fifty functioning labs in Moscow. We had what it took: plant, logo, letterhead; there was even a brass plaque Alla designed. We were a company, we were textbook.'

'The doer, the talker, the seer.'

'You do need all three.' Even now Lev has trouble believing it. 'When you think of it, any one of the three can go bad, but the seer has the most time to. We were showing losses right away. And then he was gone.' Such a big place this country, a man can just disappear, still. Twelve time zones, the biggest country in the world.

'You lose a lot?'

'The car at least was in Alla's mother's name. What's up?'

'Nothing. Just what walked in.'

Lev turns to look. The woman is not special but her short skirt and high platform soles make her pale legs look improbably long.

'St Isaak,' Lev grumbles.

'Just looking. So where are you now?'

This too had to come. 'I'm at the Indian Consulate here.'

'In *Peter*?'

'Yes.'

Now Lev has Isaak's full attention. 'You've been here since when?'

'It's two years since the company folded.'

'You've been here two years!' *And you haven't looked me up?* hangs in the air between them.

'I was lucky. They use a lot of English,' Lev offers, to pre-empt the next question.

'Aha.' Isaak knows Lev went to the English school on Zagorodny. He went to a Hindi school himself.

'You still speak Hindi?' Lev remembers.

'For what it's worth. I used to think I'd go there some day. Maybe I will, who knows.'

Now is Lev's opening but he backs off. The truth is he

can't believe he's leaving in less than a week. At some point the plan rose up, natural as a landform, but suddenly it looks insane. He still doesn't know who he's going to meet, where to go once he's there. The lead he dug out of Ramaswamy in the front office always sounded thin. And Purohit, their visiting military attaché, so crisply specific in the back seat, came up with two ministry numbers and a couple of hotels Lev could have got out of a book. His mouth goes dry at the thought. What's he done? It's madness, vanity. Just because he was not convinced of his driverliness!

But the moment he remembers the Volvo — it's always parked when he sees it, never moving — he knows why he's going: that's not his future, it can't be. It was a lucky break when it came, but that was desperation. Now Alla has a job at the china shop, he needn't carry groceries, walk the dog, fetch the dry-cleaning. He's even carried Shep's litter downstairs. A dark woman's dogshit, for godsake.

'Drink up,' he says, and reaches for the pitcher, but becomes aware of a commotion behind him. There's a man crumpled on the floor and the long-legged woman is kneeling beside him screeching. People have risen from their tables while the bartender kneels on the other side of the fallen man unhurriedly loosening his collar. The woman has risen and is appealing to the patrons for a doctor. Someone goes to the telephone.

Lev looks at Isaak who has not risen, who has in fact put out a hand to restrain him.

'I'm not that kind of doctor, Lev. Anyway, it's just a fit.'

Lev sits sideways on his chair a moment before turning his back on the incident. He lights up and smokes the first drags in silence.

'So, what kind of doctor are you?'

Tikhonov rubs his furred cheeks as if unaccustomed to the fuzz and looks intently at nothing. One hand continues on up and runs over the short nap of greying hair that covers the whole of his head except for a coppery tonsure at the back. He lets the hand rest there; its gold ring shines at the centre like the treasure in a fairytale.

'I got into trouble not long after you left. Something I said. They sent me to Murmansk.'

'Murmansk! My grandfather was sent there. He died building a hospital.'

'I built a toilet block in hard frost. And I did Siberia. They moved Isaak around.' He gives the name its full Hebrew valency, then waves the whole thing aside in disgust. 'It came right, anyway. I came back and finished what I started, went into surgery. I do nose jobs now, snip and tuck, add-ons, cut-offs. Want your dewlap fixed? Katia stood by me. She's a psychoanalyst, by the way – the real estate is on the side.'

'Psychoanalysis! There's a demand?'

'We come to everything late, right? The BMW brigade want their heads shrunk. Katia's qualified too, especially in the Freudian stuff. Good listener. Published too, but if you ask me her special talent is houses.'

Lev listens, enchanted. 'So it's turned out well for you.'

Isaak spreads his hands again, and the self-satisfied gesture makes Lev moodily envious. The empty jug rattles against the napkin dispenser as the metro passes underground and sets the paving stones trembling. Lev scrapes a cherry stone off his sole and tries to keep his voice even.

'So we're both the kind of doctor who makes you sick.'

Isaak barks out a laugh. 'Katia's the well-making kind. Come along and taste her shchi.'

'I can't. Alla's waiting.'

'Then come next week. I want to meet her.'

No way out now, Lev knows. He pushes his lips out and says meditatively. 'Next week I'll be in India.'

'*India!* You sneaky bugger! What's this all about?'

'Bit of business. Clothes.'

'Clothes?' Isaak absorbs this. 'You been there before?'

'First time.'

'You know the market?'

'You've got to start somewhere. There's a lot of stuff coming in. That shirt you're wearing is probably from there. They'll put on any label you want. The margins are good, Isaak. You buy cheap. It's the labour.'

Isaak has made a washboard of his forehead and keeps it that way, so Lev trails off uncertainly.

'Where will you sell?'

'The kiosks, Sennaya, Apraksin, anywhere.'

'Sounds like a lot of trouble.'

'Our neighbour's done all right. He's been back four times. He works from the house.'

'And Customs?'

'They take their cut.'

'And there's still enough left over?'

'Seems to be.' Anything's better than waiting in the Volvo.

'Good luck. Be sure to see the Taj Mahal.'

'You're the one who should be going, St Isaak.'

'You know, I used to think at school I would. We used to have guest speakers come from there. I remember this old woman in a white sari who'd written a whole lot of books.

For a whole term I saw myself as a doctor in some godfor-saken village spreading socialism and sanitation. One Prize Day we had a film star from Madras who couldn't speak either Hindi or Russian.'

'What did he do?'

'She smiled a lot. I can still see her teeth.'

They stand outside in the twilight. The first breath of a sea breeze flows down the street.

'You should be going to America – with your English,' Isaak says, staring at the pavement between his feet.

Lev, who has stepped back from the streetlight to hide his sneakers, would like to say he's selling his know-how, not his English. He follows Isaak's gaze and finds they're astride the fading work of a pavement artist's crayons. It's the Petrov-Vodkin painting *Bathing the Red Horse*; the copyist will have sat all day beside it with a cap to catch coins in. The things one does to make a living.

It could be the beer or the breeze playing on his seaward side, but suddenly the thought of his journey no longer weighs him down. All day he has been on edge, all summer he's been torn by conflicting feelings that always end in a paralysing nervousness. Now, standing here, he's ready to go.

'America?' he laughs. 'As in Levis? You know the denim capital of the world?'

'Don't tell me. Wuhan?'

'Ahmedabad. State of Gujarat. Population thirty-five million.'

'Is that where you're going?'

'No. I get off in Delhi. Population ten million.'

'Give or take a million.' Isaak shakes his head and shoulders. 'So when do you get back?'

'Let's see. It's an open ticket. I'll play it by ear.' Lev thinks of the phone numbers he was given and the phrase takes on a new resonance. He doesn't feel bad about lying. Biosecuritat taught him evasion if it taught him anything. Besides, he's not just romancing about the rag trade. If the other comes to nothing he'll stock up on jeans on the way back. Cover your ass: Mother Russia's taught him something too.

'You have insurance?'

'What for?'

'Accident, sickness.'

'I intend to stay healthy.'

'In *India*! I'd take out life.'

'I intend to stay alive.'

'No, no. You just take *out* a life policy, like some people I know, and take it from there. There's a lot of American companies looking for suckers: here's your chance to teach them.'

'Teach them?'

'And get rich.'

'How's that?'

'You really want to know?'

'Tell me.'

Isaak lets the command crystallize in the air between them and smiles a small serious smile.

'You have to be prepared to die, sort of.'

Lev fetches back his straying gaze and pins it on Isaak.

'Sort of?'

'Yeah, not *die* die. You disappear. It can be arranged here, but it's actually easier abroad. You know Sergei Punin? Didn't stand a chance but ran for mayor? He was a jeweller, into other things too? You remember how he was shot at his own front door? So. That was insurance. His wife is richer by one and a half million dollars. And she got compensation for harassment too – by the company. They said he wasn't dead. They always say that about Russians, so why do they keep coming back? It must be good business. Punin is wanted in France too.'

'*Is* wanted?'

'Well,' Isaak looks right and left, 'he found the right doctor.'

'Someone you know.'

Isaak repeats the same smile, no shorter or longer.

'What have you got against insurance companies?'

'Nothing. Maybe their buildings: think of our skyline. But think of Alla too. And of your new life.'

'What's it cost?'

'Your identity, basically. You'd have to relocate. You'd need another passport, but you can buy one where you're going. Over there you can buy death certificate, news story, photos, burial records, police report, the whole package. Here too, but it's harder.'

'And money?'

'The down payment. And maybe a couple more. But look at the return.'

'What's in it for you?'

'Percentage.'

'You make it sound easy.'

'It has its risks.'

Lev shakes his head. 'Thanks.'

'Well, you can always scale down to accident or sickness. If your other "business" doesn't work out.' Isaak drives the inverted commas in and Lev sees he doesn't mean clothing. He feels suddenly exposed and is tempted to come clean.

'You remember that mouse, Isaak?'

A quarter of a century later Isaak blinks just once before he remembers. The laboratory overlooking the Neva, and a mouse without its skin running loose under the tables. Isaak had meant to stun it the usual way before injecting. He swung it by the tail but the head missed the bench and the creature was unjacketed. Isaak was left holding the white pelt while the mouse ran, pink and squeaking in mortal panic. Twenty-five years and their separate skins still tingle at the memory.

Isaak plucks a card from his wallet and presses it into Lev's hand. 'Call me.'

'I will.'

But Lev is not sure he will. He walks the other way, aware that St Isaak has not taken his new address, that he must have guessed that Lev carries no card. Lev Repin, Consular Driver.

He looks at himself in the plate glass at the Rossi corner. The reflection shows a sallow troubled face lit by the glow off the rich cushions. Suspended in the dusk, it's unlined for a man of forty-six, though lately a single furrow has come to stay across the very middle of the forehead. He frowns to remove it, preferring the two short vertical folds that appear between the eyebrows instead. He has noticed the transformation before, the gravity and focus it brings to a face that left to itself drifts into melancholy.

It helps that he's kept his hair: it lies as thick as ever in overlapping tiles all across his head. All the growth points one way, forward, part genes, part Alla's handiwork: her haircuts in the kitchen are front-on raids made without a comb, with just the scissors and her fingers over three open pages of a newspaper spread on the linoleum.

He imagines himself at the interview. This is what they'll see. He doesn't expect they'll take him on right away. First the vetting. He has his notes for the briefing. Yes, he's right to be going, he has to be there, on the spot; no good angling from here. No, pick your country and go.

He turns and walks towards the Fontanka as an ambulance goes by, to the beer garden, most likely. His feet stop at the top of the slope of the Lomonosov Bridge and he leans on the rail there looking out across the dark water, and smokes a whole cigarette. All his puppet wires are tingling and there's a tremor in his stomach that complicates the hunger he had begun to feel sitting in the beer garden.

Softly the white night descends on his shoulders while the remnants of day silhouette the apartment buildings on either side of the canal. In the distance bulks the squat dome of St Isaak's. The sunset afterglow gives the further roofs and chimneys the carpentered look of a backlit stage set. Lights have come on in the windows, heightening the resemblance, yet even at this distance Lev can see that the casements are open; one that continues shut catches in its glass the pear-coloured light of the sky, a cool yellow beside the warmth of those domestic interiors. In one window a woman makes a trepanning motion as she interrogates an invisible player. On the street below, all the cars swoop madly together each time the lights change, like flocks of tin birds. In the sky above, a searchlight from the rock concert makes a lazy metronome.

Down the black waters of the canal comes a floating discotheque whose music blots out the distant concert.

Corralled on deck by strings of coloured bulbs, tourists dance under the sky. A strobe light claps a series of white masks on their faces; their heads, their matchstick limbs, appear at a bizarre new place with every flash. The boat passes under the bridge, under his feet. Its light must illuminate him as well because he is spotted leaning there by the skeleton dancers. *Jump!* they grin, *Jump!* There's an insane moment when he feels he could launch himself and land safely on deck. The boat glides on down the canal, drawing its music with it.

Lev lets fall his cigarette butt and listens for the hiss. When he looks up the cruise boat has shrunk into a circle of light. The digital lines and dots of the dancers swarm like Kurile-D. The Fontanka shivers under him, troubled as by the passage of a vivid dream. He hears the flop of the pleasure boat's wake striking the stone walls of the canal and doubling back on itself. The sound is comforting; all sound is to a man who has spent his life, spent himself, looking. Sometimes he thinks he consciously pushed Alex into music, away from the curse of sight.

The trepanner comes to the window opposite and leans on the sill, resting between cuts. She could be Alla, but has a coarse neck. Lev feels a rush of desire and tenderness. He steps across the city works trench with a sense of mission and a return of appetite. Thursday tripe and onions has him homing by the backlots shortcut, stretching his pace along the grey paving in the grey light. Diesel hangs in the shadows, and a full moon, and the idle gritty banging of a basketball from an alley where a group of teenagers find gossip more interesting than the game. Their voices rise softer than smoke into the blue night. His feet leave the paving and cross the grassed median strip of Dostoevskogo with its double row of holm oaks. Straight ahead is the old carriageway tunnel whose stone edges have worn smooth as labia; whenever Lev ducks in there he feels received into a womblike security. He steps off the flagstones into the powdery dust of the yard and the noise of the city dies behind him. He crosses the children's park where it's sandy underfoot and a young mother sits on a swing waiting while her child wrings the last pleasure of the day from a squeaking roundabout. Beyond the blackcurrant bushes shines the dull red of the Galant.

Lev looks up at the window and smiles at the shadow of Alla's head above the line of the sash. The ricepaper blind with its bamboo splints glows white, as if a projector were on in the bedroom. The head is bent unnaturally to one side, leaning away from the shadow of an arm whose hand holds a gun.

Lev's stomach drops as his brain supplies a silencer to the short barrel, but then he sees the coiled lead and recognizes the familiar outline of the hairdryer. The kitchen light is out, which means she got tired of waiting for her truant males. Tomorrow her mother arrives, with her trunks, trading three granddaughters for a grandson. She'll hold the fort while he's away, now Alla's working, and might stay on, Alla thinks, to escape the teenage girls. The girls are her pet gripe lately, Alla says, but Lev is sure Alex will set a new benchmark in grandmother-baiting.

He unlocks the common door and steps in, narrowly missing the dog turd on the mat. The whole basement stinks of it; it'll be the setter from No. 33. Did they expect it to let itself out? Savages. He shuts off his breathing, picks up the mat and, holding back the sprung door, steps back out with it, meaning to shake the mess off. But it won't come away so easily and in a temper he chucks the whole thing into the bushes. Damn the creature. They'll lose it, next thing; already it's started running loose. Since the crash last August there's been a rash of abandoned pets. The economists will have worked out a rouble–poodle index by now. Breathing again, he's glad he vetoed Alex's Dobermann fancy last summer, though the penalty was a week of heavy metal turned up high.

'They were like this,' he shows Alla, and goes through the strange embrace he witnessed at the concert. He folds his hands behind her slender neck where the hair is still wet and lets the wrist bones ride lightly on her shoulders. He brings his forehead slowly forwards to meet hers till their noses are touching and stands there.

'It feels all right,' she says. 'You should do it more often.' There's vodka on her breath.

'One by one? With each of them? It looked creepy.'

'You just keep clear of wars and disasters for me.' She kisses him gently. 'Mother's coming on Tuesday now. And my ears are ringing, Lev. Go set the table while I finish.'

He kisses her on each ear. They're little shells, her most delicate feature, growing close to her skull. It's an injustice, a weird irony, that their porcelain should suffer daily in the showroom. Every cup, every saucer, every china bowl that crosses the sales counter must be rung in the presence of the customer. Already she's come to dread a discount sale, when the chopstick never seems to leave her hand.

'You know the red setter from downstairs?' he calls from the kitchen, but she's switched the dryer back on and he lets it go. Its wail must blot out the ringing. He must talk to her about selling the Galant. The alarm system which first intrigued her now jars on her nerves whenever the hoons at No. 33 set it off.

'Do you know who I just ran into?' he says as they sit down to eat and Alex's plate shines like an accusing moon. They've taken to starting without him lately; there's no telling when he'll come in. Lev tells her about St Isaak. 'And I almost brought you home a rabbit.'

'What's wrong with lamb? We're not that desperate.'

He's describing his afternoon at the clinic when Alex's key sounds in the door. Alex comes in, drapes his jacket on the wall radio, mumbles something and goes straight to his room.

'Did he say headache?'

Alla shrugs, exhausted. 'Let him sleep it off.' She makes up a plate and puts it in the oven for him. Alex has learnt where to go when he wakes up in the night. 'And I think I'll follow his example.'

Lev is not yet ready for bed. It'll be some time before this day relinquishes its hold on him. When Alla has gone to bed he reclines on the ottoman that was his grandfather's. He thinks of the rock concert and is surprised by the anger that floods him when he reruns the humiliation of that chase with Alex's binoculars fixed on him. And he *likes* rock! He leans across and looks at himself in the mirror that the framed Japanese print becomes when the wall lamp is on. Is he really past it?

He gets up and goes to Alex's room, knocks softly. There's no answer; the light is out. He pushes the door open and goes in. Alex is lying face down on his bed, boots and all. His face is turned away, but he's so still he can only be awake. Lev goes and sits down on the bed beside him and puts a hand on his shoulder. Alex says nothing, just breathes in deeply. Lev's hand begins to massage gently, working its way towards the boy's neck.

'Where's the pain?'

Silence.

'Here?'

'Up.'

'Here?'

'Right up.'

Lev lets go of the rope at the nape, that tough and tender fibre-optic cable now uploading pain, and shifts higher up along the bed so he can use both hands.

'Here?'

A nod. Headphones of pain. Lev leans over and grips the whole shaven skull from the top down so his fingertips rest just above the ears, those woefully sticking out ears that can't come from Alla, and levers with his thumbs at the top of the cranium, making as if to lift off the headphones. He dredges up with both hands, the pressure at the fingertips, as if peeling off a cap. Alex moans, *yes.*

Agreement at last, after a year of noes.

For twenty minutes Lev sits there, his fingertips ploughing the fine stubble already returned across the scalp till the boy falls asleep. On the pillow the weird dreaming mushroom of the head is motionless, guarding its pictures. Lev sees again the headbanger this evening ramming the speakers till the band's security led him away. He's tempted to examine Alex's forehead but desists.

So what are you, puppet or puppeteer? he asks softly, and passes a hand over the sleeping body to check for strings. And more to the point, he says, looking away into the centre of the room and then down at the hand he just moved, What are *you*? No mirror he can look in here.

He slips out of the room, takes the denim jacket off the radio in the hall and carries it back to Alex's door without going through the pockets. Alex wouldn't bring drugs home, would he? He goes through the pockets, finds a metro token, a broken book of matches, a safety pin, two condoms and a snotty handkerchief. He pulls the door to, leaving a crack, and hangs the jacket on the door knob.

Alla is asleep. He hears her breath popping wetly on the pillow before he reaches the room and stops. Tomorrow, no, the day after, his mother-in-law comes to stay and the next day he's gone. He goes to the kitchen and pours himself a glass of water from the kettle. In the old days you could drink straight out of the tap, he can hear the old lady saying. She will play romances on the piano, her piano. How will Alla cope with her helper?

He washes the pot and the frying pan because he knows she'll want to do them along with everything else before going to work in the morning. When he hangs up the tea towel his day catches up with him and pushes him down onto a kitchen chair. As he sits, a still wearier pair of eyes opens in the dark, sick to death.

Meschersky. A whole Amazon of tiny rivulets drains the light from the whites of his eyes into the black holes at the centre. He has raged, he has burned, and now he has gone quiet; drugged, but not blank, just silent. Lev knows that response. How you strain to get on in this world, and how chance stands in the way. How the world's intransigence glooms over you, makes a criminal of you; how its indifference makes a monster of you!

He sees how the tension of unknowing must have told on Alla. If it left him numb what did it do to her? He rubs the puppet arm just below where the needle went in. The muscle is stiff. His chest bone is cold; all the cold of the Petersburg night has collected there, but the heart pumps hotly underneath. He sits in the dark with one arm resting on the oilcloth and listens to the tick-tock of the clock.

The Aeroflot stewardess is leaning over him with a smile.

'The gentleman behind would like to know if it's you that's ticking.'

Lev shakes his head and nods sideways at the grand-mother in the sari one seat along. Her pacemaker. Her grandson is travelling with her, each the other's escort. They're in the front row, extra legroom just for Lev. There are two empty seats on the other side that Lev has begun to covet, but there's some delay in boarding so he could still lose them. Middle block, middle seat: he's in the heart of the plane. He reclines his seatback, stretches the whole length of his body, presses deep into the seat and shuts his eyes.

The latecomers appear. He's out of luck. A family. Father, mother, and in the mother's arms, an infant. The baby's head, large and pink and vulnerable, juts alarmingly into Lev's space. The husband looks apologetic over the top of his boarding pass. A bassinet arrives and refuses to hook onto its bracket in the wall. Lev leans forward and releases a catch. The mother lays the baby in the cradle, stopping halfway when he gives a little choking cry. He swallows gummily and sleeps on.

As soon as the plane levels out Lev signals for a drink. The steward brings vodka without blinking. Aeroflot, the home carrier. Then he orders another and another. He shuts his eyes and quickly opens them. Meschersky has returned to haunt him at ten thousand metres. There is blue sky out there, above a ground of rabbity cloud, but every window has Meschersky's face. Like a bank of television screens, even those with the shades down.

Be here now, Lev tells himself. He looks at the late arrivals. Imagines them starting out in London. Immediately he sees a kitchen from an ad in a glossy magazine with this woman in it. He imagines their soft luggage going onto the scales at Heathrow. Heathrow: the very word sounds rich, and he tests it softly on his tongue. Then he sounds Sheremetev. It conjures up history, the Fontanka palace, not the Moscow airport. Sheremetev. Heathrow.

The woman turns her head a fraction. He realizes he's been whispering the names and leans over to pat his cabin bag. The husband is reading a fat paperback. He's drinking tonic water; his wife would like a Bloody Mary but is nursing. 'All blood, no Mary,' she smiles regretfully as the steward pours the tomato juice.

Dinner arrives and unaccountably skips her. She seems oddly embarrassed to ask. The husband is already eating. Lev points out the lapse to the stewardess in the other aisle and feels obliged to hold back until the woman's dinner appears. She acknowledges the gesture with a smile and a slight raising of her glass. She eats hungrily, the nursing lioness. He is hungry himself after the delay at the airport, where the flight was held up by two hours to pick up connecting passengers.

When the tables are cleared the woman leans over to look into the bassinet. Lev hopes there'll be a movie, though the screen looks too close for comfortable viewing. He'll watch it all the same, ward off Meschersky's evil eye.

So far the baby hasn't cried. It hasn't even woken up. The window shades are lowered and the lights go down but there is no movie. Lev joins the queue outside the toilets. When he returns to his seat he has to pick his way past the grandmother. She refused dinner but made sure her charge ate everything. Then she curled up and fell asleep on the carpet. The boy is playing with his panel of switches but desists when Lev returns. He takes off his headphones and creeps under his blanket. Lev spreads his own blanket and prepares to sleep, his mind swarming over the country he will wake up in. The woman beside him has put her seat back and closed her eyes. Her husband reads on in his private pool of light.

Passport, money, ticket. Lev runs through the litany of the last few days, his hands reaching for the various pockets about his person. Keys. Decoy wallet. He leans to one side and feels in his back pocket. The woman's shoulder feels warm. Heathrow. He taps the bag on the floor beside him with his foot, then reaches down and stows it between his feet. His mind goes over the contents. Files, briefing notes, identity papers, letters of introduction, including the two he wrote himself, notebooks, slides, camera, film. On and on, smaller and smaller. Shaver, cologne, aspirin. He breathes out. All there. The woman beside him fetches a slow deep breath.

Lev grows aware of the bodies all around him. He pictures the baby in the bassinet drawing its silken breath. At once the mother sits up. When she bends to look at the child Lev glances at the husband's book. He catches the top line on the far page, his first English in weeks, since the consular magazine. He reads: *on probation again – he won't kill Dixon if he* and then she sits back again.

The shoulder is warm and close. Heathrow, soft

luggage. The baby too is a parcel, tough in its own fragile casing. Again he feels the mother stir and raise her head a little, listening. What is it that disturbs her? The baby's fast asleep as far as he can tell. He opens his eyes a fraction to see what he can make out through the gauze of the bassinet. Immediately the mother sits up and leans over the cradle. The husband continues reading, a pharmacist perhaps or a town councillor. He doesn't share his wife's clairvoyance.

Test her. Lev concentrates on the child's sleeping head, imagines it glowing softly like a crystal ball. The mother sits bolt upright, leans over and peers into the bassinet. Then turns and looks directly at him, straight through his trembling eyelashes and into the sliver of eye which he dare not now shut tight. Lev reclines there breathing lightly, listening to his pounding heart. The woman looks away, looks down at her lap and carefully spreads her rug. She eases back into her seat, breathes in, and rams her shoulder into his.

Lev, who watched himself walk away from Biosecuritat as if it were somebody else, who has seen half his savings disappear in the Moscow sting, is surprised at his own next move. He leans all his weight against the shoulder. Instantly the shoulder pushes back. Lev doubles his thrust, pushing with such force that if the woman were to lean forward again he would fly into the pharmacist's lap. But she stays where she is, loyal to an instinct written into her cells ten million years ago. Pushing back with all her strength, the lioness.

Half an hour, whole aeons, raging. Against the weight of the world, the tyranny of convention. Dry-mouthed they wrestle, reduced to law, the chaos of her head millimetres from his own. But it must end, even this ancient union. He feels her slacken and go still.

He can't sleep. He sits unmoving, her pillow, afraid to move in case she wakens. He listens to the breathing of the plane, to the drone of the engines, the song of its living body, the sighs and murmurs of the passengers who are its organs. His flesh goes on cooking in its skin like a drained potato.

He feels the plane begin its descent. On the screen its graphic image swivels a fraction, an albino hawk over the bull's eye of Delhi. So he has been over the subcontinent for some time. The screen narrative flicks to continental scale and the flight path shows as a line that tracks over central Europe and Iran (Grigoriev went there, they say, and is earning good dollars for kasha), jinks around Afghan airspace and then runs straight across the Hindu Kush to India.

We're there, he thinks. This is it. And so the captain's voice confirms, first in Russian, then in English. The woman wakes, lifts her head.

Passport, money, decoy wallet. He feels the softness of her shoulder, but now his nerves are on edge, his palms wet. The wheel carriage grates into place. Local time is 2:20 a.m.

The family beside him are going on to Kathmandu. The mother takes the baby in her arms for landing. The father reads on, his seat belt fastened. Lev looks to catch the paperback cover but sees the top line on the far page again. It still reads: *on probation again – he won't kill Dixon if he.*

The husband looks across at him and holds his gaze, then smiles a little smile. As the plane lands smoothly the Russians on board applaud, a patter like rain. The wife looks up serenely as Lev joins the queue of disembarking passengers.

'Thanks for all your help,' she says. She means the bassinet, the meal tray, everything.

Irony in a second language is confusing. But he must get

accustomed to English now, and he is pleased when the response glides to his mouth without a trace of rust.

'It was a pleasure.'

Just off the plane the queue bottlenecks so he's stranded by a window for fifteen minutes looking out at the great mechanical bird he flew all the way from home on. Its belly trembles open as he watches. From the hold a coffin appears and is unloaded onto a flatbed truck by four men before the luggage is touched. Lev stares. One of the men seems to look straight at him. Lev looks away and up at a night sky the colour of sand. Then the queue begins to move and he's gone, into India.

Red City

One

She wakes out of a dream and walks with her eyes shut tight, trying to keep the dream pieces from falling apart, smack into the door jamb.

If the door had ears, she might wail. As it is she winces and rubs her forehead and wonders if there's blood. It's the electricity department's fault. The power failed in the middle of the night and she shifted to the camp cot on the terrace and fell asleep on unfamiliar ground.

There is blood, but not on the forehead. 'Shit, yaa,' she says, though the puppets are nowhere in sight, so she could be talking to the hawks roosting in the silk-cotton tree. She heads for the outdoor basin. It's a nosebleed and the water in the sink runs red for a good minute before returning to its normal grey.

There's a dust haze over the city that hasn't moved for a week. In the morning the disc of the sun comes up khaki at six and in the evening at six it goes down the same khaki edged with fool's gold. Dust mantles every surface. A black dog will change colour if it falls asleep outdoors. For a week there has been no sky.

Anyway, the knock woke her up properly. She makes tea,

a stew of leaves and milk and sugar and dusty water, and sits on the balcony on an aluminium folding chair with the same plastic webbing as the cot, only this is blue, and holds the cup by the rim and not the handle and looks out across the city wall.

The chimneys have disappeared. Two giant gushers wiped out. Ordinarily they stand there on the riverbank, grey shadows by day, black shadows by night, with the sodium lights of the power station clustered at their feet. Last night there was just a sodium haze on the bank and, floating up above, two red warning lights for aircraft.

A cool morning breeze flows from the river, then stops, flows and stops. From somewhere on the horizon a shift siren starts up and mourns and mourns and switches off. Much nearer is a monotonous squirrel chirrup. In a little while the peacocks and early buses will be shrieking. The bright pain of the knock has settled into a buzz like a wasp. She is watching a wasp ride a puddle at the water tank, imagining the thread of glass it draws up into itself. The wasp leaves refreshed, the glint lodges in her like a sting.

What sort of man shall be my lover?

That was it! That was the dream she tried to keep and lost to the door jamb. And he was there *in* it. That was why her eyes were shut so tight. To keep him there.

He must be tall, let him be anything else. Short though she is herself. He need not have her deep-set eyes either. They will come out in the child. He must have taken a great risk to come to her. In her daydreams he's climbing some sheer rock face to get to her. The only rock face around here is the red and grey sandstone of the old city wall beyond the silk-cotton. Hanging on by his fingertips. A thief of love.

In the dream he was starting to show his face, something he keeps turned away in her fantasies. Turning his head slowly towards her.

Show your face! she wants to call but doesn't because she's weird enough already to the neighbours. A young woman living by herself, making puppets. A man could sing out, shout out loud and just be a crank. A woman would be a witch.

She puts down her cup and slips into her exercises. These she does do as she pleases, undressed because it's the top floor. There's one pose she holds longer than the others. In it she becomes the woman in the colour photocopy that hangs on her wall. It is the torso of a young woman cut off at the pudendum so the clay model rests on the stumps of her legs. The head is not complete either and the arms are cut off too. She has her head thrown back so her missing eyes look straight up at the sky. She is reaching up for something, fruit or bird or plane. When she comes to that particular yoga asana this morning Maya is reaching up through the dust haze into a zone of sharp clean air.

The flat is sparely furnished, almost unfurnished, to judge by the expanses of empty floor, a grey terrazzo. It's a cement grey set off in squares with white marble chips. In the principal rooms the chips are above pea-size; on the terrace they are smaller, in the bathrooms almost invisible. Here and there a chip of yellow or green marble is cause for celebration. In the passage at the heart of the flat, which doubles as a dining room, there are two cane chairs and a cane bookcase with paperback art books such as a former student of design might have collected, one or two books of poetry on loan, and for some reason a copy of *The Marine Fauna of the Dutch East*

Indies. The adjoining kitchen is not scrubbed clean. A layer of dust and grease coats the spice jars from which the jam and pickle labels have not been removed. There is a stack of pans and dishes in the sink. In the dining space is an old cream fridge with a chrome lever handle that dates it; not new money. It holds chiefly cold water in clear plastic mineral water bottles. A bunch of spinach has wilted in one drawer, like a good intention; certain of its leaves are already rotten and have begun to stink.

Maya uses the smaller of two bedrooms. The other is her workroom. Her studio, Morgan calls it, though she resists the imputation that what she does is art.

'All right, so it's a craft, a fine craft,' he said when the argument was young. 'Potters have studios.'

'Look. It's just the puppets' room. This is my bedroom and that's theirs.'

'The puppets' bedroom!' he pronounces, with a slight lift to his chin that he reserves for mockery.

'I'm hungry. When are you going to make that famous pea pulao?'

'When the kitchen is penetrable. I'm not cooking *and* cleaning, my dear.'

But in a little while the media personality is scrubbing the pots he needs.

'You can make up my bed,' he calls, to save face, and Morgan's is a face to save, known to all who watch the morning news. Maya, who won't have television in the flat, is immune to his looks and his fame.

His bedroom, when he stays over, is the drawing room, which is entirely free of furniture. He is given a mattress, a sheet, and a pillowcase to slip over one of two cushions in the flat. The mattress he draws as far away as possible from the ceiling fan, which goes only at top speed. He must find the middle ground between getting blown away and getting bitten by mosquitoes. Such nights are especially hard on a newsreader who must rise early, and yet Morgan would rather sleep here than anywhere else. His wanderings from mattress to mattress are also legendary, Maya knows, in the capital, but she has no use for gossip. Morgan drives his Zen or takes an early taxi to the studio from the night's bivouac.

Blood returning to her nose, Maya remembers the night she found him up with the lights on, killing mosquitoes at half-past two and talking half to himself in the full, round enunciation he uses when upset.

'*Death came suddenly to two errant mosquitoes in the walled city last night.*' He is gloating over a patch of wall just above his mattress where there are two fresh smears of blood. '*They were killed in the line of duty by the debonair newsreader Morgan Fitch, who smacked their heads off where they sat on the wall and then carefully washed the bloodstains away . . .*' He's performing now, because he knows she's there, but he actually is washing away the stains with ghoulish tenacity because they're easier to treat when fresh. '*Interviewed by the press afterwards, Mr Fitch said: "Always look on the wall just above the bed.* That's *where the bastards hide."* ' He carries the mug of water back to the guest bathroom and returns. '*Never again will those two mosquitoes trouble the sleep of Morgan Fitch.*'

'Morgan . . .'

'*Never again will those two mosquitoes—*'

'Do you know what time it is?'

'Oh, I do, I do.' He's furious because there's a cooler in

her bedroom. If she was staying over at his flat she would have an air conditioner.

A jet goes over with its landing lights winking.

'Another load of disgruntled tourists was deposited in the capital last night by the truant carrier Air Tajikistan.'

'Go to sleep.'

'Boris Yeltsin is quoted as saying—'

'Morgan . . .'

' *"Morgan, come and be my Prime Minister." '*

This last in a coarse Russo-English accent, fuddled with drink, but the fact is Morgan belongs to the Russia Club, drinks vodka by preference, and knows the Russian poets. He reads them in translation but can follow the parallel text.

'Actually,' he continues, 'I thought it was later than it is. I was sure I heard the koel calling, so I thought: *Get up, kill, stay up.* But I think I will go back to sleep. No chance of Odomos? A Tortoise coil? Then why not help me fight the mossies?' His gesture sweeps over the mattress, a Berber chief inviting her.

'Go to sleep, yaa. Or you'll be reading every other line in that thingy tomorrow.'

He lies down obediently and sleeps till his built-in alarm clock wakes him two hours later and he makes himself black tea, an old affectation he's got reaccustomed to because she never has any milk even though there's a dairy downstairs. He doesn't wake her till he's ready to leave, and wouldn't at all but she must bolt the security door after him.

She stays up, ratty from broken sleep and unable to vent her irritation on anybody but herself. Though there is one lot of sleepers she could torment. She opens the door to the puppet's bedroom and peeps in.

Always she's that split second late as they shiver into stillness.

Hot stale air greets her, wadded right up against the door because the sun beats down on the roof and she keeps the windows shut against dust. She crosses to open them. These windows look straight down into the street, bare at this hour. Grudgingly the hot air flows out into the morning and she feels she hears a tiny rejoicing around her.

The room is low-ceilinged, with no skylights or air vents, the whole flat simply a suburban shoebox stuck on half the roof of a once-grand mansion. This end of it gets the afternoon sun; by evening the room is a stoked kiln. The terrazzo in this room has the largest marble chips of all, which suggests the master bedroom, but almost the entire floor is covered with a cotton durree of lime green and charcoal with terracotta lozenges. The durree is a relic of her design days when she shopped with her mother at FabIndia and the wrong green could upset either woman. They were closer then.

As if in repudiation of that past the durree is covered with heaps of textile scraps, offcuts she's collected from the tailors downstairs, and remnants from cloth merchants in the narrow gullies off Chandni Chowk in the old city proper. Voiles, muslins, coarse handlooms, georgettes, block prints, tie-dyes, shirting: she'll take the lot, cramming them into the black nylon overnight bag Morgan got free with a two-year subscription to *Update*. Into the bag also go smooth tors she finds in the grass under the old wall, mauve-and-silver tinsel propellers from an itinerant toymaker, glittering threads and crimped piping from the gully of haberdashers, a spoilt crochet cap from the devout capmaker outside the black mosque, spangled turbancloth from the wedding gully, feathers from the stinking bird market. Once the bag came home packed with coir husks from a coconut vendor's cart, another time overflowing with a carpenter's woodshavings, several times with the tailings of an office shredder on Haidar Road. From the kabari bazaar she picks up china beads, bicycle bells and bottle caps. These blue knobs off an old air conditioner will make a demon's eyes. The auto parts gullywallahs know she wants old manifolds for torsos, but she's never told them that a set of old Fiat indicator lamps made a fine pair of breasts for the eloping puppet Padmini.

She has learnt to manage the looks, the stares, the sniggers, like any photographer or birdwatcher. They come in double measure for a woman. She simply focuses and gets on with it.

Along one wall of the puppet room is a workbench. Set in the wall above it are shelves and pigeonholes crammed with the spoils of the day, the order following roughly a map of the body. Hair will go on top, eyes one shelf down (a glass jar of bright buttons), ear shells off to the side and so on. Innards to the left, outers to the right. If she wants an arm, her hand knows to reach right and up to where a box of aluminium window latches waits, hinged and ready. On the bench, among paints and tools, is work in progress. Puppets recline, sit up, sprawl, a skeleton beside a fat priest. Look, this one with his arm laid open for a muscle graft has not let go of his sword. He may be cannibalized for another puppet. A puppet is not complete until the eye is dotted. Then the soul enters in and he may not be violated.

The sewing of garments is done on the floor, on the durree where an old hand-turned sewing machine sits under its wood-veneer hood.

The finished puppets occupy the opposite wall. They hang with their strings and histories from hooks set in three tiers. The tallest hang from the top tier to the floor, a family of giants who occupy the centre for symmetry's sake. They took no stuffing, being simply sheets, dyed yellow, maroon and black, sheets with padded shoulders and hands sewn on below. It was the faces that took weeks of labour, long papier mâché shields moulded in wire mesh with great wise eyes and small severe mouths and a lamp bracket behind to light up the whole head on stage. They have no local ancestry. On either side are traditional types, the courtesan, the witchdoctor, the snake charmer, the knight, stringers from the Aravalli hills. There are clusters of miniatures on the third tier, stock types from the plains: the just king, the unlucky lover, the clown with two faces front and back, the tubby merchant, the wily minister, the resourceful princess (she of the Fiat breasts). At the far end is a menagerie, a tiger with a swivel tail who hangs beside a crocodile with styrofoam teeth, a quilted horse, a snake sprung on six dead electric heater coils. From the window pelmet hangs an aeroplane with two cutout clouds that fly with it. Maya always prods it as she goes past.

But her favourite hangs by the door, a near life-size mendicant she's done and redone, rearranging his rags of flesh, unbandaging his lean arms, painting his grotesque ribcage, hanging and rehanging his staff, his dreadlocks and his begging bowl, while he waits for eyes with the large patience of his kind.

Talk to me, Babaji.

She shuts the door on them. Inside, whole cycles of tales, stalled scenes of love and war, creak into motion again. Lost topoi find meaning, sap mounts to heads of pith. Most of the inmates have not yet had an airing. Virgin puppets, they fantasize curtain calls, an enemy's head severed from the trunk, one successful kiss.

Sometimes she stands just outside the door in a blaze of conjecture. Imagining a story from the sealed past come surging back down the strings on her wall until the whole blind circuitry is buzzing with light. The only use she has for history.

'Do you think I just make dolls?' she asked Morgan once.

'What's wrong with that?'

'They don't move.'

'Maybe you should let them go.'

'What, give them away?'

'No. Lend them to a master.'

'Those guys don't want anything new-fangled, yaa. Baldev and Sukhdev have their own ideas. I'd like to have some control.'

'Who pays the piper calls the tune.'

'Where's the money coming from?'

'Green Park.' He means her family. Jewellers for twenty generations till her father ducked into exams and ended up Chief of Police, having married jewellery after all. So Maya was sent to automatically to Risingholme in the hills. Till she escaped into design. And then escaped again and left the family wondering.

'Pocket money. No thanks.' She flicks the fingers her mother would like to see hennaed. They're long and tapering, the fingers beloved of miniaturists (her eyelids have their beloved fold too), but already worn. 'That would be worse than going back to Risingholme.'

'Be grateful it wasn't Boys' High School, Roorkee.'

'If I had a company . . . Let's start one, Morgan.'

'I'm a humble newsreader.'

'You know everybody.'

Together they dug out the government grant that staged her first show. Now she's a known quantity, has even toured, but dreads the limbo of arts grants. Today she's especially low, after a whole afternoon spent on a general's collar, getting it right.

'I feel like I'm building a museum.'

It's evening and the sun has dropped behind the office block across Haidar Road. Into the hot still air rises a bird cry that goes on and on battering at the dusty lid of sky.

Ghee chapati ka ghee chapati ka ghee chapati ka ghee!

Butter over bread, bread under butter!

Morgan grins. 'Your brainfever bird.'

He's almost a parody of the Vinay Suitings model; his chin even has the dimple that goes with the look. This year when he chanced a red tie with a black shirt for the 14 February news he was flooded with red and black valentines.

She waggles her chin back at him, still embarrassed by her mistake.

The caged bird hangs in the barbershop downstairs. It's a brown partridge whose dark chocolate mottling she can imagine sprayed on with a toothbrush dipped in paint. It is not as handsome as the black partridge; few birds are. But the black has a grudging scooter horn of a call while the brown's is melodious, earnest and full throated, if a little pushful. It's crying its heart out, even when it isn't caged.

But a brainfever bird it is not. As she declared the day Morgan first visited.

'No. *That* it isn't,' Morgan ruled. With the judicial pursing of lips that his adjutant found infuriating in Gentleman Cadet Fitch at the academy. It almost cost him the sword of honour. He rattled his mother too by quitting the army as captain, destined he felt for other things.

But they've come to call it what it isn't. So Morgan the birdwatcher, who has a pair of Russian field glasses at home, can no longer look at the cage downstairs and think: *partridge*. It's the brainfever bird now.

That's not to say the true brainfever bird doesn't visit. It comes down off the Ridge, the forested spur on the edge of the city, flying from park to park, from tall tree to tree, a shy bird, furtive in speckled fatigues, a cuckoo with a liking for babblers' nests (it could pass for a babbler with a long tail) and a call that climbs and climbs maddeningly through the hot June afternoon and the burning nights: *brainfever! brainfever! brainfever!* higher and higher till the crazed listener sits down on a stool and prepares a noose that could be either for the bird or for himself. From ancient times it's the bird of love: in Hindi it calls: *pee-kahan? pee-kahan? pee-kahan?*

Where is my love? Where is my love? Where is my love?

Two

The bird in the cage is Laiq the barber's.

Laiq has the last shop on the right of the central staircase, and the cage hangs at his door. It's a double door with white hinged shutters on the outside that match the shutters of the four main shops in the building. There are two lesser shops, holes in the wall, on either side of the staircase, one a tyre repairer's and the other a panwallah's. Laiq's is the most respectable of the four larger shops. Its shutters fold back to reveal a proper door. Door and surrounds are of panelled glass, with the large central pane elegantly bowed above and below, the bottom curve deeper than the top. That curve alone testifies to the building's age; no modern builder would bother with a bowed cut, much less the tongue-and-groove work of the side panels. Above the door is an arch filled with stucco foliage.

Laiq takes no special pride in these trappings, though he will wipe down the glass when necessary. His shop is sparsely furnished. The barber's chair by the door is the only chair in the shop; Laiq has no partners. It is wooden, a high chair on a slight cant, the front legs two inches higher so the customer is tilted backwards into Laiq's hands. The other chairs have disappeared but the framed mirror that extends along the entire wall shows that three customers might once have sat abreast. This was a respectable barbershop before Laiq was born.

Nowadays it's not just a barbershop. Two sorts of customers come to Laiq's door. Those who come for a haircut or a head massage use the chair or wait their turn on the padded bench opposite the mirror. The others are led beyond a dividing curtain into the back of the shop. Here, from behind a counter whose pink laminate top is swallowed up in the gloom, Laiq dispenses the herbs, electuaries and Yunani medicines for which he is known through the nearer gullies of the walled city. There are other barbers in the vicinity but none who can also cure flatulence and treat gout and banish melancholy or morning sickness or flaccidity and at a pinch remove an infant's foreskin.

He is a thickset man with a beard into which some grey has lately come. Hair grows luxuriantly on Laiq, as if it ordained his career; he is a walking monument to hair. For that or some other reason he has never got around to putting up a shop sign. Where the shop next door says, just under the foliate arch, DIAGNOSTICS, and in smaller letters, Pathology Research Laboratories, Laiq has no board at all. The high chair speaks for itself, and when there are no takers Laiq will stand in his door and gaze into the street, a man given to brooding. The hair on his head, a massive head, has a natural wave; he runs a comb through it and it falls in a swirl at the back that recalls the style of the Bombay film stars of his youth. With the shop came a framed illustration of European styles of the thirties at which an undecided customer might point, but it has chiefly iconic significance, and it is seldom used except in reveries.

No one knows who cuts the barber's hair. The dense beard is shaped with a razor and clipped below. Its black river goes underground at the carefully shaven neck to emerge in rapids at the chest. The white is heaviest there. Further down he is said to be clean shaven, but that is covered by his radiant white kurta pyjama.

He is not married, so the bird can count on his devotion. Every morning he takes it for a walk in the field outside Delhi Gate. There among the yellow oleander and the paths that crisscross the wiry grass he lets it out of the cage. The bird flaps its wings and puffs out its chest and kicks at the gritty soil. Then it trots off followed by Laiq, who unknowingly mimics the supercilious craning of its neck. If it strays too far he will call it to heel with a clicking of the tongue; if it disobeys or doesn't hear he stops in his tracks and calls:

Ahh *ah ah ah*, Ahh *ah ah ah*, *Ti ti ti ti ti!*

The bird will halt and cock its head. Lift one foot off the ground and bring the claws to a point. Then, as if taking its own counsel and not in obedience to any summons, it will turn back. But let it find the slightest eminence – a heap of rubble will do – and it will rush to the top and fire three machine-gun bursts:

Le sale pataka le sale pataka le sale pataka le!

Take that you coward, try this for size!

Returning to the shop Laiq will hang the cage from its hook in the lintel and replenish the feed tray and the water dish. All morning the bird watches the walled city world go by. Customers come in, grow vast as they cross the threshold, and leave the shop subtly altered. In summer its beak strains open as the day progresses, but before the sun strikes down from the meridian Laiq unhooks the cage and brings it in. It passes the afternoon suspended in interior gloom, more fish than bird. Directly the sun has gone behind the office block opposite Laiq takes the cage back out and there it hangs until the evening walk and the mellowing of its war cry into a call of anxious love:

Re more sajni re more sajni re more sajni!

O my love, o my sweet o my ducky!

Master and pet are past their prime. The partridge was once a fighting bird, even at Laiq's hands. But then Laiq saw him lose and rescued him amidst jeering and cut off his spurs. Later he put a lady in with him, but that's all done. He's bred his broods, known other ladies, and settled into the middle age of his kind, more threat than doing. There were days too when the bird was fearful for the master. Sundays past, Laiq put on a terylene shirt and went wrestling. But now he's put away that shirt and slipped into white cottons.

This Sunday the bird is again agitated. For Laiq is drawn to the lawns of the Delhi Gate park, a little iron-fenced island of grass and shrubs and benches where solitaries congregate and itinerant masseurs prowl in their blue turbans looking for custom.

Three

Lev pushes his trolley past the shoal of waiting eyes. Dark foreign eyes. Where the air conditioning ends there's a policeman on a stool whose finger says: straight on.

The heat slips on like a pullover. A hint of night moisture clings to the skin defining the space in which he moves. It's a quarter to three, his scheduled midnight arrival pushed back because of the delay in Moscow. He's tempted to wait till daylight but there's nowhere to sit in the forecourt. His tall frame stands hunched over the trolley. His shoulder still tingles from the encounter on the plane.

He buys a prepaid taxi coupon and finds a number on the back. The plates come up, an old roundtop painted taxi-yellow-and-black. The driver shoves aside the urchins squabbling over Lev's suitcase and swings it into the boot himself. Next he reaches for the briefcase but Lev holds up a warning hand. They roll out under the foreign sky.

The stream of sodium lights overhead unravels like a warranty. It cuts across the nameless dark places and rules a straight line towards the civilizing glow on the horizon. Lev goes through the routine that constant repetition has shrunk to slight shifts of hand and chin: passport, ticket, money wallet, decoy wallet. On arrival he changed fifty dollars to see him through to the city banks and put most of his rupees in the real wallet.

At the first set of traffic lights the taxi driver respects the red signal for as long as he can bear, considering there's no one about. Lev smiles. Driver Repin being driven. At the next junction the driver leaves the sodium stream and takes a secondary road. Deep night enfolds them.

There's a roadblock ahead where a sign says CHECK POST. A couple of steel barrels painted white and a cross pole. The post is unmanned at this hour. The driver dodges around the barrier without stopping and is shifting up to accelerate when a second barrier catches the headlights. This one is simpler: a fallen tree blocks off half the road. The other half of the blockage is a small white van drawn up side on. Its toy-sized front wheels are sharply angled and a man sits smoking at the wheel. He flashes his lights once. Two armed men are on the road waving down the taxi and a third is stepping from the van's slide door.

The taxi driver's first response is to veer right, looking for a way to barge through, but the men on the road lift the muzzles of their automatic weapons and he screeches to a halt. Lev's heart is beating madly. Alla, he thinks, Alex.

The unarmed man comes up and leans into the driver's window.

'Where were you off to?' He pleats the driver's shirtfront bit by bit till he has a handful. '*Hey*?'

'Just . . .' the driver cringes, folding his hands.

'ENGINE!'

The driver jumps and switches off.

Lev is thinking: to have come *all* this way! The man

pushes the driver down flat onto the front seat and comes around to the back door.

'Come,' he says in English, opening the door.

Lev steps out, leaving the briefcase in the taxi. The two armed men have come around. Lev sees the cheeseholes in one gun. 'Money?' he asks.

The man looks up at him and stretches his lips in a humorous way. Lev reaches for his wallet. In his nervousness he has forgotten which is which. He digs into his side pocket and comes up with the fatter one. The man takes it and feels the wad of notes. 'More,' he says, pocketing it.

Lev produces the other wallet.

The man pockets it without inspection. 'More.'

Lev spreads his hands.

'Shoes.'

Lev bends down and slips off one shoe. He holds it up, turns it over. 'Nothing,' he says. 'Empty.'

'Other one.'

Lev takes off the other. It's empty too.

'Socks.' One by one they come off, empty.

The man taps Lev's watch. Lev unfastens it and hands it over.

'A car.' One of the armed men has spoken. There's a headlight splitting off from the main road.

Lev's face erupts in a slap that almost topples him. His bare feet stamp gravel as he recovers his balance.

'Let's go,' the leader shouts. He reaches into the taxi and snatches the briefcase as the gunmen cover him. He swings the case into the back of the van and jumps in. They jump in after him and slide the door shut. The van is already rolling. The driver does a tight circle that opens out beyond the fallen tree and speeds off into the dark without switching his lights on.

The other car has already turned away down some side road.

The taxi driver gets up slowly and comes to where Lev is. He is standing in the middle of the road looking at the pale outline of his feet against the tar. Indian tar. His cheek, that whole side of the face, is tingling. He looks at the driver without seeing him. The case is gone. His reason for being here. The blood is singing in his ear and his briefcase is gone. It is three o'clock in the morning in India. He has been in India just over an hour.

'Sar.'

Lev looks up.

'Come.'

Lev nods.

'Sar, shoes.'

Lev obeys, sitting on the corner of the back seat, shaking out his gritty socks.

'Sar, go police.'

'Police?' Lev imagines a police station. The officer is asking him what was in the briefcase.

'No.'

'No?'

'Hotel.' He has a booking at the Rajdoot. He pats his chest; the waistcoat still has his passport, his ticket, dollars. Thanks to a nameless car.

'Suitcase not gone, sar.'

'No.'

'Sar, you have prepaid coupon?'

Lev checks his shirt pocket. 'Yes.'

'Sar, cheap hotel.'

Lev considers. Fifty dollars down.

'Yes.'

They continue on their way. The city appears, wide roads with well-lit roundabouts, bungalows with bunkers at the gate, avenues of strange trees. Taller buildings now, the odd car sweeping past on high beam. A dome, a bridge the road ducks under, a stone gateway.

'Sahib. Hotel. Cheapest and best.'

And so Lev checks in at the Serai, outside Delhi Gate. He has a cabin to himself, only slightly larger than the two narrow beds in it, but it is his own. Its boxiness satisfies an urgent need for closeting. There is a tiny window, actually a glassed vent, and the door bolts from the inside. It's one of fifty identical cabins in the walled compound.

He lies down fully clothed with his hands folded under his head. His shoes are on, but in a little while he shakes them off. As the sun comes up he falls asleep.

Four

He wakes into Sunday.

His stomach turns over: the briefcase is gone. There is some-body in the other bed. Alla. No, Meschersky. There's a suitcase under the bed he recognizes. The shoes are his. The briefcase is gone.

He has a number to call. But he has no currency. It's Sunday, the banks are closed. He left his passport at the desk as surety. He has a number to call and nothing to show. And anyway it's Sunday. He had planned to rest up, so that's what he should do. It's gone. He falls asleep again into terrible heat, nightmares.

Merchersky. Takes the Galant, dobs him in. His cheek is on fire.

The next time he wakes the heat is down a fraction, maybe two degrees. He sits on his bunk with the door open and stares. The ground outside is powdered brick, red. He needs to use the toilet. He checks the window, padlocks the door and goes in search. It's in the bathhouse block. He should bathe too, wash the sweat off. He goes back for the Serai towel, a large tea towel with rust spots, but clean.

Hunger. Can he still be hungry with the briefcase gone? It's late afternoon, judging from the sun.

He eats an omelette and buttered bread at the cafeteria, parting with a ten-dollar bill. Till tomorrow, the manager assures him, piously putting it into a separate drawer. The omelette has green chillies in it that he ferrets out after the first burn and pushes to one side of the plate. He drinks mineral water, takes the bottle with him. Checks the padlock on the cabin and goes for a walk.

Across the main street the shops and offices have their steel shutters rolled down. Most of the larger signs are in English, others in both English and a language he takes to be Hindi. He pictures the young St Isaak struggling with the script. There's a smell of waste, human waste alongside vegetable decay. The people are all a whole head shorter, but then he's tall in Russia too. They walk differently, a slackness he puts down to the heat. The men have their shirtfronts out. The saris are not as rich as in magazines. Drab is how the mass looks; individuals stick out freshly bathed, scented with oils and talcum.

He wanders past the old city gate, marooned by itself on an island in the traffic. There's a pavement book sale in progress on one side of the main street beyond the gate. The books, mostly in English, are laid out on the pavement. He sees two copies of *Anna Karenina* from the Raduga Press. Off to the left are narrow lanes that appear to tunnel into the past. An enormous tree blocks half of one and rises four storeys.

People stare at him with frank curiosity; curious, he stares back. Highway robbers, he wants to think. But they look so humdrum and preoccupied with their own narrow lives he's not convinced. Where the books end there's a footbridge over the main road but he's inclined to follow the pedestrians picking their way through the traffic to the other side. It's a strange press of humans and machines and cattle. Mingling with them he falls into a black hole of thought.

Sitting in the consular Volvo, waiting. Outside the Asian school, waiting to pick up the consul's children, he feels the street go still, the shops round about go dead. This is how a city sounds after a successful delivery of Kurile-E. Not a roof tile touched, but a schoolyard gone absurdly quiet. Peter a ghost city where the traffic lights change from red to green and back over and over. A whole office block where the computers have switched to the screen saver of a journey through deep space.

Shepherded across by the crowd Lev comes safely to the other side. In the distance he sees a fortress of red stone. It rises out of a field and curves away seemingly for miles. He's drawn towards it but the heat and traffic defeat him. As he's turning back he sees a great mosque of matching red across the way, the dome an anchored cloud, the minarets stone kites, soaring. Some other time. Early morning maybe, when it's cooler, less crowded.

He walks back on the other side of the wide street, past chemists and television stockists, Sunday-closed, till he's back at the old city gate. The gate is a monument now, protected by a high iron fence. Its large uneven blocks of grey stone are fringed with red, the red of the fort and the mosque. Life flows around it: the old city wall in which it once stood has been breached on either side to let the traffic through. Here where he stands was once wall. Not fifty metres from a police station, the pavement has been occupied by squatting teastalls and primitive eateries.

There's a park at Delhi Gate. Lev finds an empty bench under a tree. The locals are sitting out the afternoon heat. A shoeshine boy comes by. Alex's age, maybe. Lev shakes his head and shuts his eyes. He stays that way for a long time going over the night's events, the journey, the leavetaking at Peter. Someone sits down at the other end of the bench but Lev keeps his eyes shut. The person leaves.

There's something tapping at his shoe, a rat gnawing at his foot. He wakes with a shout. It's the shoeshine boy again, still young enough to expect fun on the job. The boy backs off startled, scolded by other sitters as he goes.

Lev looks around. The lawns have begun to fill up with men taking their leisure. A blue-turbanned journeyman squats down beside a client and grips the man's ankle. He twists the foot each way, plucks at the tendon and tentatively prods the calf. He massages his way up the trunk to neck and arms then sits the man up like a rag doll and starts on his head. Lev watches with interest. He feels his watching being watched by others. The masseur is aware of the crosscurrents of interest. He too begins to look at Lev as he works, hamming it up. Cheap and healthy, his eyes say.

'No good.'

The woman's voice carries great authority. Lev turns his head. On the bench beside him is a partridge in a cage.

'No good,' Laiq repeats in his clear alto and gathers up his birdcage as if to say he will have no more to do with this travesty.

'No?'

'No,' Laiq says, and places the cage in his lap. 'I know, I

am barber. I cut hairs. I give massage. Real massage. Not . . .'
And he shakes a loose finger at the grinning man on the
grass.

Lev stands up. Laiq is on his feet so fluently the decision
to leave could have been his.

'Massage is . . .' Laiq recalls when they have fallen into
step, continuing a discussion begun centuries ago, 'science.'

Lev hears *signs*, then works it out. Science. He must listen
with special care to this other English.

'Massage is art. Not for the donkeys, the owls. Doctor
of Massage, MD. Study muscles, one-one muscle, upistair,
downistair, head to leg. My shop here, just only next building.
You are Englishman?'

'Russian.' Lev is not sure why he's going along except he
feels he's owed something after last night. Some discharge
for the bile that's been building all day. He won't even think
about the briefcase. Possibly what he's looking for is dis-
traction.

'Russian!' Laiq is impressed. 'Engineer?'

'Scientist.' Consular driver no more. Immediately the
briefcase alarm sounds. Gone. Résumé, letters of introduction,
papers, briefing notes, slides, the works.

'*I* also read science.' Signs. 'Physics, chemistry, biology.
But no jobs. Lot many science graduates. Too much scientists
in India. Saloon.' He points.

Lev looks up. There's no visible shop sign. Is this a hoax?
Another holdup? For some reason he flashes back to the
pastel drawing under St Isaak's feet: a large red horse. The
barber unlocks his shutters and folds them back. Then he
unlocks the inner door; the crossbolt squeaks as he works
the leaf up and down. Laiq hangs the birdcage on its hook

and something in the act reassures Lev. The barber fills the doorway, passes through and turns.

'Well-come.'

Lev sees the high chair, the mirror, the framed vignettes of men's heads, and is persuaded.

'Please.' Laiq draws back the chair.

Lev settles into it, his long legs finding purchase on a concealed footrail. Laiq washes his hands at the basin and pats them dry on a cloth that might be his shaving towel. He comes and stands behind Lev. For a moment his hands shape the air around Lev's head as if deciding where to begin. Then they settle on the crown together, with the same calm authority as the voice. Massage is language, they state, its structure universal. All skeletons are one. But muscles overlay the universal skeleton with a grammar whose elements must be discovered afresh with every skull.

The first strokes are light and quick. Laiq's fingers are learning the rudiments of Lev's Russian head, reading by a kind of Braille that unique terrain. Laiq grips the whole head and slowly pivots it back and forth, then rolls it round in a gentle oscillation, first one way then the other. Next he leans over and clamps both cheeks with powerful hands and works the slack flesh up and down.

He works in silence. A barber talks, the masseur does not.

He goes from jowls to chin then climbs by searching handholds back up to the forehead. He pinches specific points, cheekbones, temples, the bridge of the nose, inspired fleeting pinches that rove at random across the face; he even takes hold of the eyelashes and tugs gently at the muscles used for blinking. He never kneads simply for the sake of kneading: the scalp is there to be lifted, its sheet coaxed from the skull. The broad flesh of the shoulders is ploughed with the fingertips, harrowed with the nails. The neck is exquisitely wrung, as if Lev is a swan.

All through the operation Lev keeps his eyes shut, emitting little groans that his embarrassment converts to grunts. From time to time Laiq lifts his eyes to examine Lev's face in the glass. He sees a man younger than himself by a year or two, perhaps only by a few months, and imagines him growing up on the other side of the globe, wherever Russia is. Imagines his father, his mother, his house, his school, the lab where he does his science.

A light rain of knucklebones on the roof of the skull. Lev hears a rhythmic snapping like a hundred fingers being cracked in time. Laiq goes threshing airily all across the crown with splayed fingers, a kind of soufflé saved for last. One last chop and he gives a breathless hoot to signify he's done.

'Science!' He meets Lev's eyes as they open in the mirror. Signs.

Lev is smiling satisfaction, and relief. When he first shut his eyes he felt he would open them on Laiq standing behind him with a cleaver. Then he saw Alex with his face down in the pillow. And then he surrendered to the massage, inhabiting its elastic moment, juddering to Laiq's muse.

Even with customers who expect an earful of tattle Laiq is not a talking barber. Nor does he take liberties; he might know a customer for years before he presumes to clip nostril hair. Now, the massage done, he demonstrates each stroke by way of a recap. The Mallet, he says, no longer bothering with the English, and places one fist over the other and knocks on the crown. He might use the whole hand or a part or the least fraction of it, he explains in the mirror. And each part changes character depending on how it is held. The heel of the palm is, in its declensions, cushion, pad and board; held differently it is mallet, hammer, axe. The feather of a fingertip can drill into flesh.

The Flywhisk, the Minnow, the Caterpillar. The Nutcracker, which uses an armlock. The Oxtrot. Arvind's Bicycle. Bringing Home the Fatted Kid. The Gallipot. Woodpecker's Worrybeads. And finally that rhythmic clatter of knucklebones, All Eight Udders.

For the first time Lev looks at Laiq straight on. It's a sensual face he sees, compared to his own ascetic lines.

'Next time,' Laiq says, standing there with his rhetor's composure, '*body*.'

Lev blenches. The smile on Laiq's face is almost fatherly. Or is it motherly? Or is it something else? Does he detect a gleam of daring? He stands up and bows thanks. He'd like to pay, but his rupees are gone, he says, and mimes a wallet with wings leaving his pocket.

'Pickpocket?' Laiq's eyes widen. 'In park?'

'No. Robbers.'

'Where!'

'Airport road. At night.'

'You report?'

'Gone,' Lev says, and sees the briefcase so clearly he could reach out and touch it.

'Big police station here.' Laiq points.

Lev steps off the concrete block of Laiq's step onto the pavement. 'Blood?' he asks, pointing to a red stain.

'Betel,' Laiq confesses. He's chewing it now. And there are customers who contribute their share, spitting courteously before they enter the shop. Inevitably some spots reach the step as well.

Lev steps back. The whole plinth of the building is faced in red stone; not betel red, the red of the fort, the mosque. The same red stone reappears in certain features at the second storey; otherwise the building's front is stucco, yellow-washed, with moulded cornices where the colour has streaked. Fancy pilasters divide shop from shop: barber, pathologist and tyre-repairer on this side of the staircase and on the other a panwallah, a tailoring establishment and a dairy.

At some point in the building's history the staircase off the street must have been reduced on either side, making room for the two extra shops; nothing else could explain why so grand a building should have so sorry an entrance. The upper floor and the townhouse on the roof are reached by the narrow steep stair in the middle. The puncturewallah has found its awning a convenient place to stack bald bicycle tyres. Out of the tyres rise four slender pillars surmounted by a Buddhist arch, purely decorative, with an urn and two roundels in its niche; on the arch, at roof level, sits a cube surmounted by a truncated pyramid surmounted by a cone that would resemble a duncecap but for a final piece of gingerbread, a tiny sphere. Now it's been overtopped by a rooftop apartment, the finial has a woebegone air. It could be an abandoned deity. The entranceway it crowns has all but disappeared, erased by degrees each time a pipe or piece of wiring was put in. A maze of telephone wires, rubber tyres, water meters, electricity meters, and crusted sewage pipes surrounds the only access to the former mansion of Lala Mukesh Chand Santushti Lal Jain.

A woman steps out of this passage as Laiq and Lev stand

there. She has long unkempt hair and wears a yellow T-shirt over acid-green jeans. Her suede sandals, which could be a man's, are unbuckled and she walks with one arm swinging further than the other. The other arm is impeded by a black nylon overnight bag that says, in red, *Update*. She has deep-set eyes out of which she looks intently at Lev, the kind of look few women in the old city would venture to give a stranger. Laiq she knows.

'Madam,' says Laiq, though she's a miss.

'How are things?' she says lightly in Hindi.

'Good.'

'Such heat!'

'Bad.' Laiq has turned monosyllabic, partly from his wish to stick with English, but mainly from his wish to end the conversation there. He has no wish to share Lev.

It's the foreigner who speaks. He owes it to Laiq to undo the social knot that he senses forming around him. Also, he's been loosened up. He gestures towards Laiq.

'Mister—'

'Laiq.'

'Mister Laiq has been demonstrating the art – no, the science – of massage,' he says, returning the woman's gaze. He turns to Laiq and extends his hand. 'Lev.'

Laiq bows, offended. Names could have waited. Still, if the madam stays a second longer he will have to introduce her.

She stays. She's never stayed before, breezing past his shop with that louche air of hers.

'Madam is owner of building.'

Maya wags a correcting finger. 'My mother is the owner.

I'm a tenant like you. That's not *my* flat on the roof.' She points it out to Lev as Laiq laughs politely.

She holds out her hand. 'Maya.'

'Lev.'

'Are you a tourist?'

'A visitor.'

'From?'

'Russia.'

'Russia!'

'Yes.'

'I have a friend who speaks Russian. Or at least reads it. He knows your poets off by heart.'

Laiq, who has not understood the half of what is being said, shifts uncomfortably. He feels the control moving away from him and is helpless in front of his own shop. His shop, her building. Her great-grandfather's name appears in pink capitals, moulded in cement, across the face of it.

'How long have you been in the country?'

'Since last night.'

'Last *night*! And a massage already! Well, you've come to the right place. Laiq is famous.'

Laiq strains out the same polite laugh, trapped between what he understands and what he does not. Always it comes down to this, with their kind. And maybe it's not even language. A whole era separates them: if they were being photographed now she would laugh. Laiq would grow stern.

Lev too is challenged by her speed. He looks for words and can't find them.

Maya is in trouble too, though you wouldn't guess. 'The rains are late this year,' she manages. 'That's why it's so hot.' The strain touches her at last and she turns aside. 'You must come back,' she says. 'Laiq's the best. And you must meet my friend. Well. Nice to meet you.'

'A pleasure.'

She unzips the bag and rummages in there as if she's left something behind, then ducks back into the grimed passage and races up the steep stair. She doesn't stop running until she's at the door of the flat. Undoes the padlock, wrenches the screechy bolt across, pushes in and drops the bag on the floor. Crosses to the workroom, opens the door and goes up to the mendicant. He regards her with his sightless eyes.

'He's come,' she whispers. 'Baba, he's here.'

Five

Lev returns to the Serai his head still tingling.

The air is heavy and there's a new line of black under his nails but he feels purged and rested and clear.

The briefcase is gone but he has two numbers to call, when he has changed some money. On the way back he passed a bank which will be open tomorrow. He must also call home. He can't tell Alla about the holdup: she'll be frantic. He can't tell her the briefcase is gone, but he must report safe, offer prospects, something. He will call her first. Then he can say he has his business calls to make, to the Ministry of Defence.

He has agreed to meet Laiq in the evening. And there is Maya, whose free spirit haunts him. The women he saw on his walk carried themselves differently. They were demure, looked down. She walked along looking, took control while he and Laiq fumbled. Laiq has an overbearing quality, but she had the social edge. He sees how her English, so attractive to him, is a charm that excludes. He marvels at the audacity with which she pointed out her flat. And there's her Russian-speaking friend.

Things could be worse, he falls asleep thinking. They

would have got his waistcoat next and he'd be high and dry. It's damage-control time.

He calls Alla at midday after changing money. She is well. Her mother is managing. Sankt Isaak came over. Alex is being Alex. She doesn't ask much about what's happening, but that's habit from Bio days. Still he's a bit disappointed. He's tempted to mention the robbery, but resists. He has his calls to make, he says, and she says yes, he must make his calls. He must be careful of the water. She's getting ready for work.

Life goes on, he comes away feeling. Over there, over here. Wherever you are. You sit on a plane and eat dinner at ten thousand metres as if that is where you belong. That moving point. You burrow into a stranger's flesh while her husband is stuck at page 37 and her baby is asleep at your feet. And the whole plane is held up by strings.

While Laiq's life goes on down below.

(What does she do, this woman who rents a flat from her mother?)

Laiq he's taken to. He'll go back for another session and pay this time. The body bit he's not sure about; he can't imagine the pallet. There are bedbugs at the Serai. Proximity to the walled city, he was told when he complained to the manager this morning. The bugs leap the wall.

He sits on the same park bench as yesterday and examines the strange banknotes. Buy a wallet. He makes for the yellow and black public call office across the busy street he's begun to think of as Nevsky Prospekt.

He dials the first contact number and gets a recorded message. *The number you are dialling does not exist.*

He hangs up. *Impossible!* He can *see* Purohit the military attaché in the back seat of the Volvo. Scribbling, passing the note across. This very piece of paper, his handwriting.

He dials the second number, his hand shaking as he anticipates the result. *The number you are dialling—* He hangs up sharply.

Now he's falling, spinning as he goes. Falling into his head, but if the booth were not narrow his body might topple. He leans against one glass wall. If it were a gas chamber he might be tempted to touch the black button.

The party that is dialling does not exist.

He crosses the road to his bench and sits. Yesterday he sat here and reviewed his troubles. They had seemed to him manageable then. Now he doesn't know if they are, doesn't know anything. This shoeshine boy pulling at his trouser leg knows more than he does.

'You know how to mutate Kurile-D?'

'Sahib?'

'You have the formula in your head, right?'

'Shoepolish?'

'Go on, prove it.'

The boy shrugs off the wooden rack he carries on his shoulder like a school satchel. He reaches for the tin of neutral and levers off the new lid. Normally he'd go straight for the mid tan – the foreigner's shoes are brown – but using up his brown means an investment he'd like to avoid just now. He's squatting on his hams, picking up the brown brush.

Lev leans forward and fixes him with a look that burns. 'You think I've come ten thousand kilometres just for an appointment with you? *Sod* off!'

Sod off sod off sod off sod off sod off!

The boy falls back onto his hands, turns and scrambles up and runs. Lev would like to give chase, tear him limb from limb. But the boy trips on his strings and falls again. A puppet, one of us. Little Alex.

Lev puts the lid back on the abandoned polish tin, picks up the rack and carries it across to the boy.

'Sorry,' he says, leaning over him, suddenly very tall. 'You don't get the job.'

He finds himself marching up Nevsky at speed. He could march all day in the burning sun. He could walk on broken glass and still feel unpunished for his folly. When he picked up the phone he'd actually imagined himself being given an appointment for the next day. Always, ever since the plan was born he's seen himself arriving at the ministry early, waiting his turn with his briefcase on his lap. But even without the briefcase – yesterday – he saw himself given a hearing. Always he saw a table with men seated around it, a ministry bureaucrat, scientists in the field, an observer from the lab where he might work, even a surprise Russian from his past.

Now there's nothing. He must go hat in hand to the ministry; he must work out for himself where the ministry is.

Now he sees not a table but doors. A corridor with doors. Door after door and he a scientist whose work starts when doors have closed behind him. Now he sees another sort of table. With just one man on the other side who grows increasingly curt every time Lev comes in.

He feels suddenly weary. He has been walking alongside traffic: packed buses, cars, roundtop taxis, scooters with whole families balanced on them, strange throbbing motorcycle rickshaws, pedal rickshaws, bicyclists, a volume of traffic that makes yesterday's Sunday level look civilized. Buses pouring smoke into air that is hot and grey. Sky not Petersburg blue but the colour of the dust he's walking on.

The rains are late. Where has he picked up that expression?

He feels drained, actually faint. He's arrived at the corner of a wide street opposite the red fortress he saw yesterday. JAIN CHARITABLE BIRD HOSPITAL says a row of large pink capitals perched like flamingos on the roof of the building there. The fort across the way looks impregnable; the traffic, not the moat, would save it from an army. A rickshaw cuts in front of him and brakes so he's in it before he can consider. It's a seat anyway, and now it's moving precariously in heavy traffic back the way he came. Hedged about by buses he misses the mosque but recognizes the overbridge. *Go on*, he gestures. 'Delhi Gate!'

But the rickshawman shakes his head. 'Police,' he says, his only English word. No rickshaws on Nevsky. Then he remembers another way, veers into a parallel road, and pedals away strongly. It's a long loop with shops and offices below and residences above. The noise and fumes of Nevsky drop away here; there's even a tree or two. Just as they're curving back towards Delhi Gate Lev realizes where he is. It's Laiq's street. Her street. And then he recognizes the Jain mansion.

The flat on the roof that's not hers. *Stop*, he pats the man and jumps off. The man holds up ten fingers. Lev gives him ten rupees.

Faint as he is, his legs find pleasure in stretching after the cramped journey. He's at the other end of Laiq's row of shops, outside a dairy where upturned milk cans are drying on the pavement. Next door is a tailoring establishment where half a dozen men are seated at sewing machines, their needles racing. Beyond them perches a tobacconist washing pale green betel leaves one by one before folding them away in a damp cloth.

He takes in all this through a dizzy haze. Hears the sigh of sewage in a rusty pipe beside the narrow entrance. And finds himself climbing the steep stair to the flat on the roof.

Six

Afterwards, after all the talk and the silences and the rich hesitations, when she is lying with her head on his chest and listening to his heart, Maya thinks back to this moment when he is standing there like an angel in an ikon overlaid with the soot of centuries.

The wire mesh of her security door is mounted on a grid of flattened hexagons. Dust coats mesh and grid. There's dust on him too, she notices as she draws back the bolt and he steps in.

Water he needs, more than anything, the glass you give a stranger, even an enemy who comes to your door in summer, and it does not occur to her until he asks. Afterwards she will give him water from her mouth, a long cold twisting rope that passes into him, joining him to her, so that he can never drink cold water again without wanting that.

'Some water.'

'Of course.' Water. Puppets, they enact a scene that repeats itself down the ages, by well and porch and bedside, in war and peace. As if the race were looking for a way back to its primordial element.

She hands him the plastic bottle before she remembers.

People use glasses; she's got so used to living alone. He waits till she returns and pours him a glass, then sips it in silence till it's gone.

It's then he collapses. Slowly, letting himself down by woozy stages, unable to make it as far as the nearest chair. There are no chairs in this room, no furniture at all. She brings a cushion from the next room and slips it under his head. Stands there looking down at him, then begins to pace the bare floor. Should she call a doctor? She stops. *Call Morgan.*

But then he stirs, opens his eyes. Looks around the strange room. She kneels beside him at once.

'How do you feel?'

He looks at her and smiles. 'OK. Just help me.'

She leads him to the cane chairs in the dining alcove. He sits, looks around. A bookshelf with books and small framed photos.

'I feel better. Sorry.'

She brings him a carton of orange juice, a recent indulgence. And cream biscuits. He drinks, eats.

'All right?'

'All right.'

Good boy, she wants to say. Please don't go away.

'You shouldn't go walking' – she was going to say *mustn't* – 'in the middle of the day. You get heatstroke.'

Heatstroke. It sounds old-fashioned to her, like gout or brainfever.

'I got,' he tests the expression, 'carried away.' And smiles, feebly.

'Where did you go? Where are you staying?'

'I'm staying at the Serai. I reached the fort.'

'The Red Fort? Did you go in?'

'No. I felt dizzy there. So I took a rickshaw back.'

'You speak very good English.'

Even in his state he's mildly irritated. So do you, he'd like to say. 'I went to an English school in Russia.'

She is fascinated. 'A private school!'

'No, state. It was the whole school's second language.'

'Are there many schools like that?'

'Sure. All the languages. I have a friend who went to a Hindi school.' He hesitates. '*Your* English is perfect.'

'It's not really a second language for me.'

'Really?'

'Maybe not even for my father.'

He shakes his head in disbelief. 'How is that?'

'He probably *dreams* in English. Like me.'

'And your Russian-speaking friend?'

'Morgan? He definitely dreams in English! It's his language. He doesn't *speak* Russian by the way, but he can read it. He lends me books by your poets. That's his, and that.'

She points to Morgan's paperbacks on the shelf, on the glass-topped table. Lev follows her finger and sees several Russian titles in translation. English imprints. 'I think he's trying to educate me,' she laughs. 'Chanus.'

'Chance?'

'*No* chance,' she translates college slang.

He picks up the book on the table, a paperback with a painting of the young Anna Akhmatova on the cover. That face, here! He smiles his amazement. Leafs through the book, struck by the parallel text. That script, here! He's never read a poem of hers, the poetess of his city. He reads a few lines

in his head, then out loud for her. She listens with her head
bent like a bird.

'That means,' he says, and reads from the level line across
the page:

> *'We shall not drink from the same glass*
> *Neither water, nor sweet wine,*
> *We shall not kiss of a morning early*
> *Nor glance through the window at evening time.'*

He looks up at her. 'And what does *that* mean?'

'Morgan will tell us,' she says, reaching across and taking
the book out of his hands. She goes to put it down on the
table but reconsiders and slots it among the Russian spines.
Then gives it a further little push. '*So.* You've had a massage
and you've seen the Red Fort – from the outside. You must
have seen the Jama Masjid, the Friday Mosque.'

He nods.

'That's all Old Delhi. Not *old* old. Actually there are much
older parts. At the other end of Delhi there's a thousand-
year-old tower. Built by a slave king.'

'A slave king!'

'His daughter is buried here.' She points towards the old
city sprawl whose rooftops begin at Delhi Gate. 'At that time
there was nothing here. All these old lanes you see came
much later.'

He's intrigued. 'What was she?'

'She was a queen. She was the ruler of Delhi after her
father. She was a capable ruler.'

Afterwards when he thinks back to this day Lev feels sure
that it was then, as she spoke that last line, that he fell. Down
a shaft as real and intangible as the one in his microscope.

Into a fever. She has a way of letting her head droop as she speaks while holding you with her eye. Even when her chin dips right down she's looking straight at you. So the line of the eyebrows and the line of the eyelashes meet.

Weeks later he sits her down across from him, pushing her into the same chair, and directs her.

'Lower. Still lower.'

She giggles but goes along.

'Still lower.' The lines meet. 'Now say it.'

'You're an idiot.'

'*Say* it.'

'*She was a capable ruler.* OK?'

He leans over and kisses her. It's the way she has of shaping every word, but also it's the framing gaze, sombre almost to depression, that possesses him.

'So what is so special about her?' He hangs over her chair though he's heard it all before.

'*Every*thing, yaa. She's the *only, woman,* who *ever, ruled* this *city.*'

Already as he sits there on this first day he notices the way her gaze will stroke an object. He hasn't seen such concentration before. It shifts from him now to a dogear in a scrap of paper, a flap that's caught the light. There's a tender violence to the look, as if a magnifying glass were being held there, a circle of white light brought lovingly to a point. The scrap could dazzle into flame.

'Do you have cigarettes?'

She looks up. A lag before she surfaces; it's like his microscopic falling in reverse. 'I'll get you some. There's a shop downstairs.' But the panwallah's shop is the street's gossip centre, she realizes.

'No, *please*.'

She lets it go, makes a note to pick some up from another panwallah.

He feels the dizziness come over him again. 'I must lie down.'

She pulls out Morgan's mattress, an instant bed.

'Rest. I'll wake you later.'

'I promised to meet Mr Laiq this evening.'

'What time?'

'Seven o'clock.'

'So come back here for dinner.' Her hand goes up in oath. '*No* chillies!'

He smiles up at her. 'Thank you.'

'I'll be in my workroom.'

'What do you do?'

'I make puppets.'

He stares, looking to see if she's serious, but her smile is the same brooding thing as before, and then she's shut the workroom door. Almost immediately it opens again as she comes out to fetch a bottle of water from the fridge and holds it up in a kind of salute and disappears with it into the puppet room.

Seven

Laiq looks younger, fresher than on the day before.

He's done something, plucked or dyed something, or is holding himself differently. Lev looks hard at him as he enters the shop. Laiq has had a haircut.

There are customers waiting, all to see the other Laiq. They sit on the bench in the front room but Laiq has switched on the yellow light beyond the screen, which indicates he is no longer cutting hair. By and large the haircutting happens during the day; it's in the evening that his other clients arrive. He still has the tubelight over the mirror on but the chair is tilted forward on its front legs.

He sees Lev enter, stepping easily up the high step that is a torment to old women, and comes forward to greet him.

'My lab,' he says, with a pleased smile.

Lev runs his eyes over the shelves of jars and phials and thinks of his room at Biosecuritat. White ruled there; here it's mouse brown, in the murky light of a 40-watt bulb. Laiq is occupied with bringing in the bird. As long as the cage hangs out there the shop is open.

'Come.' Laiq's English is directed, as never before, at the partridge. 'Come, my beauty-ful.'

He waves Lev into his sanctum, past the customer at the pink counter, and draws up a high stool for him behind the counter. Now Lev understands. He is the visiting physician at Laiq's clinic; Doctor Repin. He sees himself gestured at, hears the word *Rus*. The patient lowers her head, unworthy.

Laiq does not speak directly to her. She is a young woman, a mother. Her head is covered with a veil. He looks over her shoulder as he explains the measure and frequency of his prescription. It's loose in a polythene bag, a white powder into which he has just shaken a few grains of yellow. He frowns and breaks off.

'The child will *sit*,' he calls through the screen to the woman's three-year-old. 'The child will *behave*.'

Silence from beyond the screen. Laiq continues his instructions, drumming them in, never once looking the woman in the eye. When she leaves he turns and nods acknowledgement at his colleague. They are united in medicine, in their ministrations to the ignorant. Lev shifts on his stool and peers through the curtain at the waiting patients. Patience. And what a sorry bunch of puppets!

Next up is an old woman whom Laiq does look at. He pokes her, jokes with her, grips the skinny shaft of her arm and cranks her like a hand pump. She grins her toothless grin, the wet top of her tongue a bobbing valve, and grows serious only when Laiq turns her to face the physician from Rus. Her eyes fill with awe. Privileged, she folds her hands and bows. Then she knots her potion in the corner of her sari and hobbles off, groaning at the step. *He Ram!*

When the coolie and the rickshawman have been seen and a last-minute respectable chancer attended to, Laiq switches off the yellow light. He lowers the counter behind him, ushers Lev out onto the street, and switches off the tubelight. Padlocks the shutters, picks up the cage, and turns to his friend.

'Now I show you my house. Not far. Other side. Old city.'

They walk to the Delhi Gate, Laiq more erect than usual, more stern, more magisterial. The bird, which has grown restless at the approach of the park and has been treading the floor of the cage with its good foot, sees the grass recede as they cross the busy road. It goes still and fires off a general salute at any partners that might lurk on the green. The shrill clamour of it, rising above the rush-hour din, impresses Lev.

'What's the bird?' he asks, dodging traffic.

'Teetar,' Laiq replies holding up the cage so the creature can be seen. He doesn't know the English name. He lowers the cage. 'Old.'

Laiq uses the word neutrally, almost diagnostically, as if age was a disease, a sad tedious business he knows too well both in his profession and in his person. But also there's a touch of affection in that *old*, as for a first wife, a senior wife. Stricken with age, and still calling.

Here, crossing this insanely busy road which could not look less like Nevsky, Lev feels the poignancy of age come crushing down on him. It's always been something that happens to others. Something he sees in Alla or her mother, something one watches at a remove. It's keenest in someone on the brink, naturally. Keener in Alla, say, than in her mother – or the old biddy just now in Laiq's clinic, so clearly, even comically, past it – but he's never thought of himself on that edge. He's *coming* to it, always coming to it.

Laiq, now, he's there. From the first he saw him as older,

a year or two perhaps, or even a couple of months, but older. Now he wonders if he's pegging himself too low, the way he sometimes finds he's doing in the street at home with passing strangers. Ranking as he goes. Is he wrong about Laiq? By months, or even by a year?

Age. Barbering or doctoring, Laiq is the age specialist. Who else comes up so close to strangers' bodies? So every fold and follicle declares its history.

'Laiq,' Lev assays as he steps up onto the pavement on the other side. 'How old are you?'

It's not an awkward question here, he feels. The manager at the Serai asked him his income before they had been together two minutes.

Laiq blinks rapidly and pushes his chin forward as he does when he has not understood.

'Your age. How much?'

'Forty-seven.'

The relief is immediate, physical.

'You?'

'Forty-five.'

It's a small lie, by months, but it fortifies. All the same Lev is ashamed. Also he has just seen with a twinge of guilt what Laiq meant yesterday when he said: *Tomorrow, body.* Laiq meant today he would show him his other hat, his doctoring. He meant the body corruptible, his ministrations to infirm flesh. *That* body.

'This way.'

They've come to a lane heading off Nevsky, one of those tunnels into the past Lev was tempted by on his Sunday walk. The very one he noticed with the giant tree. Beyond the tree the gully narrows. Now only scooters and cyclists, not even a rickshaw can pass them as they walk. On either side are narrow doorsteps that a foot cannot mount without turning. Their varying levels are more disorienting than the labyrinth of lanes. They cut across a wider lane glittering with shops and immediately plunge back into darkness. The pattern continues: darkness, a bright lane, darkness again. Only twice does the gully itself brighten into shops, a row of butchers, locksmiths, garland-makers. Incredibly, with all its bends and twists they have not left the original gully that began at Nevsky.

'Now,' Laiq says, taking his arm, 'it is coming narrow.'

The new lane peels off behind a tinsmith's stack of watering cans. Here they can no longer walk abreast. The etiquette for passers is to wait in the first alcove or if caught halfway to pause and turn sideways; a woman will face the wall. Now and then a square of barred light from a window guides their feet.

'Finish.' Laiq is waiting at the fork.

Lev finds the lane opens out into a common yard. He breathes in instinctively; a moment ago he felt the canyon walls were touching above his head. Here the last light of day has paled to tallow. Ahead is a low stone wall topped with an iron fence. Its massive blocks of yellow stone sit silently one upon the other, older by far than the gullies he's just traversed. In the more recent wall beside him are delicate wafers of brick, exposed in so many places that the whole tottering building has taken on their terracotta glow. Where the lane ends teenage boys are playing the last overs of a game of cricket. They stop and stare.

'Go on, go on,' Laiq urges them as he works his key in the lock. 'Last ball.'

The boys scowl at Lev as if he is breaking up their game, but the partridge sends a cheery dinner summons ringing out into the last light.

Ghee chapati ka ghee chapati ka ghee chapati ka ghee!

Lev mounts the steps turning his large feet sideways as he goes. Beyond the threshold are three more steps and then they're in a kind of anteroom.

'*How's that*!' comes the cry from the cricketers. 'Clean bowled!' On the last ball.

The anteroom floor is compacted lime gone to pieces so it's always gritty underfoot. There's a door straight ahead but it's chained and bolted and padlocked and probably locked from the other side too. Lev looks for a way out, a way on, but there is none: Laiq has one room. He feels trapped, wildly claustrophobic, even though he's spent two nights in a shoebox at the Serai. It doesn't matter that the ceiling is a long way up, that it's actually cooler inside than out. This is it. This is the home Laiq invited him to.

Laiq mounts the last step to a level where the floor is sealed. He has slipped out of his shoes, put down the birdcage, and is washing his hands at a basin in a corner niche. Lev unlaces his shoes and steps up onto the rush matting in his socks. From the new vantage he sees a stair without a banister go up to a kind of mezzanine, halfway to the high ceiling, a shelflike space that overhangs the room. Now he sees that the area below is for storage. There are trunks on the floor, stood on bricks, a sheet-iron cupboard. Deep arched niches, whose whitewash sets off the dark yellow of the wall, hold prized oddments: a book, a lamp, a censer, a betelnut cutter.

Laiq climbs the steps, taking the cage with him. Lev

follows and sees a set of doors that give onto a balcony. Upstairs the floor is glazed cement spread with a rug. Here Laiq sleeps with the balcony doors open in summer and closed in winter. Here he eats, here he thinks, here he lives.

Laiq hangs the bird up there and finds two round tins in a wall niche. He breaks coarse bread from the first and dips it in the ghee of the second and passes six morsels through the cage bars.

The balcony juts over the alley that was just now a cricket pitch. It overhangs the central stairway to the house and terminates abruptly where the room that corresponded to Laiq's on the other side caved in. You can still see one of the stone brackets that held up the missing end. The pillars are of turned wood, cracked but imperishable. A grille of iron lace supports the rail, fine work from another century; every panel is intact. As if tempting fate, Laiq has loaded the balcony with potted plants.

'Only scented flowers,' he says, leaning into the night. 'Only white.'

Darkness has fallen. The cricketing boys have gone home. All around are windows, barred rectangles of yellow light, some curtained, some not, some papered over, some hung with calendars, one or two bricked in. An arm appears out of one and drops a handful of rubbish into the little square. Rubbish has built up in heaps down below. The walls of the square rise three and four storeys, flush with the stone perimeter of the ancient enclosure on three sides. By the light from the windows Lev sees two beds laid out on a plinth in the tiny yard below.

'What is that?' he asks.

'Tomb.'

Laiq rhymes it with bomb and sounds the final b. It takes Lev a few moments to work it out. The beds are gravestones.

'Whose?'

'Razia Begam. Queen of Dilli. Long time back.'

There's a stunned moment as the realization sinks in. *She was a capable ruler.* But there's no way Lev can share the afternoon's events with Laiq. Too much to explain, too few words. And he's reminded now of Maya's dinner.

'I must go,' he says after a little while.

'Stay. I will send a boy for dinner.'

'I am already invited.'

'Where?' Laiq is openly sceptical.

'The manager of the hotel is expecting me.'

'Serai?'

'Yes.'

Laiq nods. It's all right that Lev should be dining with a hotel manager. He nods again. He is in the company of a doctor from Russia who dines with managers. That's fine.

'You come again?'

'Yes.' Lev wants to make amends. 'We will have beer. Drink wine. I invite you.'

'Good,' Laiq agrees and they go back down. Laiq slips his shoes back on and waits while Lev laces up. Then they walk back to Nevsky along the gully. Laiq points out the Serai.

Where the manager is in fact waiting. Lev has still to pay him with the rupees he's carried on his person all day. The security waistcoat is wet against his skin, the notes damp. His passport is returned. He returns to his little room to freshen up. A shower, a change of shirt – the same wet waistcoat – and a dab of cologne.

Eight

'You're late.'

Lev knows that. He looks for an exclamation mark but there's none. The way he's looked at his bare wrist twenty times today expecting to be told the time. The watch is gone; what happened on the way from the airport was not a dream.

She stands there, barring his way, this truant angel. What business has he showing up now when she's spent the last two hours going from this door to the workroom and back? Back and forth she's gone like a puppet, like a *puppet*!

'Are you going to let me come in?'

He's smiling. God, look at him. Look at him, Pa. So beautiful it's not fair. She slides the bolt across, swings back the security door.

'I'm sorry,' he says, simply, quietly before he moves an inch.

She says nothing, stands aside. He shuts the door behind him and comes in. The bare room where he fainted. So this was not a dream either.

'Laiq took me to his home.'

'Oh, I know that.'

'How did you know!'

'I've got eyes, haven't I?' For you, only for you. She looks accusingly at him, her gaze shifting minutely from side to side.

'I had to go,' he says sheepishly, already the husband.

'You were in his shop a long time.'

'He was showing me his clinic.'

'Clinic!'

'Then he took me home. Do you know where he lives!' She's not interested.

'He lives at that queen's tomb.'

'Everybody in Delhi lives near someone's tomb. It's a city of tombs. Anyway the dinner is spoilt. I kept heating it and heating it, it got burnt. So, come have some burnt pea pulao.'

She goes to the kitchen and doles out a lump of rice on a melamine plate. The long grains have gone curled and crackly and the peas in it changed from the beautiful green they were when Morgan left them to steam. She's fried some paneer to go with it, cubes of ricotta that started out a light gold in the pan but are now crusted brown dice that rattle as they drop on the plate.

'Here. Dinner.'

He sits obediently on one of the two cane chairs in the dining alcove. The same one where this afternoon he sat and read Akhmatova for the first time.

'What about you?'

'In India the man eats first.'

The man, not men. It tolls over his head like fate. Da-*dang*. The man.

'Come on!' She's having him on, he's sure. 'Join me!'

She relents, serves herself, sits on the other chair, drawing one foot up under her.

'It's good,' he says, though even he can tell it isn't.

She chews in silence, her eyes wandering here and there and finding nothing to fasten on. She seems not to notice what she eats, hardly knows she's eating.

'Are you expecting someone?'

She stops chewing and looks hard at him.

'I was.'

'I mean someone else.'

'No, no one else. Just you.' The *just* is scathing. It scathes not with rage but with something like disappointment. As if they've already travelled the whole way and come back to this point.

Lev eats up, spooning peas he'd normally fork. 'Can I have some more?'

'Help yourself.'

He does. 'We have a dish like this from the south in which the rice is cooked with mutton. Children contend over the crust at the base.'

'I'm a vegetarian.'

He returns to his place and eats. Eating has made him hungry. 'Good,' he says with more conviction, his mouth full of food. She has put her plate down as if food does not concern her.

But now she's watching him with something like interest. It could border on pleasure if she let it.

'Some more?' She's standing in the kitchen door.

'All right.'

'You might as well eat it straight from the degchi.' There's the trace of a smile on her lips.

'All right!'

She hands him the pot and takes away his plate. He sits

back down and scrapes. She returns with the skillet and sweeps the remaining cheese into the pot. He eats off the wide rice spoon, scrapes and eats till it's all gone. Clangs spoon and pot together and offers them up. 'Perfect!'

Not forgiven yet, her eyes say. 'Mangoes for dessert. Langras.'

He screws up his nose, feels he can do that now. 'For me not.'

'Not for you? Sure?' Mangoes she will eat, any time. 'Try this.' One slice.

In the weeks to come, when the rains have broken and it's the true langra season and she feeds him slivers with her own hand, he's persuaded that no fruit can hope to match the mango. Not even the tiny oublepiha berry that he went picking as a boy and his mother turned into a tangy yellow jam that can still summon up childhood. Nothing will taste the same again.

'Will you *ever* be late again?'

'*Never.*'

They burst out laughing.

'I need a cigarette.' The relief has him gasping.

'Bad habit,' she rules, temporizing till inspiration strikes. Then goes to the workroom and apologizes to the clerk in the black waistcoat and takes the bidi from behind his ear.

'Just one,' she rations, returning.

He lights up, inhales deeply, enjoying the newness of it. Presently his hand goes in search of an ashtray.

'No, not that!'

The bidi withdraws but a tiny scroll of ash has fallen into the bowl on the table. She snatches it up and shakes the ash out onto the floor.

'What is it?'

It's a bowl of yellow metal, not six inches across but heavy. Devoid of ornament but polished so it holds the room's light in it like water. From where he sits Lev can see the ceiling fan turning in it. There are touches in it of copper, touches of brass, of nickel. The pale underglow reminds him of something. When he leans over it holds his yellow face.

'It's a singing bowl. Finish your bidi and I'll show you.'

He crimps his lips on the butt and drags repeatedly, watching through narrowed eyes how she hangs on the series of tiny plosives.

'It's used for meditation,' she says when he stubs it out on the floor.

Instantly he's on his guard, this puppet of science.

'You rest it on the palm of your hand, like this. Your hand has to be held perfectly flat.' She takes up a carved wooden pestle and runs it gently around the rim on the outside. The bowl begins to hum. 'And you keep rubbing, not hard.' The humming gathers resonance, filling the room. At the same time a sound that started somewhere else is travelling towards them from the corners of the room, repeating the event of the bowl. 'Try it.'

He can't get it to go, is inclined to strike rather than rub. She takes it back and sets it going again. The humming fills the room. Then she cups her hand damping down the sound and returns it to its place on the table. Sound returns to light. He prefers the colour to the sound, he thinks. Now he remembers. It's the glow at the bottom of a microscope.

'It upsets Laiq's bird. Have you seen his partridge?'

'Yes. He can hear it down there?'

'Sometimes when it's quiet and I feel like teasing him.'

He stares at the little ceiling fan in the bowl turning like a cog in a watch. Overhead the blades take the hot night air and slap it down on you. He pushes his chair back. Does she only run it at top speed? It sounds like a helicopter and sets all the papers and cloth ends jiggling; it makes even her eyelashes quiver.

She jumps up. 'God it's hot. This city! I'll turn on the cooler. Maybe some of it will reach here.'

She slips away and he hears a kind of sonic boom from the next room, the cooler coming on. The noise levels off at a drone that's louder but mellower than the whippy fan.

She stands in front of the cooler, eyes shut, body on fire. Evaporation begins. God, yes. If she has a god it's the dumpy finial on the roof she nods at half in jest coming and going.

'Maya?'

He's come looking for her. How long has she been standing there? The pain's eased, gone to mauve.

'This is my saviour,' she says introducing the cooler. 'Cooler, Lev.'

He bows. The cool blast catches his face and he holds it there. Nice. He peers in at the works. Water trickling down the straw bats, a pump spinning away behind the fan.

'What's the scent?'

'Khus-khus. It's a kind of grass. You get that when you wet it.'

They're so close to the booming it's some time before they hear the doorbell.

'Shit,' she says. 'Morgan. What's the time?'

He looks at his wrist and shakes his head. The bell goes on ringing.

'It must be past midnight,' she says. She steers him from

behind to the workroom. Pushes him in there and shuts the door. On second thoughts opens it a crack so he can breathe.

Lev hears him before he sees him, the Voice. Organ Morgan, he's called at the studio by a whispering clique. No one remembers his surname till it appears in print in the society columns. He seems to have forgotten it himself. His books are signed with just his forename, the way he signs autographs for schoolgirls, a mountainous *M* with the *organ* trailing away in a squiggle of lesser hills.

'Look, just *four* hours!' he's saying as he reaches for his mattress. Four hours to reporting.

'Sorry, Morgan. You can't just barge in any time you like.'

Lev strains to see without being seen and can catch only a moving slice of the man. Shorter than the voice, as the schoolgirls always find. Lev shifts uncomfortably. The room is unbearably hot and close. He's turning to look for a window when his heart skips a beat.

There's a man standing beside him.

The room is full of people and they are all looking at him. All except the man at his shoulder, who would appear to be blind. It's the mendicant, staring sightlessly into space, with his head at a slight tilt. The arm with the begging bowl is held up by a string.

'So she does make puppets.'

Lev picks his way past them to the window, his feet snagging in piles of fabric on the floor, opens the casement and breathes deeply. Yellow light from the street lamp flows in. Two floors down he sees Laiq's concrete doorstep with its dark stain of betel juice. At his feet is spread a puppet garment that has been cut out for sewing. The front and back of a jacket of some kind, two sleeves on either side and a collar above laid out like the pieces of a solved puzzle. Even the gussets are in place, waiting to be sewed in; she's not an amateur.

The door opens and she stands there framed in light.

'You can come out now. He's gone. Can you see? The light's fused in here. Morgan was supposed to change the tube.'

'What did he want?'

'A bed for the night.'

'He wanted to sleep here?'

'Yes.'

Lev looks at her. 'Does he often?'

'Sometimes.' She's looking closely at him, pleased. Pa, he's jealous!

'What did you tell him?'

'I said he was not allowed in after midnight.'

'Is it so late?'

'I don't know. Morgan doesn't have a watch either.'

'Have you ever turned him aside before?'

'Away, no. It's a new rule.'

She looks into the workroom. The listening puppets straighten up, the mendicant has turned his head away.

'You can meet them tomorrow,' she says and shuts the door, switches off the kitchen light and the hall light and fan and the lamp at the bookshelf. Now they're in the dark.

'You're married, na?' she says.

'Yes.'

Don't tell me about her. He sees her lips shape the warning.

He wasn't going to. Share Alla. Though she's going to have to share him.

'Over there, in Russia,' she hesitates, 'it's like shaking hands, isn't it? Morgan says it is.'

'What?' He takes her hand, touching her for the first time.

'This.' She's still searching for words. 'Here it's a scandal.'

She buries her face in his side. Now she must explain that Morgan's mattress is for Morgan. She must tell him about the pain in her joints, that he will have to be gentle. That she must remain a virgin. That he is too beautiful for words. That she's been waiting and waiting.

Nine

'You're covered in bites.'

She's been awake, watching him since first light.

His eyes open and flutter shut again. He could sleep the day out quite happily. What bites? His eye focus under their lids. It's not Alla's voice. The bed is a mattress on the floor. His eyes open wide.

A head of black hair resting on his chest.

The night comes flooding back. His arms come up and clasp her and she burrows deeper in. They fall into a light drifting sleep, the half sleep of skin on skin.

He wakes out of it before she does and looks down at her. Her body stretches away smooth and unmarked, with the fine grain of youth. Last night he felt its miracle of softness, now he sees its gold. The colour where the buttock swells is the colour of the singing bowl. Six metals.

When he wakes again she's sitting cross-legged beside him wearing an outsize T-shirt with jungle stripes across it.

'You're covered in bites.'

Has she said that before? He props himself up on his elbows and looks down the length of his body. There are pink spots all over it.

'Fleas,' he says. 'At the Serai.'

'Then sleep here.'

He looks up. 'Every night?'

'Why not?'

He sits up fully. The silence is strange after the thundering of the cooler all night. Morning has crept in to claim back its space. The air is full of strange bird cries. Automatically he looks for the time but his wrist continues bare. That happened, all that business in the taxi. He shuts his eyes. He's a scientist without a briefcase, without a watch. He's a scientist with all the time in the world. Again he sees the corridors and himself trudging. It's so real he must force his eyes open.

There she is. All that happened too. They look at one another in silence. She pushes a strand of hair aside.

'We'll put Morgan's mattress underneath,' she grins.

'He won't like that.'

'Morgan? He's a gypsy. He has fifty mattresses.'

'But this one is special?'

She considers, shrugs.

'He is in love with you?'

'Morgan! He's too handsome, yaa. Too clever. Anyway he has more women than he can handle. But he's *sweet*,' she adds, looking slyly at him.

He smiles uncertainly back, a crooked smile. Gets up, wants the bathroom.

When he emerges she's gone. He looks in the workroom, the kitchen, the bare sitting room. The dining alcove is empty, the cane chairs as before; the other bathroom door stands ajar. He goes to the front door. It's bolted from the inside, but he opens it anyway and checks the security door. It's bolted from the inside too. She's disappeared.

Returning to the dining space he sees another door. He'd taken it for a window before. It's unbolted. It gives onto a terrace, sequestered from the mansion's roof. She's sitting there, waiting.

For the sun. Sitting cross-legged on the swing seat, her eyes shut. The singing bowl is balanced on the palm of her hand; in the other hand she holds the pestle. He steps back in instinctively, his bare feet returning to smooth terrazzo.

He stands in the doorway, wearing one of the big T-shirts she gave him over his moleskins, and looks out at the world. The morning air is cool though the fabric of the house still holds the previous day's heat. The haze that hangs over everything has begun to silver in the east like a television screen coming to life. The field beyond the old city wall is dredged with grey; the distant trees are so wrapped in dust that they appear blue. Only the nearest greens are true, tree-tops and the terrace pot plants.

Bird calls sound from every side, and a high-pitched chatter that could be bird or animal. A dark clarinet call is a peacock perched on the city wall. A peacock! Moss has blackened the wall's grey stone, grass overrun its breastwork of slits and sluices. Set in the deep bayed arches down below are windows whose filtered light evokes a bridge. White bathroom tiles along one pier disclose a urinal behind cement lace. The field beyond the wall is dotted with the figures of the unhoused, defecating in the open.

The whole scene as far as the horizon, where two grey chimneys rise into the haze, has the unreality of a stage. It could be another planet, waiting to be touched into existence. The otherness might break down then. Lev retreats into the kitchen and pokes around there.

Maya begins to rub the bowl. The sound builds and hangs in the air in tiers, a ground note and its octaves ranged above it. A locomotive at the horizon answers it and among the pots in the kitchen there's one that catches its note. She varies the pitch with the pestle as she slips into the rosiny trance of it, rubbing with a new sure touch till the bowl begins to sing all its notes at once. She passes it under her chin from ear to ear and is engulfed by the sound.

'Tea's on the shelf.'

She's come in behind him. It's not a sweet voice; it grates on something inside.

'There, on that shelf. I'll put the water on.'

He watches her lips mould the air. Meditation presumably unites her with something larger. But her instinct is to seal up the air, to stamp herself on it.

'Here.' She's holding out the bowl.

'Not for me.' He means all that carry on.

'It's *yours*, yaa.'

She giving it to him, she means. He's surprised but knows she doesn't speak lightly. *Sleep here. Take this. She was a capable ruler.*

'I don't need it any more,' she laughs. 'You calm me.'

He takes it, goes looking for a neutral place to put it down on. The whole flat is a neutral place. She camps there with her three changes of clothes, her borrowed books. This tea caddy lives half on the shelf, half off, could easily come tumbling down. It does.

'Shit! Asshole!'

The tea is all over the floor. He tipped the balance. He's contrite but amused.

'Where did you learn your English?'

'Risingholme.'

She starts with what's left in the tin.

'No, wait.' He doesn't want stew. He shows her how to make Russian tea.

'Come meet the puppets.'

He follows her in, barefoot like her.

'If you spill your tea in here I'll kill you. This is Babaji.' She's stopped in front of the mendicant. 'Babaji is blind. Say namashkar.'

Lev says it.

'Babaji is pleased to meet you. He's been waiting.'

'We met last night.'

She looks sharply at him. Oh, when Morgan came. 'Babaji's renounced the world so he won't talk to you. Even me he hardly talks to.'

She moves on down the line. Now and then she pulls a string so an arm stretches out or the whole puppet bows. Sometimes they surprise her with their loveliness: the long lashes on Anarkali, she'd forgotten those.

'Anarkali dances with a lamp.'

Anarkali minces forward, bends to the ground and comes up swaying with one hand held out. There could be a lit lamp in the hook of her hand.

'Uttam Singh rides a horse. Bade Mian smokes a hookah.'

She gestures towards them with the respect one accords living people. The old man's lungs are full of phlegm, the rags inside him strain across the divide into life, into sickness.

'Janaki is in love.'

Lev sees the red rag of the heart pumping. The sawdust in the gut endures a spark of pure longing, the woodchips begin to smoke. Suddenly the tinder ignites, and there is love.

Puppet after puppet leans into life. As she bows back Maya wonders if she is not leaning into the inanimate.

They've come to the window, which she opens. A cool draught pours in as she looks straight down. 'Sweeney's in.'

'Who?'

'Laiq. His bird is hanging up.'

Lev looks down and sees the curve of the cage.

She flashes him a conspiratorial smile. 'Do you want to try out your singing bowl?'

He goes and fetches it, curious. She shows him again how it's done and gradually he gets the knack.

'Good. Keep going.'

The note swells and fills the room, spilling over to the shop below. In its cage, the bird begins to duck and scrape. Then it can bear it no more and bursts out.

Re more sajni re more sajni re more sajni re!

'See?'

He's impressed.

'Why do you call him Sweeney?'

'Sweeney Todd. He was the barber in a famous puppet show. He used to disappear his customers.'

'Disappear them?'

'He had a special barber's chair with a trapdoor. You'd be sitting there getting shaved and the next minute you were gone. Into the cellar. And that was the last anyone saw of you.' Her voice changes. '*Now Mrs Lovatt was Sweeney's landlady and she made meat pies. With a flavour never surpassed and rarely equalled . . .*' She rolls her eyes at him.

'Is that why you're a vegetarian?'

'Maybe.'

She turns from the window to where the bodice-in-progress is laid out on the durree. 'This is Ràzia's.'

'The Queen of Delhi?'

'The show's coming up soon.' She lifts the lid off the sewing machine, then turns and puts her arms around him. 'When will I see you?'

Lev wilts at the thought of the day ahead, selling his death skills. The enquiries, the taxis, the struggle just to get there. He holds her in a distracted clasp.

'What's wrong?' She kisses him lightly on the lips, the forehead, the cheeks, the chin. She's painting on his face.

'Nothing.'

'So when are you coming back?'

'Tonight.'

Ten

The day goes sour when he leaves.

When he gets to the Serai he pays for another night and goes and sits in his cabin on his bed. The longer he sits the more disinclined he is to move. By midmorning he's paralysed with indecision. Should he ask the manager? Can he say *Ministry of Defence* without attracting suspicion? Should he first get himself a map? The ministries are in New Delhi. New Delhi starts at Delhi Gate, just across the road. Should he look up all the Purohits in the telephone directory? There might just be a Colonel Purohit. Maybe all the city numbers have changed, added a digit?

In the middle of it all he thinks of her and experiences such a rush of tenderness he is overwhelmed. He drops back on the bed. Her touch is on his skin, her kisses, innocent and daring, remain fastened where she left them. He falls asleep, poor puppet, with one arm thrown over his eyes against the harsh light of midmorning. When he wakes the sun has shifted but he can't move his arm. It's stuck there, hinged wood, and he must use the other hand to free it, carefully working it loose.

The Ministry! He sits up with a start. Maya is there in

the other bed, dwindling to the dark points of her sunken eyes.

'What is happening to me?' Lev speaks the words out loud, sculpting each word the way she does. He shakes his head. He's laid wide open and he's known her just two days. He's been in India three days. He must act. Orient himself, make a list.

Map, he writes. *Manager. Ministry.*

And again he's travelling in circles. How, when, which, where? He's like the vendor puppet she showed him with the pot of curds on his head. *Dahi!* she called, flattening her voice and slackening the strings so he went trudge, trudge, trudge. Is he reduced to that? Selling his bacteria from street to street.

And he expected a car. There were scenes from an earlier play in which he actually expected – Lev cringes at the thought – a car to call at his hotel. For Scientist Lev Repin, a driver.

In the end he gets a map at the front desk and spreads it on the cafeteria table when the traces of onion omelette have been wiped away. He finds Delhi Gate just outside the Old City walls. New Delhi folds out below: long straight roads, arcs, circles, a geometry that contrasts sharply with the streets just north of the Serai. He checks the distance he walked yesterday to the corner with the bird hospital opposite the Red Fort. It's nothing compared to the expanse below. The walled city is an island in the sea of Delhi.

He decides he will not take the manager into confidence. He will go to the centre, to what appears to be the hub of the new city. There's a tourist office where he can safely say *Ministry of Defence*.

'Take a phat-phat,' Grover says. 'They drop you right at Connaught Place.'

Lev perches on the back of the motorcycle rickshaw, the fifth passenger with the narrowest seat, and the old Indian Chief roars off into the traffic. He's flying low in a chrome cage that rides on the deep beat of a wartime engine. They go pelting down the straight, duck under a bridge, and come up in Peter. Or so it seems. A mock Petersburg with a pillared arcade that goes on curving and curving until it's a circus. He half expects to see a statue of Catherine the Great.

Ministry of Defence he hears himself say when his turn comes, and the tourist office woman doesn't blink. She circles the appropriate intersection on his map with her ballpoint and goes on talking on the phone.

So now he knows, but he'll start fresh tomorrow; afternoon is not the time to go looking for an appointment. He crosses the street towards a row of trinket shops and looks in the windows, converting into roubles and dollars. Beyond is a row of garment stalls.

'*For*-ty, forty.'

'*Cha*-lee, chalee.'

'*For*-ty, forty.'

The chant comes from a trestle table heaped with shorts and T-shirts. The vendors wear a different sort of shirt but they are peddling the garments on the table with an energy Lev never sees at home. Sweat that streams from their faces, they have their handkerchiefs out, but they never stop the back-and-forth of the price chant.

The echo stands behind the table with his heel on a brick and hoists himself up with every other call. Jerked up, but he's his own puppeteer. Tiring, he breaks into a double clap. The front man takes up the clap and works in a quick middle beat that makes three of two. They do a random set of variations, syncopating, missing a whole bar, returning to the ground rhythm. Sometimes the bossman who sits on a crate frowning into a pocket calculator will join the echo without lifting his head.

Two tables down the competition has a chant going over a heap of children's garments.

'*Pacch*-ees, pacch-ees.'

'*Twenty*-five, twenty-five.' Further along are dresses and beyond those more T-shirts, more dresses, shorts, kaftans, kurtas. All the variants that four limbs and a trunk can take. Customers pick over the stock: it's moving.

Lev does a quick conversion and is amazed. You could triple your money back home. At the first stall the chanter on the brick is still bobbing up and down. Each time he retreats into his puppet solitude, he looks for a fresh start and finds it in the small variations he draws out of nowhere. Lev picks out a T-shirt and goes to hand it to him. *For my son*, he wants to say conversationally, but the man is intent on his chant and nods him at his employer without a pause.

Back on the phat-phat he hugs his purchase and his map against the windstream. Something to show at the end of the day. He smiles into the wall of rushing air and decides to stay on board to the end of the line. The Serai goes past, then the Delhi Gate, then he's roaring up Nevsky. The police station, the cinema, the footbridge; then the road bends and there's the mosque. A dome with palm trees! On the field opposite, the long red rampart of the fort. Then the busy street with the flamingoes on the hospital roof. The motor-cycle turns up it and blasts a way through the crowd. The driver, gearing with thonged feet, sits back for one last burst of speed, then cuts the engine, wheels lazily around a fountain, leaning on one handlebar as he goes, and rolls to a precision halt.

'Finish,' he calls to his one remaining passenger. Lev stays where he is, unwilling to face the crowd, to get lost. Anyway, he wants more. 'Back,' he gestures, 'Serai.'

But there are three phat-phats in the queue ahead so he gets off. On the ground he plucks up courage and strides into the crowd.

'Money!'

Ah, he forgot to pay. He pays, apologizes.

'Noproblem.' One word.

And then he's swallowed up. Once he stops to unfold his map and becomes an island. People flow around him; then he's the river again. The map says there's a shortcut home by a curving road that comes out at the next gate along, Turkman Gate. He finds the road and takes it, walking on a pavement that can break down into rubble without warning, or into rubbish. Not Peter, here. Sennaya maybe, on a market day. NEW JULLUNDER BRASS WARE STORE *Brass and Copper Sheets Coils Flats Wire Etc PVC Tubings Rubber Plastic Pipe Cork Sheet All Asbestos Goods.* Behind this very shop could be the tomb of Razia Begam, only Queen of Delhi.

The hardware shops give way to fruiterers, tailors, photographers; the first pickle rickshaw he's seen tails him curiously for a while. A stone arch right on the pavement frames a courtyard that might once have been a garden. The walls surrounding it are covered in bills and posters stuck over bills and posters, all peeling together, bark on the urban tree. Down the middle of the road, with scooters and rickshaws looping around him, comes a human car. *Beebeep*, he calls and shifts gears, *hrrrrrrrr*. He brakes, waves traffic on, reverses and cuts carefully around an obstacle, a seated bull. *Beebeep*.

The road opens up and there is Turkman Gate. A simpler, tawny version of Delhi Gate with half the traffic and no discernible wall on either side, gate only in name. At the corner where he stands a sign reads NIGHT SHELTER, in English. Lev glances through a gap in the corrugated iron cladding and is glad he doesn't sleep there. Across the way, among trees, is his own Serai, lettered in red. But I don't sleep there either, he thinks and is swamped by the memory of her. The power of a secret buoys him up.

A figure detaches itself from the idlers by the shelter and comes after him. It's the shoeshine boy, looking for revenge. He doesn't sleep at the shelter because he's underage, but has earned night money from the men who do.

'Saab.'

Lev knows him at once. He looked into his eyes yesterday.

'Shoepolish.' One word, a whiplash. He follows Lev all the way to the Serai Gate, plucking at his sleeve, just out of range.

'Here,' Lev stops. He hands him the polythene bag he's carrying and disappears through the iron gates.

Now why did you do that? he thinks in the shower, but knows that the T-shirt will fit. It wasn't black enough for Alex, probably.

Eleven

He's more thirsty than hungry when he's dressed. Maybe Laiq would like a beer.

Laiq would. He's delighted. He was standing in his doorway when Lev came up and now he puts the lock on before any customers appear. He knows just the place, though he's never been in himself. They cross Nevsky and walk along the other side past the cinema.

'Here.'

The sign says Moti Mahal. The restaurant has a pluperfect look, but it has a licence. In the old days the linen was starched and the chickens were succulent; now the reverse is true and the old waiters are caught in the ebb. But the prices! Laiq's eyes widen over the menu and he grows quiet.

Lev tells him of his trip to Connaught Place, of the pavement sellers and their chant. Beer lets him hazard mimicry.

'*For-ty*, forty! *For-ty*, forty!'

Laiq perks up. He knows of a better market. All the Russians go there, he says, for clothes.

'*This* much jeans!'

He measures a pile fatter than a suitcase and mimes

shutting the lid on them. He sips his beer, presses the napkin to his lips. He tells Lev of his time as a scooter rickshaw operator, his meter wars with South Delhi customers. He goes further back. To his year at university, pranks at the girls' hostels. Then, sobering down, he tells of dropping out, setting up shop. When the chicken comes he picks delicately at it; breaks the naan with two fingers and a thumb on the plate.

Lev eats with frank enjoyment. He's not a dainty eater. He describes the canals of Petersburg. Russian trains, the dog in space. Catherine the Great's lovers. 'Like your Razia,' he hazards, crunching on the neck.

Laiq holds up a finger. 'Razia have only one lover.'

'Oh?'

'General.'

'Army?'

'Yes, army general. Her father die. King dead. Brother want gaddi, throne. But she not want to give. She want rule. Be Queen of Dilli. Soldier queen, fighting queen. Yes? So. She say no to brother, no to uncles, no to all mens. She rule alone. But mens not liking, not let her sleep. Not let her rule. So she marry slave. Foreigner. Horseman.'

'A knight?'

'Many nights.'

'An officer?'

'No. Cleaning horses.'

'Groom?'

'Maybe. She marry him. Make him general. After many days, many nights, people say he is not general, he is slave, he is foreigner. Not caste. So both murdered, first him, then her.'

The bill comes and they arm wrestle over it under the

waiter's eye. Conviction carries Lev through, or its lack lets Laiq down. He goes down slowly, nodding his heavy head. 'Next time,' he threatens, but knows it's bluster, and realizes sadly that Lev knows too. He would like to lose, if he must, on level ground.

'Next time,' Lev agrees, dealing with the strange notes that have come back as change. 'A tip?'

Laiq lifts both hands: he will take care of it. But frowns and reaches across the table once again. His heavy hand holds Lev's face steady and he looks into the eyes. The frown deepens.

'You have pain here?' Two fingers, the same with which he broke bread, touch his own Adam's apple.

Lev is surprised. He swallows. 'Yes. A sore throat.'

Laiq nods. He gets up with his usual swift grace, happy now the balance is shifting. 'I give you something. You take.'

As they leave he plucks a fifty-rupee note from his shirt pocket and leaves it on the plate. It's more than he would spend on an entire meal, and a slight bulge of the eyes shows how it hurts, but he walks away with his dignity restored. The waiter bows deeply, Laiq inclines his head; it's worth it.

Now Lev is the tortured one. He planned to go straight to Maya, leaving Laiq at the head of his lane. But if Laiq is heading for the shop he'll have to wait, then go back to the Serai first.

They cross by the footbridge, walk up the other side of Nevsky, take Haidar Road and arrive at the clinic. Any customers who were waiting have gone home; there's that loss too Laiq's incurred. Also waiting is the bird.

'Morning, afternoon, evening,' Laiq says, measuring out a

brown powder. He drops each spoonful straight into a fresh polythene bag. 'One teaspoon. Three days.'

Lev thanks him. He has come to a decision. He will tell Laiq where he is going.

'Upistair!' Laiq is incredulous. '*Now?*'

Lev looks up at the workroom window. The light is on in there.

'She invited me,' he says.

Laiq's mystification grows. On that short introduction! Right here, last Sunday. He spreads his hands and looks down as if something fell from them. 'So.'

Lev says goodnight and climbs the stair. She's waiting at the door.

He steps straight into her kiss and there they stand. Once she surfaces to slide the bolt in the iron door; the wooden door she simply pushes to. Again they are strangers discovering one another, uncovering the strangeness, this continent. The salt sail of him, the clean curve of her coast. Everything is new, electric storms, bent trees, the harsh birds, awakened water. They lean against the wall, this rock, slide inch by inch to a grey terrazzo beach with small white shells.

They are lying where he fainted, on hard cement.

'Lev.' He looks up, but she shakes her head. 'Nothing.'

She holds him so his head rests on the pillow of her palm.

'What's this?' The soft rustle of plastic between them. She works the polythene bag free from the hand on her breast. He tells her.

'Sweeney's powders,' she says, with a wicked smile. She has a wide mouth when she lets it spread. 'Better watch out!'

She pulls him up onto his feet.

'What's it for?'

'A sore throat.' Now he realizes. If it's a sore throat he shouldn't be kissing her.

'You have a fever?'

'No.'

'Then kiss me. I want your sore throat.'

'You'll repent it.'

'Regret it. Maybe.'

She leads him through the flat, turning off the lights one by one.

'Leave one on.'

Her wide slow smile. 'Which one?'

'The puppet room,' he says. He's thinking of Laiq.

'The puppets need to sleep! How about the kitchen?'

'OK.' That looks into the street too.

'Why?'

'Laiq.' He almost said Sweeney.

She thinks about it and nods. Then they go to bed and the cooler starts up.

Sitting up in the barber's chair, Laiq looks at his watch. Midnight. He'll wait another half hour, but he knows Lev won't be coming down. When did this start? Monday? Sunday? That woman is quite something. What sort of woman – let alone a young one – would live alone without being at least, what? Circumspect. Even here, not quite in the Old City, she sticks out, with her T-shirts and men's sandals and that swinging arm. What's she doing here anyway? What sort of woman becomes a puppeteer? Well, her sort. She belongs south of a line that is Rajpath. Where his meter wars began. That whole South Delhi set with their cellphones and their

English and ponytails on men. Except her money, the family money, was made here.

He thinks of Lev and shuts his eyes. Switches off the tube light and sits there in the dark. The bird is where he left it on the windowsill.

'Anything wrong?'

It's the chowkidar with his whistle and stick, doing his night rounds. Laiq starts awake. He must have fallen asleep in his chair.

'No, no,' he answers. 'Everything's fine.'

Twelve

The phone rings.

'Hi.'

'Morgan! It's six *o'clock*!'

'How would you know? Anyway, *I've* been up for two and a half *hours*. Did you see me on the news? It's not six, it's half-past seven, by the way. Was I OK?'

He's just talking. He knows she doesn't have a TV.

'Did I make up for yesterday's mistake about Morarji? I meant Mohan Desai, the pole-vaulter. Not that I expect you to know the difference. But there are people here who won't let me forget. Can I come there and forget?'

'No.' She falls into the cane chair facing the bedroom and looks at Lev's sleeping figure framed in the doorway. He rolled over when the phone rang and now she sees the crook of his leg, a plane of back bisected at the spine, and the nape of his neck. A bridge or buttress leaning into the blank wall.

'OK. Breakfast?'

'I said no.'

'Fine. What's new?'

'Nothing.'

'What's the matter with you? Why did you throw me out?'

'New rules. You can't just stroll in here any time you like.'

He hangs up. She's sorry she said that. Now he'll stroll in here any time he likes.

He's there so soon he might have been calling from next door, not his Nizamuddin flat. Maya just has time to shut the bedroom door on Lev.

So when Lev walks in, disobeying an order she never gave — or gave the night before in another room — Morgan's face is not camera-ready.

'Who're *you*?'

'Lev.'

Morgan is looking at Maya, with new eyes and a sinking heart. Maya is looking at Lev. Can she forgive him? She can.

'I'm Morgan.'

I know, Lev wants to say, and Morgan reads that too on the invisible autocue. Lev has promised himself an early start at the Ministry and he's not going to be locked in there waiting all day.

Morgan refuses to be part of any opera either, with doors opening and shutting on lovers. He will be blunt.

'From Russia?'

'I am Russian.'

Morgan looks aghast at Maya. 'You have a Russian in the house and you don't tell *me*! *Moscow* Morgan?'

'Settle down, yaa.'

'I will not settle down. Here, you see these books?' He grabs one. 'What language is this? Whose name is this?'

She looks at him. No stopping him now, he's off.

Morgan can widen the action. 'Here.' He hands the Akhmatova to Lev. 'You tell me.'

Lev bows as if to say he's seen the book already. That bow, with the eyes shut and the head nodding slowly, galls Morgan. How long has this been going on? A verse comes to him from the movies and he turns to Maya. '*How often does this happen?*'

He looks back at Lev. '*When did the trouble start?*'

And back at Maya. '*You see my stethoscope is bobbing to the throbbing of your heart.*'

'Come off it, yaa. You want breakfast?'

'Of course I want breakfast. Do I have to make it myself?'

'No, I'll make it.'

'On second thoughts, maybe I will.'

He gets up and marches into the kitchen. He'll show the interloper. Onions, chopping board, knife, he finds them without looking.

'Chillies.' He holds his hand out through the door.

She goes to the fridge and finds a couple. 'Lev may not want any in his egg.'

Lev doesn't want an egg at all. He wants to sit in his cabin and think before he goes hunting. 'I'll have breakfast at the Serai,' he says.

'The Serai!' Morgan knows it well. He goes trawling there for foreigners when the level is low. All is explained.

Something in his say-no-more tone irritates Maya. She wants to say she was introduced to Lev. But remembers how it happened. Looking down from the workroom, seeing him there. Tall, even when foreshortened from above. Remembers running for her bag, her sandals. She wants him to know.

'I came down to you,' she tells the mystified Lev. 'On Sunday.'

She wants to say she didn't pick him up, she *picked* him. If she'd had a garland she would have put it round his neck.

Morgan is impressed, but still curious. 'Since we're all introduced now can I take us out to dinner tonight?'

Maya looks relieved. 'Why not?'

Lev is edging towards the door. He too is relieved not to have to see Laiq.

'Not South,' Maya rules. 'Somewhere nearby.'

'In that case there's only Karim's. But they're not vegetarian.'

'Are you also a vegetarian?' Lev asks, disappointed.

'No, no!' Morgan raises pious eyes. '*Strict* non-vegetarian. But Maya here . . .'

'They'll have alu, won't they?'

'Muslims have never understood the potato. But we can send out for some. So. Eight o'clock?'

Lev looks at his wrist, shakes hands and lollops down the steep stair.

Maya shoots the bolt and turns slowly to face Morgan. He's looking steadily at her with his head cocked.

'Well!'

She says nothing but her unasked question hangs in the air between them.

Morgan goes to the cane chairs and sits, careful not to face the bedroom. When she sits down opposite he jumps up and walks up and down.

'But he's so . . .' He won't say *plain*, riddled as he is with the curse of handsomeness. '*Ord*inary.' He means for her; she makes other women look like dolls.

Maya draws her feet up, pleased. Jealousy always intrigued her. 'And old,' she says. 'How old would you say?'

'Sixty-nine? Seventy? Well, at *least* forty.'

'He's forty-five. And you?'

'Ten years older than you and you know it. Whatever that is.'

'So we're all ten years apart.'

'Except you and him.'

'I meant you and him,' she says.

'*I'm* not in love with him!'

'I meant him and you and me, Morgan. Don't be like that. If you're going to be like that please go home.'

He stops pacing, suddenly tired. 'I think I will.'

He bends and kisses the top of her head. It's only when she's seated that he can do that.

'And your scrambled egg?'

'Can't you—' He stops. 'Sorry.' He takes a slice of bread and eats from the pan in silence. She watches him with tender affection. For years she's stored eggs for him in her fridge, watched him cook them in her pans – her mother would have a fit – without once being tempted to try one. It's the same when she thinks of him, Morgan; she's never been tempted. It's never occurred to her to be tempted.

'Eight o'clock.' He waves without looking back.

The phone rings before he's reached the street.

'Pa!'

'Putli. You haven't called. What's up?'

'Nothing.'

'Why don't you come over? Have dinner, beti.'

'Pa, the play's coming up in two weeks. I haven't even finished Razia.'

'You have to eat. I'll drop you back.'

'Last time you didn't even show up.'

'Called away, Putli. You know what it's like.' He sounds weary. 'Anyway the driver can drop you back if I'm not here.'

'Why would I come if you weren't going to be there?'

'Putli, your mother looks out for you.'

'She looks out for a husband for me.'

Silence.

'Pa?'

He's suddenly alert. That new tone is his little girl. 'What, Putli?'

'Pa, there's this guy.' She bites her lip. 'Pa, I'm in love.'

Her voice could fit in a pinhole. But it carried clear across the city into the receiver of the Chief Police Commissioner.

'Beti!' Mayhew Prep, St Saviour's College, and still he bridles. He sends Sunderam on an errand.

'Tell me.'

'Bas, that's it.'

'Who is he?'

'Just. Someone I met.'

'Is it someone we know?'

'No.'

'How long have you known him?'

'Not long. Shit, it's terrible, yaa.'

'But if it's terrible just break it off.'

'Pa, don't be silly. It's terrible because it's . . . not terrible.'

'Well, I suppose all the poets can't be wrong.'

'They're not.'

'I don't know, beti. I was never in love.'

'What, not even at college?'

'Well. Infatuations maybe. And then I was married.' He doesn't say *off*, but he doesn't need to.

'I don't want to be married off, Pa.'

'Who said you're going to be?'

'Good. Because I won't.'

'So. You're coming for dinner?'

'No.'

'You're having dinner with him?'

'Yes.'

'Can I send a spy?'

'No.'

'Can I come and see myself?'

'No.'

'Any chance of meeting him?'

'Not yet.' She stops short, kicks herself. What are you thinking of? He's married. 'No, no chance.'

'So, when do we see you?'

'Soon. Pa? Don't let Ma come here.'

It's the nearest she can come to telling him. That there are cigarettes in the flat now and another toothbrush.

He laughed when she found him using hers.

'I thought you wanted my sore throat!'

'I don't have any miracle powders, you know. Have you taken Sweeney's?'

'Not yet.' The rabbit nurse's gamma globulin would see him through.

Thirteen

When he arrives at the Ministry Lev gives Purohit's name because it's the only name he knows.

He's given up on the man, but he's hoping to find someone on the rebound, another Colonel Purohit, any colonel. He draws a blank. There are no colonels who know Purohit. The man at the downstairs desk suggests the Ministry of External Affairs. Lev clutches at that. He could name names from the consulate back home. Even Ramaswamy is a handhold on this blank red rock face he's climbing.

He crosses to the South Block, more red rock, and asks for the Russia desk. He is told he must return to a queue he didn't know he jumped. He must sign the book clearly and without abbreviations. Next he must name the specific officer he wishes to meet. No, the designation alone is not sufficient. He takes a chance and fills in a name from the opposite page where the word Russia appears. Now he must wait until the person's PA is contacted before he can proceed to the ground-floor waiting room. But before that there is a security check. Checked and cleared he is asked to wait till a functionary from the third floor is free to conduct him to the third-floor waiting room. The toilet is for junior staff. There is another outside, but then he will have to go through security again. In the third-floor waiting room a television set is on, playing to rigid sofas. He watches a giant panda nibble at a bamboo shoot. Twice a couple of peons poke their heads in. A junior staffer comes in and looks at him and goes out. Then nobody comes. Time passes, and still more time, and it's somewhere in the middle of a documentary on the making of tortoiseshell castanets in the Honduras that Lev realizes he has been forgotten.

He in turn has forgotten the name he copied out in the register. He doesn't want to go back to that particular man at the desk downstairs. He's seen his type at home; it's universal. He looks out the door. He walks to the end of the red carpet and looks down the corridor.

There is the very vista he saw in his dream: the same corridor with doors off it on one side and arches opposite with roll-up bamboo screens and stools for peons to perch on. They are perched on them now, shifting like pigeons, in one long vanishing perspective. He could enter the dream now, start trudging from office to office, or he could take the lift down and walk away.

He takes the lift down and steps outside.

In the distance, two, maybe three kilometres away, he sees a great stone arch. India Gate, his map says. The wide road leading to it is heroic, out of another sort of dream. Its vaunting scale is familiar: he recognizes the bullying note from his Moscow days.

In the sky above he sees another order of architecture in progress. The flat grey television screen of the past few days has changed. At the horizon it has developed a series of corrugations in a darker grey that look like a vast flight of steps mounting to infinity. Their immense gravity makes the yellow stone arch look toylike, but at the same time attainable.

He's walking before he knows it. He knows what's going on in the sky, can even remember the arrowed map he drew and coloured in for geography. It's the monsoon she's been talking about, the rains the whole city has been waiting for ever since he arrived. Up the wide road towards him a cool breeze has begun to flow laced with the moisture his skin has been craving ever since Petersburg. It's like the cooler in her bedroom, except the cooler too is a toy, a noisy toy. This is a great silent exhalation. At home in Peter there would be about now a fine spray, half salt half sweet, running on ahead of the rain cloud. Here there is only this cool steady breeze under a darkening sky. The staircase has come overhead, turned inside out, turned arch, the keystone poised to come crashing down. But it goes on building in silence, behind him now: first the stone block hung in place, then the mortar applied underneath, working against gravity till the ground is reached.

God's arch.

Lead-grey slugs. Then a hail of tracers that splinter on the tarmac. He's walking knee-deep in sparklers. Now the main body of rain, dense nets that involve him, wrap him about. Competing gusts tug at him, threaten to tear his clothes off. He's at India Gate when lightning strikes. Down the middle of the sky, a river of light stopping the storm's mouth with silence.

Next a crack like the invention of sound, as if the gate were being vaporized for fun. Then thunder, in two syllables.

That is thunder, Lev thinks in his sudden grand deafness. That was lightning.

The unruliness passes, the shifting front of wind and current moves on. Rain pours down like justice, a steady unrelenting rule of rain. His best shoes are wet through. He steps out from under the shelter and walks all the way back to the Serai thinking: This is rain.

Fourteen

Morgan is late.

Red Morgan, who took the young Marx to heart, has stopped off at the Russia Club in Chit Park and been caught by the rain. He and half of Delhi. He drives a small car now, a gold Zen, has put away the motorcycle along with certain tenets which no longer apply. The change has less to do with disposable income than might appear. It's true he has now more money than he needs, and is careless with it. But he would not have let go of his faith so easily. In the heart of his gypsy faithlessness Morgan lives by faith, and it took nothing less (his enemies say, nothing more) than the discovery of a new one to shake the old. The texts of his second faith, which is strictly his third, if he counts the religion of his childhood, are not on the shelves at the club. (Maya has some.) Morgan is in the club to browse among the dictionaries and atlases of the land he loves without ever having seen.

Tonight especially, when he is hosting a Russian, he would like to refresh his memory. Not with the images branded there by his chosen poets: the Neva with its frogging of iced willows, a widow on a bench in the snow, sparrows in a hoarfrost bleeding at the ear; those he carries with him like stigmata. Tonight he'd like just to be reminded of where the steppes begin, of where the railway crosses the Urals, how the Ob finds its way to the sea. Lev might well be from the provinces, like Morgan himself, a small town boy stuck in the capital.

Then again he might be from Petersburg. Which shimmers just above the heat haze of Delhi, so real Morgan will sometimes drive an extra block towards it.

Transparent Petropolis, he repeats, blinking at the mirage as he stands at a red light that says RELAX (Why can't he? Forever going from A to B, his zippy little car the emblem of his pick-up, his drive and derring-do.) But Morgan is working at his life; the unsteady anchorman is moving by degrees visible only to himself towards the peace he seeks. His social life distracts him, his job is a pain. But, look (behind the screen if you like; it's just a play): the ribbon of text that runs before his eyes when he's alone is cut up into discontinuous lines, the lines of his poets. They are his steadiness. He lives in fragments but knows he must learn concentration. It's why he returns constantly to Maya; she is his concentration.

Russia moves before him like a destination, that fixed other place his rootlessness craves. Some day he'll go back there and recognize a world he never knew. For now he goes from place to place searching. From friend to friend without a gift, just turning up. It's because he gives himself that the gift is invisible; he is looking for what he always leaves behind.

Tonight the stormwater under Tilak Bridge sends him all the way around via Ring Road. Water there too; at one point the Zen turns amphibious. *God Jesu*, he says, steering with crimped anus. He shakes the water off at a hundred and ten on the flyover and finds Maya and Lev waiting in the cane chairs.

'You missed some rain,' he tells them.

'No,' Lev answers and smiles. He's changed into sneakers. They park right opposite the great mosque and arrive dry.

'We're slumming,' Morgan explains to Lev as they push through the crowd, 'but the food is good.'

Karim's is a cloister with cooking alcoves and eating halls off it on three sides. Upstairs in the first hall is a gallery with five tables for families, which in this quarter means groups that include women. Morgan leads the way up, talking back down to Lev.

'I meant to tell you to watch out for pickpockets in the lane. They're artists here.'

Lev pats the new wallet in his pocket; his wrist is still bare.

Morgan turns to Maya. 'How's the artiste? You're a pickpocket too, aren't you, in a way? You can't just *borrow* the audience's heart. You have to steal it, right? *Lend me your ears* is fine, but lend me your *heart*? No. Suddenly there's a hole where my heart was and I say: My God, it was here a moment ago!' *Abhi yahan tha!* He says it in Hindi.

She smiles a queenly smile. Her two favourite men in the whole world are in attendance and she is pleased. She looks radiant, has forgiven him for being late. Has forgiven the rain for raining. Morgan beams, then saddens, her jester. Lev is Commander-in-Chief now.

'Busy day?' he asks Lev. His smile is a complex pout, pre-Lev, a simultaneous pushing out of the mouth and tugging of it to one side so the cheek on that side is drawn up and the eye narrowed a little. It's there for the whole nation to see in the last nanosecond before the camera cuts at the end of the news.

The people at the next table vaguely recognize him and he acknowledges their smiles. They're not the class that would listen to the news in English, but they've come across the Morgan features browsing through the channels. Nowhere else in Delhi do rich and poor sit together to eat.

Has he been busy? Lev wonders. The exhilaration of his walk has worn off. He's been thinking maybe he could go through the university and come at the Ministry that way. But that's for another day.

'Yes,' he says.

'Yes, what?' Morgan asks. He hasn't time for dawdlers, has begun to think of ordering.

'Yes, a busy day.'

'Good.' He hands the menu back to the waiter without looking at it and orders. Tandoori chops, kadhai gosht, seekh kababs, shammi kababs, barra, biryani, no, pea pulao. He always overorders. Oh, and alu timatar. For the lady, a dish of potatoes swimming in a red sea. And salad, though you shouldn't really, in a place like this, in the monsoon.

'Roti?' the waiter wants to know, returning.

'Rumali, of course. Six.' He calls the man back. 'First three, then three more. *Fresh.*' He turns to Lev to explain. 'Handkerchief bread. Rumal is handkerchief. You want to watch them making it?'

They troop downstairs to the courtyard to where a man stands before a domed griddle tossing a roti from hand to hand so it thins to muslin; the final toss makes a handkerchief of it. It flies up and hangs in the air, spinning into fineness. The man's eyes roll up and his mouth strains open, a mystic from a medieval scroll. The rumali hovers, a soul. Caught on the back of his forearm and flipped onto the griddle. It loses its pallor, colours up to beige, is cooked in seconds. Let it freckle and it's overdone. The man peels it off and adds it to the pile. Waiters stand by counting off their quota.

'It's not really bread, it's a state of mind.'

Morgan shepherds them back up. The food follows them, steaming. Lev has not eaten meat since the plane.

'At Karim's,' Morgan declares, 'you kiss it off the bone.'

Maya watches them for a moment, her men. She takes up a rumali and tugs, enjoying the elasticity of it. Her fingers know fabric.

'The only food on earth,' says Morgan, tearing into one, 'that looks and feels and smells and even sounds' (he flutters a strip like a prayer flag) 'better than it tastes.' He rolls up the flag and pops it in his mouth. 'Latex,' he pronounces. 'Surgical latex.'

Maya giggles. He's right. After all that mystification, it's rubber in the mouth. She finds solace in her potatoes. There was no alu timatar so the cook fried mashed potatoes in cumin seed and aromatized the dish with hing.

'No sauce like hunger,' Morgan nods sardonically.

'It's good, yaa.'

'If you say so.' He kisses off more chop. 'It's all in the head, anyway. A whole civilization can't be wrong. The lust for flesh subtilized into faith. Only a nation of vegetarians could produce a Khajuraho.'

'Khajuraho?' Lev knows the erotic sculptures. His hands describe an hourglass in the air.

'Flesh as stone.' Morgan chews latex. 'Never was desire more carefully impounded. Or less desirable.'

'Oh ho, Desire,' Maya says screwing up her nose. 'Is there anything that's not Desire, Morgan?'

'Well,' he says, looking ruefully at her. '*Satisfaction?*'

She chalks one up for him. His pout is more pronounced than ever. My destiny, it says, to be the other man.

'Morgan is an Indian name?' Lev asks.

'It is now. But it's taken three hundred years. My ancestor came sailing from England. Can you blame him? Cold wet miserable little country. Where in Russia are you from?'

'St Petersburg.'

'St *Petersburg*!' It's not fair, Morgan's tone says. So much beauty in the name, so much pain. One should not simply be from there; it shouldn't be allowed. You should earn your citizenship of Petersburg.

Lev looks amused at the reverence in Morgan's voice, but he understands a little of how he must feel. Today he's earned the right to be here: the sky of Delhi fell on him and claimed its due. But she is Delhi, this woman; she blots out the real city. He looks at her and can't swallow, his throat actually rejecting food. She is sky and cloud and wall and gate.

'Here.' The spoon was halfway to his mouth. He turns it around. 'Try some.'

Morgan's hand comes up at once and grips Lev's.

'Are you *mad!* She's never eaten meat in her life.' He looks at Maya. She is his virtue.

'She can learn,' Lev says, surprised at Morgan's heat.

Morgan looks at him, deciding just how ordinary this man is. But Lev is trying to mend, not force. He feels he has a right. He's drunk water from her lips, she can eat meat from his.

It's Maya who breaks the hold. She has shut her eyes on

them in despair. Why do men have to press an issue? Is it a gross urge, like hers to squeeze the pustules on Lev's back? Look at him, Pa, just look at him.

She puts out a hand and touches Morgan's restraining arm. Then with the hand still resting there she leans forward and brings her mouth to the tip of the spoon. Her other hand is on Lev's wrist holding it steady. She's looking straight into his eyes. This is what I meant when I said I chose you. Her lips open a fraction.

She is eight years old and her mother is trying to get her to take the thermometer in her mouth again because the last time she didn't do it right. She must hold it under her tongue but she must not bite the stem because then the bulb will burst and the mercury will run into her mouth and kill her. She must do it because she has a fever. Her brain is on fire.

She is ten years old. She is twenty-five. She is here. She will damn herself to another life on the wheel.

The tip of her tongue touches heat. Done. OK? her eyes say. For you.

Morgan realizes only when she lifts her hand off his arm that for a moment the three of them were joined. He calls for dessert, to clear the air.

'You must try their firni,' he says to Maya, as if it will change the taste in her mouth. 'Creamed rice,' he explains to Lev, embarrassed at his earlier anger. Morgan has few male friends beyond those who acknowledge his suzerainty.

The firni comes in little clay dishes sprinkled with chopped pistachio nuts. It is very good but Maya leaves hers half eaten. Lev finishes it for her, careful to use her spoon, but she won't be drawn.

'So when is the show?' Morgan asks.

'Two weeks.' She's biting her lip, a bad sign, he knows of old.

Lev, who's still new to her signs, asks: 'What show?'

'Puppets.' She's earned the right to sulk.

'Razia Begam,' Morgan answers for her. 'The Queen of Delhi.'

'Oh, the soldier queen.'

Morgan is impressed. Maya too looks at Lev for the first time since her pledge. She hasn't told him the story. How did he find out? She wants to know, is dying to know, but would sooner die than ask.

'How do you know?'

There, it's out. She's climbed down.

Lev allows himself a knowing smile. *Oh oh*, Morgan thinks.

Maya is furious. 'Well, thank you, Morgan. You can drop me home first.'

First. It stings. Fire and waterbrash.

She gets into the back of the Zen, behind the passenger seat so she can't be seen by Lev, or see him. Morgan backs out of a corral of scooters, passing a handful of change out of the window to three urchins as he does, and they're home in two minutes. Her home.

'Good night, Morgan.'

She's come around to his side. Morgan rolls down his window to receive her kiss, but doesn't return it. He will not be used.

Lev sits stunned in the passenger seat.

Morgan drops him at the gate of the Serai and beeps as he pulls away. The sodium street lights have alchemized the Zen's gold to dross. Lev hangs in the rear-view mirror strung up like an abandoned puppet.

Fifteen

'I'm not well.'

Now she's his idol, standing there framed in iron and wire mesh. Two arms, hanging by her side, no weapons.

He was not coming back, but he's back.

'Maya.'

Her listless hand comes up and slides the bolt across and drops back down.

'I've got your sore throat.'

He puts his arms around her, gently enclosing her, and kisses her forehead. It's burning.

She takes his hand and leads him to her room, trembling as she walks. There she sinks back onto the mattress on the floor and shuts her eyes.

He stands over her in silence hardly daring to move. He had pictured a rapturous amnesty. Now this. Her breath comes and goes lightly. It's a warm day but she's pulled the sheet up over her. She seems actually to have fallen asleep, instantly.

He wets his lips, looks around. No chairs, just the mattress. He glances through the open door at the telephone corner by the bookshelf.

The two cane chairs. He stares at the one facing him. There's a face in the cane back.

No. No, no, no. Meschersky.

Oh my God.

He looks down at her. She's swallowing slowly, with difficulty. Her eyes flutter open and shut straight away. The fingers of the hand nearer him come up and pat the mattress three times.

He sits there on the edge of the mattress that was his. Right where she said, by the hot hand. The slender fingers he's held in his mouth; now he's afraid to even touch them. My beautiful girl. What have I done?

'Can I get you something?'

She shakes her head.

'Have you taken anything?'

She nods. She is trying to say something. He leans closer.

'Where were you?'

Where was he? He tries to think. The whole day has collapsed into this moment.

'I went to the university. Then I was at the Institute of Immunology.'

She nods, satisfied. He was busy.

He almost smiles. His day, which her interest revived like a plant, is dismissed. Good. Let it go. No. He can't let himself think that way. He owes it to – whom? His family, he's always told himself. He shakes off the weariness.

'Would you like some water?'

She wouldn't but she nods to please him. He goes to the fridge, then checks himself and fills a glass from the kitchen tap.

'What medicine did you take?'

She smiles for the first time, a trembly smile, and points to the floor by the mattress. Put the glass down, she means.

'Laiq's powder.'

He looks at her. She's serious.

'How much?'

Her finger flickers. 'Teaspoon.'

'How many times?'

Two fingers.

He's considering. Medicine is faith, partly. 'Take one more. It's night now.'

'Did anybody see you?' It's an effort for her to talk. 'Coming upstairs.'

He thinks back. Except for the first time he's always come after dark.

'No.'

'Good.'

'You need a doctor.'

She swallows, the same elaborate dry swallow. He watches her mouth, the mouth she's given him.

'Call Morgan.'

Morgan's number is among the fainter numbers pencilled on the wall above the phone. He picks up the receiver and dials, leaves a message.

Then there's nothing to do but wait. He sits beside her. She knows he's there.

She thinks, through the shifting filter of delirium, this pain in her joints is not the same pain that torments her at the height of summer. It's a new shape laid over the old template. If the two layers matched it would be unbearable.

At some point they fall asleep. Once she wakes, drinks the water.

Morgan gets the message in the morning. He spent the night with a Saket friend and went straight to the studio. It's eight o'clock when he gets home.

Morgan this is Lev. Maya is not well. Please come quickly.

Morgan is back in the car before he knows it. He jumps two red lights, waves his fist, wheedles, is flying. You fucking Russian git, what have you done to her? I'll disembowel you. He parks in front of the entranceway and runs upstairs and rings. Walks right past Lev.

Her forehead is burning. They can't wait for a doctor.

'We have to get her to hospital.'

On the way he's been thinking, where? AIMS? Shitty, public, but the doctors are good. But take her all the way across the city? No. Apollo? Five star, but still further out. He knows doctors there too. Morgan knows everybody because everybody knows Morgan. Holy Family? Why are all the hospitals back of beyond? Now he sits on the mattress and thinks. What's close by? Of course! The hospital right across the road from the Serai. He can never remember its name. Big. Public.

They carry her down the steep stair together. Morgan shows Lev a handhold that turns four arms into a secure seat. They put her in the back of the Zen. It's before nine so, except for the dairy, the shops in the building haven't opened yet. Laiq's is shut.

'I'll be back,' Morgan says.

'No,' Lev insists. He's going with her.

'Then lock the fuck up!'

Lev remembers: they hang locks on doors here. He runs back up the stair and padlocks the open door. Then turns the giant security door key twice. It feels strange putting her keys in his pocket; they clink uncomfortably against the single cabin key from the Serai.

The Zen streaks around Delhi Gate, and in at Emergency. Morgan abandons it and picks up Maya himself. They barge into the crowded waiting hall, push a way through the families and relatives and idlers and find a seat for her along the wall. At the desk Morgan is recognized. He collars a passing intern in a white coat who looks at him and immediately forgets where he was going.

A bed is found for Maya next to a chubby moon-faced boy who is evidently dying. He is wheezing at three-second intervals as if he would like to expel a world of poison from his lungs. There is no curtain, so Morgan and Lev go and stand between the two beds. They do this together, instinctively, turning their backs on the boy and his family, the mother and a brother. The intern takes Maya's pulse, a calm young man, very thin and conscientious. He stethoscopes her chest, listening intently. It is impossible to tell from his face whether he is satisfied with what he hears. He beckons a nurse, who takes her temperature and hands him the thermometer. He looks at it, nods, and gives it back.

'Where does she live?'

'Here, near Delhi Gate.'

'Old City?'

'No, the other side. Haidar Road.'

At that moment a cry breaks from the mother of the boy in the next bed. The nurse can find no pulse; the wheezing has stopped. The intern steps around Maya's bed and puts his ear directly on the boy's chest. The mother goes on wailing.

Morgan and Lev turn to watch the tragedy unfolding

directly behind them, drawn despite themselves from Maya. Morgan looks at the boy's face. He appears asleep, with a trace of froth on his lips. Cuckoospit, one larger bubble in a cluster of small ones. Lev sees a blank puppet. He has his old sense of falling, but a strange upward falling. *Yes, God,* they think, simultaneously. *Take him.*

They turn back to Maya. She is breathing lightly, steadily. Death has touched the next bed.

The intern lifts his head from the boy's chest. He springs up and brings his hands down together on the boy's chest with such force that the mother's cry breaks off in astonishment. She watches him repeat the action, battering down the door of her son's chest. Smashing a way through to nothing. Again and again he rams his arms down on the boy who jerks up with each thrust, his rag doll's head nodding. The mother's mouth hangs open; the brother is rigid with fear.

Lev turns again. He's in the way. He steps around the intern and goes to the other side of Maya's bed. Morgan joins him there. For ten minutes the intern labours, throwing his whole weight onto his arms. Once he rests with his ear on the boy's chest, then starts up again. 'Drip!' he calls, and more nurses come running. They shift the woman aside and go to work, pricking, taping, rigging up the tubes, the stand, the bottle. A pulse has returned.

The intern stands between the two beds and shuts his eyes for a moment and brings the tip of a finger and thumb to the bridge of his nose. He is trembling. He steadies himself and returns to Maya. Her breathing is even. There's a slight frown where the eyebrows almost meet.

'I must call her father,' Morgan says and leaves Lev there. Outside the gate is a black and yellow PCO board nailed to a neem tree. Morgan dials emergency and demands the Police Commissioner's number; a family emergency, he threatens the cowed operator. Sunderam takes the call and turns to Jain. 'Sir, urgent.'

'Vir Uncle? Morgan. It's about Maya.'

The Commissioner sends a car for his wife and comes directly.

'She was delirious,' Morgan says defensively, explaining the panic, the crowded ward.

'It's probably viral,' the intern begins, but stops. The Director of the Hospital has come down, alerted to the Commissioner's presence. The lobby is swarming with Jain's armed guard.

The Director has his own brief but attends to the daughter first. He examines the young woman and is inclined to agree with the viral assessment. A colleague writes a prescription, broad-spectrum antibiotics to cover other possibilities.

'But,' the Director explains, 'we have a crisis.' He lowers his voice and steps confidentially towards the nearest wall. Jain draws nearer.

'Last night the sputum cultures of two patients showed *Yersinia pestis*. Both are plague positive. Please – her case is not necessarily connected. We have isolated those two, but we must regard all reported fevers as serious. We must isolate her – not in that ward, of course. But she must be held until we can be sure. We have still to take a culture. In the meantime she must be given presumptive treatment. And the whole family – everyone who has been in contact with her – must take antibiotics.'

To the intern he says: 'Shankar, blood sample. And throat swab.'

My little Putli. My baby. When he can think Jain says: 'We can isolate her at home.'

'It is not advisable, sir.'

'How long would she be here?'

'One week.'

'*One week!* Just on presumption?'

'Only till the report comes in, sir.'

'Impossible. Doctor Sahib, you know what hospital quarantine means. It is broken all the time.'

'I was coming to that. I was going to ask you for police cooperation.'

'Doctor Sahib, only the Lieutenant Governor can order that.'

'I have talked to the Health Minister. She says they must deliberate. Deliberate! Sahib, you know the old city. The infection could spread like that.' He snaps his fingers. 'Both cases are from there.'

Jain has stopped listening. 'Sorry, Doctor. I am taking her with me now.'

'Well. It is probably viral. But she must take the antibiotics. The whole family must. And the quarantine should apply there.'

'Here is my number. I will talk to the Lieutenant Governor. The Rapid Action Force can come.'

He becomes aware of Lev standing at the foot of the bed. Morgan has introduced him as a friend but something about the way he watches the girl suggests a concern that runs deeper. Is this the subject of the last telephone call? Jain looks away. He does not want to know whether this man, who is not young, stands in need of antibiotics.

Lev is only too aware of his position. He has been gradually backing off from the bedside and is now up against a wall leprous with rising damp. He is afraid of the speed with which things are moving, and now he has overheard the word plague. He looks at the woman on the bed; even with her eyes shut she looks inviolable. He hates his false position, his foreignness. A capable woman. What sort of man is he?

Her mother arrives, shocked into silence. The ACP escort salutes Jain.

'We're taking her home, Mummy,' the Commissioner says, calming his wife. 'But we have to take some medicines first.'

Maya is stretchered out to the police car and lifted in by the Commissioner himself, who then surprises his driver by taking the wheel. He nods at Morgan who stands with Lev on the kerb. The two men wait till the cavalcade of police jeeps and lesser cars vanishes, then turn away.

'You had better come and stay with me.' A week off work, Morgan thinks as they are issued their emergency supply of tetracycline.

Lev has just thought of something. 'I must call home,' he says, and Morgan shows him the PCO, right opposite the Serai.

It's morning in Peter; dew on the window box. A small rain prickles up out of nowhere and sets the swallows tumbling.

'I'm fine,' Alla's voice echoes off the satellite. 'Why?'

Sixteen

Morgan has a maid.

The fact can startle him still when he thinks back. So did Marx, it has occurred to him (and look what happened), but he's still not easy with the idea. Most days she arrives to find he's done the dishes, washed the clothes she was meant to wash, laid out the vegetables for her beside the chopping board. Sometimes he will be chopping them when she arrives. It's not all conscience: he likes the way a knife goes through a cold potato, delights in the crisp resistance of a cucumber. He will pare an apple and forget to eat it. Onion rings he slices for pleasure: the finer the sweeter is his theory; they should melt on the tongue like the host. He has a collection of knives – German, French, Brazilian, half of which lives at Maya's. Morgan was a boy scout.

'You like that job,' Lev says watching him sort and marshal a curious fluted vegetable so all the duncecaps are lined up.

'Yes.' The chef's knife slices down through eight in a row, a cheesy cut. The caps stick to the blade, trailing gummy threads. 'Lady's finger.' Morgan holds up the knife with its row of decapitations. 'Okra. The kidney vetch. Hibiscus family.'

Bhindi, yaa! Maya will supply the market name, impatient with his passion for nomenclature. *Brainfever, partridge,* he taunts her back, *same thing.*

'Not me,' Lev says, meaning the job. The kitchen is Alla's province.

When the maid arrives Morgan sends her away, calling from the next room. He won't need her this week, he says, unable to face her. How do you tell someone you might have plague?

He listens closely to the sound of the plastic slippers going back on her feet. Relief? Pleasure? Annoyance? She clatters downstairs, then the gate clicks and she's gone.

Sound is a mystery to Morgan. Voice, the proof and echo of being, he knows to be precious. So he is always dismayed to find himself wasting it. All his honeyed speeches, even the little ones, are ashes in the belly. Professionally he is his voice. That was one reason why the shift from radio to television was bearable: it shared the burden between voice and face. Visibility doesn't trouble him; it's sound he wants to hoard. And yet even outside the studio he squanders what he should save. That night at Karim's half of him stood apart, like the muse of silence, watching while the other drowned in words.

When he was a boy the simplest sounds gave him the greatest joy, sounds before or after words. Neem leaves tossing in the green tree, dry and trampled underfoot, crushed in the hand: the sound was sharper than the scent. The clink of bricks sweeter than the taste of them on the tongue. *Did you never lick bricks?* he chides Maya. And away he goes, discoursing, sounding off. Even now he will hear that clink at a building site and feel his being clarify. Chance sounds are purest, their disinterest a perpetual reproach to a man whose profession demands an audience. When he listens to things Morgan feels the corresponding words evaporate inside him. The longer he listens the less inclined he is to speak.

Sound words torment him especially. The sound of flesh and bone on stone, for example. Why does the language have nothing to convey this elementary sound? A sound that must surely ring through history with a special and malevolent persistence.

'Does Russian have a word for the sound of a body falling on stone?' he asks Lev.

Lev can't come up with one, but understands the urge. He too likes to pin things down. Morgan has asked Maya too, about Hindi, but she is more comfortable with English. Besides she comes at the world another way, through her fingers. Her puppets must be shaped before she can make them speak.

Morgan chops in silence: just the sound of steel on wood. Close with things. But look at the risk, even with a master. *Stone* is Osip Mandelshtam's first collection; all that follows is a few diamond-like sparks struck off the original block. A speech so spare the stone has entered into it. He's not happy with the consequences but he is a disciple.

'Why are your poets so cold?' he complains. 'Is it just latitude? When I read them the temperature in the room falls to zero.'

'I don't know. I'm a scientist.'

'What sort?'

'Research.'

'What sort of research?'

'I research bacteria and viruses for biological weapons.'

Morgan's face tilts to one side. There's the ghost of a

smile on Lev's lips; he's not sure how he came to speak this unprecedented sentence. Another time he might have said what he usually says by a reflex so deep he no longer needs to think about it. Today for some reason the words forced a way through.

'You mean as in plague?'

'Yes.'

Morgan can't help a bark of baleful laughter. The mad wild irony of it. A jest comes to mind, but he lets it go.

'So you're not here on a holiday.'

Lev shrugs.

'Maya said you were going to one of the ministries.'

'I was.'

'Not Defence, by any chance.'

'Yes, Defence.'

Morgan raises an eyebrow but says nothing.

'I don't think I am needed,' Lev volunteers. He pushes his chair back to get up and winces. He's still not used to the screech of terrazzo. Somehow Morgan's cult of Russia depresses him. Lev tries to imagine Isaak putting together an Indian flat in Peter, with Indian books and furnishings, and can't. There's a robustness to Isaak that wouldn't allow it. Perhaps some neurasthenic professor of linguistics might, but Morgan is still young, flamboyant. It could just be the way he's feeling; on another day perhaps the Chagall prints on this wall might arouse something in him.

He puts his plate in the sink and looks for the familiar tools of washing up but they're not there. People scrub dishes here, they don't wash them, he's noticed. If Morgan got that bit right he might be closer to the real Russia. But then perhaps it's not the real Russia he's after. What is he, Lev, after? Not the real India, anyway. He should be starting to think about going home. Cutting his losses, taking the hint. But the very thought of leaving is suddenly complicated beyond all volition.

He stands by the kitchen window and looks out. How is she? Where is she? In this city of ten million. He is almost sick with desire. Not for the Maya he swallowed whole in darkness, just for random glancing bits of her. The deep-sunk eyes flash and are gone. The sombre grating laugh sounds and vanishes. A wild snatch of hair. The certainty with which she faced him.

There's a man out there on a three-wheeled pedal cart pressing the rubber bulb of his horn. It's a high plaintive crane-like note. The cart is loaded with bread and eggs in stacks of grey cardboard trays and the man sits sideways in his saddle, his angular body in momentary equilibrium. He is sitting at the precise centre of the cosmos and blowing his horn and calling.

Bread and eggs, bread and eggs!

Galubchik. Where have they taken you?

Poor Lev Repin! The day will come when nothing will remain to him of this city but this moment at Morgan's kitchen window. There will be only the mournful sound of this horn. A rubber horn, blowing and blowing, calling, calling. And then tears will flow, unstoppable tears, because a moment of pure longing passed into his heart and took up residence there.

This night they sleep fitfully. Once Morgan cries out in his sleep.

Seventeen

Heat like she's never felt before. *But I'm cold.*

Orange pain, like cartoon war. Burning. Fever is a body torching other bodies. She is a charred log. She is a decaying star in a black wilderness. She is carbon.

Mother? She is in her mother's house, not the flat. She can feel her blocking the way. Someone is pushing a steel pin into her arm. There are two bones, the radius and the ulna; the ulna is what we are going to replace. Someone has made an incision at the wrist and is squeezing out the decayed bone. I'm sorry, the anaesthetic was incorrectly administered. It has the weight of plate glass so you can see everything. You will have 80–90% mobility in that arm.

Where is he? Pa, where is he? Can I sit up?

'Better not, Putli.' Whispered.

I heard that.

The pain starts at a point between the eyes, tracks up the forehead, splits open the crown and earths in the occiput. It is a wire for cutting cheese. The cut is repeated at minutely varying angles. The wire is live.

I don't make dolls, do I? My puppets talk and move, doing dolls, thinking dolls. Janaki loves. Uttam Singh kills. Babaji thinks. Are you there, Babaji? Talk to me.

Here is a bed of nails. When you turn the glass blanket will splinter and the splinters push in. The pain is accompanied by loss of focus in the eyes, reducing the world to an undifferentiated sheet of light. By night patients report a shifting curtain in the violet to indigo range. The sensorium is reported to compensate with acute keenness of touch and hearing. Noise levels should be kept low.

There's no need to shout. It's a universal cawing, like crows circling when one of their number has been shot.

The pain is exquisite at the knees. Kneecap her and volcanic sand will pour out. Detach the toes and pain will escape like green neon. This is the body that disappears when you are well, so the world can return.

Come for a walk, Pa. Did I tell you he's married? I have to finish the kamiz. The show is next Sunday. Strange, his puppet thing. A life of its own. How it fills the hand!

She lies there on the third morning, the dawn chorus in her head. *They're* birds, *yaa.* But there's one missing. *Yes.* Her eyes click open. *The bird!*

'Putli!'

I want to go home.

Eighteen

Morgan lies with his hands folded under his head, remembering.

'Bas bas bas bas bas bas basbasbas,' she stops his mouth in the middle of a line he's reading because she's had enough. She needs no reminders of eternity from his poets; she's already serious about living. Reading she does in short intense bursts, eyes wide, like a child: she'll read until she finds a line that pricks and put the book down. (He'll go obediently to the end of the chapter.) Writing's a bore. Her notes are scrawled, the pen flying over the page. She'd rather pick up the phone. *He said, she said,* hours of *saids* poured down the line till he's nodding off and swears he's going to hang up on her. And does.

Then she'll go back to her puppets or simply go collecting. Nothing's real until she's touched it to life. Her talk is a kind of touch. Her eyes rest on him and he has an almost tangible sense of being moulded. She sees on her own terms. It's why she's so difficult. (Is that why he's so easy?) But that's how he missed out. Schooled in sound, Morgan blinked. And her unblinking eyes moved on, till she found the right match for an object that was already forming in her head. *He's cute, na?*

She is for herself, like her puppets. (Janaki is for Janaki. She'll get her man.) Hubris, though: she goes and picks a married man.

She is for herself. He is for others. Who's right? Service makes you invisible, intangible. Morgan has spread himself too thin. The thought brings him to his feet so suddenly he's left light-headed.

In the guest room Lev stirs. Touched by a dream he yelps like a wired car. Wakes to a small ochre lizard on the ceiling directly above him and lies there eyeballing it. Its black bead eyes take in the whole room but are fixed on the bed. Lev is staring back but he's thinking of her.

'Tetracycline time!'

Morgan stands there, glass in hand, the pill on a plate. Lev takes the glass, swallows the pill.

Then the moment of reckoning: they call Green Park. Lev hangs over the receiver.

Her temperature is down! There's a mood of subdued rejoicing in the Jain house that travels along the line and infects the two men. They too are free, or in sight of being cleared, but must complete the course.

They watch the news, flipping between two channels.

'But Som Uncle said there's been another plague case in the old city.'

Lev thinks immediately of Laiq. 'I must see the barber in Maya's building.'

'What, a haircut?'

'No, just to see how he is.'

'You know Sweeney!'

'We've met.'

'Through Maya?'

'Well, actually I met Maya through him.' Lev hesitates. 'He doesn't like her, does he?'

It's news to Morgan. He shrugs. He didn't think liking or not liking mattered, given the social levels. All the same it satisfies him that Russia has produced this democratic blindness in Lev.

'Is that because of the Hindu–Muslim feeling?'

'Maya's not a Hindu! She's a Jain. As in Mr *Jain*, her father!'

'Are all Jains called Jain?'

'As far as I know. Which is not very far. We'll ask Maya.'

It's a moment before either of them appreciates the implications of that comradely *we*. Men-in-waiting, henchmen.

'What are they? What do they believe?'

'I couldn't tell you. God's out. They're like Buddhists, only more so. Buddhists without the mystagoguery. Or maybe they have their own mystagoguery. Probably. They believe in non-violence. I don't know how Mr Jain handles his lathi-charges. That's the Delhi joke. We have a Muslim Defence Minister, a Brahmin Army Chief and the top cop's a Jain. But they're serious about non-violence. They make ordinary vegetarians look like cannibals.'

'But she's not . . .' Lev searches for the word that will justify him.

'Orthodox?'

'No. I mean holy.'

'Not especially, no. It's just what you grow up with.'

'Did she grow up with the singing bowl?'

Morgan laughs. 'Actually, I gave her that. I picked it up in Kathmandu. It's Buddhist, not Jain.'

'She's,' Lev considers, 'not exactly . . .'

'Conventional?'

'Yes.'

'No, that she isn't. She sticks out over there. There are proper Jains all around.'

'What do they think of her?'

'I couldn't say. You know the *really* orthodox ones wear little masks over their mouths so they don't kill stray insects. Maybe even germs.'

'Like plague.'

They snicker grimly, men reprieved.

'What are you *doing* when you research germs for weapons?'

Lev looks off into the distance and squints as if trying to sight Biosecuritat. 'You are trying to maximize delivery.'

'You mean kill as many people as possible?'

'And as few germs as possible.'

'So really you're some kind of super-orthodox Jain?'

'Maybe. You don't want the germs to die in the warhead. You have to consider storage, application, spread, reception.' He searches for each word as he goes.

'Reception?'

'Immunity, for example. You are trying to develop new strains to dodge the host antibodies.'

'You've worked on new strains?'

'We all have at some stage. They move you around.'

'What have you done?'

'You do some plague, some anthrax. Then maybe some virus. Smallpox, Ebola, Marburg. They're always looking for new ways. It's like ordinary weapons.'

'How did you get interested?'

Lev pauses only to get the grammar right. 'I was got interested.'

'With a gun at your head?'

'No. They mark you. When you're still quite young.'

'What if you had refused?'

'Well, it was not the 1930s. But I could have been sent to Murmansk.'

'To Murmansk?'

'Like my grandfather was. It's in the far north.'

'The biggest city north of the Arctic Circle.'

'He died building a hospital there.'

'So what happens after they tag you?'

'It's not straight into weapons. But once you're in you're in. You start off maybe with aerosols, then germs. The new strains come last.'

'Is it tempting to try to change nature?'

Lev runs the tip of his tongue along the furred teeth at the gumline as he considers the wider question. He's been without a toothbrush, his own or hers, for three days.

'Have you ever seen a goosefoot barnacle?' he asks Morgan.

Morgan shakes his head.

'Have you seen the dorsal bone in a squid?'

'I've never seen the sea.'

'You would say it was plastic. Clear plastic. Not of nature. The first time I saw the goosefoot barnacle – it had a piece of seaweed attached to make it more confounding—'

'Confusing.'

'Confusing – I didn't know whether it was animal or vegetable or mineral. The borders are already blurred, already mutating.'

He thinks of her hands making shadows on the ceiling: wolf into tortoise into crane. Illusion upon illusion compounded.

'Tell me,' Morgan ventures. 'How was the changeover for you? From communism. How did it affect you?'

Lev has a complex smile too, when there's too much to convey. He twists both ends of his mouth down simultaneously, raises one eyebrow and focuses on facts.

'I lost my job.'

'The research job? So you did something else?'

'Yes.'

'Is there as much unemployment as they say?'

'There's *more*. It's a poor country.'

'*This* is a poor country.' Like all his countrymen Morgan is proprietorial when it comes to national poverty.

'Well, you have poors, we have poors.'

'Should we be chasing weapons?'

Lev laughs a short laugh. 'They're our best export.'

'And we're your best customer.'

'But it would be cheaper for you –' Lev ducks his head in a mock salesman's bow – 'if you bought just the know-how.'

All his adult life Lev has seen himself as a victim of circumstances, a man worked upon. The bow shrugs all that off. Freed today of suspicion of plague he's free too of the need to sell plague.

They order tandoori chicken for dinner. It arrives in a recycled foil pouch that has a tea company's logo all over it. Morgan gets to slice onions and an old cucumber that he refreshes with lime. His fridge is the red of his Valentine's Day shirt.

That night Lev dreams an old dream, his dream of the half man. He is travelling in a train by night when he's approached by a blackmailer he seems to recognize. He shoots the man and pushes him out the door as another train goes past in the opposite direction. The man falls on the tracks and his legs are cut off. At the next station Lev alights, imagining he's safe now. He climbs a high chain-link fence to enter some forbidden zone and is about to melt into the shadows on the other side. Just then a truck pulls up beside him and a figure rises up off the flatbed. It's the half man, raising himself up on his arms. He has Lev's face.

It's only ten o'clock. He steps out under the night sky onto Morgan's rooftop terrace where white bougainvillaea is flourishing in a concrete pot. A plane goes over with its row of windows clearly visible. They must be nearer the airport here. He thinks of the woman with the baby and the husband and half waves to her.

Down below Morgan is playing something vaguely familiar on the stereo.

Nineteen

'Come and see,' Jain says.

Morgan puts the phone down delighted. 'She has to rest, but we're invited to lunch.'

It's the fourth day. They've just had breakfast. Lev is sitting opposite Morgan's stereo on a daybed spread with a red-spotted counterpane examining a puppet she must have given Morgan. It's a small horse and rider, the horse a legless wonder, all mane and tail and brocade caparison. The rider has one fixed and one moveable arm. The free arm has a sword of tin and is worked with a separate string. Lev sees him sweep across a field cutting men in half, his weapon the finest that science could devise.

'She made that.'

Lev nods, her Commander-in-Chief.

They no longer use her name. She could be the centre of the known world. In their heads it's no longer she, it's *you*. Gone third person, love's dead.

Galubchik. You're well again.

Marionetki. No one else comes close.

'What does Maya mean?'

'Illusion.'

Lev swings the puppet in a wide arc over the stippled counterpane, twitching the middle finger as he goes. They watch him sweep across the field hewing men down.

'Here.' Lev hands him back to Morgan to hang back up the way he wants. Morgan likes that in him. He takes the horseman but then stops halfway to listen to his favourite passage from *Lieutenant Kije*, where the trumpet, masquerading as a bugle, peels off from the ruck of string and snare and lofts a lonely salute.

Lev has got up off the divan and is stretching, eager to be gone. He looks around at the still frozen anchorman.

'Morgan,' he says enunciating in meticulous exasperation, '*fuck* Prokofiev!'

Morgan bursts out laughing and falls with the puppet on the bloodstained field. It's some time before he can bring himself to stop.

It's a long time till lunch. Lev worries a string button on the raw-silk kurta that comes up to his knees.

'Keep that,' Morgan says. 'Blue suits you better than me. By the way, there's more plague in the old city. And the chemists are hoarding tetracycline.'

Lev thinks at once of Laiq. 'Can we find some here?' He means in South Delhi.

'We can try.'

They take the Zen to Hauz Khas where the chemists there shake their heads. They try Green Park, skirting the very house, and Yusuf Sarai, then Gulmohar Park and on through Anand Lok to GKI and II. No one in Kalkaji has heard of tetracycline either. They go out along the Faridabad Road, try Okhla. No tetracycline. Govindpuri. Tetracycline?

That's some kind of shirting? They pass the Apollo hospital and come to Sarita Vihar. Sorry, there's been panic buying.

'Now what?' Morgan turns the Zen around and parks under a neem tree near D-Block where scooter rickshaws stand. 'Shall we walk a bit?'

They walk up a narrow winding road whose half-metal surface is puddled from last night's rain. Cyclists zizz around them through the ochre pools, their tyres making momentary Persian wheels just above the face of the water. Ahead of them goes a rickshaw whose tyres have been repaired so often there's more patching than original rubber. It's a scene from a small town, Morgan realizes, not metropolitan Delhi. Here at the edge the Grey City frays into haphazard north India. The Jingle Bells warning chip on a backing car, the glue stick on the stationer's counter, the hole in the wall dotcom are all there; you can talk to Tokyo from the PCO. But the pace is different, down a notch to busy Mofussil, a metabolism he knows intimately from childhood. They walk on because the curving road keeps promising to end. Finally, at a bridge across a black canal choked with water hyacinth, it does stop. Delhi's end.

Morgan is surprised. So the hive has its horizon. Beyond the canal are fields Razia might have ridden through. A factory with chimneys, a deeply rutted causeway, and in the distance, back on the Faridabad Road, a Hyundai showroom from another planet.

They sit on the bridge sweating. The people who go by are still half peasant. Women carrying huge loads of cut grass on their heads, half-urban students with their hair oiled and combed sideways, holding hands. Men in dhotis stare at Lev. They don't know Morgan.

'Lunch time?' he asks.

Lev looks at his bare wrist and nods. They've killed two hours; a little early won't matter, surely. They start back, stop at the first chemist.

'Tetracycline?' he says. 'Sure.'

They check the expiry date. September, one month away. Lev takes a week's supply, then decides, two weeks, just in case.

Back in Green Park the frangipani is out among the Lancias and Mercedes. Lev looks out for a Galant.

'Hello, Morgan.' Mrs Jain has come to the door herself; the servants are still on leave. She smells of Yardley's and her beauty is more conventional than her daughter's. 'Welcome,' she says to Lev and at once he feels the sting of his false position as they cross the white marble floor.

Black marble in the bedroom. Jain is sitting at the bedside on a Panchkuin Queen Anne chair with cabriole legs. He got up at the bell, but the kitchen is nearer the front door so he let his wife go. The finessing, like the furnishing, is her job anyway.

Maya is awake. Her eyes birdbright and seeking. It's hard to tell who they seek out first, but it's Lev they return to after flashing at Morgan. Dark velvet pouches the skin under each eye.

'Eh, eh,' Jain says, like a man about to sneeze, 'don't forget what the doctor said.' He holds up a monitory finger. 'Rest.'

She smiles at her father, this refusenik jeweller-turned-policeman who disdains the marble under his feet. Her smile stretches to encompass her two visitors. These are her men, these three.

'*One* minute,' Jain rules and leaves them.

'Are you at Nizamuddin?' she asks them together, her eyes going back and forth.

Morgan nods, grinning stupidly. Her loyal subject.

Lev is too overcome to speak. His lips are pressed firmly together, the smile twitching at the corners between concern and relief.

'So now you're free!' she says happily. 'I have another couple of days in bed.' She sticks her arms straight out above her head, amazed that she can hold them there, and grimaces, stretching. She's wearing one of her mother's mallowy cambric Lajpatnagar housecoats that cover the body from neck to ankle but leave the shoulders bare. Pale green piping at the armholes and down the front where jade buttons make small smooth milestones. Her feet are bare, with nails her mother would give anything to paint.

'Sit, yaa!' She pats the bed, but neither man budges from where he stands. If she tried to sit up herself she'd fall over, she's so weak. 'The show's been cancelled.'

Her father broke that bit of news. All shows are, during the period of the plague.

'People are leaving the old city. Pa says it's half empty already. There must be chaos at the stations.'

'God, I should have filled up my tank,' Morgan remembers. Now petrol will disappear.

'Taken your tetracycline?'

'Yes,' Lev answers for both. 'How are you?' he goes on now he can speak.

'Better.' She thinks back. 'Much better. Is Morgan looking after you?'

'Yes. I have your keys.'

'Keep them,' she goes to say, but simply bulges her eyes because her mother has just come in.

'Lunch is ready,' says Mrs Jain. 'What can I bring you, baby?' She has wide amber eyes and a baffled air. Under her clear plastic apron are black slacks and soft leather moccasins with the wet black shine of batskin.

'Nothing. I'm not hungry.'

'You must eat something, beti, some dahi, something light.'

'OK.'

'Come, Morgan. Mr—?'

'Repin.'

'Mr Repin, come. Just a plain meal. It's such a pleasure to get into one's kitchen again. In this country you are the hostage of your cook, your gardener and your driver.'

The dining-room floor is bordered in spinach green with a motif all across it of small green squares turned on their points into diamonds. Consular Driver Lev Repin would like Alla to repeat Mrs Jain's last sentence in a house such as this. It's no more than the New Russians say, but it's too late to get in on that act. It's why he's here. It's why Grigoriev went to Iran. To become hostage to a gardener.

Fresh gerberas on the table, cadmium yellow, and a bowl of glowing pomegranates. Morgan cannot praise the puris highly enough. They are light, they are golden, they are crisp on the outside and not oily on the inside. They are like haloes on Russian ikons. Mrs Jain enjoys his raillery and he never fails to play up to her. She knows she cooks well. She serves them two rounds of fresh puris with their alu timatar and soursweet pumpkin and then takes a plate in to Maya.

Jain eats in gloomy silence, his axe of a face bearing down.

But he has made the concession of being there. The phones have been ringing all morning in the downstairs office; Sunderam and two ACPs are busy at this moment answering them. He can spare twenty minutes. He eats sparingly as a rule, with raw garlic on a side plate.

'On holiday?' he addresses Lev.

'Yes.'

'An unfortunate time. You must stay away from the old city.'

'My suitcase is still at the Serai, near Delhi Gate.'

'I see.' Jain nods deeply once.

'Stay on with me,' Morgan says.

Lev nods thanks but won't commit himself.

'Or go to Agra. See the Taj,' Jain suggests and runs a fingernail down between his front teeth to dislodge a husk of wheat. He takes rapid swallows of water from a glass, downing tetracycline, beta blocker and antacid at one go. 'Gentlemen,' he says, and rises from his chair.

Morgan cannot resist another puri when he's gone.

'Take them all,' Mrs Jain says, coming in. 'Let me pack them for you. No one here is going to eat them.' Her voice sounds resigned, and comes from a region well past boredom.

There's a white police jeep blocking the gate so the Zen must be patient. The lights on all the white Ambassador roofs are revolving; Jain's in the back of one with the curtains drawn. The whole cavalcade push off and then Morgan backs out.

They take Ring Road to Andrews Ganj and then turn north. On the Defence Colony flyover there's a huge billboard with Morgan's face advertising the morning news. He used to avoid that route at first but now he just winks at himself in passing.

'You're famous,' Lev turns to him, as if checking the features.

'Don't remind me. I go back at six tomorrow.'

'How does it feel?'

'No complaints.'

The hoarding flashes past. It's not the complex pout Morgan's developed lately, but an open unguarded smile that took three shoots to get out of him. He scoots the Zen through gaps in the traffic on the Mathura Road. The gaps get wider as they approach Minto Bridge. Past the ITO most of the traffic is coming the other way. At the Delhi Gate lights even Lev can tell traffic is down.

Morgan lets him out at the Serai gate and writes his phone number and address down for him.

'I'm off to Chit Park,' he says as he pulls out. 'I don't know when I'll be back in Delhi.'

Then backs the Zen up and says he's just going to the Russia Club in Little Calcutta. It hurts to explain the joke, but it's the second time he's looked in his rear-view mirror and seen Lev standing at that gate, a forlorn mannequin.

Twenty

There's a lock on the Serai gate.

Lev is accustomed to a shut gate at night but this is mid-afternoon. The uniformed watchman is not there, though his stool is, its polished wooden seat conspicuously bare. There is nobody about the office, visible through the gate's peephole. Feeling the strings slacken above him, Lev climbs over the spiked gate top and jumps down on the inside. He expects to be challenged from some quarter but no challenge comes. He follows the gravel path to his cabin, half expecting to find the door standing open. It's locked; the padlock takes his key.

The suitcase is under the bed as he left it. He sits down on the bed above it and thinks. Go now, cut and run. Every morsel he ate in the Jains' Green Park home stuck in his throat. The sting of that food, offered in good faith, is still in his mouth. This is how it must have been for her at Karim's. And yet it's a joint deception. She wanted him there; she's not a child. She wants him in the flat too, but he must go there and decide.

First he must call Alla. More deception. She will have heard about the plague. The world's media will be battening on the outbreak, the only time they notice countries such as this, such as his own. But what is he to say?

He goes in search of Grover. There's a lock on the office door but the manager is in his residence, a specially appointed cabin. He talks to Lev through the window with a handkerchief tied over his mouth and nose. Leave the city, he advises; the few remaining Serai guests have gone. He himself is waiting for a ride.

'One more night?' Lev asks.

'There will be nobody here.'

Lev considers his position. He must go to her flat, then. His things are there. He has been using Morgan's shaver.

'Can I pick up my suitcase tomorrow?'

'There will be a police guard.'

'If you give me a receipt I can show it.'

Grover is silent. The curtains part and he makes for the office, looking steadily away from Lev.

'Have you taken antibiotics?' Lev asks from the office door, respecting the man's fear of infection.

Grover faces down as he works his way through the desk drawers looking for the receipt book. 'Bastards are hoarding,' he says without looking up.

'Here.' Lev drops a week's supply on the desk.

Grover looks up, surprised. 'You have taken?'

'Yes.'

'Thank you.'

They part without shaking hands.

'Go and see the Taj,' Grover calls from his door.

Lev climbs over the back gate and finds a functioning PCO; the owner will be on tetracycline. Alla's mother answers. She is well, they are well. St Isaak wants to buy the car; he keeps coming over to inspect it. Plague? What plague? He must take care. Lev says goodbye, sends his love.

He pays and pockets the change, noticing how warily his money is handled. At Nevsky there are army trucks, olive green with canvas tops, parked at intervals along the wide empty street behind the Serai. Traffic has been diverted to Ring Road. A line of soldiers in fatigues extends all the way to Turkman Gate and beyond in one direction; in the other it stretches down the west side of Nevsky, the old city side. Army trucks and police vehicles are using the east side to come and go.

Cordon sanitaire. Residents are being turned back at every gully leading into the old city. The soldiers are armed and implacable. The order to return home is simple and is repeated every few minutes over a loudhailer. Health workers guarded by army patrols have begun a doorknock, inspecting every house, distributing antibiotics. They must double check every street and lane and gully to make sure no one has been missed.

But people continue to leave their houses hoping to get away. Whole families simply stand among their belongings halted in mid-flight. Every few metres there is a confrontation. Women wail, unarmed men shout and bare their chests. Wherever they look in danger of breaking through the soldiers use their boots. One man who begins to sound dangerous is pulled out of the crowd and frogmarched across the median to the police station.

The police have the pavement on the east side. Their patrols have a security brief and will be busier by night. For now they enter and search the east side pharmacies, they dragoon chemists at home with warrants; confiscate quantities of tetracycline.

Lev crosses Nevsky at the Delhi Gate end. An officer on the police station steps points his cane straight at him, waits to catch his eye, then waves him off. Lev circles around the park where he met Laiq. He is heading up Haidar Road when he sees a police patrol coming his way and turns back again. He knows another point of entry further east where a service road makes its own small breach in the city wall.

There are few people about. Two pedestrians are walking down the centre of the street to avoid infection from doorways; they are together but are looking away from each other. A man coming the other way sees Lev and crosses to the other side of the street.

Laiq's door is shut and a curtain is pulled across it on the inside, but the wooden shutters are folded back. The birdcage is not visible.

'Lev!'

It's a squeak more than a call. Then the door opens and a hand beckons rapidly.

'Be quick!' Laiq means there are germs even between door and curtain.

'Laiq, you're well!'

'God's grace. And you? Your . . .' He points at his throat.

'Oh, that!' Lev has forgotten that. 'Fine. I have brought something for you. You must take it.' He hands over the pills.

Laiq examines the foil strip. 'Same thing Gour-ment is giving?'

'Same thing.'

'You have taken?'

'Yes.'

'I also take something.' Laiq vanishes behind the inner curtain to his herbarium. Her returns with a jar of yellow powder. 'This.'

'That is not enough, Laiq. With plague you must take antibiotics. There is *no* other remedy.'

'You took other powder? Red one I gave?'

'It was taken.'

Laiq stands a while nodding slowly to some inner prompting. Finally he tosses his head sideways.

'I will take.'

He gets a tumbler and measures a rope of water into it from a brass spout. Then he takes the pill, swallows it and stands there with his lips tightly drawn. At length he nods.

'Old Arab is saying. Trust God, but don't forget to tie camel.'

'Tie it up morning and evening,' Lev says and they laugh.

'Sit, sit.' Laiq spins the barber's chair around on one leg.

Lev sits. The padded bench opposite has Laiq's bedding on it. 'How did you get out?'

'I will tell.' Laiq takes up and folds the sheet, holding the centre under his chin. 'From big-inning.'

And Laiq goes back to the last time they met, omitting his night vigil in that very chair.

He tells of the first rumours of plague. One person at the night shelter by Turkman Gate (a Bihari, the rumour went) was admitted to the public hospital and died there. Then another Bihari, known to the first, followed. A group of Bihari labourers was stoned. Two days later another death occurred in a house on the Chipwara side. The family tried to conceal the body but the following day all three remaining members succumbed and were discovered. Now the richer

sort of old city resident began to leave. Doctors were among
the first to disappear. Jewellers, big merchants and the like
had already sent their families away; some followed the same
night after securing their houses and valuables. Overnight
posters began to appear on walls advertising plague specialists
who would treat you at a price.

'One is here, on *this* wall,' Laiq points to the shopfront.
'You can read.'

Shop by shop the old city closed down. Some chemists
who stayed tried to inflate the price of antibiotics – which is
foolish, Laiq said, because people remember these things.
Perhaps they thought there would be no one left to remember.
Vegetable sellers sold their stock at double and triple the price
and disappeared. By now no one took money directly from
another; you had always to carry the right change. Still no
one knew whether to stock up and stay or clear out. Everyone
was watching his neighbour but no one dared ask. In the end
police patrols began to appear with magistrates requiring any
diseased household to declare itself.

That was late Saturday, Laiq said, early Sunday. All night
people were burning fires at crossroads to kill loose germs
and purify the air. The sky was black and red. There was one
big fire outside the house of Daniyal, the template maker,
that spread as far as the house of Saili the petty retailer in
our lane. Both are great liars and people said it was divine
judgement. By Sunday morning whole rows of houses
appeared locked up. In our building there were three locked
doors and I began to feel abandoned. From my balcony I
heard a muffled wailing in the opposite building across the
tomb and then a window burst open and a man shouted: *No,
no, no, no, no!* I immediately went inside and shut the window

in case his germs reached me. That was the trouble: nobody knew anything about the disease. That was when I decided to come here. I put my things in a holdall and put a lock on the door. The lanes were full of people carrying baggage, either heading for the railway station or for the bus station. At the same time there were people coming back saying all trains and buses out of Delhi were cancelled. And of course those who couldn't afford to go anywhere, old people, sick people, just stayed where they were. The owner of our building is rich but he has stayed behind. He said he would be there to greet me if I returned. His wife was sprinkling vinegar on the curtains.

In the lane – you remember the narrow part where you have to go sideways? – I passed a boy I know, one of the cricketers you saw that day, very sweet boy, and we hardly even said goodbye. Have you ever taken leave of somebody you love with both of you looking the other way? We passed like this, talked like this, and then he ran off. So I came here, holding my mouth in, with garlic crushed between my teeth and a handkerchief tied over my nose, carrying my holdall. And him.

Laiq points at the partridge in its cage on the window sill above the bench. A ray of late sunshine has slipped into Laiq's shop to gild the bars of the cage. The lightfall puts the bird into a fever of ducking and craning. It's time for the evening walk: what's the delay? An alarm in its body clock is about to ring out. Laiq gets up and throws a wrap around the cage, plunging the bird in darkness.

'Now they are saying: Kill your dog, kill your cat, kill your pigeon. Kill rats, mouses, birds.'

'When did the army come?'

'Before morning. After night.'

'You came out just in time.'

'He wake me.' Laiq looks warmly at the cloaked bird. Then he remembers something. 'I have something. For you.'

He goes to a shelf beyond the pink counter and feels behind the books lying flat at one end. It's a small bottle but imported and therefore smuggled, expensive, Laiq's return for the Moti Mahal dinner. Brewed twice over in the still of his beholden self.

'*Stolichnaya!* But Laiq – this is—'

'It is for you.'

'Laiq—!'

'It is for you.'

Lev bows. 'Then let's drink. You like vodka?'

Laiq shrugs. He knows rum, whisky. They sit and sip white fire. Less than a kilometre away the old city pullulates, a ring thrown around it like a second wall. The old wall broods in violet shadow, a toad. The sun is going down on the red fort, the great mosque, the flamingos of the bird hospital, on scenes of mortal confusion, and they sit drinking peacefully just outside the cordon.

'We have one poet in Urdu, Mir.'

'Mere.'

'No, Mir. Long eee.'

'Alive?'

'No, dead. Long time. He see Dilli city destroy by army. His house destroy. Everything destroy. Wartime. So he leave Dilli. Go Lucknow. But he never forget Dilli. In his heart, Dilli, Dilli, Dilli.'

Laiq quotes a couplet in Urdu, then repeats it as the fire rages round his tongue. At length a translation surfaces.

'He say: "My heart was beauty-ful red city. You come. You destroy each and every house. Now where I will live? Tell! *Where?*" '

They drink in silence after that. Lev looks for ways to tell Laiq of Maya's illness, but can't find the words or the will to express the suffering he has endured, and possibly, though he can't be sure, caused.

They step out into the night. The street is preternaturally quiet, but a curtain of sound flaps from the direction of Nevsky and beyond: police whistles, cries, the scolding of the loudhailer, dulled beyond deciphering, like the barking of a muzzled dog.

'See?' Laiq points to a poster plastered between his shop and the next. FAMOUS DEVOTEE OF HANUMANJI WILL CURE ALL DISEASES. CONTACT ROOM 313 HOTEL KAILASH.

The shop next door, the pathology lab, continues closed; Lev has never seen it open. Its sign accuses him of malingering. Go home, it always says, cancelling the summons from the lid of his grandfather's painted box.

From behind them comes the sound of a jeep horn. Then the sound of an engine mercilessly revved, gears wrenching. But no vehicle appears. It's the human jeep Lev passed in the old city, driving down the middle of the road.

'So he escaped too,' Lev remarks.

'You know him?'

'I've seen him in the old city.'

'He was very clever boy. University topper. He fail one paper. He become jeep.'

Lev looks hard at the passing vehicle, acknowledging a presence he senses at the centre of the noise. The jeep too slows, scenting a fellow puppet, then moves on.

'Good night,' Lev says, turning to Laiq.

The kitchen light is burning in Maya's flat. It hasn't burnt out.

'Good night, Lev,' Laiq replies looking up at the lit window. Go on up, his expression says. She's waiting.

Now Lev must speak of her. 'Maya is not well,' he ventures.

'Fever?' Laiq asks at once.

'Yes. Viral. Not plague. She's at home, with her parents.'

'Then you eat here,' Laiq offers immediately. 'With me.'

'Thank you,' Lev bows, without committing himself. And ducks into the festooned entranceway, feeling his way in the dark past lime-encrusted wiring. Up the cool steep stair that once again asserts its strangeness now she's not here. Down these steps they carried her in the armlock chair. He tiptoes past the first-floor residences and climbs to the roof.

It takes many tries in the dark before the enormous skeleton key finds the keyhole in the security door. He feels a gaze upon him and turns to look. A dark figure stands watching him from the balustrade. It's the finial with its sloping shoulders and melon-like head, elongated in a moon-shadow. The padlock on the inner door is easier.

He steps into silence. Crosses the empty room and switches off the kitchen light. Stands in the dark once the fridge door shuts and swigs water the way she does, straight from the bottle. The whole flat breathes her presence; if she appeared in any one place he would jump because she is everywhere. Is this how it is when a loved one dies?

But she's alive! The relief floods through him so suddenly that he must sit down. Her scent is on the cane chair, the cushions, even the runner on the bookshelf. Her impatience in the tilt of a book she half put away. City dust lies on the glass top of the coffee table: he traces an M with his fingertip. The door to the terrace was left open; he leaves it as it is: it's the one lung in a stuffy, ill-ventilated flat that absorbs heat all day long.

He looks in the puppet room and feels the hair on his forearms lift. The workbench is littered with silent carcasses, the silhouettes on the wall are still. How patient a thing a puppet! Waiting forever on the touch that infects it. Its life, its many lives, a fever of antics.

I've been hanging on a nail, waiting for her touch. He lifts his head, a scenting animal. Here her presence is especially strong, a floating nous above the reek of glue and mill fabric.

'Lev. This is Babaji.'

He nods at the blind hermit and shuts the door and goes to the bedroom.

'Cooler, this is Lev.'

The bed is as they left it, her impress on the sheets.

The phone rings, a shrill mechanical ring. He turns sharply. Now what? Is it for her? It rings and rings, then just as he finds the courage to answer it stops. The next time he's ready.

'Lev? Did you just come in?'

'More or less.'

'Are you sleeping there?'

'I don't know.'

'Sleep there. Lev.'

'Maya.'

He sleeps in the hollow she left. She's alive.

But in the morning his eyes, his ears, open on strangeness and he lies there thinking, I must go home. He marvels at the ease with which he's been deflected. Talk to her, he decides. Return her key. (How?) Take your suitcase to a hotel, make a reservation with Aeroflot, look at jeans, jackets.

He cuts through the park. At the Serai there's a police guard as Grover said there would be. Three uniformed men sitting on folding chairs at the gate; a fourth, the masseur of the park; squats on his hams working. He rolls his eyes as Lev presents his receipt. The guards are cagey; Lev must press hard, show his key. Eventually they let him in, out of boredom.

He unlocks the door to his cabin.

The suitcase is there under the bed. The old blue hardshell looking worn. He lifts it onto the bed he won't be using, and sees the film of dust over the top is gone. He lifts the lid: everything's there. But in a slightly different place.

Twenty-One

She can't wait to get back.

It's not just him, it's her, Razia. She can see the bodice laid out there in pieces waiting for the machine. Can feel the scissors in her hand already. The cool black weight of them, the grinding snip as they cut through muslin for the choli.

Back to him, back to work. She wants him there in the other room doing – whatever it is he does. So that when she hoods the raptor sewing machine and opens the workroom door, he's there.

Lev. I've forgotten what you look like. The fever burned your face away. Do you have blue eyes or brown?

Grey, of course! Grey-violet with yellow flecks. Get me out of here, my Commander. You can't imagine, you *cannot* imagine, how hard it is to be free, here.

She'll paint him, has begun already. She can see the last page already with his leg sloping down into the right-hand corner, the foot turned in so it fits. Can feel the wide brush loaded with wash. Payne's grey for the terrazzo, wash upon wash, and the bed sheets begin to glow. A grain of cobalt for the sheets and he begins to glow. Flesh tones next, his strange pale skin. Her brush must learn to mix a new colour. Guava, under peeling bark, that newness.

'Maya, kuchka, how are you feeling?'

She feigns sleep. Her mother sits down on the bedside chair. Where nightly Jain sits and reports on the old city.

'Such a beautiful baccha,' her mother murmurs. She knows she's awake. 'Such a brave girl. Rest, you're so pulled down. Dark-dark rings under your eyes.' She smoothes back the unruly hair above the forehead with a pale hand. 'Sleep. Stay here till you're strong again. Make all the puppets you want but look after yourself is what I say. When you're run down you're open to all kinds of viruses and whatnot. We'll give you the blue room if you find this too dark. Any room, kuchka, you decide.'

'I'm going back tomorrow.'

She shouldn't have said that. She was supposed to be asleep for a start.

'Baby, you can hardly walk!'

'I walked yesterday.'

'I know. Look what happened. That's why you're so weak today, bachcha.'

'I'm not weak and I'm not a baby.'

It's different when Pa calls her that. Her mother says nothing, just smooths her forehead. The forehead she finds narrow. Mukund's was wide.

'And I'm going back tomorrow.'

'See, here's the doctor. Doctor Sahib, you talk to her. She wants to run away already.'

She agrees to stay two more days, to make it a full week's rest. Her head is clear now, the fever left her days ago, the aches and pains are gone. The wobbly feeling's there, but that's because she's not up enough. Also the black marble depresses her; the mirror finish makes a bottomless pool of it.

'Lev. *Soon.*'

She holds onto the receiver long after he's hung up. She neglects her friends; only Morgan's allowed to visit. A herbalist comes twice a day. He recommends ashwaganda and spirulina and bedrest.

She calls at night; then she calls by day as well. They lean towards each other across the city, puppets on a stage.

'What are you eating?'

'I go down to Laiq's. He's living in his shop now.'

'Pa says it's almost over.'

There's no radio in the flat either. She is his news and it comes from the top. Jain knows how many dead, how many quarantined, how many estimated at the Interstate Bus Terminal, how many stranded at the Old Delhi railway station. His men do cross patrols now within the cordon. He knows where the biggest cache of tetracycline is to be found. He knows the Bihari's curse, the rat-catcher's prayer, the price of pod garlic. Tells her how much searchers and bearers are paid per body. He reads turbulence in the air like clouds. He can guess why a mysterious photo of an infant is tied with red string to all the telephone poles in Chipwara.

'Why don't I dream of you, yaa?'

'What do you dream of?'

Lev can see her lips push out that complaint. He's the commissioner of her body, knows its districts down to a mole she didn't know was there.

'Mangoes.'

'*Mangoes!*'

'The doc has put me off them. Listen. You're stuck there, nà. You know the workroom almirah?'

'Almirah?'

'Cupboard. Morgan's binocs are in there.'

'Binoculars?'

'Ya. He's a birdwatcher. So use them. And listen.'

'Yes?'

'Fill up the fridge with mangoes.'

Twenty-Two

They're Russian field glasses.

Good optics, but clunky. The first thing he picks out is the gantry on the distant power station where the chimneys are. It fuzzes one way, then the other, then comes clean, sharp, the smooth iron boss at the stairhead polished by countless hands to lustrous gunmetal. Next a pigeon on the city wall, thunderhead blue and burbling. Then a nest close at hand, a large untidy structure built at the top of a stately tree, the very top, in defiance of storm or predator. The hawks that built it roost majestically on the branches round about, but today they're not there.

He takes the binoculars to the city side, and stands at the kitchen window and focuses on the one slice of the old city visible from this part of Haidar Road. It's the lane along from Laiq's. The green uniforms of the army make a conspicuous fringe along the other side of Nevsky. There are few civilians about, and the shutters are down on the South Indian restaurant at the corner. Four men with handkerchiefs tied over their noses swim into view. They are carrying something that swings in a sheet. Wordlessly they heave the load onto the back of a truck and turn their heads aside simultaneously as soon as the job is done. A body.

It's a view from a great distance, almost microscopic, and marred with the same ambiguities. Lev can't know that it's the last corpse of the plague any more than he can guess that those men are untouchables; they are organisms disposing of an organism. He returns to the puppet room and puts away the binoculars. The air smells of DDT. The edges of the street are white with it as if marked off for some deadly game. It covers the corner by Laiq's doorstep, masking the betel stain, but there's a fresh red splash where Laiq spat this morning's juice.

By night Lev talks with Laiq, by day he sits on the cane chair reading Morgan's Russians, his own Russians, or staring at the floor where big black ants are blown about by the fan's hurricane. Over and over the ants pick themselves up and march across the terrazzo only to be sent skidding to the ends of the room. Lev's eyes focus by turns on Akhmatova and the ants: he drifts between red city and white, between Alla and that world and Maya and this.

Close your eyes, na.

He shuts his eyes, arrives instantly within himself. Alone, the strings gone from above him. A puppet has a vast solitude inside. In this void Lev feels himself stretch out after a cramped eternity so familiar he can't tell when it began. A porousness in his very bones. Here at the edge of a boundless vacancy he's past woodchips and sawdust and lead, here even the rags of fate and destiny are dissolved. What's left of will slips from him with a sigh; now the barest consciousness animates the blank that is Lev Repin. The thing in the cane chair shivers. Like the thing on the stool at Biosecuritat, a spectator at creation.

From one perspective the whole of life is a play staged for one person. The whole drama of the plague was staged exclusively for this man in the gods with opera glasses. The whole web of love and chance was spun to catch one fly.

Lev struggles. Suspended over nothing, learning to breathe like some grave staring infant.

'Lev.'

'Yes?'

'Lev.'

'What?'

'Nothing. Just. Saying your name. I need to see you. I've forgotten what you look like. Are you using Morgan's binocs?'

The next time he looks the green fatigues are gone, and the cordon lifted. There are people in the street, there's traffic on Nevsky. There's a woman brushing her hair on the roof, but Lev refuses to ogle. Loyal in unfaithfulness. He goes to the terrace that overlooks the city wall. The way along the top of the wall is choked with fresh monsoon growth. In the arched recesses underneath, right by the urinal, the stalls are back: fruit stall, vegetable stall, ironing stall. Their awnings, of bamboo and sackcloth and blue plastic sheeting, keep off more sun than rain today, the hot July sun that ripens fruit by the hour. A bar of it has slipped through a gap in the vegetable vendor's burlap and touched his cool green marrows with gold. The ironing man presses and folds, presses and folds, inured to the heat from the coals in his clanking iron. The sleeve of his right arm rolled up, a bend in his back from the five-kilo weight, he smoothes away wrinkles in shirts that will be crumpled by nightfall.

Today the hawks are there, breasting a wind that never dips below the topmost branches. One is perched on the nest, leaning in to instruct her young, the other launches himself into the air and circles the tree with scarcely visible calibrations of wing and tail, calling in his chill tormented way. A blind man might hear the keening of a human soul. Round and round it goes, this icy earthward shrilling that hovers perpetually between release and a reluctance to leave.

The hawks can go but they want to stay – and here is Laiq's partridge, wings clipped, shouting freedom.

Lev lowers the glasses. Disarmed by love, he's a prisoner in this flat. And yet it's half a lifetime since he knew such exhilaration. The old malaise, that deadness of response to everything – except discovery: of what? Kurile-E or F or G? – is gone. He can even look in a mirror without disgust.

He takes a rag and dusts down every surface in the flat. For a week now he's left her things alone. What he picked up he put back where he found it. He's used the front edge of shelves, of tables, of benches. Now he clears away, wipes down, washes. He scrubs a whole greasy huddle of spice jars till the glass shines. He scours the sink. He cleans out the cooler, the fridge, defrosts the little freezer.

'Oh oh.'

It's Morgan out of the blue one afternoon running a critical finger along a benchtop.

'Are you sure about this?'

'She's coming tomorrow.'

Lev dusts the books one by one. Morgan makes himself a mug of instant coffee and notices the spice jars. He uses them more than Maya does, but he always respected their grime.

'Are you sure you're not Portuguese?' he calls. 'I mean, you haven't come in search of pepper or anything?'

Lev smiles and goes on dusting. He carries the cane bookshelf out onto the terrace and deals with it severely. A bamboo batten comes away and he takes the opportunity of dusting behind it before tapping it back into place. Then he puts the books back, in more or less the same order they stood in before.

'After you come the Dutch,' Morgan says, sipping contentedly. 'Then the English. My ancestors. Now they really turned the place around.'

Lev puts away the duster and washes his hands at the kitchen sink. His coffee is waiting, hatted with a saucer.

'Have you been reading?'

'Yes,' Lev answers, embarrassed. 'I have been using your binoculars too.'

'They're Russian, you know.'

Lev nods. 'You're a birdwatcher?'

'I go out once in a while. I haven't been since I got roughed up by some villagers.'

'For *bird*watching!'

'I was looking at a lapwing nest. It happened to be in the field their women use first thing in the morning.'

Lev frowns, then laughs when he's worked it out.

'It wasn't funny, I can tell you.'

Lev laughs some more, so Morgan joins in, noticing for the first time Lev's long almost girlish eyelashes.

'They don't watch the English news,' Morgan explains, drying up. He claps his hands on his knees to say he's off. 'If you like we can take the glasses to the Okhla barrage. At this time of year you get all sorts of waterfowl. It's cooler there.'

'I can't,' Lev realizes. 'I'm going to watch some wrestling.'

'Wrestling!'

'With Laiq. Here near the mosque.'

'Ah, Sunday.' Morgan thinks back to the maidan in his small town. 'You know the best wrestlers are across the border now. The Pakis are the world freestyle champions. Don't know what happened to us.' He looks suddenly depressed. 'Maybe I'll come along.'

'You know Laiq?'

'Sweeney? No. Let's go down and meet him. He looks like a wrestler.'

'He won't be there till four thirty.'

Morgan hunches for a moment with his eyes shut over the game board that is Delhi.

'Well,' he straightens up, 'if I'm there I'm there. Don't wait for me.'

At half-past four he's at the other end of town, but someone else is walking up Haidar Road from Delhi Gate.

Laiq sees her coming in the distance and knows that stride at once. The brazenness of it, the raffish way the arm swings up and out, the tilt of head. Is there any woman in this entire locality who would dream of walking that way? Hair hanging loose and blowing about, unoiled. It doesn't take a lifetime in hairdressing to know that at the great divide between the classes there stands a bottle of hair oil.

The strange part is that for all his loyalties Laiq is enamoured of the other side. A lack of oil, yes, but also there's something *there*. All his life Laiq has tried to put his finger on this something. Sometimes he will be standing beside the species in the street and he'll watch narrowly — he'll actually come up close — to see what makes it different.

A cop tells the next man to move on but says nothing to this one with the something. This exempt one, extraterritorial, unaccountable, unanswerable. The one with class. He may look next at Laiq and say nothing, but his glance will say *us*. Not *them*. And, just once, Laiq would be happy to pass for one of them.

This woman coming up the street has the kind of phantom hold every tiring wrestler dreads. She goes past the barbershop and smiles vaguely into its shadows. Laiq does not return the smile. Her glance falls on the brainfever bird and she nods a greeting at it like someone returning after a holiday. Then she ducks into the narrow entranceway and climbs the stair, holding the handrail for a change.

The doorbell puts Lev in a proper panic. Morgan's been, who else can it be?

She rings again. He opens, and their soft embrace muffles his surprise.

'I had a fight with my mother,' she explains when they're sitting on the terrace in the swing seat.

'A quarrel?' He's dusted the seat and the cushions, oiled the swing with vegetable oil.

'Ya.' She stops swinging. 'What happened to the squeak?'

'I oiled it.'

'My lovely squeaky swing!'

He kisses her gently on the forehead and makes a ponytail of her hair with one hand while the other traces the outline of her face. She waits for the larger kiss and when it comes leans back against the iron flatweave of the lattice.

It's an hour before Lev remembers his appointment with Laiq. He runs downstairs to call it off but finds a padlock on the wooden shutters.

He needn't have hurried. Laiq didn't wait long when he saw Maya return. He took the birdcage off its hook and set it on the window sill and changed the water in the dish. Then he locked-up shop, spat his betel juice into the whited corner, muttered *foreigners* and walked towards the wrestling without looking back.

Twenty-Three

How marvellous to be on the east terrace when the storm is blowing from the west!

Twenty different pockets of rain visible in the lights surrounding this house; twenty dialects of wind rushing up or down a wall or lane, each driving the rain before it into a circle of light. The sulphurous halo of the street light; the green glow at the mosque; domestic neon tubes that turn night into a doctor's waiting room; an old incandescent bulb at the neighbour's scooter garage, making yellow moths of the raindrops; gold strings of festive bulbs where the other Jains had a baby boy: each lights up the storm differently. Red dots blur on the faraway chimneys, warning aircraft of danger. Even the bellpush of the Raos' estranged relatives across the lane has a tender orange mist around it. In every illuminated pocket the rain blows a new way.

He sleeps through it, my love. How gentle in sleep!

Draw him. Take your lap away. (Brush the fine spray off the cushion, slip it under his head. He'll turn on his side, the swing will rock him back to sleep.)

But when she's up she simply stands there, one hand on

the swing frame, looking at him. He draws up his knees, his breath so light it's hardly there.

The rain beats harder, the trees twist and strain to the tips of their leaves. The supple young mast trees bend almost to the ground. Only the tall silk-cotton stands up straight. Where are the hawks now? Tonight the city wall is a buffalo; its wet skin glistens in the lightning.

The workroom pulls her, the lode her sewing machine. And the sound of Mira, who loved the monsoon, from a tape she plays over and over on the crackly Aiwa portable that sits on the workbench, speckled with paint, a plastic bird pouring out bhajans. Her scissors squeak, monsoon stiff, rust on the blades, as she cuts a codpiece for the Commander-in-Chief; then the chatter of the sewing machine's teeth as she hums *Sawan de rahyan jora re*. She has no ear but is in love with the ascetic who was in love with the Lord her God.

He appears, bleary in the doorway, shaking his head at her industry.

'Bas, bas, bas, yaa.'

He's learnt her chorus, in his good accent. His arm is out, asleep in the air, extending like a wing to receive her. She simply rises and is folded into his warmth. In bed she makes a ball of herself and nuzzles into his side, falling asleep before him. Never fall asleep before her, he's learnt.

All night the small hands of the rain clapping.

She lives by another clock. Next morning she's awake before he stirs, stretching into the ninety-eight shapes of her yoga. The morning is cool and grey. An opal breeze streams from the depths of black rain clouds massed on the horizon; more rain is on its way.

Now she does sketch him, by this monsoon light which

pours from every side and leaves no shadow. His ear could be lit up from inside: her pencil point works outward from the well of it. She has a line that starts in a knot and unravels with a fluidity her drawing master half envied at the Institute. Don't prolong it for ever, he meant to warn her, and forgot. In the quiet of the morning the graphite point hisses like a fuse. Lev sleeps on, unaware of the multiple images taking possession of her page. She draws rapidly, stretching the arm his head rests on till it overshoots the page so the hand must make a separate study of its own, lower down. She picks herself up, moves to a new quadrant. This morning Lev's head is the right way up, the pillow riding up against the wall. She slips back into bed beside him.

He stirs, her lord and subject. Today she will make the general's tunic and a Russian hat of imitation sable instead of the felted Afghani headdress she planned. But first there is this new fabric, skin. He turns over to pursue a waking dream, taking the sheet with him so it billows momentarily. She hears the sigh of it settling but won't be left behind. The tortoise neck of him! The tip of her tongue tracks as far as the jugular and stops to take his pulse. He wakes and turns to her, draws her down. When they fall apart she lies on her back with her fingers in her ears, a child again, and listens to the doom inside her. The phone rings. She lets it ring.

Breeze pours in at the freed window; yesterday they put the cooler out to pasture. She rolls over on her stomach with a frown.

'Last night the storm came in from the other window.'

He explains the nature of cyclonic storms, the lull in the middle followed by winds from the opposite direction. She listens as if to a story and grows restless when it goes on too long.

'Bas, bas, bas!' She covers his mouth with hers.

He laughs under her lips. He's learning from her all the time and this one lesson she resents. A country enters through your skin, he's learnt.

This morning the wall is an elephant, coarse-skinned and long of memory.

'When I was six,' she says, 'I had a doll. My favourite doll.'

Biosecuritat, he thinks with his parallel mind as he listens. When she was six I was already there, chosen, brought in. He does this obsessively now: when she was ten, when she was nineteen, when she was two.

'God, how I loved it! How I used to brush its hair, brush it, brush it, brush it. I used to kiss its nose! It had hardly any nose to start with, so I must have kissed the rest away. I brushed the hair away also.'

She has a way of wetting her lips by pressing them together and pushing her tongue through.

'A bald doll. Have you ever seen a bald doll in a dress?'

Her eyes are focused. She's *there*, six.

'It used to scare me at night. When I'd see its head shining I'd put a pillow on it, cover it up. Or I'd pick it up in the dark and bring it right up to my face so it became huge and I'd stare and stare at it. Scaring myself. I'd start knocking it against my nose, staring at it. And I'd knock harder and harder and harder and see its face come rushing again and again and again with its eyes staring. My God it was scary in the dark with just the light on from Pa and Ma's room and their voices going khitar phitar in the background far away

and no other sound just the knocking of our noses. And then
I'd hold it there and look into its eyes, but no matter how
straight I looked it was always looking away. You try to catch
a doll's eye. You can't, you just can't. It's always looking away,
listening to something else. You're just not there for it. But
it's there. You hold it up in the dark and it's there, the bald
head shining, the eyes open, the mouth closed, the lips smiling
a little at the corners, smiling for itself. It has nothing to
say to you and you've got everything to say to it. Are you
listening?'

'Yes.'

'So you start to think that the only person you can really
talk to is yourself. That even the real people around you who
look back at you and hear you are dolls to you. Just like
you're a doll for them. Or could be it's just teaching you to
be still. To be quiet.' She laughs. 'It never taught me!'

My princess. *Talk*. Talk your head off. Talk my ears off. My
nose, my mouth. Don't ever stop. Talk me bald.

'My brother never answered me. I worshipped him, liter-
ally yaa, but I was nothing to him. He was my mother's
favourite, always the favoured one, always, always, always.
Even after he died, especially after he died. I could never
match up to him. He could do no wrong. If he broke something it was because I was standing too close, distracting him.
If he made something it was in spite of me annoying him. I
tried so hard to copy him, but even when I did something
well he didn't notice. Or he'd just claim it. Like once he
claimed a boat I made out of icecream sticks, you know a
paddlewheel boat, and Pa said, *What a clever boy!* And what
really pissed me off was that later he actually believed that he
had made it. He was perfect, so how could I have made it?

Even Pa thought I was lying. So then I started to be the opposite. The more goodygood he was the worse I became. If he studied I stopped studying, if he liked a book I hated it. I started smoking because he refused a cigarette. And then he died. Ma was just destroyed. She would keep looking at me as if to say: Why him? She still hasn't forgiven me. I don't know whether even Pa—' She begins to sob.

'Your *father*! He is your complete slave.' He is thinking of the man with chapped hands he found sitting at her bedside in silence, who stood up and said, *Eh, eh, one minute only.*

He strokes her forehead, surprised. He saw her as exemplary, as existing wholly in the present. And here she is snivelling over old wounds. Her own, of course: she's wholly preoccupied with herself. That he *wants* her to be is a separate matter.

She opens half an eye to look at him and the tear she was holding in spills out. He catches that glance – an ancient glitter – and sees she's checking her effect on him. A dramatizer! But of course, she does puppets: that's her *job*. Still, it's a surprise for a phlegmatic man who has never considered the effect he has on people.

Morgan simply laughed at her, but then his childhood inoculated him against self-pity.

Once in a childhood book Maya came upon a line about a king. *To ambition he added sufferance, but to sufferance assuredness.* She took it to mean that endurance and conviction could carry you through. Now she must prove her royal faith. Will it hold in love? In disease? Or is she a commoner after all?

'Look in the mirror.'

'What, yaa!' She cringes, but goes. There's nothing new, but she sees the nimbus he put there.

'Listen to the crows!'

'They must be harassing the hawks.'

They go and stand at the window where the cooler used to be. The cassia treetops are rippling in the breeze, pale new green among last year's darker growth. Hordes of yellow butterflies occupy the middle air as if by agreement with the crows. A dog barks a deep big dog's bark, a private well-fed rich dog's bark. At the public tap by the city wall a naked boy picks up a bucketful of water and empties the whole lot over himself at one go. Lev feels it rush over his skin; Maya's eyes shine as she watches, smiling her wide smile when she finds they are watching the same action. The boy is shouting with happiness.

She kisses Lev's hands, then each finger, one by one. She's addicted to the scent of his fingertips, spiked with the smell of each place they've visited during the night. He looks down at the tangled nest of her hair. Every night she draws him back from that arid plateau he dreamed he was stranded on. The freshness of this morning is the freshness of a youth he'd forgotten so completely its return leaves him dazed and disbelieving.

One night they sleep out on the terrace sharing her camp cot; it collapses under them. They stay aboard the wreck, complete the damage, till the snake they have become arches up and topples slowly to the floor. Cold grain of sandstone, eyes of magnolia opening in the dark. The moon stares, the sill-cotton looks on. She holds him by the root, this weird self-willed doll. Morning finds him tangled in the sheets, back in the twisted hammock of the bed. The sheets have a sun-flower pattern, yellow on a blue ground, like some small island nation's flag. Now she does paint him. Quickly, as he sleeps, so the colours run, gold into ultramarine.

'Me?' he says, waking, pleased. He was never painted before.

Three-quarter heads, profiles, any number of half-finished sketches; some hardly begun when he left what he was doing and walked away. Caught cross-legged on the swing seat, or reading, holding up binoculars, rubbing his eyes, waving her off.

Sleep is the only sin. She talks him back from its brink.

'So the older sister, the goodygood, came back to visit Leela in mid-term and brought her chocolate barfi and cashew nuts and almonds and boxes of raisins and we gorged them in the middle of the night. She was still in a state of shock and whispered all her wedding-night secrets to Leela and Leela whispered them to me and we were rolling about laughing. "*Such* kisses! So *unhygienic!*" We laughed so much Leela spilt a whole bottle of multivitamin capsules, so there we were under the beds looking for these red-and-black capsules in the moonlight because Miss Govardhan's room was six beds away and she would have *crucified* us if we'd turned the lights on.'

Leela he knows intimately, he's heard of her in such detail. He even knows what her husband looks like, for godsake. He knows all her friends, the ones she's stopped visiting since he arrived, the ones she's warned off now he's here. And still not one question about his past, Biosecuritat.

'So when we had gathered them all up Leela takes a pair of scissors and cuts open each capsule and shakes the powder into the bottle. I said: "What are you doing?" She said: "I can't take those now they've been on the ground, yaa. It's not *hygienic!*" How we laughed!'

How they laugh. She is seated in the cane chair with her feet propped one on the glasstop wicker table and one on the middle shelf of the bookshelf and her hair unbrushed so its tangles glitter in the light from the lampshade that hangs over her head like a perm machine in a foreign magazine. He is gazing at her, thinking: How can I capture this, *how?*

Time is running through his fingers. He has a visa.

Twenty-Four

'Put it down and I'll take it.'

She won't take a knife from his hands. They are breakfasting on mangoes. He has learnt to appreciate the fruit; now he must learn to accept her superstitions, this scientist.

'Don't keep saying my skin is lovely or it'll get spoilt.'

'How?'

'Just. It's called nazar, the evil eye. You're supposed to say the opposite.'

'You look very ugly in a towel.'

Her wide smile.

He touches her. 'Crocodile skin.'

She's laughing her scratchy laugh.

They walk down Nevsky now business is back to normal.

'Why are you walking like that?'

'Like what?'

'Like some kind of hero.'

'*Am* I!' He blushes because it's true he was swaggering. He wants to show her off. She wants to hide him and he can't understand why.

They pass the Changezi chicken takeaway where spatchcocked birds roast in hell and the scent to his nostrils is heaven.

'Go on. But you'll have to finish it. I don't want it in the fridge.'

They sit in the park where he met Laiq, on the very bench. Beyond the hedge the masseur with the pop eyes passes clinking his oil bottles. The shoeshine boy comes up in Alex's T-shirt and Lev lets him polish the Batas he bought in Peter while he eats.

'What are we?' Maya asks, lifting one arm and freezing like an acrobat. '*The Moscow State Circus?*'

People are staring at them as at a tableau.

Lev finds another poster in his head. '*Guard Against Feudalism.*'

'Let's go, yaa,' she says, tiring of the eyes. 'You can keep your chicken in the fridge.'

But Lev has already handed it to the boy.

'Let's stop at our phalwallah.' She means to restock the fridge with mangoes, the hot blunt langras she prefers to the civilized dasheri.

'You see that guy?' Lev nods at the masseur as they leave.

'The malishwallah?'

'He's not a malishwallah.'

'What do you mean?'

'Watch him. He'll look at us just now.'

The man circles the park just inside the hedge, clacking his oils and studying his feet as he goes. When he looks up it's directly at Lev and Maya.

'See?'

'So what! Everybody's staring.'

'But not everybody has been through my suitcase.'

'What are you talking about?'

'He followed me to the Serai. He must have got hold of the room key.'

'Are you sure?'

Lev stares at the circling man and waits to catch his eye. 'I'm sure.'

They walk home in silence. She goes to the phone and dials. Sunderam knows her voice, puts the call through.

'Pa? *Why* are you having Lev followed?' She has wrapped the phone cord around her wrist.

'Putli! How are you? We never hear from you nowadays.'

'Pa, don't maro lines. Just take your man off Lev.'

'Baccha, now you're talking in riddles.'

'Pa, don't piss around!'

'Tch tch – *language*. For this I sent you to Risingholme?'

'Oh sorry – *please* don't piss around.'

'That's better. Now listen once and for all. I am not having your friend followed.'

Maya absorbs this in silence. 'But if you aren't then who is?'

'How do I know, beti? Maybe the same people who tap my line.'

'*Your* line is tapped!'

'Routinely.'

'This one?'

Jain was thinking of the home line, but he lifts his bushy eyebrows. 'Maybe this one too.'

Maya feels a wave of panic. She doesn't know whether she should just put down the phone.

'Baccha, are you there?'

'Pa, what's happening?' Her voice has shrunk to nothing.

'I don't know, Putli. I didn't know anything about this tailing business. Listen, why don't you come and see us. Your mother—'

'Worries about me, I know.'

Jain sighs and examines his raw quicks. At times like this he wants early retirement. So he can talk to her any time, without the blank third face listening in. He needs to get something across and she won't come over.

'Listen, Putli.'

Maya knows this tone, loves it.

'All things considered, why don't you—?'

'If you're going to say "marry him", forget it.'

'Marry him.'

'He's already married, Pa.'

The Chief Commissioner is quiet for a moment while he masters his anger. Now he *would* like to put a man on this foreigner. He'd do more.

'Pa, don't jump to conclusions.' Her voice breaks, the Risingholme toughness gone. 'It just happened, yaa. I made it happen.'

Again Jain is silent. He could try his posh college form; he was secretary of the Wodehouse Society. He hears the words before they leave him and cancels the whole line: *You're supposed to go for the unmarried ones, Putli.*

'I don't know, beti. What can I say? I don't understand. Anyway, this is not the place. Just come and see us.'

He puts the phone down. Maybe his wife's way is better after all. He swallows and tastes banter gone sour. Is this also the legacy of Jeeves? The curse of the English Medium? Which travelled here like some vivid exotic lily to choke the waterways of his forefathers' clear faith. He's tempted to scold

Sunderam for something, anything, so sends him for a walk instead.

'Another father would thrash sense into her,' Mrs Jain complained this morning, in English.

'Another mother—' Jain stopped himself before he said something irretrievable.

He closes his eyes. And knows why he can't marry his Putli off to any of the candidates Madhu produces. His wife speaks out of frustration, not anger, but he wants to tell her what she seems not to have noticed, that this child – not the other, who died – is extraordinary. How can she even begin to consider her latest find? They're so bland, these stripling foreign service mannequins. So common, these glossy boys from princely schools. Or the interested neighbour's interesting son. How can they give her to some hot senti-mental sportsman who stammers out endearments she'll only laugh at?

And this girl goes and falls for a foreigner twice her age!

Twenty-Five

'There's a place I want you to see.' Morgan has turned up in his red silk shirt to take them out.

'What's the matter?'

'Lev is being followed.'

'Followed?'

Morgan's smile dies. He looks across at Lev and then down at his keys, which he examines one by one. 'I suppose,' he says, picking his words, 'if I carried the recipe for anthrax biscuits in my head I would expect to be —' he looks especially hard for inspiration — 'marked.'

Lev's eyes are shut, wishing the world away and himself with it. At the word *anthrax* a thousand red dots seethe up under his eyelids. Can Meschersky be far behind? He isn't. Lev flinches and opens his eyes wide.

'What's this?' Maya asks, seeing there's something Morgan knows that she doesn't.

'Know-how.'

Lev has spoken at last. He has a sudden urge to check his ticket and his hand goes halfway to his waistcoat before he realizes he's not wearing it. He's got careless lately. Lately! The whole month rises up and accuses him.

Maya makes the connection now with the Ministry of Defence. She's never bothered to ask him how it went, or why he lost interest, and she looks guiltily at him.

'We'll think of something,' Morgan decides. 'There must be someone we can talk to.'

He takes them to Hex, the new discotheque in Saket. They drink vodka under a neon ceiling of lime-green snakes and tangerine ladders. Maya dances with Morgan because Lev won't dance. Her dance is a wild free thing beside which even Morgan's looks tinged with self-regard. Two European women come in. Morgan beckons them over; one of them he knows.

'Your countryman,' he says, indicating Lev and the women are instantly on their guard. One glances down at her skirt.

'Lena and—'

'Lydia.'

'—Lydia are on holiday. They know this city better than I do.'

Lena is a bleach blonde from Kiev. She has done nothing else to her hair; here she doesn't need to. In a cableknit sweater she would look like a librarian, but in a black satin halter, the bow drooping between her shoulderblades, she could be an indulgence. Lydia, who looked down at her brief skirt, is little more than a schoolgirl. Her holiday has just begun, but in two weeks' time a policewoman in a khaki sari will escort her to the airport. The girls exchange wry words with Lev and move to a far table. In twenty minutes they have left with separate men.

'Two thousand rupees,' Morgan says on the way home when Maya asks how much they charge.

'Which one?'

'Lena, if you must know.' Morgan looks out at the

recurring ads for seven-rupee softserve cones stapled to every lamppost on the median strip. They flip past like game cards. It was a favour, he would like to explain, an extended loan. When did he ever have to pay?

Lev turns his head to face the window.

'Too much, or not enough?' Morgan wonders sideways at him but gets no reply.

Maya, who can read dudgeon in her man, asks from the back seat: 'What's the problem? Think of all the people who sell their minds every day.'

Morgan winces. So Lev hasn't told her, then. He drives deeper into the black night.

'Look!' he points.

Rising out of the dark scrub Lev sees a floodlit tower.

Maya looks too. It's not often she gets to come this way. The tower looks like an inverted telescope, ribbed and fretted redstone, the eyepiece at the top worked in ivory. 'The Kutub Minar,' she says, 'Razia's father built that.'

Morgan feels a stab of pride: show the foreigner. 'It's a thousand years old.'

Lev raises his eyebrows and seems to answer Morgan's unasked question. 'We were just building Moscow.'

'Delhi was already old,' Morgan brags, but checks himself. Parts of *New* Delhi already look decrepit. Night is the time to show Delhi off.

'It's our Eiffel Tower,' Maya says. 'There's one in white stone at the northern end of the city.'

Morgan looks at her in the mirror. 'And one in black in the west,' he adds.

Lev turns in his seat. 'And the pink one. Where is that?' He's learnt her ways already.

'Swallowed up in history,' Morgan says. 'Or romance, whichever came first.'

'I thought poetry came first,' Maya ribs him.

'True.' He raises a solemn finger. 'First and last.'

'False.' Lev hesitates only because he can't use his own language. 'Matter is first and last.'

'Science offers proof.'

Lev shrugs. 'Crash this car and you'll find out.'

'The poetry of instant death.'

'What's poetic about death?' Meschersky looms up before Lev's jaded eye like a roadblock. 'Have you watched a man disintegrate?'

'Ah, I said death, not dying. Dying you can do in many ways, but *death*? Only through poetry.'

'Come on, yaa. Talk about things.'

'Poetry *is* things. As close as words can come.'

'QED!' Maya shouts and claps her hands over Morgan's eyes.

'*Yesu Masih!*' He slams on his brakes and veers blinded to the left. 'Are you fucking *mad*!'

The Zen stands trembling in the starlight and Maya is laughing deliriously. Lev, shaken, manages a weak smile. Morgan leaps out of the car in a rage and wrenches open the back door.

'*IDIOT!*' He wants to drag her from the car and shake her and cover her in kisses.

Lev gets out. The tyres on his side are inches from a ditch, not deep but deep enough to have rolled the car. He leans up against the back of the Zen and lights a cigarette. He is thinking he would like to live here where the air is warm, but he'd like to die at home, under his own sky.

'What are you thinking?' Maya has pacified Morgan and come around to join Lev.

He tells her.

'What does it matter where you die?' she says lightly. 'You die in your body. Not in Russia or India.'

They have left the main road and its lights. Beyond the floodlit minar and the aureole that surrounds it, there's a brown wash of secondary light that turns grey to indigo. Indigo thorn trees and bushes throng the middle distance; only the nearer vegetation looks plausible. A nightjar is hooting monotonously. Here, in this seeming wild, is where Delhi stood a thousand years ago. Razia would have ridden over this ground.

A man comes by pushing a heavy load on his bicycle. He looks like the malishwallah and for a moment Lev has a mad impulse to knock him over and accuse him.

Maya has walked a short way along the road and is looking around her, like an animal scenting the air. *Here*, she is thinking, and *here* and *here* and *here*.

Beyond the roadside ditch is a shadowy heap of stone; this corner of Delhi is littered with medieval monuments. She can make out a small dome and what might be a ruined arch. In the arch she fancies she sees a standing figure. The more she stares the more it looks like the eroded godhead on her roof. As if all imagining, every image or figure or puppet, were a quest for one irreducible shape. She turns and runs towards the car, waving her arms spookily and hooting.

'*Hoo-ooo-ooo!*'

Morgan sees her come and turns his back on her. She comes running up behind and jumps on him, clawing at his shoulders and hooting. 'Churail! *Churail!*' He gallops a short way with her then snorts and pretends to throw her. Lev watches them indulgently.

'Chalo,' Morgan says, depositing her on the car bonnet. 'I'm hungry.' They climb back into the Zen. He switches on the ignition and turns to her. 'You die in your *mind*, by the way.'

He heads for a roadside stall by the Mehrauli fire station for kathi kababs wrapped in rumalis. The kebabs cheer Lev more than the kutub, and there is a skewered cheese variety that satisfies Maya. Fed, they drive to Vasant to the bouncer-ringed ironclad Fly and drink tequilas at the bar. This time Lev does dance, on a strobe-lit floor, the broken puppet dance that passed beneath his feet on the night-black Fontanka. Maya's teeth flash on his disintegrating form; later she will put him together again in the dark.

They're singing madly in the car on the way home, film oldies no one knows all the words of. Even Lev recognizes one from a time when Bombay movies were popular in Russia.

Na yeh chand hoga, na taaren rahengey,
Magar ham hamesha tumharey rahengey.

Maya, strapped into the front seat now, turns around to translate for Lev. 'He says: "There won't be this moon, there'll be no stars, but wherever I am I'll always be yours."'

'From *Shart*,' Morgan hazards the movie.

'Rubbish! From *Awaara*. Raj Kapoor is sitting on the roof with what'shername.'

'Raj Kapoor, I know Raj Kapoor.'

'*Shart*, men! Hemant Kumar did the songs.'

Morgan looks sideways at Maya. She's started on another

song and is laughing out na-nas for the words she doesn't know. He switches off the AC because she's rolled down the window to share her tuneless voice with the night. He looks in the mirror. Lev's face is shining, this knight of the sorrowful countenance. His head is thrown back, his eyes shut tight and his mouth open in a howl of pure pleasure.

Poor puppets! Nobody here will be as happy again.

Morgan drops them at the foot of the stair and beeps as he drives away. He has the whole city to cross all over again, but the drive will soothe his sudden fretfulness. Maya feels about in her bag for the huge skeleton key.

'Shit! Look what I brought home.' She holds up an ashtray of brushed aluminium whose wings conjure a stylized fly. Lev remembers watching her fingers stroke its veined facets at the bar. Upstairs, she puts it down on the cane bookshelf.

'Morgan will take it back.'

The resignation in her voice says: *I suppose I must tell you.* She looks at Lev, undoing his laces. One month. They must compress everything into that space.

'I pick up things. That's why I don't go into a new place by myself. The shopkeepers around here know me. I've warned them, they know. But it's still hard – because of Pa. They know who I am. So I've told them, Morgan's told them, to take whatever it is off me or else to put it on my bill. They think I'm mad anyway. Maybe I am. Am I mad, Lev?'

'If you're mad . . .'

His voice trails off. What hope is there for me? he was going to say. When did he ever know anyone so independent of things? He lets it go. Almost everything important between them will remain unsaid.

She shakes her head in turn because he never completes a sentence; because, already, she doesn't need him to.

Then she lifts a hand and rolls down the shutters of his eyes and he knows why. The slow sad material dance of undressing. She still can't do that in front of him.

Lev's security waistcoat is sweaty, his passport slicked, the ticket damp. Maya unhooks her earrings and lets them drop on the dressing table beside the singing bowl, seed pearls in gold. For the first time she notices a territoriality to the dressing table top. His things, hers.

In the bowl is another jewel: a beetle, interstellar blue. Its armour is minute and impregnable, dead armour. The beetle's upturned legs wave a semaphore: not dead after all. Something in the bowl attracts insects that the monsoon drives in out of the rain. Beetles, hoppers, even moths, seek out the bright fatal well of it. Witched there by the radiance in it, or the pleasure of those treacherous smooth slopes. Fragments of emerald and turquoise and coal, they bring their strength and beauty to its depths and discover too late its hold. Of late Maya's taken to watching them toil up the sides and slip back down again and again. By morning, mostly, they're still. Or they expire in a blaze of wings.

'It's quiet nowadays,' Lev nods at the bowl from where he lies in bed with his arms folded under his head. He too has noticed the trapped insects. That have found heaven: they can have anything except their freedom.

Her shrug says it's just a thing, like the ashtray. Morgan gave it to her and she's passed it on. It could be a floating trophy. *I have you*, her eyes say. You *calm me*.

What do you see *in me?* When she looks at him he has that sensation of falling, an actual physical faintness. A tissue-like thinness all around him. Already the city, the flat, this room, has the feel of a stage. Her certainty, he sees, the certainty that he fell in love with, enables the illusion. It has made the pretended more real than reality itself. Wherever that is.

Dance and vodka are still in their blood, warm under his sliding eyelid, prickling in her fingertips. The humidity is so rich it all but condenses on the walls. A scrappy lightning looks in by a different window each time. The table lamp on the floor vibrates to a growl of thunder; the red shapes they make play on the ceiling.

'Talk to me.'

He wakes with a start and slides back into sleep.

'Lyovochka, talk to me.'

He forces his eyes open but can think of nothing to say. All his life it's struck him that there's less to say than appears, less than people make out. And he's never liked the diminutive she dug out of him.

'I have trouble talking. Even to my son.'

'I don't want to hear about him.'

'What can I say?'

'Something. Anything. Try. You're allowed to make mistakes.'

He takes her face between his hands and feels the past dissolve. 'Maya.'

'No, not me. You're changing the subject.'

'What's the subject?'

'You. For a change.'

'I'm the subject?' He panics. But there's nothing there! he wants to protest. He's always been invisible to himself; if he had his way he'd be invisible to others too. 'All right. Tell me. Why did you pick me?'

She needs no prompting. Immediately she's back in her workroom on that first Sunday, looking down at him.

'Because you looked so . . .' For once she will wait as long as it takes to pin that moment down. 'Patient.'

And at once he sees it. He is her natural opposite, this little woman who flings herself into things, who barely comes up to his chest. Again he's impressed by her way of going right to the heart of the matter. He lies there full of admiration, as if he were the younger, callow one.

'You were standing there like a tree, yaa. And old Sweeney was going on about something, and you were just nodding and listening.'

She's found her listener too, this talker. 'You looked so . . . calm.'

'Maybe.'

He's not just calm, he's content. She lets him forget. He hears her out and knows she's listing qualities she covets. But she needs to be happy, not content; look how quickly she goes from gloom to bliss and back. As if her happiness were simply a forgetting of unhappiness.

The lamp is off but Maya's eyes go on drawing in the half dark. Lev is fast asleep on his side, with one arm extended so the hand hangs off the mattress and the middle finger brushes the floor. Her own finger traces his outline just above the skin. The line her drawing master noticed was a line of longing that pushes out interminably. A lover is a painful thing, but it's not him she's drawing. She's tracing a sorrow that runs ahead of separation.

She leans over him in the dark. What business has he appearing whole like this? He belongs in her dreams, always about to appear.

She's alone. Has always been alone with her longing, a hunger that any present lover could only kill.

She passes a hand over him in the dark. No strings there. He too is alone.

She lies down beside him on the mattress with her back to him in animal resignation and draws up her knees till they are almost under her chin and pushes back the hair from off her forehead and falls asleep with one hand resting lightly on her own shoulder.

Twenty-Six

Mist – in summer! in Delhi! – at four in the morning, and a damp chill under the fan so the lovers draw closer and fit together like the pieces of an ancient puzzle. Above the mist the clouds regroup and agree to rain at daybreak, not pelting monsoon rain but an even fall, light and cool and steady as Petersburg wet.

The young pipal tree on the roof trembles with pleasure. It puts out one sticky pink heart and watches it turn green. Its roots dig deeper into the crack they've made in the grouting. What does it care for the ruination of a house? What does it care for lovers? Its lover is the house it destroys. It could hug this mansion to death.

This morning, after she has watched him shave because she loves that, Maya decides she will make Lev parathas for breakfast. She promised them, rashly, the morning he made little blinies they ate with mango jam. Also, she has noticed the neighbours looking curiously at her and knows the smell of cooking will travel downstairs in a kind of vindication. Distant relations, and poor, the downstairs Jains regard her with a compassionate scorn she finds infuriating. Anyway, she associates Sunday with parathas from Risingholme. There are some leftover potatoes she can use for filling and the rest she will make plain.

He watches the hawks while she works.

She starts with more dough than she needs because she decided to empty the flour jar; it seemed pointless to leave three-quarters of a cup at the bottom. The potato filling is frying with coarsely chopped onion and fenugreek; it catches while she rolls the dough, so some is lost. She spoons the remainder in equal portions onto the rounds and wraps each into a bundle for flouring and rolling afresh. Tedious work. The frying she learnt from her mother, watching out of the corner of her eye. The trick is to dry cook them first on one side before spreading the oil. They come out well: four filled parathas her mother would be proud of. The plain parathas are less successful. They must be folded and greased like pastry; oil squirts annoyingly from the folds in rolling. The first one is passable, a cone more than a quarter circle. The next rolls out like a map of Africa. She could stop here happily.

Lev wanders in, the field glasses in his hands. 'Smells good,' he says, kissing the top of her head.

She is trying to rescue Africa and warns him off with a tiny toss of the head.

'Africa!'

Another day she might have laughed; today it's a compressed smile. Six to go. How she hates cooking! Is this the other side of the love tape?

'Australia,' he suggests the next time, looking over her shoulder, and he's right again.

'Piss off, Lev.'

It's a new tone; he blinks and stays away. Her map-making

continues. The terrible thing is she hears his voice in her head: South America, Borneo, Madagascar. Please God, unGod, release me. But the dough balls are an impassable chain of mountains; she's stuck in this kitchen for ever. To crown it all he's been cleaning in here again, scrubbing the benchtops, polishing all available glass, scouring the taps. He's even taken down the old thermos, unscrewed more plastic bits than she knew it came in, and washed the silver bubble of the vacuum flask; it lies on its side in the dishdrainer like a submarine from – her latest misshape tells her – Atlantis.

It's hot work, even with the exhaust fan going, but it will end. It has to. Then why are there still two lumps of shitty dough?

And then it's done. *Done!*

She wants to sweep the whole lot, rolling pin, pan, stove and all into the sink, but contents herself with chucking the slotted spoon. Its handle nicks the flask, which miraculously doesn't break.

They eat at the glasstop wicker table to Lev's loud compliments. Potato pancakes to rival the ones his mother used to make.

'Parathas, not pancakes.'

'OK, OK.'

Just then there's a shattering sound from the kitchen, a glassy explosion like a light bulb bursting, but loud. They rise together and make for the kitchen and stand there staring.

The room is utterly transformed. It's covered in tiny mirrors scattered like confetti. Shrapnel, millions of pieces – not thousands, not hundreds of thousands – millions and millions from the exploded flask. They lie in drifts on the floor, on the benchtops, on any level surface, a dust cloth of powdered glass spread over everything. The scene is strangely inert; it might have happened ten thousand years ago. They're in a prehistoric tomb. With simple breakage you see the line where the material gave. This is destruction of another order, atomic, irrecoverable: matter has simply collapsed. The only recognizable pieces are from either end. Lev's image appears in the bottom, upside down.

'Poor flask!'

There's blame in that cry. Flask, this is Lev; Lev, this was flask.

She switches on the light and the room blazes up like cold fire. Glass dust cascades off the light switch.

'Well, you like cleaning up,' she says. 'I think I'll take a walk.'

'But you—' Lev's mouth drops open. He points to the slotted spoon. He saw that happen. It's still lying where it fell, only now it's coated with glass.

'The flask didn't *need* washing, Lev.'

And she steps out, hating herself because now she's committed to going. She could still stop, but she has her pride.

She walks without seeing the world, looks through Laiq, who looks through her.

When she returns the mess is cleared away, the dishes done. Lev is sitting on the swing seat writing something. Today the Cyrillic script is a blind wall, not the beautiful thing she sees in Morgan's books. A wall topped with broken glass for keeping out.

'A letter home?'

He looks up at her. Is this Maya? The voice, not just the tone, has changed. She's never mentioned Alla before, even indirectly.

It is a letter to Alla, but here is an irony: in it he was trying to express Maya. Trying also to express himself, his awe, his gratitude, his need, without causing pain. He was stuck because he was trying to say all that without saying it, to confess without confessing. Maya, now, would just say what had to be said; there's a purity of response in her that puts him to shame. But is her certainty just inflexibility? Has she had time to discover her limitations? She has the courage of her intuitions, but look, she picked a married man.

'As a matter of fact, no.' He holds it up. 'A memo to myself.'

Faultless idiom always sounds strange on his lips, she thinks. So does a lie. But she will forgive him because he so often overlooks her little sins.

'Lev!' She drops into his lap, onto the letter. 'I'm sorry.'

He folds his arms about her and they sit swinging in silence until she starts to giggle.

'What did you do with the pieces?'

'They're wrapped in your latest newspaper.'

Merited sarcasm: the paper is three months old. Morgan must have brought it, because she doesn't get one delivered. The world could be ending and she wouldn't know. There's a war on the border and Maya hasn't heard.

Twenty-Seven

A drum is beating somewhere and it's not Lev's heart.

It's further out, and faster. The beat is not battle red or doom black; it's the white of invitation. Something Morgan said to him runs through Lev's head as he walks towards the drum. They were talking of Delhi's invaders and Morgan spoke of Timur the Lame.

'Tamburlane. They said of his battles that on the first day all his tents were white. The second day they were red. The third day, black.'

Lev walks towards the white sound. Sweat dripping off his forehead into the ginger of his eyebrows. He's walking to clear his head. He is running out of time. What he wants is years, what he has is weeks. He has just called home to see if Alla got his letter. She did.

Silence. Explain yourself.

But what can he say? He's here but he's stopped looking. He's found something, though it's not what he was looking for.

There are two sides to his brain and she fills all of one.

'Look at you!' Admiration blazes up in him.

He just left her at the corner of Nevsky.

'What?' She can sense nonsense coming and smiles in advance.

'You make everything look cheap.'

'What are you talking about?' But she knows.

'Everything around you, the whole city.' He gestures. 'All this.'

This Nevsky or that, he's played the scene over twice. The sides are reversible.

Now he's walking to clear his head. This drumbeat has nothing to do with her, this railing owes her nothing, the red stone beyond it was here centuries before her.

It's a man in a skullcap with a long drum strung about his neck and a curved drumstick like a floating rib. He is standing at a gate above which a banner has been stretched announcing some event in two sets of script. Lev can make out neither: no English here. Behind him three ragged boys plead with the ancient gatekeeper. The drummer drums with his back to the gate, a poor puppet not dressed for the occasion, simply hired and stood there and told to drum. He bows ceremoniously as Lev comes up but doesn't waver in his drumming.

There is a grassed amphitheatre beyond the gate with four poles marking a square of raked earth at the centre. The poles are bandaged in red and white cloth below and strung with bunting up above. Tied to one of the poles is a loud-speaker.

'Kushti,' explains one of the urchins, and demonstrates on the friend who hangs about his neck. Wrestling.

'Five rupees.'

The old man's legs, clad in spotless white pyjamas, form a wicket. Lev buys a ticket and ducks under the gate chain.

The legs swivel to let him through and return to lock the urchins out. They could be made of iron. There are perhaps a hundred people already there, seated on grassy knolls, and more are trickling in. On the far side, directly in front of the pit, are benches, but these have already been taken. The few empty spaces on the front bench are evidently reserved and nobody is inclined to try them. A figure detaches itself from the crowd and comes forward.

'Laiq!'

Laiq is wearing his white pyjama kurta and black Quo Vadis sandals. He has left the caged bird on the ground before his bench seat. He leads Lev back to the spot and makes room for him. Laiq is one of the notables. When another retired wrestler comes in with his trainees in tow, the boys duck their heads and make to touch Laiq's feet. He stops them ritually, casually, but heads turn in the crowd. The boys strip down to their clouts for the early rounds under his eye. The microphone squeals as the announcer warms up.

'Put some go into it,' he heckles the drummer. 'No, put some come!'

The crowd like that. The size of the purse depends on the takings at the gate. Laiq turns to Lev. It was just as well you didn't come the last time, he says. The show was cancelled. This is the first wrestling since the plague.

A referee has entered the ring, a man with a beard and clean upper lip and a way of hanging his head as if embarrassed by the whistle that never leaves his mouth. He is immediately thronged by boys in clouts looking to have their bouts numbered. He doles out sanction, the whistle piping softly with each breath, and they pair off, shake hands at the sideline, and line up from light to heavy.

The boys wrestle first, two matches at a time because there are many and because it's the heavyweights the crowd has come to see. The very smallest grapple like spiders, so light their strength must be taken on trust. The slap their thighs and feint like adults but fall so lightly it's all the crowd can do to keep from laughing. The middleweights, young men of nineteen or twenty, lift the tone. Their muscles are real, their grappling a thing the eye can follow. Circling, their feet come down with a caution that draws Lev into the fight. One pair come to grips so quickly the announcer is won over.

'Here's wrestling, friends! Saharanpur has brought some goods to town.'

'Black one from Saharanpur,' Laiq informs Lev, 'other one Delhi.'

The Saharanpur man is stringy, a head taller than his opponent. He has the advantage of reach but is thrown from below when Delhi sneaks a side-on tackle. But a lightning hand to the ground saves the visitor. He springs back up and pins Delhi on the rebound.

'Wrestling! Wrestling!'

The fight has gone out of the ring and the referee leads them back to the centre with his breathy whistle and his shamefaced smile. *Here!* his finger admonishes and the men begin again. It's a draw in the end, the first of the evening, after a line of throws and miracle escapes. The announcer commends both men to the crowd as the referee holds up their arms; the award is equal money to each.

Laiq joins in the applause reluctantly; at one time he would have called for the fight to go on to the finish, but now he nods slowly, peaceably, the nod of middle age.

Just when the heavies are due a black raincloud ships up

and stands over the arena. The announcer conjures it away with his patter. Vendors move through the crowd selling paper cones of roasted gram. Laiq buys one and offers it to Lev, but Lev is cautious now. The bird isn't: it swallows grain after grain and when it has had enough lifts its head and sweeps the crowd with a vicious fusillade.

Le sale pataka le sale pataka le sale pataka

The heavyweights come up, a single pair whose bodies the crowd's eyes have kept returning to as they stood waiting on the sidelines. Big men, their shaven heads only make them look bigger. The shorter and darker of the two has two rolls of muscle where a neck might ordinarily narrow. The taller has his reserve lower down, spread across the shoulders and again below the shoulderblades. He has an arrogant eye and bearing and has not once looked at his opponent since they shook hands at the pairing off. His opponent is less aware of the crowd; he appears to live inside himself, looking out from time to time at the uncut monsoon grass, the pit, the man he is to fight. His meekness does not bode well.

They enter the ring and are introduced one by one, the taller of the Bulbuliya ghotal behind the great mosque, the shorter of the Hanuman ghotal in Shahdara across the river.

'Shake hands. *Go!*'

The referee chops lightly at the air between them and steps back.

The men dip heads and lock eyes, transformed into a single slowly revolving creature. Their feet lift in slow motion, their hands make dreaming passes. Head, neck, head, a grapnel hand strikes and falls, strikes and falls. The tall one slaps aside the other's questing arm and charges in. A simple lover's grip: the hands clasped behind the other's back and straining downwards, lifting the other to pull him down, looking to break him where he stands. The crowd make disbelieving noises; even the announcer is silenced by the brazen unorthodoxy of it.

It doesn't work. It's too early for that. They part and dip down again, then rush in simultaneously and tuck chin for chin into the shoulder opposite. The dark one looking down the tawny slope of the other's back, the other's eyes fixed on the distant wall of the Red Fort.

Lev is reminded of Maya's way of looking up from under a lowered forehead. Laiq too is focused on the taller man; he has money on him, but more than that he seems to be looking through the man's eyes. He's twenty-six again, a young lion staring over the shoulder of his opponent – at what? At what, Laiq? He still can't say. All his life he's closed with bodies, and made do with their surfaces when part of him would like to – what? Storm through to the other side? God forbid! He jerks his head, a middle-aged man's tic: What then? He shuts his eyes. To burrow in, turn himself inside out? The uncle who raised him, whose room he now occupies in the house where Nabi was doorman, taught him the art hold by hold in a marrow patch, but couldn't help him there.

Laiq opens his eyes. The grass has grown under his feet. Lev is sitting there spellbound by the Bulbuliya's eyes. Another clasp has come apart and the men are grappling once more.

'Tall one looking for this,' Laiq says and taps Lev's shoulder.

'Shoulder throw?'

'Dhobi pat. He is good dhobi. Wash clean.'

But the bullneck will not be thrown. He rams his head between the other's thighs – suicide, suicide! – and goes to lift him from underneath like a table.

'Coolie!' a wag calls from the crowd.

'Fool, fool,' Laiq mumbles, pleased for the lion but sorry for the bull. The Bulbuliya at once locks the offered head in a nutcracker grip that has the man's eyes bulging. Lev can feel the beleaguered blood banging on the eardrums and is relieved when the head slips out and rests a moment, dazed and defenceless. Instinct keeps the man on his hands and knees, and for a long interval the two are a nest of tables, the Bulbuliya on top. Then, casually, the tall one rises, holding the other one down with one hand. The bull makes no attempt to rise. The crowd see his predicament and murmur.

'Bullfrog,' the wag calls.

Get up and fight, the lion mimes. He grips the man's red clout and drags him back into the centre of the pit, his buttocks in the air, then kicks the man's legs apart, little delicate kicks at the ankles, almost lover's kicks.

The rested bull turns and attacks. He scissors the lion at the crotch and turns him in the air so the two flip over. Now the red langot is uppermost, but only for a second: Laiq's man slips out so nimbly the crowd applaud without the announcer's prompting. He turns at once and gets his washerman's grip. The red langot flashes through the air. It's all over.

Or is it? It's a short whistle.

The bull landed on one shoulder, the referee rules. The two men face off again, resume their circling. Then the Bulbuliya stops. He takes a handful of earth and applies it to his opponent's sweaty shoulders, one at a time, then to the man's head. The bull replies in kind, but the crowd snigger. And in no time he's back on his hands and knees, the safest refuge for a tired man.

The crowd lose patience, the Bulbuliya walks away in disgust and returns with a double handful of earth that he pours ceremoniously on the other's head. It's a draw, the referee rules to end the stalemate. The bull gets up but the other won't shake his hand.

The light is failing and the crowd begin to leave, unsatisfied. The masseur is there, Lev notices. There's a sullenness in the air despite the antics of the youngest wrestlers, who have taken over the arena. Laiq and Lev make for the gate, passing the bull who glooms, tamping the ground under his feet. They've reached the gate when the crowd appears to have turned back. The warriors have agreed to one more round. Laiq and Lev return to the ringside. No sitters now; the crowd press in close.

The wrestlers lock at once. The Bulbuliya is on top again, the other man back in his bullfrog position. This time the lion rides across the red langot and hooks the man's right arm from underneath. At once Laiq knows what he's about. Little by little the Bulbuliya pulls up on the arm while forcing the other down with his hips; little by little he works the arm up and grasps it at the wrist with his free hand. Now his left arm is free to hook the man's head. Laiq nods approval at the cunning of it.

'Science.' He taps Lev on both shoulders as if to say: it's all over.

Signs, Lev hears. Bit by bit he sees the bullfrog's shoulders topple towards the ground. But there's a stubbornness in the man which refuses defeat. From time to time the Bulbuliya applies pressure on the right arm, as if to say: Roll, I have you. But the other won't roll. No pain will make him give in. And then there's a snap, the dull unmistakable clack of bone dislodged. The crowd sighs and freezes. A howl breaks from the injured man and trails off into moaning.

The Bulbuliya springs back, letting go the arm. It falls like a useless thing, a broken doll's arm. The crowd press forward to inspect the damage, even as the referee tries to push them back. The announcer is pleading with those in front to move away. Laiq steps back and away from his sometime protégé. There are tears in the lion's eyes; he can't understand why the man refused to yield. He's amazed at how quickly the moral ground has shifted.

'You can do something,' the announcer turns to Laiq, the bonesetter.

Laiq is reluctant. Someone from the injured man's side, some relative, should ask.

'He is one of us,' the announcer counters. He means one of the family of wrestlers.

'He won't wrestle again,' Laiq says and kneels beside the prostrate man. His knees sink into the soft familiar earth as he shuts his eyes. He is trying to reconstruct the hold from memory, precisely as he saw it happen, the exact direction of the pull. Next he opens his eyes and studies how to redo what was undone. Only then does he touch the man. He holds the shoulder steady, grips the puppet arm just below the joint, pictures the glistening spring onion of the ball, the gaping socket, takes a breath, and deaf to the man's whimpering, stopples the arm home.

At the click a relative steps forward. 'Take him for an X-ray,' Laiq advises.

All bets are deemed cancelled. The victor is dressing on the knoll where he left his clothes. His friends console him as if he is the loser. But the crowd has lost its sullenness, divided now between those who blame the lion and those who blame the bull.

There are many ways to hurt a man, Laiq tells Lev back in his shop. The Bulbuliya should not have pressed so far. But the other was stubborn. The fault was his. A man should know when to give up.

'A man should have more than one chance,' Lev answers. He is sitting in the barber's chair with his back to the mirror.

'Maybe. But world not forgive weak man. Science not forgive.' Laiq gets up and crosses the room. He runs his hand up the back of Lev's neck. 'You need haircut.'

Lev flinches. 'Tomorrow.'

'Tomorrow, tomorrow, tomorrow,' Laiq laughs. He takes Lev's right arm playfully and draws it up in the classic hold they just witnessed. 'This called Catching Kite. Very easy, very hard. Frog not learn it. Frog fool. No – not fool.' He searches for the English word to convey weakness, innocence. 'Small sheep – *lamb*. Frog lamb!' He laughs a high hysterical laugh and pulls up on the arm so now Lev is balanced on the edge of real pain. Then he drops the arm and slouches across the room and falls onto the discoloured Rexine seat opposite.

'Lev,' he says. 'Lev, Lev, Lev.' He rises and picks up the bird. Time to go home. 'Hour is late.'

Once in a long while it happens that the same dream will visit two dreamers simultaneously. Tonight it happens. In Laiq's narrow pallet that overlooks the grave of Razia, and in Maya's bed on the roof of the Jain mansion, two figures are wrestling on raked earth. It is high noon above the arena but the light is violet, an eerie eclipse light that has sent the crowd scurrying home and turned even the watching birds into feathered stone. The wrestlers alone continue their slow-motion dance, their arms reaching out for a first hold behind the other's head.

'You need haircut,' Laiq, in the red langot, says to his opponent, his lips moving slowly as the dreamsound grinds down to an electronic mooing.

'Yes,' Lev agrees, but his head is as clean shaven as Laiq's, so clean it catches the eclipse light and shines like a bald doll's head in a nursery. Green comets race across the nursery ceiling above a cardboard city wall. The wall is a dragon.

'There are many ways to hurt a man,' Laiq's slowly moving lips say, and he locks Lev in a simple lover's hold. 'Here is one.'

Pain, comet greet, shoots up Lev's spine, leaving him rigid, unable to move.

'Here is another,' Laiq says and removes one of Lev's arms. This time there's a click but no pain. 'But it can be repaired.' Another click and the arm goes back. Even in the dark X-ray light it's clear that the arm is on back to front; there's nothing for it now but to leave it that way. Lev can never wrestle again. But the men continue to circle one another in slow motion, two decrepit nations under the black sun.

Twenty-Eight

Lev wakes sweating in the dark, his mouth dry. He's alone on the mattress. He sits up at the sound of voices. It's the middle of the night but the light is on in the puppet room.

He goes and looks in the door. Maya is there, standing over a man seated cross-legged on the floor. The man nods slowly, meditating on her questions. When he answers he raises his face towards her but doesn't seem to see her. His voice is deeper than hers but comes out of her mouth. It's the sightless hermit, her old confidant.

Maya looks around and sees Lev standing there.

'Babaji is advising Razia to marry a man who can help her rule. He says: Look for the man who has fashioned the sharpest sword. Did I disturb you?'

'No. I had a strange dream. I need a drink of water.'

'Oh, poor bachcha. Come.' She goes to the fridge for a bottle, turns off the light and leads him back to bed where leaning up against the wall she makes him drink. They have run out of time. They have only the present, that clear cool rope of water that unites them, travelling from her to him and down into his being. He is infected with love, he knows. It rages in his body, the way her fever must have. It's why he's still here, writing useless letters home, making phone calls in bad faith.

Sitting there, drunk on water, he sees in a flash the whole distance between Petersburg and Delhi, every mountain and river and plain made simultaneously visible. The vision fades. Does he need a plainer diet?

'Tomorrow,' she says, 'we'll finish Babaji. I've found a part for him in the play.'

'I love you.'

She looks at him in the dark with a smile that says: *Of course!* Her eyelids droop, the heaviest thing about her. So lightly she travels.

'Don't let me fall asleep,' she says resting her head on his shoulder. She must have worked all day, cutting, tacking, sewing.

He sits there smoking while her breath comes and goes. It's raining now and he imagines the ochre soil of the arena turned to mud. He remembers the waking fragment of his dream and looks down to check his arm. Her head rests on the shoulder Laiq dislocated and remade. She's remade him too, but has he touched her life at all?

He looks down the length of her body. The dowdy shift she wears at night covers her legs but bares her thin arms. He lets her sleep; she will be tired. How she works! Undoing, redoing, twice, three times, forever jobbing for the stories she invents. Her useful life is just beginning; his is coming to an end. The skin of her! A line from Blok slips out of one of Morgan's books like a bookmark. *You are all that is left of my youth.*

'I fell asleep,' she says, shaking herself. And dozes off again. She's murmuring something in that borderless world.

He bends to hear it. Her eyes rove lightly under the fine skin of her lids; slowly her lips push out an old boat: 'Marry me.'

Night smells come in singly at the window, released by the rain. Frangipani, beetles, urine, drains. Lately, the inquisitive wife from downstairs has been hanging her washing on the roof, nosing around.

A lone frog rewinds its ratchet up. *Vod-ka, vod-ka.*

Lev lights up a new cigarette, admiring her feet in the orange flare. He should have put up or shut up long ago, he knows. Instead of useless declarations of love. He deserved that smile. She's teaching him, this girl half his age.

'Yes, marry,' he whispers. If he had Morgan's tongue he'd argue Morgan's case – as if that wouldn't send her running. Refusing takes up so much of her energy; it *is* her energy. He wants to see her safe, less exposed – to what? It's a foreign country, he doesn't know its dangers, but he feels it's harder on a woman alone. He's seen the bus stops of this city and the women who stand there waiting, always outnumbered, always outrun, outclimbed. He's watched them give up, turn away, go back to waiting for the next bus. She does that.

And yet. Married, she'll become ordinary, tamed. This gypsy rooted only in herself.

He looks around the bare room and sees in its scant materials what he first admired in her. Her making do is part of her making up. Her daily discoveries of function and beauty in the discarded, her intractable, impulsive nature all point to a formidable faith in herself. Her wild dancing, her continuous present, even her love for him – she loves only what she has made – are part of this sufficiency. Would she throw it away in marriage?

He stubs out his cigarette as sleep comes over him. As he goes to lie down she wakes up.

'Talk to me.'

He yawns. The day's tensions have left him drained.

She shakes him. 'You never say anything.'

I do, he thinks, sometimes. When I can get a word in.

'Don't go to sleep.'

I'm already asleep.

'Say something, Lyova.'

Go to sleep.

'Maybe I should smoke.'

God Almighty.

'All right, go to sleep. What do I care?'

One more word, just one more word from her . . .

She begins to cry, silent bitter tears. When she cries she makes a fist in front of her mouth and runs the knuckle of her index finger over her front teeth, back and forth, harder and harder. She knows he's tired, knows it's unreasonable. How do you explain the way this life is ordered to a man accustomed to working from a certain hour to a certain hour? Hers is a life lived in snatches – the way she swooped down on him. This Razia play, every play, is patchwork, random glints and flashes. She must watch and wait; the job is the watching. The workaday puppet room is just a waystation. She is loitering with intent outside another mansion. Sometimes a calm comes over her and in this calm all the bolts and latches in the mansion fall away and the house stands open. She simply glides in and inhabits it. He broke in on that state just now, and the fantasy simply dissolved. She let him in. (How all the puppets go dead when he comes in! It's why she never lets Morgan in there.) And now he rolls over and goes to sleep!

'Fine. You sleep, I'll go and make some tea.'

Through a fog of sleep he sees the kitchen light go on, hears tea-making noises. In a little while – or is it much later? – there are other noises, clatterings, bangings. Then a weird luscious slicking that settles into a steady rhythm. It's like a pair of knives being sharpened against one another.

He sits bolt upright. Morgan's knives. He jumps up and goes to the kitchen.

She is standing there in a kind of trance with the two largest knives, stroking blade with blade.

'Maya.'

'I just want to make a little cut here.' She holds out a wrist, fragile as a child's. 'Should we make a little cut, Lev? You make one, I'll make one.'

That's when he decides to go. Tomorrow he'll check with Aeroflot.

'Maya, come on. We'll sit here and talk. If we lie down I fall asleep.'

She puts the knives down. 'Poor Lyova. I scared you, na? Come, we'll sleep.'

But in bed they fall on one another, wrestling like knives rubbed together. Then fall asleep, like knives, instantly.

In the morning Morgan arrives fresh from the studio.

'Good morning, India,' he addresses the last flat in the nation without a television. He turns to Lev. 'I think I know somebody who can help with your tail. I'll take you to see him after breakfast. He's expecting us.'

'We were going to finish Babaji today,' Maya says.

'We'll be back, never fear. You get ready, Lev. I'll make breakfast. We shouldn't be late.'

'I can't leave the clinic,' Maya announces in Laiq's squeaky voice, and sails towards the workroom looking serenely right and left. It's so Laiq both men laugh out loud. 'You're coming to the show?'

It's a command more than a question.

'Of course.'

'Friday. Keep the evening free.'

'What time?'

'Eight o'clock.'

'Where?'

'In the Foara gully. God – I've got to see the tentwallah.'

'Eggs Benedict!' Morgan calls presently. They draw up chairs around the small glasstop table.

'Where are you going?' Maya asks. Cheese toast for her.

'To his farm.'

'A farmer?' Lev is surprised.

'Not that sort of farm. A hacienda. A Xanadu. He's an arms dealer.'

'An arms dealer!' Maya smiles at him as if to say: Trust you. 'Big time or small time?'

'On the big side.'

'What does he look like?'

'On the small side, actually. He's no film star. I think of him as Hobbesian man.'

Lev leans forward and raises his eyebrows.

'Nasty, brutish and short.'

Maya laughs delightedly.

'But *he* would say – candid, virile and stocky.'

She mimes applause because she knows his wit's on

display for her. His bow says: *At your service*, her nod says: *I know.*

'Drive carefully,' she calls and turns to face her world. The puppets lean towards her from their hooks and hangers. The great grave-sheeted ones, the little twitchers, the animals, Babaji.

Morgan takes the Ring Road down to Ashram, then picks up the Mathura Road, buzzing past the mansions of New Friends Colony and a pullulating slum at the Okhla flyover.

Lev stares. 'You thought *we* needed a revolution?'

'Ours will be late,' Morgan answers. At the red light is a woman with three heads: her own, a goitre and a baby. 'Too late for her, anyway.' He buys a paper off her that shrieks of war.

Then they're out of the city in a landscape of scrub and grey rock.

'The red stone of the fort was not from here?'

'That's Agra stone. It came up the river. This is the local stuff. See?' He points to the walls that have begun to appear on either side with hacienda-style gates of the same grey stone. 'These are all farms that grow nothing. You're nobody if you just have a house in Delhi. CV not only has a farm, he has his own lake.'

They take a side road and follow it down a steep grade. A thorn forest swallows them up as the road drops further. Sunlight flashes off distant water through the grey-green scrub. A great grey pile looms up behind a fringe of bamboo.

'Is this it?'

'This is the gatehouse.'

The gatekeeper is a grumpy garden lizard, a man of proleptic and pre-emptive ugliness. Vetted, they follow a gravel drive, descending all the way till suddenly the forest falls away and acres of level lawn surround them. Gardeners squat at intervals like withered topiary. On the far side of the grass rises the first of a series of white domes.

'Not small time,' Lev agrees.

'He doesn't do machine guns. But I don't know if he's in the submarine class.'

At the portico the parking valet is disdainful of Morgan's Zen but limits his disapproval to an insolent click of the keys in his palm. A young man with a ponytail greets them as if he merely happened to be passing and offers to conduct them to the boss. Together they traverse the length of a hallway hung with large contemporary canvases and step out at the back door. There, spread before them, is the lake, with pavilions and guest houses scattered about its margins. CV's residence is in the next building under a smaller, more exquisite dome. The hollow square beneath harks back to both the Haryana thakur's citadel and a Petersburg mews. A fountain bubbles pointlessly in the domed atrium; the living quarters, when CV is visiting, are further back: a row of six rooms with a shared veranda in front and independent courtyards behind. The doors of each room stand open so you can see right through into the backyard. There is a hookah and a charpai set in the nearest, so splendid in isolation it could only be CV's. But then as they pass the next door an identical hookah and charpai appears framed there. The master himself could be in any one of the yards. The ponytail knows which one today.

Wrapped in a sheet in the centre of this yard of swept earth, under the blue Haryana sky, is a figure in an upright chair. There is a man leaning over the seated figure and a pool of sky at the seated one's feet. CV is having a haircut. Lev recalls last night's glimpse of Maya bent over the hermit. Morgan is reminded of a ventriloquist's dummy.

'Gut morgen, Morgan,' CV calls without stirring. The barber freezes with scissors and comb aloft. He could be a mannequin. CV continues to look in the mirror he holds between his immaculate running shoes. 'You told three lies this morning.'

'Just three!' Morgan is astonished. 'I must have a word with my scriptwriter.'

'*Are* we still holding the Gurukul Pass? Art Master – this is Art Master – you know Morgan and this must be Lev – Lev, Art Master; Art Master, Lev – Art Master, will you have some chairs sent out?'

The ponytail summons a row of chairs that have been waiting for his nod. They file out and array themselves in a semicircle facing the haircut.

'Art Master is in charge of acquisitions,' Morgan explains as they sit back. 'I see you have a new Kidwai.'

'It's of the lake,' CV says in Hindi. 'He sat right there at the back door and did the lake. For three days we had to go around through the dining hall. I said, "Why the lake? I can see it any time I want just by turning my head." He said, "Chowdhury Sahib, the real lake will now be indoors." I said, "But I carry the lake in my head." He says, "Now you can put it down. Or move it around, or even sell it." I said, "But it doesn't *look* like a lake," and he said, "Thank you very much." Finished?' His pop eyes swivel up.

'Almost, sir,' the barber replies and comes to life. He makes a single snip and goes to take up the mirror.

'Never mind, never mind,' says CV, and springs out of

his chair. On his feet, without the barber's sheet, he is in fact stocky and not especially short. After the gatekeeper he is personable but entirely bald. An ancient retainer mimes sweeping up the clippings.

'Would you?' CV offers the barber around.

Morgan declines.

'Lev? A memory to carry home? Of course you must – an alfresco haircut. Let us change places. Or better still, he will come to you.'

He has switched to Russian, which he speaks so fluently that Lev is surprised into acquiescence.

'Now what is this tailing business?' CV draws his chair up opposite as the barber sends for a fresh sheet. His head is still, but little muscles skip all across the dome, along the jawline, at the temple, on the wings of the nose, in the porches of the ears, the embrasures of the eyes fixed on Lev. Lev describes the masseur who shadows him, the business with the suitcase.

'Nothing was taken?'

'No.'

'You're sure?'

'One or two things I can't be sure about. They may have been in the briefcase.'

'What briefcase?'

As the sheet is wound around him Lev shuts his eyes and describes the robbery on the airport road.

'What did they take?'

'The briefcase. Money. My watch.'

'The watch too? Nice.'

Lev lifts his head enquiringly. The mannequin pauses, then resumes his clipping.

'When they *show* some intelligence. Usually they are so stupid. Passport, ticket? *No!*'

'Another car showed up.'

'Lucky. And you stayed on. Very brave. But you should leave as soon as possible. While the war is still undeclared.'

Morgan, who has been following the conversation with difficulty, butts in. 'It was the same crowd?'

'No,' CV replies, returning to English. 'To me' – the *me* is light and sure – 'this second attempt sounds like somebody else, less professional. I would say this is local, political, some neta out to make mileage. The war makes it easy for him and dangerous for you. The *other* lot may or may not need you, depending on what they find. You were carrying classified material?'

'Some.'

'Good.' He looks away delicately. 'You are aware that your special knowledge may be redundant?'

Lev shrugs.

'What I mean is that their use of you may also be political – but not local, like the other. In neither case is the sleep of science disturbed. If I were you I would leave before either party acts. I can't help you once they do, but I can get you a seat on Aeroflot. Which is harder than you might imagine at short notice, Lev.'

The mirror empties of sky and shows Lev his chastened face. But he smiles faintly. It's a more open face than the one in the plate-glass window at Rossi's on the Fontanka.

'Saturday or Sunday,' he says finally.

CV nods. It's done. The Aeroflot boss golfs here, on these grounds.

The ancient returns with broom and pan and fixes rheumy eyes on the ginger harvest.

They make their way to the lake where even Morgan is surprised to find Lena and Lydia swimming.

'I've fallen into cliché,' CV says regretfully, looking over the yellow hair. 'But you know in Africa they would be enemies. Her country's fighter pilots are flying for Ethiopia and hers are flying for Eritrea.'

They watch the healthy frolic, then turn aside.

'Stay for lunch,' CV offers. 'I'm told Nguyen has something special planned, but I have to be in Calcutta.'

He brushes aside Lev's thanks. 'Your country has been good to me.'

'You thought *I* was a Russophile,' Morgan says to Lev in a stage whisper. 'But don't ever mention SWEDEN.'

CV laughs. 'Bofors is for children. Naughty children. Now I must run.' He bounds away down a lakeside track, his neat round stomach jogging a little ahead of him.

After lunch they drive back to Lajpat Nagar to an address Lena gave them. The smell of leather greets them at the bottom of the staircase. Lev drives a harder bargain than Morgan imagined, but he has costs to recover. Six jackets could recoup the outlay on this whole trip; the jeans from next door – where they use the Levis patches replicated on these premises – are a kind of insurance on top. Lastly they pick up an expandable cabin bag.

'Maya knows?' Morgan says as they test the zippers on the bag.

'We have always known.'

Morgan endures the hyperbole with forbearance. It has been a long monsoon.

'Well, I think even she might notice your luggage.'

Lev smiles. 'You're lucky,' he says. He means Morgan has the words to express what he feels.

'I'm lucky!' Morgan guffaws. 'You've got her and *I'm* lucky?' But it's true, he feels lucky, especially now.

Lev shakes his head. 'I haven't got her.'

'Then nobody has. *She's* got her.'

'What does she *want?*' Lev's voice expresses utter prostration.

'You and me and Babaji and none of the above.'

Lev nods: he wants two wives. Morgan, who has many wives, wants just one.

There's a shave in progress at Laiq's. It's the masseur, who averts his head and shrinks into himself. 'That's him,' Lev says under his breath. Laiq notices the change in Lev at once and bends to his job, his face burning with rejection. It's when he refuses to look up that Lev remembers his haircut.

How to explain? He simply lugs his bag upstairs.

Maya is out, somewhere. She never leaves notes, but the flat is full of the burnt starch smell of rice boiled over into the flame. There are delicate papery frills down the side of the pot.

Morgan has come up to borrow back one of his books. He retrieves it from the bookcase and turns to go, brushing aside Lev's gratitude.

'Your country has been good to me,' he intones, holding up a finger. 'Don't forget to call Art Master.'

'Here, take these away too.' Lev hands him back the set of knives from the kitchen.

Morgan looks searchingly at him then leaves, letting a

theatrical silence spread in his wake. At the top of the staircase he turns and sees Lev standing at the security door.

'All in all,' he calls out, 'you got off pretty lightly, didn't you?'

Lev's English is not quite up to the idiom, and Morgan doesn't finish the sentence. *For a plague doctor.*

Puppets both! Lev is not quite off the hook, Morgan. Thanks to CV he will be upgraded to Business Class, but the flight will leave without him.

Twenty-Nine

Is the foreigner moving in?

The other Mrs Jain, of the downstairs Jains, has watched Lev and Morgan arrive and noted the heavy bag. When she sees Morgan leave alone her curiosity is piqued. Her husband, a clerk, clearly does not approve of the goings-on on the roof. He says nothing but his old mother has been threatening to write a letter to the landlady.

'*She* is the landlady, Mother. Landlady's daughter, landlady, same thing.'

'Nonsense. You think her mother would allow all this carry-on if she knew?'

'These are big folk, they're different. Leave them alone.'

The wife, a broad smooth woman with sly somnolent eyes, adds a dish of special lentil halwa to the evening meal. After dinner, when Maya is back she takes an offering on a stainless-steel thali, a single serving, upstairs.

Maya answers the door.

'Just a little halwa we made specially today,' Mrs Jain says, fussing her way in. 'My mother-in-law was saying, "That girl is looking so thin, we should do something or she'll fade away." But really you should look after yourself. Why don't you come down and take your meals with us? How can you cook for just one, day after day? It's not economical.'

Lev, who was sitting at the glasstop table, has retreated by old habit into the puppet room. Maya goes to take the offering but Mrs Jain holds on to it and sits herself down, still talking, on one of the cane chairs, warm from Lev's presence. So this is the kitchen? She jumps up to look. She has studied home science, nutrition, cookery; she sends away for free recipe books; her spices are in a uniform set of PET jars. From the kitchen she sees the terrace and is entranced by the swing seat. Very nice. This must be over her own bedroom, right? Now where would Maya's bedroom be? That window, surely, with the cooler outside it. Number one bedroom, no? She glances at the en suite bathroom. Nobody there. Off the hallway is another door. A common washroom? Excellent idea! Every flat should have one Indian-style pan. And this room?

'My work room,' Maya says, barring the way. It's enough that the puppets have to contend with Lev. Sometimes she pictures the consternation among the puppets when she herself enters the room without sufficient warning.

'By the way,' Mrs Jain remembers, turning innocently aside, 'we heard some clattering up here in the middle of the night and I was worried. This city really isn't safe for a single girl.'

'Last night?' Maya tries to think. She is ushering her visitor back towards the cane chairs when Mrs Jain hands over the thali and dodges back in.

'You have a museum!' It's a gasp of genuine amazement. If her hands were not full Maya would seize the woman bodily and drag her out. It's then she notices Lev has disappeared.

'The bulb is fused in there,' she protests but is drawn by the strength of the stranger's will.

Puppets are nourished on half light. Every night when the room light is switched off there's an instant of profound darkness. In that limbo human and puppet alike stand blinded. Then Maya pulls the door to behind her – leaving a crack – and the world resumes its workaday disparity. But behind the door a balance has been tipped and as the light from the street lamp returns, stealing across the wall where the puppets hang, life ebbs into the puppets.

A head creaks on its neck, a finger twitches. A tiny throat is cleared.

But sodium light turns all colours to mud. All puppet finery is bled of glamour; that is the price a puppet pays for life. Look at poor Janaki's crimson sari! Done down to beige, the pallu muted. Even her gold is gagged. Rana Pratap's armour of crushed silver paper is suddenly tarnished, like some crazed old mirror. It's a half-life of veils and intentions. Long shadows strike across the wall: noses, spears, a moustache tip stretched longer than the moustache. Front on, each face divides into night and day.

The downstairs Mrs Jain steps carefully along the row of silhouettes. The puppet faces watch her come with fractional turns of the head. Their eyes track her with the frowning attention of an honour guard. Maya who has followed her through the flat hypnotized by her vulgarity notices the woman has fallen silent. Mask after mask refines her fear. Each time she crosses the divide from the dark side of a face she pauses and absorbs its gravity. At the sheeted papier mâché group her eyes travel down the tallest puppet. Modelled in the orange light she sees a pair of calves so real they leave her faint with desire. The legs are on the wrong way: which way would the manhood point? She trembles and moves on, her arms rigid against her sides, then returns along the other wall. Past mounds of fabric scraps any of which might conceal a body. Clear of the room she breathes again, but hasn't recovered her voice. She rocks her head sideways at Maya and presses her palms together and flees.

'She saw your legs!' Maya laughs. 'But I don't think she took in anything. She was hardly breathing.'

'I didn't have time to turn around. She came back in so quickly.'

'She must have thought you were a churail! Their feet are turned backwards.'

They laugh together on the mattress. He describes his torment, smothered in a sheet, mosquitoes fastened to his ankles.

'Poor bachcha. Go to sleep, jaanu. Tomorrow we're going out early.'

'Where?'

But they can't sleep; he won't let her, and she won't be let. Downstairs, Mrs Jain is unusually quiet. It's only when she's in bed and her husband has turned out the light that she says softly, looking at the ceiling. 'That girl is a witch.'

Thirty

They take a rickshaw to Turkman Gate.

The rickshawman's thin legs stand on the pedals, his chequered lungi flaps in the cool morning breeze. They sit side by side on the shiny narrow seat whose padding, covered in blue Rexine, has been compacted to stone; there are enough brass-tack arabesques along the front to make it a wedding seat. Where the gully ends Maya hops off.

'We're getting married,' she laughs.

He raises an eyebrow but follows her.

'Relax, galubchik,' she says. 'Just business.'

Two steps up from the gully is an old door set in an arch. They go up and in.

A man with a machine gun stands against the far wall of the courtyard, his face streaming with blood. He is firing a whole stick in orange tracers at an invisible foe. A coral-pink giantess looks the other way, his heroine. The gold and orange lettering of another hoarding flares up against her cheek. The painter is on all fours in the middle of the paved yard.

'Still not finished!'

Gurmeet jumps. The work is done, he signs with both hands; these are simply finishing touches. He holds two brushes crosswise in his mouth, one pink paint and one white, but he's mute anyway; what was once a stammer has congealed into silence.

There are three backdrops: two hang suspended from their dowlings, a riverine landscape and an urban view of a medieval Delhi centuries older than Shah Jehan's red city. The first shows a river flowing across a plain of stunted trees with a low range of hills on the horizon and a bridge of boats in the foreground. In the other are turquoise domes, red stone pillars, a courtyard, an arch. The arch frames the Kutub, Razia's father's tower.

Maya is delighted. She marches up to the bridge of boats, and enters the landscape. Lev stands on the riverbank and watches. He sees the morning sun fall on the mustard fields, sees it flame up on her kamiz. She moves in slow motion across the courtyard of the second painting and her footsteps echo among the pillars; he could swear she disappeared momentarily behind one. He crosses to where she stands, afraid of losing sight of her. It's the first time he's seen her in her element; usually Delhi disappears around her. Giants up against the canvas, they do violence to its puppet scale. But see how the perspectiveless scene draws them in!

'Delhi,' Razia murmurs, and runs a finger over a blue tile in a distant dome. Its glaze is cool and vitreous, no canvas in it. She is showing the city to her foreign lover; she had hopes of him.

The third painting is spread on the paving. It is of the grove where Razia and her lover meet their end. Here the trees have eyes for leaves and the swordgrass makes a vicious hedge around a pool. Gurmeet has added a solitary crane in the shallows; it was this that he was working on when Maya surprised him.

'Just one?' she tilts her head. Meaning, they are always paired.

Gurmeet shakes his head vigorously. *Look carefully.*

High up in the sky, in what is clearly another moment in time, for the sky is another colour there, is the mate, circling.

'Friday morning,' Maya says. 'Bring them to the flat. No later than ten.'

Gurmeet spits on his palm and returns to the crane's pink legs. His fingers are of different colours; his palm is a palette and spittle his glue.

By Turkman Gate a familiar T-shirt shouts out a greeting at the rickshaw.

'Plague Master!'

It's the shoeshine boy, grinning; to him it's a nickname. Lev waves back, but Maya wonders where the boy picked up the phrase. She doesn't translate it for Lev. In the short space since the sun came up it's gone from cool to hot: too soon. In these fickle days at the end of the monsoon that can only mean more rain.

'Let's walk a bit,' she suggests, and leads him up the old city side of Nevsky. The cream Doric columns of the grand police station across the way look serenely down on the jumble of closed shopfronts. Maya looks away whenever she passes. The Changezi chicken rotisserie is only now coming to life. Defiantly she takes his arm in public. Behind the Golcha cinema hangs a stink of greenrot where the old flower market is given over to vegetables. In the cobbled square – just where portage required a level surface – the ground has heaved. Coolies range across swells of black stone armed with hooks; one comes at Lev with his steel point glinting. Dodge or be trampled is the rule: a fifty-kilo sack of potatoes is nothing. Framed in dust an old man squats gravely polishing an onion, its red gold skin a Kremlin dome. More domes, ribbed white ones, deck the stall behind him, prize garlic set in tiers. Their sloughed skins go gusting across the square. Maya picks up one complete with spire, faithful to the lost shape.

'Plague Master!'

It's a group of urchins, three boys for whom it's still a joke.

'Let's go home,' she says. 'Looks like a storm coming.'

They return past the first open shops. Lev notices the way people gather at shop-window televisions, but Maya is not interested in the war. She hangs on no radio bulletins, but can hear the word *martyr*. In the undeclared war there are no soldiers, only martyrs. Morgan, who was a professional soldier, balks daily at the word in his script.

Under the Nevsky footbridge an ambulance, its siren going, is caught in traffic. Maya looks at it wedged between the median railing and a Blue Line bus, with a car for a chock front and back. That's her, exactly. Her love an ambulance that can't get through.

There are mangoes on the other side, a new pale green and yellow variety.

'Chausa,' Maya says. 'These you must try. They come at the end of the season. After this it's apples and pears and crap.'

She buys two kilos, then two more, and fills her black shoulder bag. Lev knows better than to offer to carry it. They've turned away when she decides that's still not enough.

'We'll fill the fridge up.'

She hands him the garlic-skin dome and goes back and buys two more kilos. Now just bread and smokes. Wind whips at their ankles as the storm builds. Maya forsakes her grocer for a nearer man.

The shopkeeper has his eyes on a small screen on the counter. He is telling a customer what should be done with the new bomb.

'*Nuke them.*' Maya translates as they step out of the shop. 'That's what he said. He says: *The best weapon is surprise.*' Suddenly everybody is mouthing slogans.

Weapon. The word brings Lev up short. Weapons have come to mean swords and shields. He has helped Maya cut them out of cardboard and stick the silver paper on. The Commander-in-Chief's scimitar. Razia's damascened blade with a jewelled scabbard. Her golden shield with a blood-red rosette at the centre.

Her hands full, Maya insists on stopping at the tailors for offcuts. She's looking for a last-minute addition to the general's armour. A buckram piece for chain mail. It's the first time she's gone to the shop with Lev. For some time now the tailors have been sniggering when he passes; now they sit there, treadles working, grinning like satyrs at a wedding.

Every time she walks by, Maya feels their envy, these bondsmen nailed to their stools. What yearnings they must hide! Lev too contemplates their eternal leglessness. They seem no more capable of standing up than Maya's puppets. Maya sees also their scorn, and lately something like judgement. Despite herself she minds what they think, so as she goes to hand her shopping to Lev she hesitates. It's the bread and cigarettes, a light bulb and a hundred-gram pack of butter;

basics, on view through the flimsy polythene. To hand this mundane bag to Lev would be an acknowledgement that he is staying at the flat. It's a moment of reckoning for her as the owner approaches with his pile of offcuts – does she put her bag down or docs she hand it to Lev? It's vexed by another question: what is she to this man at her side? And another: what is he to her? What she now does will decide those questions.

The tailor is holding out a bag stuffed with yesterday's clippings. The satyrs are watching.

She hands the shopping over. Lev takes it, implicated but oblivious to the moment, its impudence and its holiness. Poor puppets! Bound by an alternating current.

'Friday night the new puppets have their show,' she tells the owner conversationally, 'in the Lane of Watering Cans.'

The storm breaks as they top the stair and come out on the roof. She traps him at the door, mad with the electricity of it. The garlic-skin dome disintegrates, but she laughs it off. The city is spread before them like a battlefield: thunder and lightning and rain like hissing arrows. The little pipal tree will be gloating.

Inside she puts on her favourite tape and sings with Mira:

> *Peacock mourns, Koel sings, Brainfever puts her question*
> *Raindrops peck at the wanderer*
> *God of Mira, God of Mira*
> *When, oh when, oh when, oh when?'*

'What's the instrument?' Lev is looking at the cassette case. Even he can tell she has no ear.

'She carried an ektara. One string. I should make one for Babaji. Next time.'

So little time. She turns to him, almost bashful. 'Will you wash my hair?'

My beautiful girl. And again as he's working the lather he's thinking: God in heaven. How do I preserve this? Her head is bowed before him, her face hidden, her unruly hair hangs down wet and straight, the shampoo running onto her feet. There is no way, he knows. And the sadness of it slows his fingers till he's all but stopped and simply standing there beside her musing, the water drying off on his body.

'Finished?' she calls, from behind the screen of her hair. Shouting as if from another shore.

'No.'

Her bird neck. He releases the nape, applies more shampoo, enriching the mix. He is holding the skull of her in his hands. Little by little he works the foam down the fall of hair, rubbing as he goes. And then he's reached the end.

'Finished? All right, pour!'

He scoops mugfuls from the bucket and pours. He's forgotten any other way of bathing.

'More, yaa!'

He scoops faster and watches her hair return from white to black. He feels her enjoyment and is piqued. Is staying easier than going? Or is there only this rinse water running through her hair, now and now and now?

'POUR, yaa!'

He picks up the second bucket and empties it over her in one go from up high. She shrieks, laughing.

'Enough?'

'Yes, baba! Your turn now.'

They have Russian tea and bread and butter on the terrace, rocking on the swing. The storm has moved on and the air is moist and limpid. The brainfever bird calls, the hawks have vanished.

'Now I have a script to by-heart, OK? Relax, use the binocs, read. We can go for a walk later.'

He sits in the cane chair with Morgan's Mandelshtam and muses on the cover. Why do they use only the youthful photos for the covers? Look at the Akhmatova, look at this man. Didn't he grow bald and middle-aged? Beauty is youth, bas. He reads the Russian, looks to the English for help and is turned back. Will he ever read another line of poetry? He is doing everything one last time.

Lunch is mangoes, a yellow dream. The last mangoes.

'One more week and they'll be gone,' she says before she knows what she's said.

He says nothing to that.

'Or overripe,' she soldiers on. 'You always end up buying one bad lot.'

She has changed into a tiger-striped T-shirt and he reaches over and paints mango whiskers on her.

Dinner must be more substantial. They go up the road for dosas and at last he discovers Indian food he likes. Too late. The first dosa is the last. They return to the safety of the Jain mansion.

The Hans Dairy brothers grin as they go by, the tailors ogle. *Sex*. She shakes her head. Do they think of anything else? What *do* they think of as their hands adulterate the milk, as their fingers guide the fabric past the whirring needle, the endless knop-and-flower of their tapestry work?

'Hans means swan,' she laughs at the crude bird in the sign above the dairy. 'In our mythology the swan can tell milk from water. These guys can't.'

Upstairs he does the day's dishes but is careful not to exceed his mandate. They are both walking on water, but her concentration is greater. She comes up behind and puts her arms around him as he works, resting her head against his spine. She is saying goodbye to the strange thudding of another heart. Sometimes she will be alone, working in the puppet room or just walking, and she will feel a remote pulsing reach her from some unrecognizable source. Then she leans forward and listens in this way, this mediated way, alert and a little afraid.

'What's Petersburg like?'

'Cold.'

'And white?'

He shuts his eyes. 'Brown, actually. Like old snow.'

'Is there always snow?'

'A lot of the time.'

'I'd like that.'

'I like this.'

She thinks: Live out your life in one place. He mops the sink with the dishcloth and runs the cloth along the rim.

'*Come*, naa!' she tugs. He resists force with force till he has spread the rag on the edge of the sink and rinsed off his hands and shut off the dripping tap and wiped his hands on his jeans and turned around.

Now she hesitates. Takes him to check the front door but pauses, imagining a man – or two – standing there, beyond the grille. She opens it. Nobody there. It's bolted. They go to bed.

'Last year,' she says, when they're in bed, 'I went to Bali. With the troupe, four of us. You'll meet them. First time abroad for any of us. It was like a tour, government-sponsored, to show them our puppets. Theirs are flat, shadow puppets, made out of leather.' She wets the pebbles of her lips. 'Their stories are borrowed from us from our epics. *Ramayana, Mahabharata,* the battle of the Pandavas and Kauravas. With them it's all shown on a screen, with an orchestra. I use recorded music mostly, when I have an engineer, sometimes just a drum.'

'What are you using this time?'

She rolls over onto him.

'Music. Leela will be here. She couldn't come today but we'll rehearse tomorrow and again on Friday morning. She's good fun. She's the one I told you about—'

'I know. Her sister's husband is impotent.'

'Well done!'

'And she used to eat toothpaste at school when she was eight years old.'

'Good boy.'

'And you fried banana chips in Vaseline one night.'

'Full marks!' She laughs out loud, a little put out because he's teasing.

'Go on,' he gloats, 'surprise me. You can't!'

'She can.'

The man's voice comes from behind her.

Lev starts, his heart racing, but sees she hasn't moved. She's grinning widely now. He realizes he felt her diaphragm tighten as she spoke. The lips didn't move at all.

'Don't forget I do all the voices,' she laughs. 'I'm not just a puppet-maker. Razia's voice, her father's, the general's, Babaji's—' Her voice changes again, grows old. ' "The armourer's job is to fashion the sharpest sword." That's Babaji, when the general confesses he has an unethical weapon.'

Lev looks up. So she has been thinking about what he did for a living. Does. Did.

'Senapati's is the lowest voice. He's the general, the Commander-in-Chief. That's the hardest one for me. But it's not a ventriloquist show, thank God. I'm hidden with the mike in the wings. Anyway Leela's going to be there so it'll be easier. We cover for each other. In Bali we left the puppeteers at the show and went off to the beach with two guys on motorcycles. We were the only women left anyway. We sat under the palm trees and drank beer and told them all kinds of lies. My guy was very handsome.'

Her chin is resting on his chest, her mouth at the nipple, and she's watching him through the slits of her eyes.

'We got back after midnight. Baldevji – you'll meet him – didn't speak to me on the whole journey home. He fancies himself my protector.' She rolls off him onto her back. 'Why do I always attract father figures?'

She's back in Bali, reworking a father puppet. But it's not just puppets she makes; it's the illusion *they* make. They're just dolls until they start to move. She's an illusionist. It's like her magpie gathering, he thinks, a rearranger of matter himself. All the bright bits and pieces she lines her nest with are nothing till she reshuffles them. She's reshuffled him. She shuts her eyes, he's gone. She could fall in love with the same man twice: in her eternal present he's a different man each time.

Am I? Lev wonders, breathing in molecules of green jasmine that go wending through the night. A dotted path that closes up behind. Is his past like that, an illusion, or is he accountable for it?

She left the light on in the puppet room, meaning to work on the chain mail, but gets up now and turns it off.

'Close your eyes, naa.'

As the eyes open in her hands. She has a painter's fingers, a barber's nervous thumb, a tentwallah's calluses. A milkman's blind measure. She's a tailor sewing kisses on his ribs, machining him to the bed. She's a shopkeeper who will deploy the ultimate weapon.

As a child she was amazed that other people exist. She still is. *Lev, my love, my marvellous doll.* She falls asleep – a steep, violent fall, like her descent into love – and stays that way until dawn.

First light, white in the window. Garlic-skin cope of sky. Blue salt-lick of his shoulder.

My God! Chain mail for it.

Thirty-One

'I'm calm.'

She knows he's going the day after tomorrow. She's watched him pack the jackets, seen the jeans, heard about CV and his Aeroflot connection. She knows he picked Saturday so he can be here for the Razia.

She's done her share of adjusting, because she saw this coming. She brought the show forward a whole month when September would have been better for an outdoor venue, with the rains safely gone.

But even as she walks this morning under a low grey sky, avoiding the puddles on the uneven street (in this season when nobody walks in a straight line except the human jeep: watch him stop and reverse come up trembling alongside because he loves the sight of her!), she's not worried. Worry would mean the world beyond her fingertips really did exist. She is prior, and therefore deserving. Fair weather is her birthright.

Worry has nothing to do with it: it's anxiety, which has no focus and thrives in the present, that produced her declaration of calm. Fate, she's declared, is injustice looking for a victim: so she must not look like one. But when did she ever?

It's why her mother is afraid of her, why her father is afraid for her. Why Lev made his declaration of love and Morgan is recklessly unfaithful. Why the human jeep stands in one spot with his engine racing long after her eyes have smiled on him. Only anxiety is not deceived.

'I'm calm.'

Men hauling crates of iced sea fish swarm around her. The stink causes schoolchildren in their navy and white uniforms to hold their noses as they sit in a row of rickshaws that inches forward through the market, but it doesn't bother her. Everywhere is wet and sloppy underfoot, though the rain stopped an hour ago. There's a little hubbub as small sellers bid for remnants from the emptied crates; the strange dead oddments have only that spumy seagrey scum and their stink in common. She breathes deeply, tasting it. Her mother would faint here, retch, truly.

Then she's past the fishmarket and the bottlenecked rickshaws, bearing left towards Soldier Gully and across Chitli Qabar Bazaar to the Lane of Tinsmiths where the first alley on the left ends in a private courtyard owned by a family friend.

Here in this cul-de-sac she has permission to stage her puppet show.

It will mean blocking off the main entrance to the friend's courtyard for a few hours, but then weddings do that all the time. A covered stage will back on to the elaborate old arched gateway and face out into the alley where the audience will sit on durrees spread directly on the paving, an aggregate of concrete and brick and stone slabs and gouts of tarseal. A marquee will provide shelter for some in case of rain and there will be standing room beyond, where the lane's doorsteps begin.

Maya paces the alley picturing the stage, working out the lighting, wondering if the two hundred-year-old murals around the gate, late additions, might be worked into the set. There is a row of painted soldiers and two sentries, one on either side. A householder in kurta-pyjama appears on his steep doorstep.

'Have you heard about the puppet show we're putting on here?'

'I've seen the poster.'

'You don't mind a loudspeaker at your front door?'

'Blast away. My children can't wait.'

He mounts his scooter and rides off. Good, she thinks; neighbourhood goodwill is important. Word of mouth will run ahead of the posters, and there'll be a drummer. If it works here she'll do another show in another alley. This is the heart of the old city: Delhi Gate lies one way and the Friday Mosque the other. Just beyond the wall of the friend's courtyard is the resting place of Razia herself.

On the way home she calls in at the tentwallah's apartment above his shop in Sitaram Bazaar.

'Day after tomorrow, sisterji,' he assures her, pushing a drawer of air at her with his callused hands. 'I'll drop off the poles and canvas in the morning. I know the place, Soldier Gully, just off Watering Can Lane. Have a cup of tea. How to tell you? I'm an educated man. This tenting is just the way my life has gone.'

At home the doorbell rings.

Lev lets it ring, as he was told to. It stops ringing. After fifteen minutes it rings again. He ignores it. It stops. Fifteen minutes later it rings again. He lets it ring till it stops, then goes and listens at the door. There is somebody out there. He waits for the next ring. Fifteen minutes. It doesn't come. The noises have stopped. He waits a space, then opens the door to see.

Two men are standing there. They are as tall as he is — he's accustomed to looking downwards at Indians — and have loosely tied turbans that take them above his height. Both are gaunt-faced and have black handlebar moustaches and a grizzled six-day growth. Their sunken cheeks are smiling but when they see Lev the smile vanishes. They look alike and speak together.

'Mayaji nahi hain?'

Lev gestures: gone out, but lets his finger circle back. Schooled in gesture, they understand at once. By way of introduction they take two puppets out of their luggage and jiggle them. Lev unbolts the door.

They come in and squat on the floor on the empty sitting room in their dhotis and crimson turbans and jodhpuri slip on shoes. They address Lev in Hindi; he answers them in Russian and both sides are satisfied. He has learnt to offer water to callers and they drink by turns from a stainless-steel tumbler, throwing back their heads and pouring the water from a great height like conjurers so the vessel can be seen not touch their lips.

'Where's the TV?' they want to know, and are immediately disappointed in Delhi.

'Sukhdev Bhaiya! Baldev Bhaiya!' Maya greets them, coming in. 'At last! I should have known you'd come at the last minute! Is that your luggage outside? This friend is a

Russian scientist. Yes, from Russia! Let me make you some tea, then I'll show you the puppets. We can rehearse in here,'

She flips the Mira cassette in the Aiwa and gets busy in the kitchen like a model homemaker.

Lev feels himself in the way and goes downstairs to see if Laiq has arrived. He must say goodbye. Yesterday Laiq looked steadily away each time he passed with Maya.

It's early but there's no lock on the door. The shutters stand open yet the glass door is bolted from the inside. He knocks lightly, then a little louder. At the third knock there's a groan as of someone waking out of deep sleep. A shuffling, then silence.

Lev is preparing to turn away when the bolt is drawn behind him and the door opens.

A young man stands there frowning from under level eyebrows. The frown involves the whole of his angelic face as if the pursed lips and the folds in the forehead were tokens of profound turmoil; even the rounded, perfectly symmetrical cheeks are implicated. He wears a white crocheted skull cap that hides part of a fringe and accentuates his prominent ears. The beginnings of a beard darken only his chin. He might be seventeen.

'Come in.'

The voice is Laiq's, from behind. He is sitting on the bench seat where his customers wait. His kurta is crushed and he has not combed his hair. He does so now, looking sourly in the wide mirror.

'Sit.' He indicates the barber's chair with a resigned gesture.

Lev turns the familiar chair around and climbs in. The boy has got busy in the dispensary with his back to the men.

Laiq lets his eyes linger on that back but finds they slide down to the floor with the weight of his morning head. He has been drinking. He puts the comb down with great care on the Rexine seat beside him, nodding ponderously to himself; it could be a holy relic. At last he lifts his head and lets his eyes meet Lev's. They say: What can I do for you?

'I came to say goodbye.'

'You are going?'

'Yes.'

Laiq considers this development with raised eyebrows, then nods. There is a silence which only Lev appears to find uncomfortable. It's clear the boy's ears are listening.

'It is better,' Laiq says at length. 'The malishwallah was here.' At the word malishwallah the boy bristles. 'He was telling bad things. About you.'

Lev looks down, when he should look up. 'What did he say?'

'He say you are Plague Master, you bring plague.' Laiq looks for the word in his far-off student curriculum. 'Bacterias.'

'It's not true.'

'He say government make him follow you.'

'Maybe.'

'Why?'

Lev lifts his hands in the local way. 'I don't know, Laiq.'

'It is better you go. Many people die, Lev. This boy's brother.'

The boy puts the phial he is dusting down on the counter and turns around. He crosses the room and carefully shuts and bolts the glass door beside Lev. Then he turns again and stands there barring the exit.

'So,' he says to Laiq. 'What are you going to do?'

Laiq waves him aside, but the boy will not be moved. He ignores Lev and continues to address Laiq in Hindi.

'Last night you had a lot to say. Go on. Do something.'

He steps behind the barber's chair and pulls open one drawer after another, rummaging with an agitated hand.

'Here.'

He picks up Laiq's razor and holds it out.

'You little pubic hair! Put that down.'

The boy ignores Laiq. He opens up the razor and holds it out again.

'Go on. You were going to teach him a lesson. You were going to circumcise him, right? You said you would keep the rose to sniff at. Or was that vodka talking?'

Lev has gone rigid in his chair. He understands nothing but the menace in the bright steel edge that flashes at his ear.

'Come on, then,' the boy taunts Laiq. 'Or you hold him and let me do the job.'

Laiq too has frozen. There's pain and a new rage in his concentration. 'All right,' he says quietly. 'I'll do it. For you.'

He staggers to his feet and crosses to the barber's chair.

'You hold him,' he says and takes the razor.

The boy pins Lev's arms behind the backrest. Laiq snaps the razor shut and smacks the boy with the back of his hand.

'Madman! Looking for jail bread? Go on, piss off or I'll set about you properly. Silly bugger! Who taught you to tie your langot? Forgotten?'

The boy undoes the bolt and lets himself out, glowering.

'All talk,' he sneers from the doorstep. 'And African hair.'
He nods at the floor where Laiq is standing and stalks off.

'He is right,' Laiq says when he is gone. 'Laiq only talk.' He looks down at the bush of kinked hair at his feet, last night's body shaving, and bursts into tears. 'Laiq only dream.'

Lev takes his arm and leads him back to the bench seat. The birdcage rests on the window sill above, the bird is doing a frenetic dance.

'Maybe we can meet tomorrow,' Lev offers. 'We can have lunch. Moti Mahal?' He finds himself trembling uncontrollably.

Laiq rocks his head. Maybe.

'One o'clock?' Lev says and shuts the door behind him. He lifts one finger and waves briefly through the glass.

Laiq sits there red-eyed and impassive, framed in the fancy woodwork.

Lev stands a moment at the bottom of the steep stair where old bicycle tyres hang in festoons. A toilet flushing rattles down the black pipe beside him. Shaken by his manhandling he is still able to notice the horrid gurgling, to picture the squat toilet and to reflect that he's now comfortable using one. His arm smarts where it was pinned against the chair back. She's up there rehearsing. The puppet room is up there, the swing seat, the mattress on the floor, the cane bookshelf. All that will be there when he is gone. The tailor-mermen are already at work. The murmur of their machines reminds him of how far he is from the sea. In the next shop along the dairy brothers are pressing cheese. He goes upstairs slowly and finds the rehearsal in progress, so steps out onto the terrace and sits down on the swing seat. He pushes all the way back with his feet but then locks his knees and holds the swing poised as he stares out across the city wall.

Thirty-Two

Where's Morgan when you need him?

Maya looks at the telephone guiltily. She knows she has only to call. Still, it's been days. She can see Lev's restless and this morning Sukhdev and Baldev are coming early. The sets arrive at ten, that Leela should be here; she ditched yesterday. The last thing she wants is Lev mooning around the flat. If she could send him out sightseeing. But there's danger out there.

Conscience afflicts her: she escapes into her work, which is love poured into something else; where can he go?

'I'm going for a walk.' He's stopped pacing. 'As far as the chimneys.'

'They're further than you think. They're right on the river.'

'Good. I'll go down to the river.'

'Be careful.' She has a sudden vision of someone pushing him in. Of crocodiles.

She watches him from the window where she saw him the first day. He looks in at Laiq's and lifts one finger; they're meeting for lunch, she knows. From the terrace she watches him take the short cut by the row of stalls where the press-wallah is already at work. He passes the vegetable stall whose pumpkins dream in the blue morning shadow of the wall. This morning the wall's a python. At the urinal, whose stained tiles are also steeped in shade, he slips into sunshine, stands there, legs apart, tall, ginger-haired, unmistakable. She watches with girlish fascination the little jerk with which he finishes. Then he turns and steps through the gap in the city wall and is gone.

Lev crosses the uneven ground where Laiq walks his bird and follows the wide road that divides North from South Delhi. She lives on the border, he realizes, in the shadow of the wall. At the lights of the Ring Road intersection he crosses to the greener side and makes for the chimneys of the power station. He realizes they'll be off limits but in his mind he'd like to touch the smooth rail of the gantry he's seen so often through Morgan's binoculars. The chimneys recede before him like a mirage; behind him the malishwallah keeps a fixed distance. At the first bridge there's so much traffic between him and the power station that he gives up and decides to go down to the water instead. He goes clambering over culverts and along paths the monsoon has churned to mud. The river is full, a swollen stream, but the inlet at his feet is edged with froth and choked with flotsam. The bank is lined with faeces. It's not the Neva at Peter.

He follows the bridge road back to the city. On the city side he finds a fruit juice stand with a local telephone sign and rings Art Master's cellphone. *Not to worry*, Art Master says. *Just report early to the Aeroflot check-in counter on Sunday. Ask for Sergei. He'll take care of you.* Lev risks a glass of sweet lime juice, freshly squeezed. It tastes so pale and comforting and northerly he has a second glass. He orders a glassful for the malishwallah, and walks on. Now to call home. There's a

PCO opposite the Income Tax Office. The line is bad and
he can hardly hear his mother-in-law but she says she can
hear him clearly. Sunday, he says over and over, he's arriving,
not Saturday, and puts the phone down. Then he turns back
towards Delhi Gate along the busy link road where the newspaper offices are. INTERNATIONAL DOLLS MUESEUM, says the
incongruous sign. How can he pass it by?

He knows how she feels about dolls and doll-makers but
as he goes from cabinet to cabinet, enduring each off-centre
stare, his nerves are soothed and a kind of peace steals over
him. He steps out oddly becalmed. The malishwallah is there
with his bottles, waiting patiently. They exchange the forgiving
look of executioner and victim.

Lunch with Laiq is a sombre affair. They sit at the same
table as before, the first on the left, and drink beer and eat a
single kathi roll each. By contrast the wholesale merchants at
the next table are working their way down the menu, trying
all the short eats in turn. Their leader's cellphone keeps ringing
and he answers each call from the same reservoir of patience
with which he sends back a tray of tandoori chops that are
too lean. Laiq is impressed by the man's confidence; that's
himself, he realizes with a shock, ten years ago, but without
the money. He even shares the build. Where has this new
money come from? Where has his youth gone? His gloom
deepens. The waiter wears a bottle opener in his breast pocket
like a decoration. He must reach for it in his dreams.

'Russia is cold?' He makes Russia rhyme with Razia.

'Very cold. Six months of snow. In the north, eight
months.'

'Eight months!' Laiq shivers and makes a funnel of his
lips. 'Russia have rockets, yes?'

'Yes.'

'We also.' There's pride in his voice. 'They are telling war is coming. No good. They have bomb, we have bomb. So, OK. Why this fighting? Country is poor! Russia is our friend, yes?'

'Yes. Russia is also poor.'

'*Russia!*' Laiq smiles disbelief. 'Russia have science.' Signs.

'You have science too.' A weapons programme, Lev thinks bitterly.

'We have scientists,' Laiq corrects him. '*This* much scientists, *this* much science.' He marks off one big and one tiny measure along the edge of the table and laughs for the first time. As the world firms around him he remembers: 'Madam is having puppet show.'

'Yes, tomorrow. Razia's story.'

'Razia Begam?' Laiq's plucked eyebrows make an arch.

'Yes. You will come?'

'I will try. Friday is busy night for me.' He slumps a little at the thought and sits there unprotesting while Lev pays. He looks shrunken, Lev feels. As if he's read Lev's thoughts Laiq springs up and walks out stately as ever.

They cross Nevsky by the footbridge no one uses. A small crowd has gathered at the bus stop on the other side. The crowd is looking with the oblique glance of a collective doll at an object in the street. As Lev descends the steps from the bridge he sees a sight so horrific that he tries to spare Laiq it by pulling him away. But Laiq has seen it, and he has recognized the man he shaved. It's the malishwallah, or his remains. He has been run over by the bus that is standing there and all his sorry wadding has scrolled out.

The bus driver has absconded, as every driver in the land

knows he must if he is to escape lynching, even though it appears this one was not at fault. The malishwallah's box of oil bottles lies smashed in the gutter, the oils and the blood run together. Laiq takes Lev's arm and steers him homeward. When they have left the clamour of Nevsky behind he slows a little and explains.

'They are telling he was pushed.'

At the Jain mansion they part.

'You *stay* upistair,' Laiq warns. He returns to his shop and drops onto the bench seat, his brain tingling. His whole frame sags as if he had let out a long breath, the breath of his life. A couplet of Mir's which he has often repeated without understanding returns to him with new clarity.

> *Already you complain of blistered feet?*
> *It's a long way to Delhi yet, my son.*

Thirty-Three

Upstairs the rehearsal is over. Sukhdev and Baldev have gone back to the Serai. Maya can see something's wrong.

'How was your lunch?'

'It was all right.' He stands before her.

'But?'

'I just saw something horrible.'

He tells her. She listens appalled.

'This is crazy. I can call Pa.'

'And what?'

'Have him put a man downstairs.'

'Last time you told him to take his man away.'

'It wasn't his man.'

He looks down. 'It's just two more days. Three.'

She puts her arms around him. 'You stay here, then. Just don't go out.'

'And tomorrow?' He means the show.

She winces, then smiles placatingly. 'Pa will be there. There'll be cops all over the place. Stick with Morgan.'

He nods. 'Go rest. You must be tired.'

'You too.'

'I have to check all the outfits. Today Leela found Razia's

shield hanging by one thread, can you imagine. We're having a full dress rehearsal in the morning. She's very keen to meet you, by the way. I've told her she's not to run off with you. She's too much, yaa.'

She rolls her eyes at him and slips away. An hour later she calls from the puppet room. 'I don't really *mind* Russian tea.'

He makes it. They drink it on the swing seat, looking out at the chimneys.

'How was the river?'

'Dirty.'

'Be grateful it was the monsoon. It's even dirtier when the level is low.'

He remembers. 'I went to the dolls' museum afterwards.'

'You went *where?*'

'I was trying to get away from the – guy.' He can't bring himself to say malishwallah. That defunct mannequin.

'I've never been in there.'

'I'm sure.'

'Maybe I will.' *After you've gone,* hangs unspoken. There's little they can safely say. It's as if they're already moving apart. In pure geometry they passed that point weeks ago.

'Your hawks are back.' Neutral ground, up a tree. They watch the male feather the currents in a wide circle around the silk-cotton while the female roosts in the nest.

She gets the binoculars but focuses on a garden lizard sunning itself on the compound wall.

'God! I had forgotten how powerful these are.' The spiny ridge along the lizard's neck mimics the glass shards embedded in the cement. Its red throat has gone cement grey. 'You want to see camouflage?'

He spots it right away. 'He has his own armour.'

'Shit! That reminds me.'

She skips to the workroom to make the general's chain mail. Her scissors cut out a buckram vest that she smears with rice paste. She applies the paint while it's half dry and watches the silver glug into the mesh, hole by hole. Then gets busy tacking on Razia's shield. Then there are Babaji's wooden clogs to mend: he's the only one in the play with feet. *Clack, clack, clack* go his chattis. When she looks up the sun is low behind the office building opposite.

'I'll go get some peas.' Their last dinner. She wants to make a special effort. Tomorrow night the friends who own the haveli are having a feast to celebrate the show. 'Is panir all right?'

She fetches her black bag and comes back and kisses him. 'Bolt the door. I'll give three short rings.'

He returns to the field glasses. Laiq's bird is calling from beyond the city wall, the hawks have settled down. A plane goes over and he focuses on it; its windows catch the light of the setting sun. The city wall glooms in evening violet, a salamander. In a little while Maya appears at the sabziwallah's stall under the wall. Her magnified back, her wild hair, her shoulders, quake in the grainy circle of light. She could be a rogue cell trembling in the dish. Chattering to the sabziwallah as she splits open a peapod and rolls the peas down the green chute into her mouth.

The doorbell rings, once.

Lev lowers the glasses and turns his head, considering. When he trains the glasses she's gone. He goes and sits on the swing seat, on the edge. The bell rings again.

He stays where he is, focusing on the hawks but not

seeing them. The sky is a pale yellow behind the tree and pale blue above, and the tree itself is a dark shape. Again the bell, a single ring. He gets up and shuts the door to the flat and goes and stands at the edge of the terrace and waits there.

The bell keeps ringing at intervals, growing more peremptory.

Maya is at the Hans Dairy downstairs. Hurry up, she thinks. The younger, slower brother is minding the shop. He takes up a handleless knife and carefully cuts a wedge off the chalk-white round of cheese, then another thinner slice to make up the weight. Now it's too much. He cuts a cube off the end. OK, OK! At last the needle finds the mark. White plastic bag, red rubber band, pink polythene carry bag. Come *on*! She pays and finds herself running upstairs.

Lev hears voices at the door. Then Maya's three short rings.

It's Morgan with her, indignant at having been kept waiting.

'Where did you park?'

'At the other end of the universe. *Well* past the Crab nebula.'

'Good. My sabziwallah was looking at me strangely just now.'

'So. Now you have security.'

'*You!*'

He looks at her witheringly. 'Not just *me*. Not *just* me. *Not* just me. Haven't you noticed the cop?'

'What cop?'

'Across the road.'

He leads her to the balustrade where the downstairs Mrs

Jain has spread her sari to dry. Lev hangs back. There's a constable on patrol in the street below.

'Pa must have put him there.' Maya squeezes Lev's arm. 'Now we can relax.'

'So you don't need to lock yourselves indoors,' Morgan says, turning. 'In fact I came to remind you of the shower.'

'What shower?'

'The shower everybody's talking about. Didn't you hear me on the news this morning? The meteor shower.' He stops short and points. 'Shouldn't you remove that?'

It's the self-sown pipal, no longer little. It has doubled in size since the return of the rains. The stem is now fatter than a finger and the topmost leaves are chest high.

'But it's lovely!'

Morgan looks at his love and shakes his head. Lev smiles, his first smile of the day.

'Look at it!' Maya strokes a young leaf, pink and silky with a tender tail.

The roots have burrowed deep into the roof.

'Another week and it'll be taller than Lev.'

Who won't be here, waves like a flag.

'It'll grow back,' Lev says, 'unless you remove the roots.'

Morgan turns his thumb down. 'Lev?'

Lev nods.

'OK,' she shrugs. 'Murderers!'

Lev goes and ferrets among her tools. He returns with a screwdriver, a small trowel, and a broken dinner knife, and begins to chip away at the weathered roofing. Glad at last to be doing. Maya watches, surprised at his deftness. While he works she tells Morgan of the downstairs Mrs Jain's visit. They laugh together, Morgan uproariously. In twenty minutes

Lev has tracked down all the cunning roots and completed his surgery; the plant lies on its side, a fresh corpse. There is a deep gash in the roof.

'What's down below?' Morgan asks.

'Mrs Jain.'

'Oh dear.'

'You can pot this, you know,' Morgan says. He takes the sapling to the kitchen and sticks its mandrake root provisionally into a mug of water in the sink. When he returns Maya and Lev are standing at the grave, musing.

It's then that Mrs Jain comes up to get her sari. She stops and stares at the hole in her roof. Morgan is the quickest off the mark.

'We found them just in time,' he says confidentially to Mrs Jain in his slightly formal Hindi.

'Who?'

'The thieves. They were trying to get into the flat below. They must have heard there was gold.'

Mrs Jain looks at him in dismay. She's seen him up here before and she's definitely seen him on TV.

'But *when?*'

'This afternoon, in broad daylight. You see that policeman downstairs?'

Mrs Jain goes to look. Maya looks at Morgan and tugs his sleeve. Enough, silly.

'Don't worry about it,' she says to the alarmed woman. 'I'll have the hole filled in tomorrow.'

'There might be rain tonight, though,' Morgan forecasts for Mrs Jain. He's never done the weather before.

He cooks the pea pulao; the panir he does in a tomato purée from a Godrej carton. Monsoon onions, but that can't be helped; what he's missing are his knives. When they've eaten Lev washes up. Morgan decrees that the place to watch the meteor shower from is the terrace and the best position is flat on their backs.

'Where's my mattress?'

She pushes him down onto the swing seat. 'I'll take care of that.'

Morgan's mattress, now hers – hers went to Lev – comes dragging out behind her, travois fashion; then she returns for the other. She pulls both out well past the terrace awning and spreads a sheet crosswise over them.

'There.' She stretches out and looks expectantly up at the sky. 'Bring a cushion. When does the show start?'

'Two o'clock. No matinee.'

'*Two!* How am I supposed to stay awake?'

'First one asleep gets sixty lashes.'

Lev comes out wiping his hands.

'Any meteors?'

'No. Come and lie down.'

They lie looking up at the faded yellow of the sky. It's the exact yellow of the Jain mansion, with the same moss-black streaking lower down, as if the mansion has expanded to include everything. The day's fluffy cloud tents are now pitched on the horizon, cloth of gold but empty of rain, leaving a clear field overhead whose argent is already darkening. Every now and again a single cloud detaches itself from the massed tents and drifts over them, coming apart in a plasmic haze through which Morgan notices suddenly a wan last quarter moon. A plane goes over, its red light winking. Morgan says nothing; he's learning quiet. It's Maya who's tempted into facetiousness.

'Shh.' He puts his finger to her lips.

Silence. The heavens open, the dark cloth of sky flaps and the stars come swooning down. Lev sees entrails looping, an intestine that winds from star to star in Cassiopeia. Maya has found a cluster to focus on, a tiny web of light directly overhead that offers no purchase for the eye but is magically there. Morgan is trawling the Milky Way. *Whey,* he always thought as a boy. Tonight his asthma is no worry at all; he's so sure about it he's left his spray behind. He goes sailing through the constellations, yet every time he blinks he's back on earth beside this woman. Spider-like he slips back down his silk and turns his head to look at her. That profile like a range of low familiar hills. She grows conscious of his gaze and answers it without looking, with a quick squeeze of his hand.

'You could reach up and pluck one,' she says.

'*They* reach down and pluck you.'

Lev, who cannot shake off the entrails, says to clear his head: 'Maybe it is tomorrow night?'

'No,' Morgan answers from across the hills, 'tonight. Two o'clock.'

Two o'clock comes, then half-past.

'Don't let me fall asleep,' Maya says.

Just then a point of vivid light streaks clear across the sky. Up, then across, then down: simple bisection.

'There!' Maya calls, and claps like a little girl.

All three saw it, have seen nothing like it, ever. They tense themselves for more, but no more come. There are one or two small sparks but they are ordinary falling stars, isolated, removed.

'A shower of one,' Maya grumbles.

'You want fireworks,' Morgan reproves her. One, that one, was enough for him. More would, he considers, reduce that one.

Lev is so still it's possible he's asleep. Maya turns and looks at him. He is. His head has rolled to one side so the chin is almost resting on his shoulder. The twist is exaggerated and has the effect of a broken neck.

Maya feels sleep descending. Her forehead drops onto Morgan's shoulder and stays there. He feels its warmth and goes still, afraid to move, afraid she'll move. Slowly his anxiety vanishes; she's fast asleep. Now he's alone with the weight of that one touch. The night reclaims him and he lies there under the sky, sifting, sifted. A poem is coming to him.

The Glasscutter nods, dull with too much light, tired of being a mystery to himself. He lays his setsquare finger flat on the void. *There!* his diamond glides. We hang on the snap of black glass. He falls asleep, spares us the scalding.

At four thirty Morgan gets up, careful not to disturb her. He slept in his clothes so he'll just have to use the studio wardrobe. He makes himself black tea, drinks it in the kitchen, and wakes Lev to let him out. His finger is on his lips. Don't disturb her. Her big day. Together they pad to the front door and Lev draws the bolt.

'GOOD MORNING, INDIA!'

The voice booms from behind them, making them jump. Maya is up. Her delivery is so perfect, exactly Morgan's practised locutions, that he rounds on her laughing and grabs her by the shoulders and shakes her. Then he remembers Lev's presence and is suddenly shy.

Maya sees the bashful look and is pleased. Pleased in him, more pleased by that than by anything he's ever done.

'Eight o'clock,' she warns him. 'Don't be late.' To Lev she says: 'Should we stay up?'

'It's still night.'

His wrist still bare of time. If she had a watch she'd present it to him. They go back to sleep in yesterday's clothes.

Morgan drives the empty avenues on automatic pilot. There are moments, he is thinking, when you stand open to the universe. Last night, this morning, he had one such, *and* he felt love in the squeeze of her hand, *and* he received a poem. It's no wonder he's carrying himself like something precious when he steps from the car. The sky to the east is taking on a pale mucilage yellow, so the big jamun tree at the edge of the studio car park has just begun to stand out trunk and leaf. How can Petersburg compare with this city where every tree is Maya?

Thirty-Four

'Maya.'

She looks up at him against the sky. It's morning. She strokes the nap of his still new haircut and holds his gaze.

'Maya . . .' Russian or English, he's tongue-tied.

She kisses his shoulder. 'Chalo. Or Baldevji will be breathing down my neck. You're invited to a special performance. In fact I'll do the seating right now.'

She goes to the dining space, picks up one of the cane chairs and carries it to the front room.

'There!' She bows and sweeps one hand. 'Chief guest.'

He sits in the centre of the empty room. 'And breakfast?' He's hungry.

'Oh yes. Bring the chair back.'

She sets about stewing tea. He goes and sits on the swing seat with the binoculars. The hawks are circling. The sun is well up, already hot. The few clouds left over from last night are white and skimpy. Someone is splashing water in the yard below. A bucket is set down on gritty concrete. Horns, radios, water pumps, bells: the sober percussion of a city coming to life. Then Laiq's bird sounds its war cry from across the wall. A hawk swoops down and plucks up something from the neighbour's yard. It's the garden lizard from yesterday: the hawk has it by its wiry tail. Its red throat flashes as it's carried away, astonished, choking with cold rage. If it could bite off its own tail it would and fall to the ground but it can't reach. It arcs right up in desperation, balanced on one muscle. And then it's in the nest where the young hawks are waiting; the meal commences at once. Lev lowers his glasses.

Leela arrives early. With her china-doll features and fine blowy hair cut pixie short, she makes Maya look plain. Silver of her own device winds about her wrist, her neck, and every other finger. Her nails are grown long but not painted. Her earrings don't match; one is very large and petalled, one just a stud.

'Condensed milk on bread!' she screams. 'I'm next. This is like old times, yaa. Do we bunk maths today?'

She dangles a condensed milk cigar as she sets up her equipment, then takes one of Lev's cigarettes.

'Is this breakfast? You haven't taught Maya how to cook?' she asks, flirting outrageously, the old school pal pledged to share everything.

'She makes excellent parathas.'

'Parathas!' Leela affects shock at betrayal. 'Maya! I'm not going to talk to you.' She puts on her headphones in a sulk.

'*This* one not talk!' Maya points with her chin, bringing out the puppets. 'Some chance. You think *I'm* a chatterbox.'

The bell goes again, Sukhdev and Baldev. They've brought their own puppets for the run up. Their Anarkali is cruder than Maya's but lighter on the fingers. Hooks for hands because she carries a lamp while dancing. Baldev produces the lamp and wants kerosene for it.

'Will cooking oil do?' Maya asks.

'Chalega.' Will do.

'Jalega,' Sukhdev chimes in. Will burn.

They too have their impromptu act, an older rapport. Today they're freshly shaved so their moustaches look even bigger, their legs longer and leaner in fresh dhotis. How they come to life as their fingers touch the strings! Each puppet is lifted out and unravelled till it hangs true. Each is tested — left arm, sword arm, bend sideways, bow, lean back, *charge!* — and laid down with the strings extended.

Suddenly the room is filled with a high piping. Baldev answers with his reed and the two men talk in squeaks and grunts, squeaks for discourse, grunts for threats. The squeaks fill the upper air like circling seagulls; knives could not be sharper. The grunts, which come when all patience is lost, actually bring relief. The puppeteers' arms go out as their puppets rush apart and turn and fly at each other.

Swoosh and thud. Grunt.

Swoosh and *THUD!* Harder.

In the middle of this, the doorbell. It's Gurmeet, the painter, with the backdrops rolled up like wallmaps. They're almost as wide as the room, and heavy.

'Lev,' Maya calls. My general. 'Can you hang this up? Use those windows.'

Lev hooks the dowling over the pelmet boards. It's the panorama of the Yamuna floodplain. There's a medieval town in the distance with its domes and red stone tower, and the river muscling up on either side in the foreground. The field in the middle is both battlefield and cropland, so when the lights come up they will find the farmer puppet, Bodh Ram, who is both chorus and tiller, tilling his narrow tithe.

Baldev and Sukhdev have finished their Anarkali rehearsal.

The room is turned around. Maya has laid out her puppets at the other end and the brothers come over to inspect the late addition. She picks up the farmer and introduces him.

'Bodh Ram, this is Baldev, and this is Sukhdev. Bodh Ram says namaste.'

'Namasteji,' his puppeteers reply.

'Bodh Ram will be ploughing his field,' Maya says, handing the peasant over to Baldev. 'Here is his bullock.' She hands the creature over to Sukhdev.

The men's fingers slip into action, finding natural knots and stays, and Lev watches amused as the old peasant goes riding on the ploughshare behind his beast, up and down, up and down the little stretch between the two arms of the river.

'Music up,' Maya signals, 'and count ten furrows, five this way and five that, OK? Then go down and I start. All right?'

All count ten furrows. Bodh Ram rides his plough, twigging his bullock from time to time. He turns to the audience.

'*In the year the locusts came I was a small boy.*'

Lev stares at Maya. Her voice has changed completely. She might be changing into a wolf, he stares so hard. It isn't the deep voice that surprised him last night but a mellow tenor.

'*That was the year the great Sultan of Delhi, Altamsh, died and was succeeded by his son. But the nobles of the land disliked the young man and rose up and killed him. It was then that his sister Razia became queen.*

'*She was a capable ruler. Oh yes, she was strong and good and just and wise and fair. She ruled from her throne in the palace over there in the shadow of the Kutub Minar, but equally she ruled from her saddle, for she was a fine horsewoman and wore a sword as sharp as*' *a razor and as bright as the sun and as strong as the ancient iron pillar that stands hard by the great minar.*

'*Such harvests my father reaped in those years! Such butter my mother made from our cow's milk! Golden the sugar I sprinkled on her cakes!*

'On *cakes* music up again and Bodh Ram rests in the shade of that tree. All right, Baldevji? Lie him down there and then we start where we started yesterday. That's the only new bit. OK?'

Lev looks at her. Some time yesterday she sat alone and worked up a puppet and wrote the new bit in her head. Yesterday! Just like that. And said nothing about it.

On stage Bodh Ram leaves his bullock and sinks down under the feathery thorn tree Painter Gurmeet has put there. The bullock waits, its tail flicking this way and that.

'Now lights down. And disappear the bullock.'

Leela nods. There is only one floodlight and she will work it from beside her console. She makes notes on her script. Maya's script is in her head.

'Then enter Razia. All right, Sukhdevji?'

Razia enters alone, riding out of the city gates to stage left, making for the bridge of boats. She sees a peasant asleep under a tree.

'*Ho, peasant!*'

Maya calls in her own voice now, but immediately drops into a third register, that of Bodh Ram's father.

Tulsi Ram rises from his slumber in a coughing fit. A red turban has been slipped over his head.

'*What is it, woman? HIGHNESS! Forgive me.*' He prostrates himself, '*I thought it was my wife. She is a very troublesome woman, highness, a very stupid woman, a very coarse woman, a most rude and vulgar—'*

'*Enough, peasant. Did you see a riderless horse pass this way? Oh, never mind.*

'And then she crosses the bridge and exits on this side.'

Maya feels Lev's gaze on her as she comes out of the scene. His admiration is a palpable thing and she is accustomed to the pull of it. She rides it, drawn into extemporisms that strain the manipulators, pushing the illusion, performing with a strength and assurance she dare not stop to examine. She would like to touch him in passing, but won't in front of Baldev and Sukhdev. Village men, her manipulators judge harshly of the city. They are part-time tillers who have sat in a plane. So she simply glows and endures the look.

And now night has fallen.

Maya watches Lev from the wings where she sits with the microphone. He is seated on the soft carpet at the front, off to one side. Morgan is coming in now to join him, late as usual. There is a sprinkling of South Delhi types among the gentry at the front. The friends whose haveli gate she's turned into a stage are there, and in their midst she has spotted, with a sudden thudding of heart, her parents. Her father catches her eye with a look that says: *You didn't expect us to miss it, did you?* and she parries with a nod at the cop nearest him: *You and half the force, I suppose.* He shrugs, *Well, you know.* He has seen certain posters, not just the ones advertising the show. Of course she's grateful. She bulges her eyes at Morgan. *Late as usual.* He gives his pout.

'Apparently,' he says to Lev squatting down beside him, 'Thailand got the best view of the meteors.'

The drummer is still drumming at the head of the lane

as folk drift in from the precinct. Families sit down on the durrees, solitaries stand along the sides of the marquee, urchins crowd the rear. There are watchers from roofs and balconies and terraces and windows; the small children of the street are perched on high doorsteps. The drumming stops.

Leela turns down the flood and they go straight into Anarkali. Such fights! Such horsemanship! The prince leaning the whole horse over as he rides in hot pursuit: Maya's fingernails drum the board under the microphone. Battlecries, death groans, whisperings, cacklings, evil laughter. Then the lights go down and in the dark a single footfall with anklebells. *Chhang!* Then another, flat, *chhak*, then *chhang!* then *chhak* in the silence as step by step Anarkali comes on and begins to dance. Applause when she picks up her lamp, murmurs as she holds it out in front of her and makes a perfect circle. Horror on small faces as she is bricked into the wall alive.

Laiq has missed the Anarkali. He heard the drum and did intend to go but a kind of helplessness has seized him. It's the hour for doctoring, not for cutting hair, but he sits in the barber's chair all the same twiddling the clippers. He has herded the shaving brush and stick into a corner of the laminated benchtop along with the dish of talc and the fluffy powderpuff and the hairbrush and comb and the clothes brush and the large safety pin, as if in readiness to lock up, but he sits there toying with the spring arm of the clippers, watching the teeth glide back and forth. If a customer came by for a cut he might sit him down or he might turn him away and take down the cage. There he's his own man, untroubled, secure. The smell of the shaving stick never leaves him and he loves it. What's bothering him is the doctoring. Ever since the plague his faith in his potions has been shaken.

He's the only one who knows about the tetracycline lapse –
apart from Lev – but that's all the more galling.

What *if* the powders in the jars are just powders? He
jumps up at the unbearable thought and stands in his door.
The bird, walked and watered and fed, imagines it's time to
be taken home and darts him an expectant look. It begins
to jib like a compass needle, but Laiq just stands there. The
thought, unjust as he knows it to be, recurs and he leans over
and spits out a nervous jet of red. It's then that he notices
the poster. He steps down on the pavement and reads the
letterpress Hindi.

WHO HAS SENT SABOTEURS AMONG US?
WHO PUSHED THE MASSEUR KARAN CHAND?
WAS THERE A FOREIGN HAND IN THE PLAGUE?
You Who Suffered and Lost Loved Ones
Be Vigilant!
THE MOTHERLAND IS IN PERIL

Laiq reads the poster through twice, the blood rising to
his face. He knows mischief when he sees it.

He takes down the birdcage and locks up. Lev will be at
the puppet show. He must get to him before someone else
does. He hurries down Haidar Road and crosses Nevsky. By
the time he gets there the show is almost over.

Razia and her lover have come to the grove that is Babaji's
retreat. The old mendicant squats outside his cave trying to
rekindle a fire. He leans right down to the embers and blows.

Maya blows beside the microphone. Her voice grows
ancient.

'*All cunning is low,*' Babaji is saying. He looks up at the
kneeling queen. The general stands back, motionless. It's a

tricky moment because Sukhdev, who is handling both lovers, must go between them when they're apart, hanging up one and taking hold of the other, while his brother manipulates Babaji.

'*You must do as your inner voice dictates.*'

Laiq has made his way through the bystanders along the edge of the marquee towards Lev's ginger head at the front. He sees his friend sitting with Morgan, crossing and uncrossing his long legs because he's unaccustomed to sitting on the ground. He catches his eye and beckons.

Yes, *now*. It's *urgent*.

Lev gets to his feet. Morgan looks up, annoyed because it's a critical moment in the play. He sees Lev confer with Laiq and both men turn away. He sees Maya's attention waver and her eye follow Lev's retreating figure. It's a long moment, but she must end it.

'*It tells me that hesitation is weakness,*' Razia says.

'*Then do not hesitate.*'

'*Even to do wrong?*'

'*Act boldly. Your enemy may be preparing a greater wrong. History will judge. And time will seal up the judgement.*'

Razia remains silent a space, considering. Now it is her turn to kneel motionless. It's then that fate strikes. A drumroll, a clash of cymbals. *A-hhh!*

The Commander-in-Chief gasps and staggers. For the first time in the scene he turns his back to the audience, and there it is, an arrow new-fletched and sunk to the depth of half its shaft, a red stain around it. He cries out and falls where he stands.

Immediately Razia is on her feet, sword in hand, rushing

wildly about from side to side. But the assassin is gone. Slowly she returns to kneel at her lover's side.

Death music snakes up from Leela's console, unaccompanied shehnai. The holy man crosses slowly to his cave and sits in the cave mouth. The lights go down and then it's time to roll up the grove backdrop.

The final battle is fought before the panorama of the Yamuna banks. Trumpets blare, battlecries resound. Dust and din and derring-do. Razia falls.

Lights down to black, then up again.

Now the battlefield is bare.

Now it is cropland again, and Bodh Ram wakes from his slumber under the thorn tree. The bullock is discovered grazing.

Laiq and Lev thread the narrow lanes in the dark.

'Here is *hundred* per cent danger for you,' Laiq says walking rapidly; his testes have drawn up into the cavity of him like machinery. 'You please *stay* in Madam's house.'

Lev says nothing. He feels suddenly foolish and exposed. The lights of Nevsky ahead are a comfort. They cross the thoroughfare at Delhi Gate, cutting through a string of pilgrims who carry brightly decorated pots of holy water. Every bush in the corner park is an assailant; at the Durga shrine the goddess brandishes ten deadly weapons. The sabziwallah's stall is curtained over, the presswallah has gone home. They have just reached the urinal when a scooter pulls up and the pillion rider jumps off. In the half dark Laiq recognizes something in the masked man's shape, some slenderness of frame, intimately known. Yet instinct makes him lift an arm to ward off, not to welcome. The lifting breaks a circuit: the assault is halved, but half is enough. The stranger shakes out his bottle and jumps back onto the pillion.

Lev gasps and bends double as the night enters his eye. Pain so excruciating he wants to scream and opens his mouth but can only gasp again. The eyeball instantly molten, the eyelid unwilling to shut or stay open because a burning wind is pouring through the space it guarded. He clutches his face where the skin was and the affliction comes away on his hand.

Laiq half shouts after the disappearing scooter but turns back to Lev. He sees him clutch at his face and knows at once what it is. He throws an arm about his waist and hauls him towards the light of the shops in the Jain mansion. There he sits Lev down on the kerb and rushes into the dairy.

'Water! Quick, water! Someone's thrown acid.'

The only water is in a large storage tank even now being filled from the mains tap. It is too heavy to shift, much less to carry.

'*Any*thing! Quickly!'

Lev has rolled over onto his side. His head lifts and drops as he moans a terrible soft moan, his hand clenches and unclenches. He does not know where to put his pain. Droplets of acid have burnt through his polo shirt on one side and are eating into flesh. The dairy brothers grab their catch-all degchi of rinse water and heave it onto the counter. Laiq takes it from them and pours it over Lev, over the dark rose of the eye and down the face and across his chest. The tailors have jumped up and come out of their shop and are watching in consternation. They have legs, if only Lev could see.

'More,' Laiq calls, handing the degchi back. He lifts Lev back up into a sitting position and tenderly removes his tattered shirt.

The degchi is filling, too slowly. The brothers hesitate, then reach together for a brimming milk can. Carefully, with Laiq directing, they pour milk over the affected parts until the huge can is empty.

'Take him to the hospital.'

'Get an auto.' The younger brother goes running to the stand.

Laiq is squatting beside his friend holding his good arm, trying to imagine his pain. He has a flask of jojoba salve on his shelves in the dispensary, but is it any good? He gets up, goes from foot to foot, staring down at Lev. He would use the lotion on himself, but can he trust it on his friend? There's a single spot of acid on his wrist which is worrying its way through skin and he dabs at it with a wetted corner of his kurta, but the torment of indecision is greater. The autorickshaw arrives. The word *hospital* sounds again. It carries more authority than anything he could hope to offer.

Laiq wraps Lev's bare chest in a sheet the tailors have provided and sits him in the auto. The gutter is running with milk. The auto driver speeds away.

It's the same emergency room they brought Maya to but Lev will never know it. Laiq carries him through the press of waiting folk. A bed is found and Lev is lifted onto it. A sedative is administered, a basin brought, and irrigation commences.

Laiq stands by and watches his unconscious friend. The face he so admired is spoilt on one side, the skin of the cheek gone, the eye destroyed. For half an hour the laving continues, then the basin is taken away. Lev's breathing is so light Laiq fears for his life, but there's nothing he can do. He must return and inform Maya.

The auto drops him at the haveli gate where the stage is being stripped. Maya and Morgan listen distraught to his account and all three climb into Morgan's Zen. Outside Emergency Maya prepares herself to see Lev's ravaged face. It's a strange moment for Morgan too who was last here carrying Maya.

Laiq leads them through the stained white door and stops short. His mouth falls open.

Lev is gone.

The bed is empty. The pillow bears not the slightest impress of that head he has barbered and massaged and cherished and held in an armlock, and brought in ruins to this place. The linen has been changed, the undersheet so perfectly smoothed down it could be a slab of white marble.

Thirty-Five

Maya blames Laiq.

Over and over she replays the moment when Lev's head tilted to catch what Laiq was saying from the edge of the marquee. She sees him rise and turn to Morgan before following the barber out. That's the last glimpse she got of him. It's the last she'll ever have.

'*Discharged!*' Laiq and Morgan mouth together. Maya doesn't know what to think.

The duty nurse is adamant. Yes, the intern confirms. A van came for him, along with an official car. They had the authority. He saw the papers himself.

Day after day Maya waits for word. No pain like waiting. '*Pa?*'

'Putri. Nothing. I asked again. Same thing.' The Ministry is stonewalling his source. The undeclared war drags on. The fate of a foreigner, and a suspect one at that, counts for little at a time when the blood of martyrs is being spilt.

What has the war to do with me? Maya asks. Columnists, shopkeepers, even her mother, can tell her. But fear of the stranger is what it comes down to. Love of one's own gods. That demoted godhead the finial could tell her.

Secretly she imagines he'll turn up somehow the way he did that first afternoon with Laiq. Who sold him out, she's sure. She's so sure she jumps up and runs downstairs meaning to confront him. But Laiq's shutters are closed. He'll be out walking the bird.

She goes walking, muttering to herself, couldn't care less about the looks she's getting. Finds herself seeing in superimposed slides. Nevsky traffic is flowing across her stage, making for the bridge of boats. Her heart is beating strangely, a muffled gabardine thumping with a stitch across it, knop and flower, knop and flower. She stops, listens. A singing in her ear. A tingling floods her body from her scalp to the soles of her feet. She must turn back or fall. She returns to the mansion, climbs the steps slowly, her heart pumping as never before, an irregular thrumming as if it's worked loose of its moorings.

Pain she can read like a palmist. She's takes regular counsel from her joints, knows their advice down to a twinge. This is different, like a whisper of war. Sitting there with her eyes shut she feels with clarity the onset of some mortal attack.

She goes to the bedroom. Rest will cure her: she hasn't had much sleep lately. She lies down square in the centre of the mattress, alone. But as she's dropping off the doomy tingling surges up and threatens to engulf her. *Stay awake*, her body signals: *this current drowns*. She fights off descending sleep, forces her eyes open, lies there wondering. God, round-shouldered finial. What is happening to me?

Then the miasma lifts. Hope jumps in. There's nothing wrong with me. How *can* there be? I'm all there is.

She scans the familiar gauzy chains that float across the surface of the eye, guardian spirits since childhood. Singles one out and tracks it. It skates just ahead of true focus, but it's there, a rope of stars she can twist with a flick of the eye. She shuts her eyes. Galaxies on black velvet.

Laiq took you away. Led you into that attack. Your poor face.

Strength has pooled again in her body. Again she goes out walking. Again the shop signs fuzz, faces blur. So. It was not a dream. It's still there, the malignant thing, swirling up like radioactive dust. On her way back she sees Laiq standing in his door, his face unassailable. He steps back into his shop. He must have seen her too. She has nothing to say to him.

The birdcage hangs from its hook; behind the blur of bars the bird comes into focus like an idea.

She climbs the stair, her mind made up, weakness guiding her revenge. She goes to the kitchen. Where are Morgan's knives? They've disappeared. Is she going mad?

No matter. She knows now how to hurt the man downstairs.

'CV doesn't have a clue,' Morgan says, coming in behind her.

She doesn't even jump.

'You left the door open, by the way.' He looks at her. 'You haven't slept.'

'No.'

But she is eating, constantly. Even the dairy brothers have noticed: she buys quantities of panir, curds, milk, cream sweets. Morgan holds the fridge door open and glances at her. There's a box of chocolate barfi in there with the top layer gone. She doesn't see any difference, she's just obeying her body.

'What happened to the knives?'

'I took them back.'

She looks at him. What has Lev told him? He avoids her gaze; he wants to stay and comfort her but is afraid of intruding just now.

She goes downstairs with him when he leaves and looks to see if the birdcage is up on its hook. It is, but Laiq is there. No matter, she'll bide her time.

She's up and down the stair all week, checking. She just needs to be lucky once. Whenever the tingling abates she goes for a walk and returns by way of Laiq's saloon. Let him just step out and leave the shop open.

And then he does. He's stepped into the alley to urinate. Maya looks along the row of shops. Nobody out. She steps up onto his doorstep, unhooks the birdcage, and sneaks it upstairs. Sets it down on the glass table. Stares at the bird.

Brainfever.

The bird cocks its head, stares back through one eye, then the other. This is not the face, the hand it knows. It backs off and stands still, only its head shifting at clockwork intervals. For the first time Maya sees its plumage up close, the fine tiling of the neck, brindled on the feather, terracotta. Spots of tan making chain mail of the coverts. That ridiculously exposed throat.

Now what? She's never considered what she'll do.

The bird stretches its neck and flaps its clipped wings and appears to want to rear up. As if clearing its throat to speak.

What if it should start to call!

Maya grabs the singing bowl. Her sudden movement checks the bird; the drone stills it as she begins to rub: it's never heard the strange wailing from so near. The sound goes through it, a knife without edge or point. The red eye blinks, the head droops and comes up again, its feet begin to tread the floor in a witless dance: it is possessed, it is being called. The bird is being sung. Maya goes on rubbing, working the people till the bowl is singing on three levels at once. The whole flat is ringing like a bell.

She lets the sound die. Takes the cage to the top of the stair and opens the cage door. The bird stands dizzy at the edge of freedom and refuses to move. It sees a dark shaft, a fog of light at the bottom. Maya tilts the cage and the bird tips out onto the top step. Then spreads its clipped wings and half sails, half tumbles down the steep well with a feathered thudding of warm flesh and bone on stone.

The cage she'll return another time.

Thirty-Six

Laiq is leaning up against a pillar whose murals occupy him as he waits his turn.

Pillar and wall are covered in paintings of wounded birds and their healers. The number of times he's passed this building and read the lettering on the roof that says in capitals, JAIN CHARITABLE BIRD HOSPITAL, without giving it a second thought! And here he is waiting to collect his doctored bird. Saturday is discharge day for treated birds; it is six days since he brought the partridge in after carefully trimming the spurs. He wants no lectures, especially not from a fellow doctor.

In the weeks since Lev's disappearance he's passed through many moods. Something like equanimity has returned as he leans there, his eyes wandering peaceably over the painted scenes. The bird was a shock when he found it on the pavement, the cage gone, but he's been twice to visit it and after the first time, when he learnt it would live, he stopped worrying about the motive. The tailors are more exercised over that. When the cage turned up Laiq formed his own conjectures.

She picks up things. But he's her tenant.

He looks at the crested hoopoe laid out in the mural, a

stream of blood gushing from its chest. Strangely it's not his partridge he sees in that bird, and it's not even Lev, whose dark rose and pale rose still trouble him. He sees himself: *he* is the wounded hoopoe. He realizes that he has loved and that love is not a thing he would care to handle again. It has seethed in his body like a fever, it has tormented him with ecstasies. Now he has returned to life, tepid life, after an eternity of burning and freezing, and it is here that he chooses to remain. He has felt the halting return of the normal, and is grateful. The painted vet leans over the hoopoe with a bandage in one hand and a thermometer in the other. A stethoscope dangles from his neck and he wears – a further badge of doctoring – horn-rimmed spectacles. Laiq has often fancied a pair himself. They would lend a professional gravity he sometimes feels he lacks. Perhaps nature will oblige and blur his distant vision. Already he sees things differently. He will not abandon his jojoba and his roots and his cassia seedpods. But look at the line of this tabletop under the bird in the mural! It's distinctly odd. Even, come to that, wrong. Lacking something, the way the lines reject infinity. He hovers on the edge of a judgement altogether new to him.

He's so absorbed in his thoughts his name is called twice before he hears it. The bird looks bright of eye and happy to see him; it has had a trying week among twitterers and warblers. Laiq has brought for his mended mate a special offering of the best chickpeas, bruised and soaked overnight, so they smell of heaven and earth and life itself, and have made him salivate as he stood waiting his turn. He bows and makes his offering. The bird cranes its neck over the cupped palm as if to nuzzle or inspect, appears to inhale with heartfelt gratitude, and then scatters the lot with a sudden furious kick.

Thirty-Seven

The doorbell rings just as Maya puts the phone down.

It's Morgan, framed in the grille, a foot lower than Lev, and annoyed because she's standing there gawping.

'Are you going to let me in? What's the matter?'

She draws the bolt. '*Lev* just called! Just now.'

'He's back home,' Morgan says lightly.

'How did *you* know!'

'I've just come from CV's. He had news from Petersburg.'

She's turned away. 'It was a bad line. I could hardly hear him.' The monsoon has leaked into a jelly-filled cable laid last year.

'What did he say?'

'I couldn't make out anything. I think he said he arrived yesterday.'

'Yesterday! From where?'

'I don't know. He kept saying: *I'll write*. Then the line got cut.' She sinks into one of the cane chairs and breathes out a long exhausted sigh.

Morgan sits down opposite her. 'So.'

She glares at him. '*That's the end of that.*'

'I didn't say that.'

'No, you just said: *So.*' Her voice mimics his exactly.

Morgan pushes the whole argument aside with both hands. 'Poor Lev!'

He sees a new puppet on the glasstop table, a Frankenstein monster with a lightning conductor in his head. He sees she's been whittling away at the Commander-in-Chief; the medieval tunic has been replaced by a modern suit, no tie.

'A lightning rod in the head,' he notes drily. 'Who needs an umbrella?'

She doesn't reply. She's thinking of a childhood toy and wondering where it went. You pressed all sorts of plastic eyes and ears and noses into vegetable heads: potatoes, carrots, brinjals. She can see the ski nose clearly.

Morgan is thinking too. Love strikes like lightning, the deserving and the undeserving alike. He classes himself among the deserving, but beyond his usual chaffing propositions he's a paralysed suitor.

She jumps up. 'Chalo.'

'Where?'

'Just.' Her gesture of one hand flitting. Out.

They stand at the top of the stair the bird tumbled down. 'Have you told Sweeney?' she asks.

'I met him on the way in.'

'Then we'll go the other way.'

Past the tailors, towards the footbridge. She leads him across Nevsky, behind the great mosque, and into the old city. Past shops so specialized that a larger button must be sought next door. Past morose peddlers of dancing dolls that twitch on invisible thread. A walking skeleton whose ribcage is his livelihood, a ghastly peepshow. It's the hour of jasmine chains and incense and dust and a blue monoxide haze. Veiled women look askance at her, a mask seller goes to call out but lets it go. She is walking with no fixed purpose. Just looking to shift the weight of the past. Deeper and deeper into the red city that the fading light is turning brown. They pass under frail balconies sketched in tailor's chalk, old walls with the sag of canvas. They have entered the reverse of the paintings she visited with Lev: no bright morning view, no colour brighter than this shelled tamarind.

Presently the lanes begin to widen, the air to brighten as if the day were going backwards. A flock of mottled pigeons explodes off a cornice and goes wheeling through falls of yellow air. They come out on a bridge beyond the railway station; Morgan recognizes with a start its mock castellations in the distance. Here it is still evening. Colour has returned to the sky, and just where the yellow runs into blue there hangs suspended, wet and vulnerable as a gland, the evening star.

They are at the old city wall again, that dun camel. On a kind of embankment that overlooks an open field. Behind an immense tangle of pink quisqualis are the portals of an old hotel. *Casimir Hotel* says the blue and white sign; the compound behind is an island of green. Tempted by its air of sedate oblivion, they make for the gate without a word. They must go around the building twice before they spot the sign that says *Office*, tucked behind another swale of hot pink flowers that hats the portico.

In the vestibule an umbrella stand greets them with white china knobs on its coathooks and a cravat of viridian tiles; the mirror offers no reflection. Oxblood wainscoting dogs a red cement floor. The desk is ornate, heavy and tooled with a device that dates it to the twenties. Bureaux, dressers, a keyrack that might be a dovecote, a mahogany and rosewood telephone console, all stand untouched by time. But the custodian behind the desk looks chastened, a man once enormously fat, from the way his flesh hangs off him like drapery.

'You would like some tea?'

He leads them into the parlour beyond where there are one-legged tables and spindleshank chairs. The air is at blood heat. He switches on a ceiling fan the colour of old ivory.

'Some cakes?'

Again he doesn't wait for an answer but sets about fetching cups, plates, forks. He might have been waiting all his life for this moment.

'Did you notice his eyes are of different colours?' Maya whispers.

Morgan nods and smiles, as if the phenomenon were familiar to him. The cakes arrive, a two-tier plate of pineapple pastries, so called, the sponge the exact colour of the sky at the horizon in the open window.

'I'll have a nimbu pani,' Morgan decides instead, and the manager removes his cup.

There are no waiters in evidence. From the dark pantry comes the rhythmic tinkling of a teaspoon in a tumbler, sugar being stirred into fresh lime and water. It's a sound so plain and comforting that for the first time in months Maya feels the return of normality. What, she wonders, as the glow fades around her, *what* was that raging? The pale green tinkling from the pantry excludes the indifferent world, but does not deny it; it has its part in the vast repertory of sounds that she has unconsciously muted during this past summer. The once-fat man returns with a frosted glass on a tray. It is the colour of the evening star. He switches on a brace of dim lights in the centre of the parlour and leaves them.

'You know he was a plague specialist?' Morgan says because Lev still occupies the air between them.

Maya looks levelly at him. 'Everybody's something. Some people read the world's bad news.' She won't say *even*, or *badly*, but he hears the reproof. 'Some make dolls,' she adds to soften the blow.

'Oh, I wasn't judging. I just wondered if he talked to you about it.'

'No.'

'Well, I suppose he wouldn't. He probably didn't talk to himself about it.'

'I'd say he did nothing but.'

'Maybe.' He sips in silence, then thinks out loud. 'He might even have forgiven himself if that . . . thing hadn't happened.'

She winces. 'What sort of person would throw acid at somebody?' She shudders at the picture she carries in her mind of a destroyed face. Then she remembers the bird and the bowl and stops short. She wants to cry. Her sort of person. Looking to balance an unfairness beyond redress, some wretched imbalance in the universe.

The man at the desk is listening to short-wave radio turned down low, more atmospherics than music. A snatch of something familiar alerts Morgan. *Listen*, he goes to say, when the manager twiddles Prokofiev away. How a line of music can recur and recur through your life! It was the piece he was playing for Lev when Lev jumped up exasperated. This woman was coming out of sickness then, this matchless woman looking at him from under the line of her eyebrows.

'I hate that flat now.'

He spreads his hands. 'Come and stay in mine.'

'And Pa?'

'Not him as well.'

'Idiot.'

They sit quietly listening to the assorted music of the world, the BBC, VOA, China, Germany, happy in a pallid way, the air cleared a little.

'I mean it,' Morgan wants her to know. 'He doesn't have to know. It doesn't have to be all the time. In any case you need your studio.'

'Workroom, moron.'

Suddenly it's Morgan who wants to cry. He feels his life splitting open and he can't tell if it's from emptiness or hope. There's a freshness to this hot sweaty evening that he dare not identify. Such is his superstitious dread he dare not even think of it, and in his confusion gets up to pay. The manager looks for change and can't find any.

'That's all right,' Morgan says. He would leave a hundred-rupee tip, just now, two hundred. He would leave his whole wallet and throw in his watch.

'Come back some time, men.'

'We will.'

Outside the gate the hard-worked world returns. They pause and look back at the door where the custodian vanished.

'One of these days,' Maya says, 'someone will come along and demolish it.'

'Or trash it up with granite and mirrors.'

Dusk has fallen. A lone fruit-seller stands by his cartload of bananas, selling them cheap because they're ripening by the minute. Mangoes are gone, that hot yellow sweetness.

They pick a pale hand and the man blows on the edge of a fresh polythene bag to open it with a tiny puppet-piping.

'So where are you parked?'

'Faridabad, more or less.'

'Walk it or take a rick?'

'I've walked enough.' He flags down a rickshaw.

'You have a spare mattress?'

'I have a spare room.'

'So what's for dinner?'

It's then that Morgan remembers. 'God, I have to go out!'

'Where?'

He hesitates. 'I'm meeting Leela.'

'You're *WHAT*!'

'Just—'

'No just,' she rules. 'The sneaky bitch! When did this start?'

Morgan is worried, but not excessively; it was tentative, he can still call it off. As the rickshawwallah makes his way through the late evening traffic Maya lets their knees touch. She feels herself waking out of a dream. There's no severance: you are oriented just as in the dream, but the other world is gradually asserting itself, the sounds of traffic – the human jeep, pulling over to let her rickshaw pass – the smell of this mad city, the rickshawwallah's shiny legs working like pistons.

'Nothing you want to pick up from the flat?' Morgan asks as they approach the Serai. The Zen is parked there.

'No. I can always come back tomorrow.'

After dinner they go out onto Morgan's terrace and smell queen-of-the-night from the garden below. A plane goes over with its landing lights on.

'Poor Lev,' Maya says, following its descent. 'His suitcase

is still in the flat. All those leather jackets! There should be some way.'

Her hand grips Morgan's arm as the idea takes hold. She turns and fixes him with a setter's eye. He gags and goggles and puts out his chin, but the look is still there.

'Oah no,' he laughs, '*oah* no.' The whole history of their friendship stands transfixed in that look. 'You must be joking.'

White City

Morgan is walking along the Fontanka with a spring in his stride. Maya put it there, Russia has kept it there.

This bright pane of an November evening, vinegar sharp and dazzling with zigzags of low late sunlight in a band of gold that moves with him on the water, could lift him clear off the pitted stone beneath his feet and he would walk on, on air.

Not since the day he put in his papers and stepped out of the whitewashed gate at brigade headquarters in Dehradun has Captain Morgan Fitch felt so transformed, so – there is no other word – justified. The poetry he proposed to write that December day ten years ago remains unwritten, if you don't count the loose-leaf folder that travels everywhere with him (it has travelled here, to Petersburg), and yet he feels closer to accomplishment than ever before. His heart clears a space before him, he strides through the gap and colonizes all he sees. Here is his start.

For one thing he is no longer a face. Ten days ago he resigned as anchorman at Channel X. Never again will he mouth even in jest the greeting that so stuck in his professional throat: *Good morning, India!* Schoolgirls will learn to live – they have already adjusted – without the Morgan pout; their valentines will find another target next year. The hoarding at the Defence Colony flyover already has someone else's face. He has escaped the double prison of his face, which was always a kind of mask, and his voice; he has slipped into anonymity and plain speech.

And then he's here, at last, in Russia.

In the city that went ahead of him like a mirage on hot August days in South Delhi when it was 39 degrees beyond the glass and the Zen was hemmed in and slowing to a halt at a red light that said, without winking, RELAX.

White City of his dreams.

Here is one, in black and white. It's a recurring dream.

He is walking along an embankment of the Neva in the heart of winter. Black water, black as bled engine oil, moves the river on. Flake by flake the snow descends, every crystal a Petersburg. Black trunks of willows, bench slats. A widow on the bench in a black coat and hat, lost in contemplation, the poet-queen of this city. There are no passers-by on the embankment. All is quiet. Here the Neva flows under a carpet of ice. The woman stirs, rises, makes for the street. It's a busy street, Z—, swarming with black cars and buses. Snow dapples the beams of the oncoming traffic, icicles epaulette the railings. Here her courage fails her. How to cross? Morgan offers an arm. They step off the kerb together and walk. Halfway across the poet stops in her tracks, unnerved.

Come on, the dreamer urges. *You can't stop here.*

A bus is bearing down on them.

For godsake, move!

The bus is almost on him. He can see the whites of the driver's eyes.

But where's the woman!

Morgan remembers this dream. It came early in his obsession with this city. The obsession has changed, of course. For what goes before Morgan now is a mirage of the red city, Maya's city, a shifting scarp of red rock. But here he is at last in Peter. In the past week he has discovered other colours, the brown city, the fluorescent pink, the industrial grey, the violet. The pink was in a Peterpunk's hair (*'Will you buy me an aa-icecream?'*); the violet was in Lev's one good eye against the brownstone beer garden where they met.

'Morgan.'

'Lev.'

What to say? How are you?

'How are things?' Morgan gestures at the present, a short wave that does not devalue the past.

'OK.'

Lev wears an eye patch. The acid has burnt an Africa-shaped scar on his cheek. There are angry pink splotches in the hollow below the jawline and spots down the neck.

'How is Maya?'

'She wants to know why you haven't written.'

Lev's eye drops to take in the purple stains on the paving stones. It's then that he remembers that this was where he met St Isaak that night before leaving for India. St Isaak who bought the Galant, after coming over to inspect it, not once but many times. So many times that now Alla lives with him. His Katia has moved on, into real estate. Lev has the Repin flat, which he shares with Alla's mother, who has stayed on because of Alex. St Isaak won't have Alex now the boy's gone all Aryan. Alla too is not sure she can handle him. Only her mother can, the mother who couldn't take three granddaughters. There's some obscure understanding between the boy and his grandmother. Perhaps she sees the world his way and he senses that. He comes and goes, is not disrespectful to his father. Especially since Lev came back battle-scarred from a dark country. There's almost envy in the eye Alex turns on his father's face. As if his own tattoos are cosmetic beside Lev's.

'It's been –' Lev searches for a word – 'complicated here.'

Morgan nods. It's been complicated at home too. But he can imagine this, here.

'Is there pain?'

'Not now. I have a friend who can do plastic surgery.'

Silence.

'Tell Maya I will write.'

Morgan nods, then looks straight at Lev.

'She's with me now, Lev.'

Lev's eye holds his, then drops away to the cherry stains. It's hard to hold with one eye. He's still not got used to the wall of darkness that travels with him on the left. He turns his head sharply to that side to check that the world is still there. It is.

Cherry tree, railing. Peter.

Morgan too has turned aside. He's drifted back to his flat, where Maya is standing in the kitchen leaning up against the sink so its jut fills the small of her back. Tiny, this consummate woman. With her he can forget he's not tall, if she lets him. Today she will. They've just quarrelled over nothing and she's admitted she was wrong. He's so surprised he's inclined to score.

'Which means you were latching some other grievance onto this.'

'Ya.'

'Which means there's still a debt outstanding.'

'Bas, yaa.'

'Which means—'

'Shut up, Morgan!'

He's been edging closer, wagging his finger, perplexed by the way he is suddenly opaque to her. For the first time her look stops at him. He's accustomed to another focus.

Now, at no distance at all, she melts. And Morgan, who has read a hundred signs of acquiescence in others, won't trust this moment. Morgan, who lives by postponement, backs off. Smaller pleasures he'll take as he finds them; what is precious he puts off. He sees the surprise in her eyes and must explain himself.

'The banana and perfection,' he pronounces, peeling one, 'have just one hour together. Maybe just one minute. The ripe moment is actually ungetatable.'

So she kisses him first, to stop his mouth. Amazed at how simply the other dream passes. The bonesetter's click with which she snaps out of it. Pain there still is, but balance is restored. She has exchanged an impossible love for a possible one.

And Morgan, pinned at the limits of eloquence, finds she is solid to him too.

It's then, when they are lovers, that she tells him of the menace she feels in her body, the fatal thing that tingles all down her limbs even now as they lie together.

'But how can you be sure?' Morgan demands. There's petulance in his question, and fear and disbelief, that something so hard won can be taken away.

'I just know,' is all she says. But it lifts a ban that Lev learnt to accept; now she wants a child.

'You can't diagnose yourself. It's dangerous. Never mind the pathology – it's bad psychology.'

She won't argue, and he lets it go; neither can convince the other. She's felt the stirrings of it before; maybe it'll go into remission again.

'You know that virus she got?' Lev has to get this off his chest.

Morgan flicks back to the white city. He heard the question, the whole of it. He nods sharply. 'Yes?'

'I *think* – I don't know – I may have carried it to her. There were two cases of rabbit vector flu here while I was in India. One was the nurse who gave me my inoculations. She wanted to give me the rabbit too.'

'You were immune?'

'Yes.'

'What happened to her?'

'Both cases were fatal.'

'Could it trigger something else? Later?'

'It's hard to say. Probably not.'

Morgan clutches at that. She's mad, she's wrong, she's imagining things, his dramatizer, his illusionist. His little marvel, bigger than Russia.

'You could have stayed with me,' Lev is embarrassed into excuses, 'but it's a small apartment. My ex-mother-in-law . . .'

'I'm very comfortable, you'll see.' Morgan's fingertips leave the table. He's staying in CV's apartment. 'CV's here, by the way. In Russia, not in the flat. He has a dacha near Pushkin. I had dinner with the consul the other night and he was there. He dropped me home.'

He doesn't tell Lev what CV told him, except to check one detail.

'He says you were reunited with your briefcase.'

Lev smiles the ghost of a smile, the same smile with which he picks up the suitcase and lugs it from the stoep to the taxi outside CV's apartment house.

'They held him for six weeks,' CV had said, struggling with the seal on a bottle of cloudberry liqueur. It was Finnish, for Morgan; he was not drinking himself because he was driving back to Pushkin and the GAI were targeting foreigners. 'Not that *they* need evidence,' he parenthesized. 'It's just as well you're not driving. You look *thet* Georgian. You heard about yesterday's bomb?'

No. Morgan was there to get away from the news.

'Anyway, they held onto your friend. At the facility itself, wherever that is. Hospital-shospital hoga.'

'Why didn't they just keep his notes?'

'They didn't need his notes, they needed him.' CV gave up and put the whole bottletop in his mouth, gripped the cap with his teeth, and turned the bottle with both hands till the little joins at the collar gave in an enfilade of tiny clicks. 'Voila! The benefits of a Heidelberg education. And Haryanvi teeth.' He flashed the teeth, unscrewed the cap and poured. 'He was on show.'

Morgan's head tilted like a listening dog. CV trod a tight expository line. The night before he had sat in silence as the consul sparkled and the talented Purohit, bowtied and shoeless, served wine custard; now his low-slung back paced the hearth rug with a sherpa's assurance of being followed.

'You see, the facility does not exist. Or rather it exists as something else. Every other year an American team – all right, a UN team – headed by a senator goes scouting for biological weapons. Now our Ministry have to assure the Americans that they're not in the business. That's where your friend came in. They simply held him till the inspection team arrived. In any case he needed treatment. They got a specialist in, looked after him. And when he'd done his bit they let him go. By then his burns were healed.

'So. The night before the showing they apologize. *We are sorry about the robbery. Our man got carried away. But the acid attack had* nothing *to do with us.* He knows that anyway. They give him back his briefcase intact, return his money, his watch, whatever else got taken. *Is everything present? Please overlook the error. But you can tell the Senator anything else he wants to know. OK?* Pride is salved. Etiquette is satisfied. And the bandages have come off.

'So the Senator arrives. *Aha! A Russian! What are you doing here? Who did this to you? What have you given away? What are you being paid?*

'And your friend – here is the masterly part – simply tells them the truth. The truth will set him free! *No, sir. They were not interested. I tried. God knows I tried. Here is what happened to me.*'

Morgan rolled the clingy green liqueur around the glass and stared at the emerald wash of tension where it rode a millimetre up the crystal walls.

'Does a weapons programme exist?'

'How should *I* know?' CV looked genuinely puzzled at the question. 'I take it you mean biological weapons. I hope not. I have a stake in the other kind. I'm a conventional man. Your friend has been closer to it than I have. I just have my contact.'

'So what does the facility produce?'

'*What* facility?'

CV smiled and shook his head. He turned and reached up and leaned with both hands on the mantelshelf and blew a speck of dust off the model aircraft-carrier there then he dropped back onto his heels and turned to face his guest and grinned and patted his pockets. He bent over a bowl heaped with cherry tomatoes and picked the reddest and popped it in his mouth and straightened his face into an iron mask in line with a row of six on the wall behind him. Then he ran a finger under his collar where a band of heat was trapped.

Could he have a touch of the flu?

Morgan watches Lev's taxi disappear and decides to return to the Fontanka. He's not quite walked out yet. Besides he's grown attached to its civilized progress through the city, especially in this long stretch where the Yusupov Palace hangs reflected on the water in the distance in one direction and the other way presents a succession of iron bridges. Impossible to believe it was once just an arm of a raw delta. Yesterday he crossed it and found himself in Sennaya among the new poor. Long silent rows of citizens outside every metro entrance winding all around the block, women in headscarves standing clutching broken sets of dinner knives for sale. A young man selling a single hairbrush. A rag-and-bone market by a row of half-demolished houses where sellers squatted on boards over pools of foetid water. It made the one in Old Delhi look rich. It made Morgan grateful to have been born in Roorkee. Into the shabby-genteel family Fitch, his mother the widow of a postmaster.

This evening he would like to see, though he's left it a little late, the Sheremetev Palace, where the poet-queen lived.

His map tells him it's on the Fontanka, so he has simply to follow this embankment. Tomorrow he can go in and see her flat, turned into a shrine no doubt; this evening he'd just like to stand at the gate. He has a sense of freedom now he's handed over the suitcase. He was afraid it might be opened at the airport, but no one bothered. He's seen Lev in the flesh again and can report back to Maya that he is back on his native soil, managing.

He's not down to his heirlooms. He can't see Lev in that row outside the metro, but equally he can't see him stuck behind a rack of leather jackets in a market square. Lev will chafe and chafe in silence, and he will come up with another scheme.

Morgan strokes the still faintly warm stone of the parapet, and feels a contentment that almost robs him of the desire to move. The sun has gone, leaving a light the colour of the elderflower cordial his first night landlady dosed him on to check a slight cold, a teaspoon of Vladimirskaya balsam extract clouding the mixture while the radio played the romance, 'What is love?'. Installed at CV's, he's escaped those ministrations. Now he's his own man he'd like to look around. CV can organize foreign exchange. *Bring Maya here*, he thinks, *show her this*. (Go to Indonesia, let her show him that.) For now he's content to praise.

Look, he says. He leans on the parapet and shows her the canal. Evening has silvered the water and a loose wind goes skittering across it, feathering the surface. The air is sweet in a temperate way, clean and chill and moist with the steam off buckets of boiled corn at corner foodstalls. The facades of the apartment houses on this side reflect the dwindling elderflower light, those on the far bank are already a gloomy brown escarpment with lights coming on above the cavernous black mouths of mews. From a pushcart comes the semeny smell of roasting chestnuts. Morgan turns and walks along the embankment.

At the next red light a wheelchair beggar dares motorists head on. His wife wheels him straight at the bumper of the front car, then jinks around to the driver's window and looks in. A coin is passed out. Morgan buys a cob of corn and looks for a spot where he can sit and eat. Beyond the bridge is his favourite reach of the Fontanka, a gentle curve in the river that ends at the bright lights of Nevsky Prospekt. It's a sequestered stretch, treed and cobbled, with landings for boats that the pedestrian must go around. Morgan goes down the four steps to the landing every time and up the four steps on the other side where the railing resumes.

Night has fallen. The streetlamps have a gaslight look that coats the bare trees with its phosphorescence. By the Anichkov bridge is a tour boat with coloured lights strung from mast to mast. Morgan sits down on a landing step and bites into the still hot corn. It is mildly sweet in a bland northern way that he likes. He eats along the length of the cob as is his way, not around it; it steams in the faint white lamplight. A group of young men are singing some boisterous song as they cross the distant bridge. They turn off Nevsky and come along the embankment shouting their song. Morgan sees them come and his soldier instincts tell him he is exposed and vulnerable. There are four of them and they are drunk. He could get up now and walk back the way he came, or he could walk past them, timing his ascent of the steps opposite. Captain Fitch would risk the second course, but the civilian he has become decides to sit it out.

The men spot him in the lamplight and gravitate towards him, drawn by the magnet that is the figure one. They keep up their singing as they approach, but don't slow down, except for one who goes quiet and slows down and splits off from the rest. The others sweep around the landing and march past above Morgan, their boots winking at eye level. The fourth stops at the top of the steps opposite and waits determined to make the stranger look up. Morgan obliges, lifting his eyes from the corn.

And sees Lev, unblemished. Lev as he was. But no, it's a boy with a shaven head and Lev's mouth and Lev's spaniel eyes. His hands in the pockets of a black pea coat.

Morgan smiles his guarded smile and goes on eating. The boy comes slowly down the steps and stops halfway across the landing.

'You're not Georgian by any chance?'

Morgan shakes his head.

'Not Azerbaijani'

Morgan shakes his head.

'Lucky.'

The other three have halted a short way along, half waiting for the boy. They've stopped singing and slipped into loud horseplay at the edge of the railing. The boy climbs the four steps beside Morgan brushing against him with the same stagey menace and goes to join the cockalorum game.

Here is where Morgan's good sense deserts him. The way is now clear. He must rise and walk straight across the landing and up the steps on the other side and make for the lights of Nevsky. Instead he becomes a puppet. He is free to give up his freedom. He sits there, his whole spirit rising up in protest, and stolidly finishes his corn.

The boy says something to the others and they look back at Morgan and laugh. Morgan hears the direction of their laughter and bristles but stays where he is. An animal would know what to do, but Morgan is suddenly burdened with a surplus of humanity. Even that might save him, if fate is on his side.

The men round back to the landing together, the front-runners punching one another as they come.

'Hey, you didn't plant that bomb in the Metro yesterday, did you?'

Morgan's Russian is not up to this speed, so he must run the sentence by again to catch the key words. He shakes his head again. The speaker comes and sits beside him. His mate sits one step down and looks up at Morgan. The boy in the peacoat returns to his position facing Morgan.

'Cat got your tongue?'

'You some kind of Roma?'

'What colour were your mother's eyes?'

Morgan hasn't read the papers. He hasn't seen the blonde maiden the media have singled out among those who died in the explosion. Her father, paid for the use of her photograph, sitting there numbed with grief, another puppet. Morgan knows nothing of this. He's given up on news. He feels the boy's boot press down on his toecap and lets it. He looks to master his breathing, sure now that any sign of weakness will trigger something terrible, but then it's past managing and he reaches casually into his shirt pocket for the asthma spray. The man below him holds out his hand. Morgan points the spray at his mouth and mimes pressing the nozzle. The man shakes his head and his hand remains open. Morgan goes to spray anyway but the hand closes over his and relieves him of the canister. The fourth man is somewhere behind him out of sight.

'Oh!'

Mock alarm as the canister bounces towards the edge, a cast die. All present watch it go. It might stop short or swerve away, but it doesn't. It rolls over the edge, and its going is like a gong.

'Duck the Roma,' calls the man from above, as if the choice is no longer theirs.

The boy releases Morgan's foot and the seated men ease Morgan towards the edge. Now Morgan does make a run for it. But at close quarters footing is always half luck. The boy is there to deflect him into the black water.

The men melt away into the shadows, their boots clicking as they run.

Morgan falls without a cry. That much he can refuse. He's not a swimmer, but even if he was the shock of the water, colder than anything he's ever known, simply stops his heart.

When CV identifies him the next day it's by his pout. For the rest he appears at peace, open in his closedness, and anonymous at last.

Epilogue

Petersburg

Dear Maya

You have given me up I think but I was not yet ready in my mind for writing of a letter. It was indeed a great shock, the death of Morgan, but the connection in it of my son I still cannot begin to understand. Just you can imagine how am I feeling even now. I know only details what came out in the enquiry and these you know from the consulate. I can imagine your response because he told me of what was between you. He did not say much, just in one sentence, but I understood and accepted that it was a better thing than the impossible relation between you and me.

It is good you did not see me after the attack in India. I have had surgery again on the area and it was a success, 70–80%. The surgeon is my old university friend. He has made no charge, or maybe the charge is my wife who is now with him. Well, she knew about you, I sent the letter, and she was antagonistic. Maybe I did not deserve her. Also he has done some arrangement for the boy, our son, because he has many resources. Here you can disappear just like before but now you can change your identity. Of course you must go to some faraway city. I even do not know where the boy is. He was too young to spoil his whole life with prison, Maya.

I wish the suitcase did not come back with Morgan. It is still here and everything in it. You can understand Petersburg is spoilt for me. I think sometimes I will sell the apartment, it can fetch a good price because it is in the centre of the city. The deeds were given so simply for such small a payment I am sure it can not be for ever, nobody knows. So better to sell and neighbours are selling for very much to buy somewhere else. Also the climate does not suit my circulation like the tropics. You were right my Maya to resume your heart but what you gave was precious and it is still alive. We will continue I know to value one each other. We have a saying of Indian summer (*babye lete*). Just before the winter there are a few days of clear warm weather. So when I was young I had my summer and then again came this season, short short short. This you were to me. I do not know still what I was to you.

Lev.

Delhi

Lyova,

I have had your letter in the Bali wallet for a long time now and should have written before when there was just one of me. But I went and left it too late and now I have only short intervals of peace when I can sleep and sit and think and read (Morgan's books, what else?) and write.

Masha was born on the 26th of June in a clinic not far from here as the crow flies (not the one we used to pass at the sabziwallah's corner). In fact I'm not in the flat at the moment but staying with those friends whose haveli gate we used for the puppet show. Of course Ma had a fit and I too got on my high horse so I've left the flat, but all my samaan is still there, the puppets and all (except for Babaji) so it's not a total break. But she didn't want the neighbours talking and neither did I. In the end she wanted me at home but that I didn't want, so here I am in my own little room overlooking the Kabootar (Pigeon) Bazaar. All the children of the gully remember me. They call me Razia Madam. The adults are as usual. Sometimes I think they punished me by punishing you.

Morgan is here in many ways, not just his books. He was always parachuting in at strange hours and continues to do so. He was my steadiest friend and still is, though Babaji is still my counsellor. What were you? A visitation? You came and disappeared like an angel. How is your eye, my poor Lyova? You don't mention it. I have left Babaji's unpainted and I've got used to seeing him that way. Maybe he has too, though some nights I feel him leaning over me as I sleep and eavesdropping on my dreams. Maybe one is better alone. Marriage is an imperium, Morgan always said. He was buried in the cemetery by the Ridge. Did he ever take you bird-watching on the Ridge? He dragged me there once and I complained all the time. *Imperialist! Let the birds get on with their lives.* Laiq's bird is still calling away. (Laiq is still barbering and quacking.) Morgan's mother came up from Roorkee. She took away one or two of his things, medals and keepsakes, and gave me the books and sold the rest. Tough old lady. Pa took care of everything. He didn't want any loose talk. Chanus. He retires this year. Pura stickler, my Pa.

Masha is beautiful, of course. So grave and lovely and (mostly) quiet. Do you know your hair falls out when you have a child? Not all at once, thank God. Nobody told me that. I had a visit from a eunuch the other day, very obstreperous creature. He came when I was alone and demanded money. Kept lifting his sari to show me how he couldn't have a child. Wouldn't go away when I gave him a hundred, wanted a thousand! Said he'd come back with all his eunuch friends and dance outside and disgrace me and put a curse on the child. So we settled on five hundred and even then he went off demanding a sari and jewellery and all sorts of stuff. Said he takes five thousand for a baby boy. Anyway he hasn't been back so I don't need to bother Pa.

My room is at the back of the haveli and during the day I can see a bit of the Red Fort above the roof of Haji Asgar's restaurant which is a hotchpotch of corrugated iron and grass matting and plastic sheets weighed down with bamboos and bricks and stones and broken chairs and rusty tins and any old rubbish chucked up there so it's out of sight to everybody except me. It makes the cagewallah's roof next door look civilized because he just has cages piled on top, all sorts of cages, wicker, wire, bamboo, even flat sheets of tin with gaps cut out. My friends send up my meals, now they know I want to be alone. They are Muslims but cook specially for me. Bread and condensed milk for breakfast! You would want to go down to Haji Asgar's, Lyova. Pura non-veg. It's almost midnight and his tandoor is still turning out rotis. No fun for the rotiwallah, it's a hothot night. Asgar is sitting on his marble counter and ladling from a row of eight degchis. The boy who scrubs them every morning is looking very sleepy.

A little later, I'm watching a long-haired beggar hold out his bowl for gravy. He holds it out for a second spoonful (given less willingly than the first) then goes looking for a clean space to sit down. (Not easy.) He has a fistful of rumalis from some other restaurant. He puts the bowl down on the ground between his feet and dips the roti into the gravy. A stray dog has come up, strong and healthy-looking, with muscly balls, and he's edging in with his tail twitching.

4 a.m. Have just fed Masha. The yard is finally asleep but not quite dead. There's a truck backed in unloading huge bundles of some dark soft material. The rickshawwallahs are going back to sleep after shifting their rickshaws to make way for the truck. Two cocks crowing, answering one another across the yard, one high, one low. The shop lights are all out so the garbage is invisible at last, but I can smell soured biryani. Bit of lightning in the sky: it's black over the fort. Another rickshawwallah singing, pedalling by in his rickshaw, taking himself somewhere. I think I'll stay awake. In any case the crows are starting. Actually the cook is already up checking his gas tubes for leaks. Now he's got his whole arm in the tandoor, fishing around for lumps of charcoal. Sky's still black, one bright star and a few faint ones. Asgar's workers sleep on narrow benches one span wide (your span) with their arms folded. Luxury. The rickshaw-wallahs have their feet up against the handlebar and their backs arched over nothing. That's how the body is, no? If we had eight arms we'd still be uncomfortable.

Are you well? I mostly all right. Sometimes I think my tingling has entered a new phase. Every now and then I get these dark pins and needles everywhere. What will happen to Masha? She was my gift to Morgan. Bas. One day at a time. What else?

Last night I dreamt I was back in the flat and Babaji came and leaned over the bed the way he does. He leaned further and further and then overbalanced and fell and I woke up with the pillow on my chest!

I better post this. What are you doing? Academic question, yaa. Don't answer. I'm not a letter-writer, Lev. I'll trust you're OK. So take care. God, it's a whole year! Light-years. It was good, na? One last kiss.

Maya.

Acknowledgements

My fairygodmother, Joy Michael, lent me her Delhi flat in the hot summer of 2000 and my wife and daughter gave me three months' leave to go there. Without that concord this tale of two cities might never have got written.

One-time fellow collegian Ashok Sajjanhar and his family made me welcome in their Moscow apartment, and Natasha Sudrovoy made a delightful interpreter during my time in that city. In St Petersburg, Natalia Osadchenko gave me the divan in her little flat and would not be moved from her kitchen bunk. The Gangulys of the Indian consulate were lavish hosts and raconteurs.

Anybody who read Richard Preston's vivid article 'The Bioweaponeers' when it appeared some years ago in the *New Yorker* will recognize the ghost Meschersky. For details of tropical medicine I troubled the genial Dr Icchpujani of the National Institute of Communicable Diseases in Delhi.

Laiq's couplet from Mir appears in Khurshidul Islam and Ralph Russell's *Three Mughal Poets*, while the lines from Anna Akhmatova are from Pete Norman's translations appended to

Lydia Chukovskaya's wartime diary, *The Akhmatova Journals, 1938–1941*. To the dead poets of the two cities, Red and White, I owe much that might be quoted, but to the living muse of Delhi Gate I owe more than I can say.